# A
# SANTORINI
# SECRET

BOOKS BY ROSE ALEXANDER

*The Lost Diary*
*A Letter from Italy*

ROSE ALEXANDER

*A*

# SANTORINI
# SECRET

bookouture

Published by Bookouture in 2025

An imprint of Storyfire Ltd.
Carmelite House
50 Victoria Embankment
London EC4Y 0DZ

www.bookouture.com

The authorised representative in the EEA is Hachette Ireland
8 Castlecourt Centre
Dublin 15 D15 XTP3
Ireland
(email: info@hbgi.ie)

ISBN: 978-1-83618-006-7
eBook ISBN: 978-1-83618-005-0

# FOREWORD

The Special Boat Squadron was formed in 1943, and from then on embarked on a series of remarkable exploits, going from island to island in the Mediterranean and wreaking havoc with piratical activities that were unorthodox, secretive and utterly ruthless. Though it never numbered more than around two hundred men, the SBS was able to tie down large battalions of German forces, thus preventing them from swelling the ranks of those fighting further north.

The hit-and-run raid on Santorini in April 1944 was one of the renegade band's most daring and audacious. Though fictionalised in this book, the key events and facts are true, not least the reliance the battle-hardened operatives had to place on local people to help them achieve their aims. Sadly, the reprisals unleashed by the Nazis in the aftermath of the attack are also true, and one can only wonder at the bravery of those islanders who took the opportunity to stand up to the occupier in the hope of liberating their homeland.

*A Santorini Secret* is the story of ordinary people caught up in extraordinary events, and forced into remarkable situations in the interests of regaining their freedom. Perhaps it's the case that no one knows what they are capable of until put to the test.

A note on pronunciation. The town of Oia is pronounced Ia (Ee-a), although the lovely, friendly Greeks understand and put up with the way many tourists say it as something more like Oy-a.

*She loved me for the dangers I had passed,*
*And I loved her that she did pity them.*

— *OTHELLO*, WILLIAM
SHAKESPEARE

# PROLOGUE

VOURVOULOS, SANTORINI ISLAND, JUNE 1944

It's dark in the room, just the merest hint of sunlight filtering through the chinks in the shutters. Usually, the young woman sitting at the rough wooden table would have thrown the windows open to welcome the day inside. But today she does not do that. The task she is involved in requires the utmost secrecy. Because writing this letter is dangerous in the extreme. The moment she puts her name on the paper she is signing her own death warrant, were it to fall into the wrong hands. There are more soldiers on the island now, and reinforcements still arriving. The Nazis are angry after recent events, which is hardly surprising, and fear stalks the landscape, looming over quaint alleyways, casting shadows over village squares, making everyone aware of the need to watch their backs.

The thought of this momentarily stills the blood in the young woman's veins. She lifts the pen from the paper and holds it there, paralysed by a sudden terror. And then she bites her lip, moistens the nib with a quick touch of her tongue, and determinedly carries on writing. She takes her time, deliberating over every word. It is essential that she gets it right, that everything she says is crystal clear. Any misunderstanding could spell disaster. Any mistake could be fatal.

A sudden noise from outside makes her jump, electric waves of shock radiating through her. The pen drops to the floor and skitters noisily across the tiles. Frozen to the spot, she listens. Is someone watching her? Waiting for her? It would be no surprise. In an island under occupation, walls have ears and eyes and no one is ever safe. She has felt observed for some time now. The fact that nothing has happened so far doesn't mean that it won't. Being discovered, captured, tortured, is always possible.

After a couple of minutes during which she strains her ears for the smallest sound, but hears nothing, she allows herself to relax. She has to go through with this, no matter what. There's no question of backing out.

She can't leave him, the love of her life, the man she adores, to die.

Finally the letter is written. Her pupils contract as she leaves her home's dim interior and steps out into the bright sunshine. She locates her little cousin and his friends, playing football in the square outside the church. They seem so innocent. They don't deserve to be mixed up in all of this. But what choice does she have? She calls the oldest over to her. Promising treats as a reward, she slips the letter into the child's hand and tells him where it must be delivered. Surely no one will suspect a ten-year-old? If she has put him in danger, if anything happens to him, she'll never forgive herself.

As the boy sprints eagerly off along the dusty road, there's nothing the young woman can do but wait. Wait for darkness to fall and for the next part of the plan to begin. As she waits, she thinks of the man, so handsome, so calm, so strong. It's vital that he gets away while he has the chance. The future of the war depends on people like him – and she's the only one who can help him, the only one who can ensure his survival.

Even if to do so puts her in mortal danger.

# CHAPTER 1

CARRIE, 2024

The rain was persistent, driving into Carrie's face as she pounded along the rough, pot-holed track, stinging her bare arms. She could have worn a coat but even her most waterproof one couldn't withstand this kind of downpour. Better just to get wet rather than to try to run enveloped in sodden layers. It was hard to see through the veil of water before her eyes and Carrie cursed out loud when her foot slipped on a loose stone, and then felt relief flood through her as she quickly righted herself. The last thing she needed was a twisted ankle; she was down on her luck enough as it was.

Having reached her goal of Four Mile Clump, high on the Marlborough Downs and surrounded by farmland and race-horse gallops, Carrie gratefully turned round to head towards home. Now the rain was coming from behind, battering her back, and large puddles had formed in the path, which she did her best to avoid, leaping and jumping round and over them.

Finally reaching her small two-bedroom cottage in a hamlet so tiny it contained only around twenty homes, Carrie fumbled in her pocket for the back door key and let herself in. It was marginally warmer inside than out, but the difference was barely discernible. Living in the sticks meant no mains gas, so the house was heated by ruinously expensive heating oil. Carrie rationed it as much as she could, only putting the heating on for an hour in the morning to encourage her fifteen-year-old daughter Nell to get out of bed, and two hours in the evening for when Nell got home from school. The rest of the time the two of them hunkered down by the open fire in the living room, or used electric blankets and hot-water bottles to keep warm. Carrie was sure that the cold wasn't good for Nell, with her heart condition, but there was little she could do about it. She'd bought the house when pregnant, a nest for her new baby, with no idea that the baby would have a health problem.

Nevertheless, despite its defects and all the mod cons and amenities it lacked, Carrie loved her home with a passion. It was her and Nell's safe haven, their sanctuary, their only certainty. Whatever else happened, however hard things were, however great her struggles as she tried to be a good mum and to make ends meet, Carrie had kept a roof over both their heads. Sometimes that struck her as her only concrete achievement.

Soaking wet, Carrie shivered violently as she stood dripping in the kitchen. She took off her shoes and socks and ran upstairs to the bathroom, where she used the last of the morning's hot water to shower. Back downstairs, she brewed a pot of coffee, poured herself a cup and, as she waited for it to cool, fetched the post from where it lay in an untidy, and somewhat soggy, heap on the front doormat. As she leafed through the fliers and circulars, she came across an official-looking letter and, with a sinking feeling, immediately knew it was her council tax bill. She opened the envelope and saw that not only was she right but also that the sum they were asking for was as out of reach as it had been the last time she looked. She'd been in denial about it but now it was a final demand, so she'd have to engage. Or in other words, she'd have to go further into her overdraft to pay.

There was another letter, innocuous enough in a plain

white envelope. Without paying much attention, Carrie ripped it open. She expected to be able to quickly dispatch it to the recycling bin and her eyes drifted over the page. At first, the words she read failed to make sense. But then, all of a sudden, they came into sharp focus. The remortgage she had taken out amidst the Covid pandemic, at a super-low interest rate, would end in a few months' time. The new rate was far higher than the one she was on now, increasing her monthly payments threefold.

The figures danced and spun before her eyes. They couldn't be right, could they? Carrie reached for her phone, opened the calculator app and did some rapid sums.

The numbers were correct.

As she continued to stare at the page, a terrible, ominous sensation of dread trickled through her veins and settled deep in her stomach. This was a disaster. A catastrophe. Making the new payments would take almost the entire salary she earned as a deputy manager at the local leisure centre, and the extra she gleaned from working some Saturday night shifts as front of house at the local gastropub. She had taken on this additional work with the intention of setting up a savings account for Nell's university education, but this letter had well and truly put paid to that idea. She didn't even have the option of changing to an interest-only mortgage, because she'd already done that.

Feeling a sense of utter despond, Carrie threw the mail down onto the table. Blinking back tears – because what good would crying do? – she pulled her sleeves down over her hands in an attempt to glean an extra modicum of warmth and cradled her coffee mug, every now and again taking a morose sip. It was miserable, being cold and skint, but she normally managed to put on a brave face, for Nell's sake if nothing else. But now the awful spectre of losing the house, of being homeless, rose up before her, with all its indignity and uncertainty and insecurity, with Nell wrested away from her school and her education, with Carrie trying to keep their spirits up while living in mouldy temporary accommodation or a B&B. It was everything she had always dreaded, everything she had always worked so hard to prevent. But, if the house was repossessed because she couldn't afford the mortgage payments, homelessness might really happen, might become a reality.

The prospect was utterly terrifying.

With trembling hands, Carrie reached out to the coffee pot for a top-up. Listlessly, she poured the milk. Could she be bothered to put the bottle back in the fridge? Did it really matter if she did or didn't? It was so cold in the kitchen it wasn't going to go off. The energy required to get out of her chair seemed akin to climbing Everest; impossible.

But eventually, Carrie rallied. If she gave up on the little things, the big struggles had no chance. She pushed her chair back, stood up, seized up the milk and headed purposefully for the fridge. And that was when she saw it, where it must have fallen to the floor as she'd walked back into the kitchen earlier.

There on the ancient, well-worn quarry tiles lay a postcard from Greece.

Carrie knew the country immediately; there was no mistaking the iconic whitewashed buildings with domed roofs of azure-blue, the splashes of brilliant fuchsia-pink bougainvillea and the expanse of turquoise sea that stretched to the horizon. Her heart lurched as she reached to pick the card up and, as memory after memory assailed her senses, she stared long and hard at the bright, vivid colours sparkling in the Mediterranean sunshine that was so different to the filthy, bleak day outside.

Eventually, Carrie turned the card over to read the back. It was from Xanthe, an old university friend. She was Greek, born and brought up in Athens, where she now lived, but had written to Carrie from Santorini, the island her mother's side of the family came from and where she was enjoying a spring holiday. Xanthe's news was brief and joyful; the island was beautiful, the weather perfect if occasionally rather windy, the local wine superb and her new boyfriend quite lovely. As well as relaxing by the pool or on the beach, they'd been enjoying learning more about the island's history, particularly the idea of whether it really was the mythical Lost Atlantis.

For a brief, shameful moment Carrie was suffused with jealousy. Why wasn't she having a mini-break in an idyllic and culturally rich location with a gorgeous man? And then she shoved such uncharitable thoughts to one side. She couldn't be more delighted for Xanthe, who was a lovely person inside and out, and who so wanted to meet someone to settle down and have a family with. Perhaps this short visit to her homeland had brought her a little closer to her dream. Carrie hoped so.

Shivering again as she imagined that gorgeous Santorini sunshine, Carrie drank some more coffee and fell to reminiscing, her thoughts stretching back over fifteen years to when she and Xanthe, plus two other girlfriends who Carrie had long ago lost touch with, had spent their first – and what turned out to be Carrie's last – university summer holiday island-hopping through the Dodecanese and Cyclades. She stared anew at the picture, drinking in the beauty, the incandescent light and the endless blue skies, remembering those heady days of youth and freedom, the feeling that anything was possible, that life was good and would only get better, that nothing was going to sully the perfection.

On Santorini, they had sat up late into the night on black sand beaches, drinking rough red wine as they listened to someone strumming 'Redemption Song' or 'Viva la Vida' on a guitar, talking and laughing, not a care in the world. Carrie had met a Greek boy called Kyriakos, who came from a village close to Xanthe's. He was devastatingly handsome, exuding allure from every pore of his deeply suntanned skin. How Carrie had fallen for him, hook, line and sinker. But after five glorious days, her friends had wanted to move on and, fearful of being left behind on her own and too young and immature to really understand whether she and Kyriakos were experiencing true love or a holiday romance that would never last, Carrie had gone with them, leaving him behind.

And that had been that.

It had been too brief for them to keep in touch and anyway, Carrie was at uni and, on returning for her second year, she'd almost immediately met Jack…

Carrie's reminiscing came to an abrupt halt. She thought, not for the first time, that perhaps she *should* have stayed on Santorini with Kyriakos. Things might have worked out better. They could hardly have been worse. She might not be facing imminent homelessness, for one thing.

Immediately on thinking that, she scrubbed it from her mind. If she'd stayed on Santorini, she wouldn't have had Nell, and there was nothing bad about that aspect of Carrie's life. Nell was the most wondrous thing that ever had happened or ever would happen to her. But being a single mum wasn't easy, that was indisputable. And Nell's difficult start in life had plunged Carrie into the adult world of responsibility, fear and frantically mugging up on 'atrioventricular septal defect', how it was treated and – most terribly – whether it was survivable, long before she was ready for it. Hearing her mother, Harriet, use the old-fashioned definition 'hole in the heart' to describe Nell's condition had brought it all home. Nell's heart, the organ that symbolises life itself, was defective, not quite right, not quite complete.

Carrie's own heart turned over inside her chest as she recalled being told the news by a softly spoken doctor when Nell was newborn, the panic she had felt, the desperate, protective love that had surged through her, as if the sheer force of it alone could make Nell better.

As well as there being no Nell in the world, it occurred to Carrie now that, if she'd stayed on Santorini, would she ever have written her first children's book? Probably not. She had taken up writing in all the evenings when she couldn't go out like her twenty-something friends went out, because she had a baby to look after, and a baby with a heart problem to boot.

Becoming an author was a wonderful by-product of being a parent and for a few years it had given her enough money to live on, albeit frugally. But this was no J.K. Rowling rags-to-riches story; it was a long time since Carrie had had a bestseller, or any kind of seller at all for that matter, to the point that she was sure her publisher had given up on her. She'd dropped out of uni during the pregnancy, so she didn't have a degree or any particular skills to offer. The only thing she was any good at was writing – except that she wasn't even good at that any more, if recent sales were anything to go by.

Sadly, Carrie picked up the postcard again and studied it anew. In tiny print, Xanthe had squeezed in a few final words: *I'll be back here in the summer – why don't you come and visit?* The very thought set Carrie's heart racing. How marvellous that would be. But almost before the idea had even begun, she dismissed it. There was no way she could afford a trip to Santorini, not when every penny was needed right here.

She toyed with the card for a few more moments, turning it over and over in her hands, before determinedly getting up, propping it on the windowsill and setting about tidying up the breakfast things. Her kitchen was so old-fashioned that she didn't have a dishwasher, so the first job was to do the washing-up. Carrie plunged her gloved hands into the sudsy water, warmed by the remainder of what was in the kettle, and before she knew it her mind was wandering back to Xanthe's invitation and her reference to the legend connected to the island of Santorini.

Against her better judgement, and almost as if she had no

choice in the matter, once the chores were done Carrie found herself opening her aged and battered laptop, cranking it into life and googling Santorini Lost Atlantis.

A plethora of pages with enticing and intriguing titles such as 'Santorini and the myth of Lost Atlantis' and 'Santorini the legend of Atlantis' popped up. Carrie was aware of the story that told of an ancient kingdom, powerful and advanced, that many millennia ago had sunk in a day and a night into the sea. But that was all she knew. As she clicked the links, she quickly discovered that the idea that Santorini could be the famed but ill-fated Atlantis was due to a cataclysmic event that had occurred around three-and-a-half thousand years ago, when the enormous volcano on the island then called Thera had collapsed, wiping out the Minoan town of Akrotiri and splitting the landmass into four parts ringing a caldera that was the deepest in the Mediterranean Sea.

Carrie's mind was already whirring, inventing a female protagonist, a young girl from bygone times set an impossible mission to save her island home from destruction in order to preserve its riches and knowledge for the future. If she could pull it off, writing a new book might help her earn the money necessary to pay the new mortgage.

It might be the answer.

As she sat and mulled over the numerous ideas jostling for her attention, Carrie had a sudden urge to contact Xanthe. She couldn't remember the last time they had spoken; it must have been at least a year ago. The time flew and Carrie's life was so unremittingly dull and mundane that she had nothing to talk to anyone about. That shouldn't stop her from communicating, and finding out about her friends' so much more exciting lives, of course, but somehow it did.

No more.

She reached for her phone, opened WhatsApp, found Xanthe's details and pressed call. The phone rang and rang but there was no answer. Not to be put off, Carrie sent a message instead.

*Hi Xanthe,* she typed, *I just received your postcard— it was so lovely to hear from you. It's been too long. When you have time, give me a bell. I'd love to catch up and hear all your news. Love Carrie, xxx*

Message sent, Carrie's mind returned to the book idea. She pictured again the Greek girl of her earlier imaginings, dressed in a simple white tunic, carrying a stone water pot back to her home for her mother to use for cooking the—

Her thoughts were abruptly interrupted by the loud ringing of her phone.

She glanced down at it, and her heart sank. Not Xanthe. Nell's school. Tentatively, she picked up the handset and answered. It was the head, Mr Donovan, a man who Carrie always thought seemed far too young to have such a position of authority, and who Nell wasn't remotely scared of. Which was a pity, because it meant that the punishment that came with each misdemeanour was like water off a duck's back.

'Mrs Corduner?' Mr Donovan sounded vaguely bored, as if making this call was the last thing he wanted to be doing. 'I'm calling about Nell,' he continued. 'Don't worry, she's perfectly safe. But do you have a few minutes to talk?'

Carrie's stomach lurched. As she had expected; definitely a problem. This wasn't the time to remind him, yet again, that she wasn't a Mrs. 'Um, yes, fine.'

The head proceeded to inform Carrie that Nell and some friends had been caught vaping behind the sixth form block, even though all forms of smoking, be it cigarettes or vapes, were strictly forbidden on school grounds. Nell was therefore suspended for the rest of that day, and the next, and Carrie needed to come and collect her right away.

'I'm so sorry,' Carrie managed to enunciate, while thoughts of the dire consequences she would wreak on her wayward daughter swirled around in her head. This latest infraction came off the back of getting drunk in the Priory Gardens a few months ago, and a more recent incident involving ingestion of magic mushroom tea that had made Nell both copiously sick and scarily high.

Hauling herself up from her chair, feeling about a hundred years old, Carrie grabbed her keys and coat and headed for the car, rushing to get the door open as the rain lashed down. Thank goodness she wasn't working, or she'd have had to say she couldn't come. She willed her ancient VW Polo into life and set off into Marlborough. Why was Nell so wilful and disobedient? Of course the teenage brief was to push the boundaries, but did Nell have to follow it quite so closely? Carrie had never been like this when she'd been that age, wouldn't have dreamt of it. And for Nell, who needed to be extra careful of her heart, illicit substances were even more dangerous than they were for others. Carrie frequently found herself tearing her hair out in despair, and blaming her daughter's undesirable friends for being bad influences. But she knew what others thought. That Nell's misdemeanours were because Carrie was a single mum and Nell didn't have a father constantly on the scene to enforce discipline.

Carrie had always railed against the stereotypical view of the single mother, seeing it as one of the many ways in which society vilified people like her. As she'd always belligerently insisted to herself, she could do just as a good a job as a traditional couple, if not a better one.

But what if that wasn't true? What if it *was* her fault?

And then a feeling of even greater despondency assailed her. If it was the lack of a live-in father that was the problem, there was little Carrie could do about it. For good reason, her relationship with Jack was almost non-existent, and there was no way she could ask him for help. Recently Nell, who loved her dad and was in constant communication with him over the phone and internet, had been agitating to know the reason why her parents had split up before she was even born. Perhaps that and the acting out she was doing at the moment were related. It was a reasonable assumption.

Carrie slammed on the brakes and jolted to her senses as the car in front swung a left turn without indicating. There was no excuse for Nell's behaviour and that was that. And as for her demands to know more about her parents' relationship, that was a non-starter. Though she hated the fact that she couldn't give Nell clear answers, there was no way Carrie could tell her the truth.

Not now.

Not ever.

# CHAPTER 2

## CARRIE, 2024

'It's raining again,' observed Nell, as she sat at the kitchen table staring at her phone while her arm mechanically delivered dripping spoonfuls of cereal to her mouth.

'Yes, I know,' replied Carrie absent-mindedly, as she added a few notes to the scrawling pages she'd already covered in her notebook. She was still thrashing out the concept for the Santorini/Atlantis book idea, which hadn't yet crystallised into something solid enough to submit to her publisher. Her years of faltering success had sapped her confidence and now she was doubting herself at every turn.

She opened her laptop as if perhaps typing might be more productive than handwriting, but found herself staring at the screen without adding anything of any worth. She snapped the lid shut and turned to Nell.

'Right,' she said, 'as soon as you've finished eating, we'll get going, OK?'

Nell nodded wordlessly, not taking her eyes off her phone screen. Carrie shook her head and left her to it while she went to her bedroom and threw a few items of clothing and toiletries into an overnight bag. They were going to her parents' house and would stay the night. Carrie was looking forward to it as Harriet and Bill's home was always warm, Harriet's cooking was incomparably better than her own and Nell tended to become marginally less recalcitrant when with her beloved grandparents. Though if truth be told, she had been a little better since the vaping incident and her two-day suspension from school. Carrie had ripped her to shreds over that. But maybe that was what Nell had needed, as she did seem to be knuckling down to her schoolwork now, and not a moment too soon. The exams were only two months away.

Half an hour later, they were ready to leave. Nell slouched into the hallway dressed in the regulation jeans that were about three sizes too big and held up by a shoelace round the waist, and a top Carrie hadn't seen before.

'Nice tank-top,' she said, gesturing towards it. 'They were popular in my day. Have they come back in again?'

Nell fixed her with a reproving glance. 'It's a sweater vest. But thanks. I got it for a fiver from the charity shop. It's merino and lambswool.' The latter was thrown out with a nonchalance that made Carrie want to giggle. She doubted that Nell even knew what these fibres were. But what was she calling the garment again? Carrie frowned.

'Sweater vest? Where did that name come from?'

'I dunno.' Nell shrugged. 'It's a sweater without sleeves, so a vest. Makes sense.'

'Precisely. Or to give it its proper name, a tank-top,' replied Carrie with a smile and a roll of her eyes. Nell, predictably, ignored her, and glided regally past pulling a little suitcase that Carrie hoped was laden with revision materials rather than more vintage clothing finds.

An hour or so later, ensconced in her parents' conservatory with the rain once again beating down on the glass roof, Carrie told her mother about her Santorini book idea. Harriet had always been her biggest fan and reliably wrote her great reviews and told all her friends about her clever daughter's amazing writing. Not that it added up to any sales, but it was still good to have the affirmation.

'Santorini.' Harriet frowned, her brow creasing as she seemed to be searching her memory for something. 'You went there when you were travelling, didn't you, with that lovely Greek friend of yours? And it only occurred to me afterwards that I'm sure your Great-Uncle Sol was there, during the war, when he was with the Special Boat Squadron.'

Carrie gave her mother an enquiring look. 'Really? Why would he – or they – have been on Santorini? I didn't realise the war went anywhere near such tiny, far-flung Greek islands.'

Harriet shook her head. 'I don't know much about it, if I'm honest. In common with many of that generation, Sol didn't talk much about his wartime antics. He let the name "Santorini" slip a couple of times but then acted quite strangely, really secretive, as if he'd made a mistake to mention it. He never spoke of it in any detail, and I didn't ask. It felt like prying, somehow – though now I wish I had found out more. There were so many things about Sol that I didn't understand.'

Carrie's brow furrowed in puzzlement. 'Like what?' she asked, as she recalled her great-uncle, who both she and her older sister Jenny had adored, how he had spent hours reading them stories by the fire, or entertaining them by plucking coins out of their ears and confounding them with card tricks that they could never work out, generally being the sort of kind and funny uncle that everyone should have. Not only that, but it was an unexpected legacy bequeathed in his will that had enabled Carrie to scrape together the deposit to buy her little cottage. She had so much to be grateful for when it came to Great-Uncle Sol.

'Oh, I don't know,' Harriet sighed, as she plucked at a loose thread on her cardigan sleeve. 'It's hard to put into words. He had such a sunny and friendly disposition, but then he'd suddenly go quiet and even morose, for no discernible reason. It was as if there was something in his past that he couldn't confront, couldn't contemplate. Something that had left an indelible mark, that was always there, haunting him.'

'Gosh,' mused Carrie. 'How mysterious. I wish we knew what it was. What he'd been through that might have affected him so much.'

'I agree,' replied her mother. 'He said something so cryptic once. *Don't let opportunity pass you by*. I really had no idea what he meant, but for some reason I didn't ask. If only I'd been more inquisitive, probed him further. But you know how it is. One always thinks these things when it's too late.' She paused, her expression wistful, as if remembering all sorts of occasions when not enough had been said or asked.

Those questions could not be asked directly now, for Sol had died twenty years or so ago. At the time, Carrie had been wrapped up in schoolwork, friendship groups and her obsession with the band Keane – the preoccupations of teenage life – but nevertheless she had felt deep and profound loss at his passing. His funeral had been the first one she'd ever been to, the first time she'd seen a coffin, witnessed a burial. She wondered how many deaths Sol had seen, during his wartime service, and felt an irrational irritation at her mother for not being more curious and talking to him about his experiences. The war generation were nearly all gone now, which made it seem even more impor-tant than ever to capture the stories of those who had been involved, to find out everything possible about them.

'We've still got lots of his things in the garage from when we packed his house up,' Harriet continued, eventually. 'I was his only living relative and he was my last connection to the past. I should sort through it all, or get rid of it, I suppose. I always meant to but somehow I never got round to it, so it all came with us when we moved and it's still sitting there...' Her voice tailed off as if the thought of dealing with Sol's belongings was too exhausting to contemplate. Anxiety grabbed at Carrie's heart. She'd noticed her mother, who was in her late sixties, slowing down recently, finally starting to show her age. But Harriet could not fade. She could not *die*. Neither Carrie nor Nell could bear that. It suddenly felt imperative to discover more about Sol's past, for her mother's sake as much as her own, to fill in the gaps in the family history, to make it complete while she still had the chance.

'Can I have a look through his stuff?' asked Carrie, as a rush of nostalgia flooded over her for those childhood family gatherings characterised by Sol's magic tricks and general congeniality. He'd always been so interested in whatever she and Jenny were doing, so amenable to playing Cluedo or endless games of Monopoly with them, forever patient and loving. But now her mother had pointed it out, she also recalled him suddenly falling quiet, his kind eyes behind his glasses taking on an absent expression, gazing at something that no one else could see. What had been on his mind at those times? Would there be any clues in his stash of possessions in her parents' garage? 'See if there's anything that could shed some light?' she added, willing her mother to agree.

'Of course you can,' answered Harriet. 'By all means.'

Fired up by curiosity, after they'd had a simple lunch of home-made bread and soup, and Nell was installed in Bill's study doing her homework, Carrie announced that she was off to the garage to have a poke around.

'Here you go,' Harriet said, handing her a black bin bag. 'If you come across anything that is clearly rubbish, chuck it. I'm feeling terribly guilty about what a job you're going to have if me and your dad fall off our perches. Any inroads you can make will be worthwhile.'

Carrie rolled her eyes in mock dismay. 'Don't even think about expiring before everything is shipshape,' she replied. She made it into a joke, but it wasn't really. She didn't want to contemplate her parents' mortality for the second time that day; she had no idea how she'd cope without them. They had always supported her and, when Nell had been born, had always been on hand to help out, even though Carrie knew that her mother secretly disapproved of single mothers. She greatly appreciated the fact that Harriet had put her deep-seated belief in marriage and the nuclear family to one side to come to her daughter's aid in her hour of need, especially as it must have been so hard for her not to interrogate Carrie about why she and Jack had split up. But Harriet had refrained from pressing her on the matter, recognising that it was something private between Carrie and Jack, and Carrie was so grateful for that. There were so many reasons why she never would or could reveal to anyone what happened between her and Jack. Even after all this time, the thought of anyone knowing, especially her parents, made her feel physically ill.

Shoving such unpleasant thoughts to one side, just as she'd resolved not to dwell on the impending mortgage disaster this weekend, Carrie focused on the garage. Like many such buildings across the land, it was used to store anything and everything except a car. It took a while, and much moving and repositioning of various crates, broken items of furniture, faulty lamps and all manner of other rubbish, for her to reach Sol's possessions right at the back. There were a dozen or so large cardboard boxes, piled haphazardly one on top of another, and looking far too heavy and unwieldy for Carrie to handle alone. For a moment she considered leaving it for another day, but immediately told herself not to be ridiculous. She couldn't give up that easily.

Bracing herself, she grasped hold of one of the boxes and, with a great effort of strength and will, managed to heft it down to a small patch of floor space that she'd freed up. Red in the face and sweating, Carrie opened the flaps and gingerly reached inside, pushing aside a layer of crumpled newspaper pages to reveal what lay beneath. She soon discovered that the entire box seemed to be full of crockery and cutlery, none of which was of any interest. The next two boxes were no more fruitful, containing nothing but ornaments and bric-a-brac, kitchenware and flower vases.

It was in the fourth box that Carrie found some more intriguing items. A magician's handbook made her laugh; was this how Sol had taught himself the tricks that had so entertained her and Jenny? Perhaps it was the solitude of the garage, or the nostalgic journey she had embarked upon, but the thought of her sister pierced through her like an arrow to the heart. She'd glossed over the memories earlier, refused to fully engage with the image of her and Jenny, laughing and giggling, gazing at their uncle with adoring eyes. One year they'd saved up their pocket money so that they could play a few tricks on him, and had bought a severed finger and a whoopee cushion from the toy shop in town. They had fallen about laughing when Sol feigned terrible embarrassment after he sat on the cushion, or pretended to call an ambulance when Jenny presented her apparently injured hand.

If only her relationship with Jenny hadn't gone as sour as that with Jack. Carrie would have loved to be able to compare parenting notes with her sister, who had two girls a little younger than Nell. How amazing would it have been for Nell to have had cousins to bond with and grow up with? It was another of Nell's oft-expressed grievances – that not only did she not have any siblings but her mother had deprived her of the two cousins she did have. A twist of agony wrenched at Carrie's insides. It was all so rubbish, so terrible, so hideously unfair, because it wasn't *her* fault, wasn't Carrie who was responsible for the rift with Nell's father and aunt; but she could never explain that properly to Nell, because it *had* to remain secret.

For a moment Carrie paused, arms deep in the box, a crushing weight of disappointment and failure pressing down on her. It was all so messed up and time hadn't healed, not one bit. She'd loved Jack with an intensity that seared through her soul. She'd thought he'd felt the same way. And then it had happened, that terrible betrayal, that moment when Carrie's entire world had come tumbling down around her ears, when her utter despair had seemed bottomless and immeasurable. The emotion was as raw now as it had been then. And that had been the end of her and Jack. It had felt like the end of everything.

And then she'd discovered she was pregnant. She'd had a vomiting bug which must have rendered the pill ineffective, leading to Nell's entirely unintentional conception. She'd vowed from the moment she knew that she'd have this baby and love it to the end of the world and back. Even if she had to do it alone. She'd pulled herself together and forced herself to carry on, for the baby's sake.

For Nell.

Distractedly, eyes brimming with tears, Carrie pulled another book out of the box and gazed blearily down at it, wanting something to take her mind off the awful memories, blinking hard and fast in an attempt to see clearly. It was around A5 size, with thick paper; a sketchbook, Carrie realised, old and worn, with faded covers and dog-eared corners. On opening the book she found drawings, lots of them, compelling images of young men, in groups or alone, sailing ships, cleaning guns, trekking across hostile landscapes, weary eyes in sun-scorched, weather-beaten faces showing steely determination. She'd had no idea that her uncle had had such artistic talent – and who were these people? Sol's fellow soldiers? They weren't in uniform, but perhaps that brigade Sol had belonged to didn't wear them. What had her mother said it was? The Special Boat Squadron, that was it. She'd look it up online, later.

Gazing at the pictures, she imagined the campaigns these

men might have been involved in, the danger they must have confronted, risking their lives on a daily – nightly – basis.

She flipped through the book until another image jumped out at her, completely different to those that had filled the preceding pages. This one was of a young woman with beautiful almond eyes and glossy hair that curled fetchingly around her heart-shaped face. The portrait was stunningly lifelike, making Carrie feel that the woman was there with her in the half-light of the dusty, fusty garage. Peering down, she saw that the drawing was captioned *VK, Santorini, 1944.*

So Harriet had been right. Sol had been on the Greek island during the war. An image of Santorini formed in her mind from all those years ago, or perhaps from Xanthe's postcard, of a village of brilliantly whitewashed houses clinging to steep cliffs that plunged down towards the sea, with here and there splashes of colour from shocking-pink or purple bougainvillea and blue-domed church roofs, all sparkling in the glorious Greek sunshine.

A shudder ran through Carrie; she'd been hot earlier, lugging the boxes around, but outside the rain had begun to fall again and it felt suddenly chilly in the dark garage. She was about to leave, go back to the house and have a hot drink, when she decided to have a last rummage in the box. There were some more books, earnest and weighty tomes including Gibbon's *The History of the Decline and Fall of the Roman Empire*, and a few inconsequential knick-knacks. Then she pulled out a cloth bag, inside which was a man's shirt made of rough brown cotton, with buttons that seemed to have been whittled from wood. It was faded and worn, with deep crease lines where it had lain folded for so long.

Carrie opened it out and gave it a shake, then examined it more closely. It was entirely handmade, each stitch painstakingly neat and even. Someone had sewn this shirt with great care, and, though it seemed that it had already been long past its best when Sol had packed it away, he had not consigned it to the rubbish bin. For a few moments, Carrie stared at the simple garment, wondering why her great-uncle had kept it safely tucked up in the bag for what must have been many years.

After a while, she gathered together the shirt and the sketchbook and took them with her back to the house. Inside, all was quiet and still, Nell apparently poring over her books in the study, both of her parents napping in the conservatory. Carrie made a cup of tea and inspected the portrait again. This time, in better light, she noticed something she hadn't seen before.

Round the young woman's neck was a small pendant. Carrie fetched her mother's magnifying glass from the sitting room and focused it on the necklace. The picture on the pendant was of an old-fashioned tall ship, which immediately brought to Carrie's mind images from history lessons of the British navy confronting the Spanish Armada. She grabbed her laptop and googled 'tall ship Francis Drake'. Immediately, multiple hits showed her the back of a pre-metric halfpenny coin featuring the *Golden Hind*. She looked again at Sol's drawing. It was the exact same image.

Carrie's eyes filled with tears again.

In her mind's eye, she saw Sol, sitting in the high-backed armchair in her parents' living room, staring into the distance, his usual jovial expression transformed into one that was absent and wistful, as if he were remembering something ineffably sad from a long time ago.

What had been on his mind in those private moments of recollection? The need to find out burned inside Carrie like a fire.

# CHAPTER 3

## VASSIA, 1944

It was a beautiful morning, the air bright, light and hopeful, a fresh breeze rustling the vibrant pink bougainvillea blooms, the first of the spring, that spilled over the courtyard wall. Everything was perfectly normal.

If there was such a thing as normal with an enemy army in occupation.

Vassia bent, plucked a pillowcase from the laundry basket at her feet, then reached up, pegs in hand, to secure it on the line. Despite still being tired after the celebrations for her father's name day two days earlier, she had woken early and decided to get a wash done. She continued with her task, rhythmically plucking and pegging, until a strange, uncanny sensation stopped her in her tracks.

Stilling, Vassia listened, heart pounding, the overpowering sense of being watched intensifying by the moment. Holding her breath, she waited. There was no sound, no sign of movement in front of her. But behind? She hardly dared look. She had no reason to be scared because, of course, she had done nothing wrong.

But ever since the Italian troops had landed on the island

three years before, and the Germans a year ago, everyone had become wary. The best strategy seemed to be to keep your head down, attract no attention and attempt to carry on with everyday life, and that was what Vassia and all of her family – her father Ianos, her mother Thalia, her brother Andreas and his wife Athena – had always tried to do.

There was nothing to worry about, Vassia told herself sternly as she stood, damp pillowcase in her hands, summoning all her courage. Taking a deep breath, she turned round, almost impossibly slowly, her eyes darting here and there, searching for whatever it was that had instilled the troubling feeling that she was not alone.

A blackbird trilled, piercing and shrill, from atop the grapevine pergola that shaded the door to the house. Usually the bird's presence comforted Vassia, but today its call sounded like one of alarm rather than joy. Her gaze moved on, to the staircase that led up to the roof, upon each tread of which stood flowerpots that brimmed with aromatic herbs and bright geraniums. Nothing amiss there.

The entire courtyard was serene and calm under the steadily rising sun.

Finally, Vassia turned towards the cobalt-blue door that gave onto the street outside. It was ajar, as it often was, the catch being old and worn. That was nothing unusual. But as Vassia's eyes settled upon it, icy terror ran though her veins. Because, inch by tortuous inch, the door was opening. Fixed to the spot, Vassia could hardly breathe. She watched as, there on the threshold, a man was revealed, rough-looking with weathered, leathery skin.

He was holding a Luger pistol, and it was pointed at her.

Vassia's hand flew up to her mouth as she emitted a small, stifled scream. Immediately, the man strode briskly towards her, gesturing at her to be quiet. Legs trembling, Vassia bit her lip and helplessly waited to see what the man was going to do.

Kidnap her? Shoot her? Sweat broke out on her forehead and the palms of her hands, though it wasn't hot yet, the sun only a mild, considerate presence at this hour in this season.

The man looked about him, then stepped to the side of Vassia, scrutinising the house and the courtyard as if he owned the place. The cheek! Vassia's mood changed in an instant. Who did this person think he was, coming onto the Kourakises' property without a by-your-leave?

In a moment, she had her answer.

'My name is Spyros Papadopoulous,' he said to her in a strange, murmured hiss. Immediately, from his accent Vassia placed him as from the mainland, Athens she guessed. 'Is this the home of the mayor, Ianos Kourakis?' An increasing urgency tinged the man's voice.

Vassia hesitated. Was this a trap? Should she tell him who lived here? But it seemed he knew already – and he had that gun. She cast a wary eye at the weapon, hanging loose in his hand but surely put to its purpose in a matter of seconds should he wish to do so.

'It is,' she answered. And then, more boldly, 'Why do you want him?'

Spyros shook his head. 'I can't tell you now,' he replied. 'I just need to see him. He's your father, I take it?'

Vassia nodded, narrowing her eyes and inspecting the man more closely. He was not wearing a uniform, and he looked as if he hadn't shaved in a week, but there was something about him. Something that told her that he had a genuine purpose, and that it was serious, and that she should trust him.

'I'll fetch my father,' she said. And then, thinking that the courtyard walls were not high and that anyone of a reasonable stature could see over them, she continued, 'Why don't you come inside?'

But Spyros had not waited to be asked. He was already making for the door. Vassia followed him.

'Close the shutters,' he instructed her.

Doing so thrust the kitchen into darkness, but Vassia understood that she should comply.

'Would you like coffee?' she asked him. It was not right, impossible even, for a Greek to invite someone into their home and not offer refreshment. 'Water? You must want water.' She bustled over to the sink where a freshly filled pitcher stood.

Spyros waved her away. 'Just get your father for me.'

As Vassia left the room, she heard the glug of water being poured; Spyros was helping himself.

Her father was up and out of bed, thank goodness. Once Vassia had explained, in a few breathless words, that he was needed and why, he hastily pulled on a jacket and headed for the kitchen. Sensing that she should make herself scarce, Vassia went back outside to the washing. Her insides burned with curiosity. Of course her dad, as the mayor of Vourvoulos, should deal with this enigmatic stranger, that was only right and proper. But how Vassia longed to know what was going on, what this impromptu and peculiar meeting was about.

The washing line was nearly full up now and she found herself right up under the kitchen window, trying to find some extra space to hang the last few items. In such close proximity, it was impossible for her not to overhear the rumble of low, male voices that drifted through the chinks in the shutters.

'...arrived this morning by schooner...', '...mission...', '...Special Boat Squadron commandos...', '...tonight...', '...utter secrecy...', '...garrison in Fira...'

The words were weighted with meaning but Vassia could not quite decipher it. What was the Special Boat Squadron? Where had the men come from? What was their purpose or intention, here on Santorini?

Desperate to know more, and no longer pretending to herself that she wasn't eavesdropping on purpose, Vassia hung around under the kitchen window, but the voices had fallen suddenly even softer and now she could barely make out a word. Had Spyros Papadopoulous and his band come to rescue the island, to free it of the Nazi oppressor? Was that what this was all about?

As she strained in vain to hear more, her mind strayed to her idyllic childhood, growing up with her brother Andreas and their loving parents. Thinking back to that time was to conjure up perfection, when Vassia had had not a care in the world. In the summer, she and Andreas would play for hours on the black sand beaches, swimming and diving, laughing and splashing. They had a little boat that, when they were old enough, they would sail along the coastline, visiting secret coves accessible only by sea, or across the deep, dark waters of the caldera to the other islands in the archipelago. Sometimes the breeze would bring the faint smell of sulphur from what remained of the volcano and Vassia and Andreas would imagine it as the last, dying breaths of the monster that had once caused so much destruction.

When the tourists came, which they had occasionally done in the 1930s, if they were exceptionally adventurous, drawn by rumours of Santorini's simple beauty, its sunshine, the villages of cave houses and churches, the impossible blue of the sea and the fiery colours of its spectacular sunsets, the siblings would giggle at their sunburnt and sweaty faces, their crumpled and dishevelled clothing that was limp in the heat, and then scamper away, losing themselves in the warrens of tiny cobbled alleyways that wound between the buildings.

When the wild winter winds began to blow, they would hunker down inside, early to bed and early to rise, getting on with the business of living, going to school and learning their lessons, or spending time with their huge extended family of grandparents, uncles, aunts and cousins.

That life had been swept away in 1941, with the arrival of Italian troops and their freedom further curtailed by the Nazis.

Since then, Vassia and Andreas had often huddled together, plotting ways to force the occupier out, from poisoning their food to contaminating the water supply. But of course the reality was there was nothing they could do. Their father, the mayor, shared their frustration – and their sense of impotence. The dark cloud of occupation cast its shadows over everyone on the island and for a long time now there had been little hope of reprieve.

In recent weeks and months, the Kourakis family had been distracted by a piece of good news – Andreas and his wife Athena were expecting their first child. The announcement of the pregnancy had been received with great joy on all sides. But now that too was marred by anxiety, because the baby was nearly two weeks overdue. Athena was huge and uncomfortable and Andreas simultaneously popping with excitement about the impending birth and riven with worry about the lack of signs that labour was imminent.

A sudden, loud expostulation from inside the house tore Vassia's thoughts away from the past and her brother and sharply back to the present. Her attention had drifted – what had she missed? She leant even closer to the shuttered window.

'We are sheltering in a cave nearby,' Spyros was explaining. 'There are nineteen of us, under the command of Captain Andersen – as I am Greek, he sent me out to find locals to help us. We need food and water, plus guides who can lead us to the locations we are to attack. They must be brave, knowledgeable – and entirely trustworthy.'

A thrill of fear mingled with apprehension surged through Vassia's veins. Guiding Allied forces in a mission of destruction against the Nazis? This would be incredibly dangerous for anyone involved. Who among the villagers, all of them simple farmers or fishermen, winemakers or quarrymen, would Ianos put forward?

Vassia's breath caught in her throat as she waited for her father to answer.

The voices dropped once more and a few agonising minutes went by, during which Vassia's entire body was coiled tight as a spring. And then she heard footsteps from within, her father's distinctive, heavy tread, followed by the door swinging open.

'Vassia!' Her father peered round the door. As his eyes fell upon his daughter, he raised his hand and beckoned to her.

Filled with nervous trepidation, Vassia followed him inside.

# CHAPTER 4

CARRIE, 2024

Next morning, Carrie woke to the sound of a notification as a message pinged onto her phone. She reached out to pick it up, blinking blearily to clear her eyes. It was from Xanthe.

> *Sorry for the late reply, I've only just had my phone repaired after I dropped it – whoops! Are you free for a call now?*

Sitting up in bed, Carrie checked the time. It was eight o'clock. A bit early for a Sunday, she thought, before remembering that Greece was two hours ahead.

She messaged back, *Give me five minutes. And not Face-Time... I'm still in my jammies!*

Armed with a cup of coffee, she went back to her bedroom to take the call, and crawled under the covers into the snug cocoon of the bed. She answered the phone as soon as it rang and she and Xanthe chatted for a short while, catching up on the health and well-being of family members and themselves, before Carrie asked about Xanthe's new man, Spencer.

'He's really great,' Xanthe enthused, excitedly. 'We've been getting on so well. But sadly he's got to be in the States for six weeks over the summer, so we're going to have to be long-distance for a while.'

'Oh, that's a shame,' commiserated Carrie. 'You'll miss him.'

'I will,' agreed Xanthe. 'But, as I'm a digital nomad these days, I'm going to base myself in Santorini while he's away – you know, I mentioned it in my postcard? Athens is far too hot, crowded and polluted in the summer, and it was only when we went back to the island for that short break that I remembered how much I love it. I've no idea why I've stayed away for so long.'

'Well, if you have the chance to ship out of the city, why not?' agreed Carrie, suppressing her envy. How wonderful to have an island paradise to escape to.

Carrie heard Xanthe beaming at her across the airwaves. 'I know I asked you already when I wrote, but I'm going to ask again – why don't you come out for a holiday? You and Nell? I've rented a one-bedroom flat in Fira as it's more convenient for work, but my grandparents' house is empty. You might remember it from all those years ago. It's only small but the village is lovely – a proper, traditional one – it would be perfect for you and Nell, you could live like locals!'

Carrie's heart leapt anew at the suggestion. She could feel the warmth of the Santorini sun on her skin, taste the delicious Greek food and wine, feel the tension and stress of life melt away... It would be a chance to get Nell away from her undesirable friends, and perhaps she could also glean some inspiration for her Art A level from the distinctive scenery and architecture of the island.

It was a marvellous idea. But, as always, the problem was money.

'I'd love to, but—' she began, but Xanthe interrupted before she had a chance to finish.

'There'd be nothing to pay except your flights and living

costs when you're here,' she said, coaxingly. 'So it wouldn't be too expensive.'

The offer was so tempting. Carrie would so love to go. Nell's exams would be finished by mid-June, so they could travel before the school summer holidays started, which would make the flights cheaper. She'd get her wages from the leisure centre on Friday; one of her colleagues had been off sick for a few weeks now, so Carrie had worked lots of extra shifts – she could probably scrape together about £450. But even so, it wasn't enough. And there was still that council tax bill looming, not to mention the new mortgage to arrange and somehow, God alone knew how, to afford. If Carrie lost the house because she could no longer pay her way, it would feel like a betrayal of Sol, of his legacy, as if she had not only let her daughter down but her great-uncle as well. She had been so, so lucky to inherit enough money to put down a deposit and the guilt she felt as she contemplated the squandering of that good fortune was all-consuming. She *had* to find a way to get the cash together to save her home. She just had to.

'Look, I'll think about it and get back to you,' she stalled, not wanting to offend Xanthe or seem like she was snubbing her friend's generosity. The thing was that other people, her friends with good, graduate careers and no dependents, had no idea how hard it was financially when you were stuck in a low-paying job with a child to fend for as well as yourself. That wasn't a criticism – merely a fact of life.

'All right,' agreed Xanthe, clearly seeing that she wasn't going to get Carrie to commit right then. 'So,' she continued, breezily, 'what about your love life? Anything doing?'

Carrie gave a derisory snort. 'Absolutely zilch,' she replied, flatly. 'The only love in my life is Nell – and she's enough for the moment.'

Xanthe's silence was more expressive than words.

'What about that lovely man you hung out with in Santorini?' she said eventually. 'Kyriakos. He was a hunk, wasn't he?'

An involuntary snort of laughter burst out of Carrie. 'Goodness, that was so long ago!' she exclaimed. 'I'd almost forgotten about him.' That was an out-and-out lie. She'd thought about him the moment she'd received Xanthe's postcard, and in lots of moments since. But Xanthe didn't need to know that; Carrie was convinced it just made her look sad and pathetic, hankering after a transitory holiday romance from over a decade and a half ago.

'He might still remember you,' rejoined Xanthe. 'Wouldn't it be fun to meet up again, rekindle that spark?'

This time Carrie's laugh was long and loud. 'You are ridiculous,' she said, when she'd recovered. 'Insanely ridiculous.' She heard her mother calling to her from downstairs. 'I better go,' she said. 'It was so lovely to talk.'

'Lots of love,' cried Xanthe, blowing kisses. 'See you in Santorini!'

*If only*, whispered Carrie to herself as she hung up.

From the kitchen, the welcoming smell of toast and bacon wafted towards her as she descended the stairs. She settled down at the table, picked up the newspaper and began half-heartedly flicking through it, not really taking anything in.

Harriet noticed her preoccupation. 'What's up? You're very quiet this morning. You look as if you're pondering something.'

Carrie sighed. She recounted to her mother the phone call with Xanthe and the invitation to Santorini.

Harriet sighed. 'Oh, Carrie, I'm sorry,' she said. 'I wish we could help. Perhaps Dad and I could scrape...'

'Stop!' Carrie interjected, cutting her mother off. 'Don't even think about offering me money or apologising for the fact that you can't. You do so much for me and Nell, there's no way I'm taking any of your retirement fund.' She didn't mention her fears that she wouldn't be able to manage her new mortgage payments. Her parents didn't need to have that anxiety in their lives, and it was entirely Carrie's responsibility, not theirs.

Harriet sighed again. 'There's no need to be so proud, Carrie.'

'I'm not proud. But I'm also not a charity case.' As soon as the words were out, Carrie realised that they might sound harsh. 'Mum,' she went on, softening her voice, 'I so appreciate the support you give me. But you're going to need all your money for your own futures. Please don't think you owe me anything.'

Nodding, Harriet fell silent, contemplatively spreading butter on her toast. 'Maybe I could persuade your father to go to Santorini one day,' she said wistfully. 'But you know what he's like. If it's abroad, it has to be France. Switzerland at a push. I've always had this strange feeling that if I went to the island I might understand Sol a little better.'

'Understand what, exactly?' Carrie asked.

Harriet sighed. 'All those oddities about him that I've already mentioned. He always makes me think of that quote from Winston Churchill – "a riddle, wrapped in a mystery, inside an enigma". Churchill was talking about Russia but it could just as well be about Sol.'

Carrie gave a half-laugh. 'Since you mentioned it I realised that, even though Jenny and I were only children, I did recognise that beneath his rambunctiousness there was a sense of something missing. I don't know how to describe it. An emptiness, maybe. He'd be roaring with laughter one minute and then suddenly fall silent, and he'd get this expression on his face as if the world had fallen in.'

'We were taught to be so wary of the war heroes we grew up among,' Harriet said, as if explaining to herself as much as to her daughter. 'Told that they were not allowed to share their experiences because of secrecy laws, and that anyway talking about the bad times would make them worse. No one understood then that burying trauma can be so damaging. It was all stiff upper lip and get on with it.'

'Do you think he was traumatised?' asked Carrie.

Her mother sighed. 'I don't know. I really don't. If he was, I'm sure he never spoke to anyone about it. For all the reasons I just gave, and also because – well, who would he have told? He didn't have a wife to confide in, as perhaps many men of that era did.'

'Yes,' agreed Carrie. 'Everyone else we knew was part of a couple, and even as a kid I remember wondering why there wasn't a Mrs Sol.'

'Exactly.' Harriet shook her head before continuing. 'I never understood why he didn't marry.'

Carrie's heart lurched at these words. They implied that Sol had been lonely, which felt so sad, especially for someone who had so obviously enjoyed company.

'Perhaps he never met The One,' Carrie suggested, at the same time as thinking that he'd surely not have been short of opportunities. A brave soldier, returned in one piece from his heroic service in the war, handsome, generous, intelligent; what was not to like? There must have been no end of young women who'd have been only too pleased to become Mrs Sol Baker.

Harriet smiled pensively. 'Possibly. He had girlfriends, certainly,' she said, affirming Carrie's suppositions. 'There was one I remember who he saw for a long time – Jean, I think her name was. She was lovely. Pretty and lively and friendly and she clearly adored him. I really thought he'd make the move with her. But they never so much as got engaged, let alone married, and in the end she gave up. She and Sol parted company and the next I heard, she'd found someone else. Her wedding to the new chap took place within six months of meeting and they soon had two children – and far from being jealous or realising he'd missed out, Sol was genuinely happy for her, sent her a wedding present and everything. I could never work it out.' She stared into her teacup as if there might lie the answer, then added, 'And before you ask, I really don't think he was secretly gay. I'm absolutely convinced that wasn't the case.'

All of Carrie's synapses were on full alert listening to this, and the portrait of the young woman leapt to her mind's eye. She got up and went to her room to fetch the tattered sketchbook and the handmade shirt, and brought both items downstairs to show to her mother.

As soon as she laid eyes on the picture, Harriet gasped and clutched at her throat. 'Gosh, what a beauty.' She fumbled for her reading glasses, put them on and examined the woman more closely. 'Exquisite. And so wonderfully drawn.'

Carrie nodded. 'Do you think Sol was in love with this girl?' she suggested.

Harriet considered this for a moment and then shook her head. 'It's a nice idea but I doubt it. I shouldn't think he had time for love. When he was in the SBS – well I don't know much but I do know that they never stayed in one place for long. Certainly not long enough for relationships.' She pursed her lips. 'As I said before, it's a mystery.'

'And there's this shirt as well,' Carrie said. 'It's all handstitched, but it's pretty old and worn. There must have been a reason for Sol to keep it.'

Harriet frowned. 'I didn't even know that was in there,' she murmured, examining the shirt. 'Perhaps someone special made it for him. Who knows? Now I feel even more terrible about all the unanswered questions.'

She shook her head as if chastising herself anew for her negligence. And then she clapped her hands together, making Carrie jump. 'Wait a minute!' Her tone was suddenly urgent. 'Gosh I must be getting old – I forget things for years and then all of a sudden they pop up in my head. And I've just recalled...' She got up and rushed out of the room, her final unsaid words left for Carrie to guess at. Except that she couldn't think of what could possibly have so excited her mother.

She didn't have long to wait. Within five minutes Harriet was back, clutching a small dark green box, the sort used by jewellers to hold rings or earrings.

Plumping back down onto her chair, Harriet held it out to Carrie. 'This belonged to Sol. But I didn't collect it up along with all the rest of his possessions. He gave the box to me, just before he died. He told me it was very precious, that I should hold on to it and give it to you or Jenny. It had completely slipped my mind but thinking of him again now, and seeing that stunning picture of the young woman... it suddenly brought it all back.'

Gingerly, as if scared it would bite, Carrie opened the box and stared at the ring inside. It was a simple gold band, studded with five diamonds, a picture of understated elegance and beautiful because of it.

'It's lovely,' she murmured. 'I wonder what the story is behind it.'

Her mother narrowed her eyes in puzzlement. 'I think,' she began, and then started again. 'He said something else,' she muttered, thinking hard. 'That he should have given it to someone but wasn't able to, never had the chance or something. I can't imagine why I just forgot about it – so much was going on at that time, when he had that final illness, you and Jenny with all your schoolwork and exams, plus there was some issue with your dad's job... I wasn't paying attention, is the truth.'

Carrie eased the ring out of the slit in the box's padding that held it in place. She turned it towards the light and the diamonds sparkled and shone like the eyes of a person in love.

'Do you think it could be anything to do with the woman in the sketchbook?' she asked, slipping the ring onto her finger. It fitted perfectly. 'Could Sol have bought it for her?'

Harriet gazed at the ring. 'As I said before, I can't imagine how that could be the case. I can't see how he would have got to know someone in Santorini that well.'

Carrie removed the ring from her finger and scrutinised it more closely.

'Wait,' she said, excitedly. 'There's something engraved inside it.' She held the ring up to the light and screwed her eyes up as she tried to decipher the engraving. 'No, it's no good,' she concluded. 'It's not English.' She turned to her mother. 'Give me a pen and paper. I'll try to copy it out.'

Painstakingly, Carrie copied down the words as best she could: πίστις, ἐλπίς, ἀγάπη.

'I hope I've done it correctly,' she said, once she had finished. She studied the letters closely. 'I think it's Greek,' she concluded. 'But I've no idea how to translate it into English. I don't think my ancient laptop has a facility to change to the Greek alphabet.'

She and her mother sat staring at the piece of paper as though, if they looked at it long enough, the meaning would suddenly become apparent. It didn't.

'I'll work something out,' Carrie said, more to herself than Harriet. She took some pictures of the piece of paper she'd written the words down on and the ring, then placed it gently back in the box and snapped shut the lid. 'I want to go to Santorini even more now,' she groaned. And then added quickly, 'and that's not a cue for you to offer money again.'

'Don't worry, I won't,' responded Harriet, smiling and shaking her head. She put the box onto the shelf where the eggs and water jugs lived.

Carrie drank the last of her coffee. 'I'm going to try to get on with some more work on my book idea,' she said. 'If you're sure you don't want any help with Sunday lunch.'

Her mother had already told her that she was more than happy to do the cooking on her own.

*I like it, it relaxes me*, she'd insisted, which was inexplicable to Carrie, who hated cooking. In her bedroom, she sat on the bed, propped up against the pillows, and opened her laptop. She read through what she'd written so far and tinkered around with it a bit, but her heart wasn't in it. It no longer seemed right. Putting her head in her hands, she tried to concentrate. But all she could think about was Sol.

The portrait, the ring and the handmade shirt danced around behind her eyes, tantalising her. There was a story here, she knew. And in that moment, it became obvious. The book she wanted to write was not about a young girl in 1600 BCE, even though she was sure that could be interesting. Instead, much more compelling was Sol's story. This was what she needed to focus on. A real story, not a made-up one, one that would hopefully captivate readers' interest just like it was captivating hers.

What had happened during Sol's brief time on Santorini? Who was the girl in the picture? Why had he bought the ring but never given it away? Where had he acquired the shirt? In what way were these items connected?

Carrie wanted, no, needed the answers to these questions. If she could find them, and she could turn them into a book, she might be able to save her house and ensure that she and Nell, with her poorly heart and sensitivity to the cold, still had a roof over their heads for the coming winter, and all the ones after that.

Going to Santorini might enable her to get closer to those answers. If only she could find a way to make it possible.

# CHAPTER 5

## VASSIA, 1944

'We will do it.' Ianos' voice was raw and gravelly with emotion. 'For your food and water – we will give you everything you need,' he said. 'My family will put together a package of provisions and my daughter, Vassia here, will deliver them to you within the next hour. And we will provide you with guides.'

Vassia's heart seemed to stop beating as she heard her father's promise of her services. Of course she would gladly give these brave men assistance. But she would be lying if she said that the prospect didn't terrify her. Never in her life before had she done anything that could possibly put her in this kind of danger, but now she was being thrust headfirst into the lion's den.

Steeling herself, Vassia watched as her father sketched what looked like rudimentary maps, drawing lines and marking spots with a thick, blunt pencil. Spyros peered at the maps, waiting for her father to finish them. Vassia began running through in her mind what supplies the kitchen cupboards held and how she could make them into dishes that would be easy to transport and that would fill the commandos up. There were dolmades and *koulouria*, stuffed vine leaves and sesame seed rings, spanakopita and baklava, spinach and feta pie and sweet pastries... all left over from Ianos' name day celebrations; that was lucky, that this event had coincided with the arrival of these mysterious men. What had Spyros called them? A boat squadron? Something like that. They must be here to attack the Germans. But how, when they were so few in number, only nineteen? Her mind returned to the food; this was safer territory than ambushes and sabotage, or whatever Spyros's gang had planned. Cold would have to do for now; later, she could make something hot and take it to the men in the big cooking pot, if she could carry—

Her father's voice cut through her feverish thoughts.

'This is the location of the barracks in Fira,' he instructed, pushing one of the maps towards the commando and plunking a finger in its centre. 'Here is Lieutenant Schwarz's residence. And' – he ruffled through the pile to locate the paper at the bottom – 'this is the radio station at Imerovigli.'

Vassia clenched her palms. So the infiltrators had not just one but three targets to hit. The audacity of it! The bravery... She could not imagine having the courage to do what these men did.

Spyros swept the maps off the table and tucked them securely inside the breast pocket of his shirt.

'I must go before it gets any later,' he said, brusquely. 'Thank you for your help.' He pushed his chair back, its legs scraping harshly against the stone-flagged floor.

'I will find the guides by midday,' Ianos asserted. 'All will be totally trustworthy; do not worry about that.'

The two men shook hands and Vassia wondered who her father was going to suggest should take on the dangerous, and crucial, role of assisting the soldiers. A second later, she had part of the answer.

'One will be me,' he concluded. 'Now go and Godspeed.'

A surge of emotion rose up in Vassia's chest, almost overwhelming her. At the back of her mind she had known that her father would volunteer his own services, but, now that the words had actually been said, their full force hit her like a violent winter tempest. Biting her tongue, she stood back as Spyros left, and waited until his footsteps had receded beyond the courtyard gate before addressing her father.

'Dad!' she cried, unable to temper her anxiety. 'Please don't do it!' She chose her next words carefully, knowing her father's sensitivities about his health. 'Let the young men do their bit. They will revel in the glory of being involved much more than you would. It will be their chance to prove themselves, which you, as mayor, don't need to do.'

Her father frowned, put a hand to his forehead and then let it fall to his side. Vassia took in how tired he looked, and older than his forty-five years. His diabetes had worsened lately, and he was beginning to feel the strain on his heart. Though he did everything he could to cover up his symptoms and carry on as normal, Vassia knew that he wasn't feeling well.

'My dear,' her father responded, his voice quiet and low, but firm. 'I cannot ask friends and family, men of the village, to do what I will not. It is my duty to lead by example.'

Vassia lifted her arms in a gesture of exasperation and then dropped them again. She knew her father, knew that voice. He wasn't going to budge.

'What will you say to Mama?' she asked instead. Her mother would be appalled, horrified. But she would also understand Ianos' insistence.

Her father opened his mouth to reply, but was interrupted by two people entering, Thalia from the inner realms of the house and Andreas through the courtyard and then the kitchen door.

Both the newcomers immediately picked up on the atmosphere in the room.

'What's happened?' cried Thalia. 'Who's died, what's going on?'

Despite the situation, Vassia had to suppress a smile. Her mother lived in perpetual expectation of their elderly relatives, of whom there were many, dropping down dead, despite the fact that they were all as strong as oxen and fit as fiddles.

At the same time, in a voice that was full of concern, Andreas asked, 'Why do you both look like you've seen a ghost?'

Ianos dropped down heavily onto one of the old wooden kitchen chairs. He indicated to the rest of the family to also sit, then explained briefly what had happened that morning.

'Oh! Oh!' gasped Thalia, her hand on her chest as if to stop her palpitating heart from escaping. 'A soldier of the British forces in the house! Did anyone see? What will we do if anyone saw? How—'

'Shush,' Ianos interrupted, 'don't be so loud. I need to think, to make a list of those who could help and then decide who will be best, alongside myself of c—'

'Dad,' said Andreas, cutting across him, 'you cannot do this. You are not strong enough.' His protests were exactly those that Vassia had made, but she grimaced at the bluntness of her brother's words. Her father would not like it. He did not appreciate direct comments about his strength, or lack of it, especially not from Andreas, for whom he always strove to be a role model.

'And you are about to be a father,' countered Ianos, calmly.

Andreas ran his hands through his shock of dark curly hair. Vassia felt a sudden stab of empathy for him, her handsome, hard-working brother, toiling endlessly to provide for his wife and child. He worked as a waiter in a restaurant in Fira, which was secure employment in such uncertain times, though even with the long hours he put in money was always a struggle.

The financial burden had been eased a little of late because the restaurant was a favourite of the German soldiers, and in turn Andreas had become a favourite of Lieutenant Schwarz.

Vassia had encountered Schwarz on a couple of occasions when she'd been drafted in at short notice to cover someone's absence due to illness or some other calamity, and she'd immediately hated him, his sneer of cold command, his merciless eyes.

Andreas didn't like Schwarz any more than his sister did, but the commander took a keen interest in the young waiter, asking all about his family and always leaving Andreas a large tip. Vassia knew, because he'd told her, that Andreas was in constant conflict about the preferential position he held and hated taking Nazi money. But he did so in order to provide for Athena and the coming child. It worried Vassia that her brother was the subject of so much attention, knowing how easily such situations could go sour. Today's chosen one could quickly become tomorrow's scapegoat.

'That's irrelevant,' countered Andreas to his father's remark about his impending parenthood, though it clearly wasn't. 'And the thing is this, Papa,' he went on. 'You are the most senior person in the village, you know everyone, you should be the mastermind of the operation. Don't you know that delegation is the secret weapon of successful people?'

Andreas paused for a moment, as if hoping his words would sink in, before continuing. 'Apart from anything else, I know Fira much better than you do.' The capital was only two or three kilometres from Vourvoulos, but it was true that Andreas, by dint of his job, went there far more frequently than his father did. 'I know all the backstreets, the short cuts. We owe it to these brave British soldiers to not just give them help, but give them the best help. You can't argue with that.'

Ianos and Andreas were facing off to each other now, both equally stubborn, equally determined. And then Ianos let out a huge slough of air and closed his eyes, his heavy lids sinking tiredly down.

When he opened them again, Vassia saw that he was defeated.

'All right,' her father agreed. 'You can take my place, Andreas.'

Vassia's stomach turned upside down. She was torn between her love for her father and her brother; she didn't want either of them to put themselves into such obvious danger. But it had to be done, there was no doubt about that.

Steeling herself for what was to come, Vassia set about preparing a basket full of the snacks she had identified earlier. Drinking water was essential, too, and she put two covered jugs into the pile she needed to pack. After all that time spent dreaming up impossible ways to get rid of the Nazis, now out of the blue had come the opportunity to actually do something for real.

Finally, this was her chance to play a part in the war effort, and she was going to grab it with both hands, no matter the danger. There would be no holding her back.

# CHAPTER 6

## CARRIE, 2024

Nell had an Inset day on the Monday, and Carrie had rearranged her shifts at the leisure centre so she didn't have to work until 4 p.m. That had given them the opportunity to stay another night with Harriet and Bill, and avoid the Sunday evening traffic. And, Carrie would be the first to admit, to keep Nell away from the undesirable friends for another twenty-four hours. Nell had been studying hard all weekend – or at least she'd been sequestered away in Bill's study for hours at a time, so Carrie could only hope she was actually revising – and Carrie was keen to give her every opportunity to continue.

The extra night also gave her the chance to enjoy a little more time with her mother. After going for a long, early-morning run, she sat with her mother at the kitchen table as Harriet looked through the post, which largely comprised colourful seed catalogues.

'So much to do in the garden,' Harriet sighed, flicking through pages displaying sumptuous arrangements of annuals and perennials, before moving on to the next envelope, which she opened, perused and then put to one side.

'What's that?' asked Carrie.

Her mother started guiltily. 'Nothing. Just—'

The arrival of Carrie's dad, back from walking the dog, interrupted Harriet's flow and the conversation moved on to other matters. Carrie got up from the table to go and gather together her and Nell's things, which seemed to be strewn all over the house, asking first whether she could take Sol's sketch-book with her.

'Of course,' her mother readily agreed. 'I'd give you the ring as well, but I have to be fair to both of you. I should get it valued first.'

'Jenny can have it,' replied Carrie, affecting an air of care-less magnanimity. She would love to have the ring. But the last thing she wanted was for Jenny to think she was laying claim to an item of Sol's that Jenny didn't even know about, getting more than her fair share.

'We'll discuss it properly when I know what it's worth,' replied her mother with equanimity. She hated the feud between the siblings but was always careful not to judge, or get involved.

Carrie opened the box, which was still sitting on the kitchen shelf, to take another look at the flashing diamonds and the mysterious inscription that must mean something special. This wasn't just any old piece of jewellery, it was classic, elegant and surely chosen with love. The kind of ring Carrie would love to receive. She'd never been one of those young girls who dreamt of her wedding day, a huge white frock, handsome beau and bridesmaids aplenty. She'd never thought she was that bothered about getting married. But something about this ring had caused her to recognise her sadness that she'd missed out on the chance of matrimony, because for sure no one was going to ask her now, at her age, and anyway she never met anyone new to make a marriage possible.

An annoying voice in her head niggled away at her, telling

her, *you wanted to marry Jack. You thought he'd ask you. You would have loved a ring like this from him.*

Angrily, she silenced the voice.

Checking her watch, she saw that they had half an hour before they needed to hit the road. She turned to her laptop to add more flesh to the new book idea. The more she thought about it, the better it seemed. A mystery from the past, a true family story... God, she needed it to work out, to be successful.

She closed her eyes momentarily to blot out the mental image of herself and Nell, packing only the possessions they could carry and saying goodbye to their little cottage before heading off to who knew where. Sol had thought his bequests would give Carrie and Jenny security for the future. She couldn't get out of her head how shameful it was that she'd let this opportunity slip through her fingers. It demonstrated how useless she was, how she'd failed at her career, failed at earning enough money to survive, failed at life. Dropping her head into her hands, Carrie ground her teeth in suppressed anger and self-condemnation.

By the time they came to leave, it was raining heavily again. Nell hugged and kissed her grandparents and then ran to the car, diving inside as quickly as she could. As Carrie turned to follow her, Harriet thrust a piece of paper into her hand. She looked down. What was it? Then she registered that it was a cheque. Who used them any more? Carrie had almost forgotten what one looked like. But a cheque it was, and for £600. She gasped out loud when she saw the sum – and gasped again when she clocked the signature.

Jack's.

She glared accusingly at her mother, and then back down at the oblong piece of paper. What was this about? She didn't take money from Jack, everyone knew that. She didn't take *anything* from Jack. She could look after Nell by herself, thank you very much.

'It's for you and Nell,' explained Harriet, keeping her tone neutral. 'It arrived in the post this morning. He asked me to give it to you.'

So that was what had so preoccupied her mother, amidst her concerns for her flower garden. Carrie had wondered what it was.

'Jack wants you both to have a holiday after her exams,' Harriet continued.

Carrie's mother was the one who had insisted from the beginning that Carrie allow Jack a role in Nell's life. She hadn't pried into what had caused the break-up but, ever the voice of reason, had persuaded Carrie that it was wrong to deny Nell the right to know her father, that Nell could well end up resenting Carrie in the long term. Carrie's stubborn, terribly hurt side wanted to counter that what Jack had done was wrong, and he should pay the price.

But Harriet had gone on to sensibly explain that being a single mother was incredibly hard – something Carrie soon found out she was absolutely right about. If Jack was willing and able to do some of the caring for Nell, Harriet had said, that would surely be a bonus for Carrie. And so Carrie had, reluctantly, agreed to Jack having access one weekend a month and for at least a week in the Christmas and Easter holidays, and two in the summer. He travelled a lot for work and Carrie had been incredibly accommodating in arranging and rearranging these visits to suit his schedule.

Carrie recognised that reminding herself of this now was an attempt to justify taking the money. She didn't like being beholden to Jack, hated it in fact. But she had to admit that her mother had been absolutely right to force Carrie to include him in Nell's life, however hard it had been to do so. Jack indulged Nell in all the right ways, encouraging her love of sport by playing football with her, which Carrie never did, being unable to kick a ball more than a couple of feet and always in the wrong direction. The two of them adored the American TV programme *Gilmore Girls*, which Carrie really couldn't relate to, and had watched all seven seasons several times. All in all, the pair of them had a lovely relationship that undoubtedly was of huge benefit to Nell.

Nevertheless, Carrie continued to stare dubiously at the cheque. She shouldn't take it. And if she did take it, she should put it in a savings account for Nell, for her future, not fritter it away on foreign travel. Although perhaps it wasn't strictly frittering if it was helping with her book project, which, if successful, would give Nell greater financial security; and then there was the goal of filling in some family history, which was invaluable in its own right, though really the bills should come first... It was hardly worth thinking about the mortgage as £600 wouldn't cover even two weeks at the new rate she'd be charged.

In the end, Harriet sealed it. 'Jack has asked me to make sure that you do use it to get away for a break, not for anything else. Certainly not for paying the bills. It's his only condition.'

Carrie set her mouth in a determined line of defiance. She wouldn't take it.

Observing her, Harriet pursed her lips, clearly focusing on choosing the right words. 'He knows how hard you work, Carrie, and how much you do for Nell. So just take it and enjoy it.' She paused before issuing what were plainly her final words on the matter. 'No buts, no arguments.'

Reluctantly, Carrie threw the cheque another accusatory look and then stuffed it into her bag. She'd think about what to do with it later. In the car, Nell was engrossed in her phone.

'Everything all right?' she asked, without glancing up from the screen. 'What was the hold-up?'

Carrie shook her head, not that Nell was looking to register such a gesture. 'Nothing,' she replied. 'Nothing at all.'

But as she fired the ignition and put the car into gear, she was already picturing Santorini's whitewashed walls festooned with flamboyant bougainvillea flowers, the hot sun in a blue sky, a black beach where gentle waves lapped the shore... and, just as vividly, the woman with the almond eyes and glossy hair, and her Uncle Sol, so kind but so unfathomable, who had drawn the portrait with such delicate skill.

Would it be so terrible to use the money as Jack had instructed? To take Nell on a foreign holiday for the first time? What might Carrie discover while there, treading in Sol's footsteps? Her whole body thrilled with excitement at the prospect of uncovering the layers of mystery that surrounded him.

# CHAPTER 7

VASSIA, 1944

'You're not going alone,' Thalia whispered to Vassia, as she helped her daughter put the finishing touches to the food basket. 'Whatever your father says.' From a drawer in the kitchen dresser, she fetched her set of prized linen napkins, which had been part of her trousseau when she had got married. 'Kostas can go with you.'

Vassia merely nodded. She'd lost the power of speech in her fear about what she was about to do, and she couldn't deny that having next-door neighbour Kostas's reassuring presence near to her would certainly be welcome. He was a few years older than Vassia and Andreas and he and his younger brother Evangelos had regularly played with Vassia and her brother as they grew up. There had always been an expectation among both families that Vassia and Kostas might become a couple. But although Vassia sometimes suspected that Kostas did like her in that way, she could not reciprocate. She loved him very much but did not harbour any romantic feelings for him at all. There was a part of her that hated to disappoint Kostas, or either of their families, as they were so very close, but she couldn't manufacture emotions. Nevertheless, she knew that Kostas was trustworthy, reliable – and courageous.

Once, in their boat as children, a sudden storm had come over, bringing with it a howling gale and torrential rain. Vassia had been terrified, but under Kostas's command they had reached shore safely, if a little shaken and very wet. He would undoubtedly be a valuable companion.

Taking the water jugs from her and carrying them himself, Kostas led the way out of the Kourakises' courtyard and onto the cobbled street. Without so much as a surreptitious glance around him, he strode purposefully off in the direction of the beach. Vassia followed more tentatively. She supposed that Kostas was right to act as if there was nothing untoward going on at all, just the normal daily business of a Santorini village. Creeping along like fugitives would be much more likely to arouse suspicion, if a German soldier happened to be in the vicinity. But still. Being brave wasn't easy.

There were several caves along the shore, hewn into the black, volcanic rock, but Spyros had described the location of the one the men were sheltering in with precise detail. It took a good fifteen minutes of fast walking to reach it. The whole way there, Vassia maintained the same cracking pace as Kostas, desperate to keep up with him. She was nervous about the kind of men these commandos would be and did not want to have to face them alone. Spyros would have told them that villagers were coming with provisions, so she assumed they wouldn't rush out and shoot her and Kostas... But should they be waving a white flag or something?

Doubts continued to assail Vassia the whole way there, but she refused to give way to them. This mission was so important, and it had been entrusted to her by her beloved father. She could not let him down.

As they approached the mouth of the cave, Vassia saw that her fears were baseless. Of course the men had posted a lookout and, as soon as Vassia and Kostas came into view, he gave them a cheery wave. Vassia almost laughed, such was the release of tension. It felt surreal, to be delivering food to the sworn foes of the enemy occupiers.

She could not even imagine the fate that would befall her and Kostas were they to be captured.

The lookout gestured them inside and, tentatively, Vassia entered the cave. Her arrival was met by eighteen pairs of eyes, whites gleaming in the half-light, staring curiously at her. Almost collapsing under the combined weight of their scrutiny, she deposited her basket onto the gritty floor. As she registered the men's rough and ready appearance, she clenched her fists until her nails bit into her palms. Then Kostas stepped in to join her, and the tension seemed to break. One of the men stood up to greet them.

'Captain Andersen,' the man said, holding out his hand.

He was very tall, dressed in well-worn trousers and a shirt made of a coarse khaki fabric. From the corner of his mouth dangled a cigarette and, once she had noticed that, Vassia became aware of the thick pall of smoke that filled the space, spiralling upwards in grey eddies.

'Vassia Kourakis,' she replied, struggling to keep her voice from wobbling under the pressure. She shook his hand and it was cool and huge, strength rippling out from every nerve and sinew. Vassia had a sudden understanding that this was a hand that could take a life, had before, and would again when the need arose.

Kostas introduced himself and then Captain Andersen began asking him a series of rapid questions, translated by Spyros. Vassia was ignored, and her attention drifted.

Through the haze, she took in the rest of the group in more detail. All were clad in similar clothing, faces darkly tanned apart from one man, who had strawberry blond hair and a liberal covering of huge freckles across his exposed skin. Most of the men were seated close together and Vassia noticed a couple of card games going on. She wondered how they could concentrate when they were on a military operation, but she supposed it helped to pass the time.

Her eye was drawn to the far corner of the cave, where one man sat slightly apart from the rest, seemingly absorbed in a book. Vassia was even more surprised that someone could read; she knew she wouldn't be able to focus on a single word in such a situation. But then she noticed a pencil in his hand, and how it was moving across the page, so lightly, almost flying, and she realised he was not reading but drawing. As she thought this, the man became aware of her gaze and looked up, and for a second their eyes met across the dim and murky cavern.

Instantaneously, the strangest feeling subsumed Vassia, so intense that she felt her legs weaken beneath her and her knees wobble. A prickling of sweat gathered on her forehead, and a thrill of electricity passed through her. She had an almost overwhelming urge to walk towards the man, as if drawn by some magnetic force of attraction. His gaze did not waver, and neither did hers, until suddenly it was too much.

Confused, Vassia turned abruptly, then sank to the ground beside the basket. She pulled out her mother's treasured napkins, then the jugs of water and the dishes of tempting savouries that she had so carefully put together.

'Please,' she said, in Greek because it was the only language that she knew, 'eat.'

The men did not need to be invited twice. As one, they lunged forward and piled into the food, heaping the napkins high with the dolmades, *koulouria* and pie. Vassia poured water into tin cups that were thrust towards her, replenishing some two or three times.

Once the men had had their fill, she sat back on her heels, not sure what to do next. Captain Andersen, Spyros and Kostas were still deep in conversation and Vassia felt suddenly vulnerable and on show, kneeling in front of this tough and battle-hardened bunch. Those eyes that had stared at her when she and Kostas had arrived must have seen so much, things she knew nothing of. Ever since the war started, she had just been here on Santorini, but elsewhere, terrible events were taking place on a daily basis.

'Efharisto.'

The voice from behind her made Vassia start. Desperately trying to recover her composure, she turned to see the sketching man lean towards her, holding out one of the napkins, still clean and neatly folded.

'Thank you,' she replied, nonplussed. For a few seconds she fussed elaborately over the stowing away of the napkin, until she had regained her composure. When she glanced up again, she saw that the man was beckoning her to come closer.

Once more, that extraordinary feeling coursed through her veins, a feeling that she and this man had met before, in some past life, that she had some deep and as yet untapped knowledge of him, his soul, what made him who he was.

As if in a trance, Vassia went over to him.

'I'm Sol,' he told her. 'I know a little Greek. Thanks for bringing us the food and water.'

Vassia smiled, her nerves evaporating in the face of Sol's friendliness. She was surprised that Sol spoke any Greek at all, but also delighted, as it meant that she could communicate with him.

'I'm Vassia,' she replied. 'My father, Ianos Kourakis, is the mayor of Vourvoulos. Spyros Papadopoulous came to our house this morning, to ask for our help. So of course we gave it.'

Sol smiled back at her, and Vassia had a moment to fully take in his kind face with its generous smile.

'Vassia,' he repeated. 'What a pretty name.'

He had brown hair bleached blond at the ends by the sun, a high forehead and glasses with small, round metal frames.

There was something so innately attractive about him that she could barely tear her eyes away. In addition, he was imbued with a sense of calm unflappability, which impressed Vassia. She knew that, if she had only hours before having to embark on a mission that could be fatal, she would be collapsing with nerves.

'What are you drawing?' asked Vassia, gesturing towards the sketchbook that lay face down on the hard rock of the cave floor.

Sol reached out to pick the book up, and shrugged. 'Just this and that,' he said. 'It relaxes me, takes my mind off all of this.' His hand swept around the cavern and the assembled men, most of whom had gone back to their card games. Captain Andersen, Kostas and Spyros were still talking; what could they possibly be discussing for so long?

Sol handed Vassia the sketchbook and she opened it infinitely gently, as if afraid the covers would snap off or the paper tear. Turning the creamy-coloured leaves, she skimmed through pages of skilful line drawings, recognising some of the faces of those lounging around her in the cave. The final sketch depicted a group of men creeping along a beach lit only by the palest of moons, with two sailing ships far out at sea, heading away from land.

'That one's not quite finished yet,' explained Sol, almost apologetically, as if Vassia might be disappointed to see a work still in progress.

Incomplete or not, Vassia was so struck by Sol's skill and talent that she could hardly drag her eyes away. She herself couldn't draw for toffee and she was always full of admiration for those who could.

'Vassia.' Kostas's voice rang out, echoing back from the cave walls. 'We should get going.'

Reluctantly, Vassia gave the book back to Sol. She wanted to stay here in the cave, admiring his artistic talent, hearing stories of his brave exploits with the SBS, the other islands they had been to, but also of where he came from, his background and history. She wanted to know everything about him.

'*Vassia!*' Kostas's voice was sharper now. 'Come.'

Still lingering, Vassia held out her hand to Sol. They had not shaken on first meeting, which was perhaps rude, but then again, what were the rules of etiquette in a situation such as this? Sol's hand closed round hers and again there was that electricity, tingling all through Vassia's body, from the tips of her fingers right down to her toes. Their hands lingered together, a little longer than necessary, but nowhere near long enough.

And then Kostas was gathering up the basket and the water flagons and gesturing to Vassia to follow him.

All the way home, Vassia's thoughts remained with Sol. His drawing danced in her mind's eye, so realistic and evocative, and her right hand still felt hot from his touch, as if scorched by the contact. Entering the village, she was miles away, dreaming of him, only noticing her young cousin Nicholas when he was almost next to her. He was clutching something close to his chest, and a look of fear and concern was etched across his innocent, ten-year-old face.

'What's up?' asked Vassia, anxiously. Had he hurt himself?

'Look, Vassia,' he replied, urgently. 'Kostas, too. I found this baby bird under the fig tree in the square. I think it must have fallen out of its nest or something. I couldn't leave it there for a cat to get at.'

As he opened his grip, Vassia saw the tiny fledgling that he was holding so tenderly. Nico stroked its baby feathers and it chirped plaintively. Instantly, Vassia's heart melted. Her cousin was an avid animal lover and horse-mad, too. He kept a chestnut pony called Apollo in a paddock on the edge of the village and was always out and about on Santorini, spotting seabirds and geckos and any other natural flora and fauna that caught his eye. Of course she would help him save the bird.

'The mother won't come back for it now,' she explained to the child. 'So we can't take it back to the tree. And you're right, a cat would certainly kill it if we left it there. We'll take it to my house, put it in a box with a saucer of water and feed it until it gets stronger. You'll have to find insects for it to eat – can you do that?'

Nico's chest puffed out proudly. 'Of course!' he exclaimed. 'As soon as we've got him settled, I'll go straight out. I know where to find caterpillars, lots of them!'

'Of course you do.' Vassia chuckled. 'Well done.'

Back at home, and with the bird, who Nico had named Chicky, safely ensconced in a box, Kostas went off to take over the afternoon shift in his family's grocery store and Vassia set to cooking something delicious to take back for the SBS men later in the day, to fortify them before their perilous mission ahead.

As she chopped and fried, seasoned and tasted, she thought of Sol, his lovely kind eyes behind the metal-framed glasses, his dextrous, muscular hands that wielded such obvious talent and skill, the way he had listened to her as if he were really interested in everything she had to say, how he had complimented her name. She wished she could have a chance to get to know him better. But the commandos would leave in less than forty-eight hours, when the boats that delivered them came back under cover of darkness to pick them up. They would move on to the next assignment, wherever that might be.

Vassia would see Sol one more time at most, and then he would be gone.

# CHAPTER 8

CARRIE, 2024

The heat enveloped Carrie the moment she stepped out of the aircraft and onto the metal steps that led down to the tarmac. It smelt of dust and aviation fuel and anticipation. This was Santorini and it wasn't a dream, it was reality.

So many things had happened over the past few weeks that Carrie was still struggling to keep up. Nell had somehow managed to stay out of trouble in the run-up to her GCSEs, which Carrie had to grudgingly accept had been helped by the fact that Jack had put a stop to all his work trips during her study leave and suggested she stay with him, out of harm's way (and far from the Undesirables), for the final two weeks leading up to the exams. As a result, Nell had done some supercharged revision, and Carrie had everything crossed for passable results when they came out in August.

In addition, she'd worked up the idea for the book about Sol into a synopsis, augmented by research into the Special Boat Squadron in the Second World War that she'd done online and through books. Xanthe had confirmed the use of her grandparents' cottage, plane tickets and insurance had been bought, suitcases packed and expectations raised to the highest level.

And now here they were, actually in Santorini.

Carrie could scarcely believe it. She and Nell had never had a foreign holiday together before. Unbelievably in this day and age, it was the first time Nell had been on a plane. She'd gone on the year 6 trip to an adventure centre in France, and on a cultural exchange to Spain, but both of those journeys had been by torturous coach and ferry – and both had been paid for by Harriet and Bill, as Carrie couldn't afford it. Carrie had thought an actual aeroplane would blow Nell away – not literally, obviously, just metaphorically. But throughout the flight, Nell had acted with her usual casual indifference towards anything that excited her mother.

'Mum, stop embarrassing me!' she'd said on various occasions, such as when Carrie was trying to get her to actually watch, and pay attention to, the safety demo, when she handed her a packet of sandwiches, prepared at home so as to avoid having to buy extortionately expensive aeroplane food, and when Carrie asked the couple behind if they could possibly stop their child from relentlessly kicking the back of her seat.

'Don't be so judgy, Mum,' Nell had hissed, emerging for a few moments from underneath the hood of her capacious sweatshirt.

'I'm not being judgemental,' remonstrated Carrie. 'I'm just fed up with being clobbered.' But Nell had already retreated back under the sheltering hoodie and didn't answer.

Now they had finally arrived, and waiting for them as they exited through customs was Xanthe, smiling and waving.

'It's been too long,' cried Carrie, as they hugged and kissed. 'Thank you so much for inviting us.'

'Thank you for coming,' replied Xanthe, turning to give Nell a huge embrace. 'Now, let's get you to your des res accommodation and then we can decide where you want to eat and what you want to do.'

As the taxi pulled out of the brightly lit airport environs and into the countryside, Carrie stared out of the window, lapping it all up. Guilt still flooded through her periodically, telling her she should have defied Jack's instructions about what the money should be spent on and put it towards all the many financial commitments that weighed upon her shoulders. But then she'd remind herself that this holiday was for Nell, and for Sol, and try her best to convince herself she had done the right thing.

It was early evening, the sky heavy with the dusk, the rugged volcanic landscape softened by a shroud of semi-darkness. The village of Pyrgos was exactly as Xanthe had described: a whitewashed picture of perfection, all cobbled streets, tiny churches and traditional houses. As Xanthe led Carrie and Nell through a maze of alleyways, Carrie hoped fervently that she'd remember the way back out again; she had an appalling sense of direction.

They arrived at a blue-painted door beside which a potted bougainvillea with purple flowers had been trained to frame the entrance.

'And here we are!' declared Xanthe with a flourish. 'I've given the whole place a good dust and put fresh sheets on the beds so it's all ready for you.'

Carrie felt overcome with gratitude. Xanthe had reminded her that they had visited her grandparents' house during their brief time on Santorini all those years ago but Carrie had no memories of it. Now she could hardly take in how gorgeous it was. She would love it here. So would Nell – wouldn't she?

The door opened with a deep click of the lock, interrupting Carrie's daydream, and Xanthe turned to usher her guests inside. The interior was thankfully a little cooler than outside, courtesy of the thick walls. Carrie paused to look around her. They were in a small sitting room with a sofa and a couple of easy chairs. A door at the back seemed to lead further into the house and Carrie followed Xanthe through it. A kitchen lay off to the right and a bathroom to the left and in the middle was a narrow flight of stairs that took them up to two bedrooms, both with a double bed.

'You'll probably want this room,' Xanthe said to Carrie, 'as it's the biggest. It has a lovely view out back, too.'

Carrie's head was still reeling, taking in the simple charm of the little house. 'It's amazing,' she replied, temporarily lost for words. 'I love it already.'

Xanthe flung open the wooden doors to reveal the balcony and Carrie stepped outside. They were on the outskirts of the village and quite high up. Below them on one side, the lights of homes and tavernas twinkled and sparkled and a soft murmur of voices from those dining and drinking rose up to them. On the other side lay open land, beyond which Carrie could just make out the stretch of dark velvet sea. She breathed in deeply, inhaling a scent of heat and dust and the appetising aroma of barbecuing meat, the latter reminding her how hungry she was.

Seeming to read her mind – or her stomach – Xanthe came to stand beside her as she admired the view, and said, 'Shall we grab something to eat somewhere close by tonight? There are a few nice places – I can show you the bright lights of the big city, i.e. Fira, the capital, another day.'

Carrie nodded. 'Yes, please. It's been a long day travelling and I won't say no to an early night. Plus I'm starving. And we have so much to talk about – I need all the latest on Spencer, for a start.'

Xanthe grinned. 'Poor Nell – she's going to be bored out of her mind. You have got roaming on your phones, haven't you? Give her something to do while we natter.'

'Thankfully, yes,' answered Carrie. 'I sorted that out before we left. But talking of Nell – where is she?' She went back into her bedroom, and then the one opposite. There was no sign of her. She went back downstairs and found her daughter in the sitting room, staring around her with a disconsolate expression. Sensing trouble, Carrie looked over her shoulder to see where

Xanthe was. If Nell was in a mood and about to be rude, she didn't want her friend, who'd been so generous in offering them this place, to witness it.

Xanthe was descending the staircase while also typing on her phone. 'I need to make a quick call,' she said. 'I'll be five minutes. Then we'll head off to find somewhere to eat.'

She disappeared through the blue front door, leaving Carrie and Nell together.

'What's the matter?' asked Carrie, warily. Nell, in common with many teenagers, was apt to be volatile, and Carrie had hoped so fervently for a quiet, easy time on this holiday.

'Nothing,' responded Nell, sulkily.

Carrie held a swift internal debate with herself about whether to pursue the matter further or just drop it. Deciding that the latter would only lead to trouble further down the line, she took the former approach. 'There's clearly something wrong,' she persisted. 'So please tell me. I don't want Xanthe to pick up on any bad feeling when she's been so generous.'

Nell shrugged. 'It's dead round here, that's all,' she said. 'What am I going to do for a whole two weeks?' Then her petulant tone altered to one that was almost pleading. 'And I'm sure this is the kind of house that's going to have spiders and you know how much I hate spiders. They're so scary!'

Carrie began to laugh but somehow managed to swallow it back and change it into a cough. Mocking Nell's paranoia about creepy-crawlies would be guaranteed to make things worse. She tried to remember what she'd read in the parenting manuals. *Try to be understanding and empathetic, even towards things that seem trivial or ridiculous. Recognising a teenager's pain is really important to them; it doesn't mean you're giving in.*

In that spirit, 'I'll check your room every night for spiders,' she reassured Nell. 'And every morning, too, if you like.'

Nell sniffed. 'I really wanted a nice hotel with a pool,' she added, her voice full of woe. 'Like all my friends go to. Chloe's going for three weeks to an all-inclusive resort in Turkey with its own water park!'

Carrie felt her heart split in two. Bloody Chloe, of course she was. She always had the latest everything; phone, trainers, holidays, you name it, Chloe had it. On the one hand, Carrie fervently wished she could provide Nell with the same. On the other, Nell's ingratitude infuriated her. Thank goodness Xanthe hadn't been present to hear it. This was the trouble with teenagers – their ability to spark wildly conflicting emotions in their nearest and dearest was both legendary and exhausting.

Suppressing the urge to give a sharp response, she put her arm round Nell. 'We'll have a great time, don't you worry. We'll go swimming at the beach, and often you can use hotel pools if you buy a drink or a meal. And I know it might seem a bit quiet here, but even if we were in Fira you're too young to be going out to bars and clubs, and you wouldn't want to do that on your own, anyway.'

At that moment, Xanthe put her head round the door. 'I'm done. Are you ready?'

Carrie nodded and, propelling Nell forward, they emerged back out onto the street and into the soupy heat.

Xanthe locked the door and handed Carrie the key. 'That's yours now for the duration,' she said, before setting off downhill at a fair lick. Carrie had to practically run to keep up, at the same time as trying to memorise the way and any landmarks she could navigate by; a huge prickly pear or a house name here, a church or shop there.

They ended up at the bottom of the village, in a lovely taverna lit by fairy lights strung along the grapevine pergola. On every table stood pots of thyme and oregano, and Greek music played gently from a sound system.

Once they had ordered, Carrie and Xanthe fell immediately to catching up on their news. Nell, Carrie noted, was engaged in a WhatsApp conversation with her dad. Well, she could hardly object given that her conversation with Xanthe held little interest for a teenage girl.

'So – Spencer!' Carrie began. 'I'm sure there's lots more you haven't revealed yet.'

'Oh yes, Spencer,' replied Xanthe dreamily, fluttering her eyelashes and fanning herself with her hand to indicate how thoroughly hot he was. 'He's intelligent and kind and thoughtful and rich... I think he's gorgeous, obvs, but he's probably not to everyone's taste... did I mention he's rich?'

She laughed her throaty, devilish laugh and Carrie was instantly transported back to their university days, to that summer travelling in the Greek islands, Xanthe leading the way as she was the local and the one who spoke the lingo. On Santorini, as elsewhere, they'd stayed in a hostel as there wasn't room in Xanthe's grandparents' house, but her grandparents had taken them all out to dinner one night. Though she didn't remember their house, Carrie did remember that. It had been the best meal they'd had in two months of travelling, when often they'd lived on bread and olives. She could still taste the fresh sea bass and grilled vegetables.

'You know I'm joking about the money,' Xanthe continued. 'But that aside, it is nice to finally have a partner who's solvent. I've met so many bums I can't tell you, men living off their parents' success... it happens a lot in Greece.'

Carrie harrumphed. 'It happens everywhere,' she responded. 'And so... is he the one? This Spencer? I wish he were here so that I could meet him.'

'Vet him, you mean,' guffawed Xanthe.

Carrie grinned. 'Of course I would need to check that he's suitable for my friend,' she answered with faux primness.

'I think you'd like him,' Xanthe said. 'And I certainly hope he's the one. It's about bloody time. If he doesn't come back from the States with a ring for me, there's going to be trouble. Big trouble.'

At this, they both burst into loud gales of laughter, until Carrie caught Nell squirming in her chair in embarrassment and quickly quietened down. Poor Nell. Carrie couldn't even suggest she go back to the house after they'd eaten because she had no idea if Nell would ever find it on her own – and even if she did, her arachnophobia would more than likely mean she wouldn't be able to cross the threshold alone. She'd just have to put up with the boredom and inconvenience of being with her mother and her mother's friend for a bit longer.

The food arrived and a few minutes passed while dishes were explained and passed around. The waiter poured more wine into Carrie and Xanthe's glasses and brought another Coke for Nell. The ban that Carrie normally imposed on fizzy drinks had been lifted for the duration of the holiday and Nell was making the most of it.

'So tell me more about this book idea you mentioned,' asked Xanthe, lifting a skewer of meat and halloumi to her mouth. 'If you end up writing it, you better make sure I get a namecheck in the acknowledgements.'

'Ha!' responded Carrie. 'Of course I will.' She took a gulp of her wine and them embarked on the tale, explaining how the discovery of the sketchbook had made her change from a book about Atlantis to one about her great-uncle. When she'd finished, she added, 'Remember I mentioned before that I was hoping that I might be able to find a guide, someone who could show me around the island, who might know where I could unearth anything further about Second World War history here? That's still my aim, but I'm not sure where to start looking.'

Xanthe exaggeratedly screwed up her forehead as she contemplated this request. 'As it happens,' she said eventually, 'I did have a few thoughts on that one.' She gave a small smirk of a smile.

'What's so funny?' demanded Carrie. 'What are you looking so shifty about?'

Xanthe shook her head. 'Not shifty at all. Just pleased that I've found someone who might fit the bill.'

'Hmm,' replied Carrie, sceptically.

'Leave it with me,' insisted Xanthe, with an air of finality. 'Now, tomorrow – I've got a whole raft of Zoom calls to make until lunchtime, so you could chill out, or I thought maybe an excursion to Megalochori might fit the bill. It's another traditional village, and the Lost Atlantis Experience is on the outskirts, so we could meet there about two. The museum has only been open since Covid and I've never actually been inside, but I thought you and Nell might like it.'

'Fab,' agreed Carrie. She wanted to do everything, go everywhere, see all that was to be seen during the time that she and Nell were here.

Later, back at the little house and having conducted a thorough and comprehensive spider search while Nell waited nervously outside, Carrie stood on her balcony and gazed out at the star-studded night sky. The peace and quiet was deep and profound.

Just being here, with the heat and the promise of day after day of sunshine, with her book project to work on and Sol's past to investigate, and Nell safely away from the influence of her smoking, drinking and drug-taking friends, perhaps she could relax and enjoy herself.

After all, what could possibly go wrong?

# CHAPTER 9

## VASSIA, 1944

It was not yet dark when Vassia returned to the cave. Andreas was with her. He was reluctant to leave Athena, who'd been complaining about stomach ache all day, but wanted to help his sister transport everything given that Kostas wasn't available. With her brother by her side, and having already done it once before, Vassia didn't feel quite as scared as she had that morning, but the state of her nerves was immaterial anyway. It was her job to deliver the food and she would do it, come what may.

The basket was much heavier this time, as it held a big iron cooking pot with a lid. Andreas carried it, while Vassia took the water jugs. As soon as they arrived, Andreas left, anxious to get back to Athena. Inside the cave, Vassia was surprised to find most of the commandos sleeping. How could they rest, on enemy territory, about to face a battle against the Nazis? She couldn't imagine being able to get a single wink if it had been her.

Once more, Vassia emptied the basket of the food she had so carefully prepared; the beef stew stifado and bread. Of course she had surreptitiously checked Sol's whereabouts as soon as she entered the gloomy space, but he too was dead to the world, stretched out with his head on his pack, his face looking different without his glasses. She wondered what would happen if he lost them or they were damaged. Would he be able to see his way out of danger? Shoot his weapon? Tell the difference between friend and foe? She was lucky, she knew, to be blessed with perfect eyesight.

Next to Sol, she spotted the sketchbook. Her fingers burned with the desire to browse through it again, taking in the tiny details of Sol's skilful drawings. Though she knew she probably shouldn't, she reached out for it, picked it up and opened it. She paused on a couple of the most striking images. One was unmistakably Captain Andersen, a pistol in one hand, a hunting knife in the other, and a look of utter ruthlessness on his face. Vassia's stomach turned over as she studied the picture, and eventually she had to look away, overcome by the power of the image. From beneath her lashes, she surveyed the group, some still asleep, most now waking up, perhaps roused by the delicious aromas emanating from the pot of stifado. They were all capable of killing, must have killed multiple times before. She wondered what it took to kill a man, and knew she didn't have it in her. With all her heart, she wished there was a way to end this war without any more bloodshed, but knew that there wasn't.

One by one, Vassia filled the commandos' metal mess-tins that they carried in their kitbags and poured water for them. Captain Andersen ate little, but smoked lots. Observing his brooding expression, Vassia wondered what was going through his mind.

Serving Sol, she acknowledged him with a shy smile as butterflies frantically fluttered in her stomach. There was no time to talk as she was so busy making sure everyone got fed. Only when the stew and bread were all gone, and the men were sitting back and lighting cigarettes, did she quietly inch closer to him.

'That was delicious,' he said, patting his belly appreciatively. 'They say an army marches on its stomach – we'll be going at a hundred miles an hour now we've been so well refuelled.'

Vassia felt a blush spread over her cheeks. 'Thank you,' she answered, demurely. For a moment she was tongue-tied, unable to say anything further. There were a hundred questions that she was desperate to ask but none of them seemed appropriate. What right did she have to interrogate this soldier about his past, his background, his life? They were ships passing in the night, that was all.

As if reading her mind, Sol reached out a hand and placed it gently on Vassia's arm. 'It's good to see you again,' he murmured. 'You are brave to be doing this for us. We are very grateful.'

Vassia's blush deepened and she hoped fervently that the light was too dim in the cave for Sol to spot it.

'Y-you're very welcome,' she stuttered, trying desperately to dispel her self-consciousness and behave like a normal person.

'Everywhere we've been in Greece, people have been so hospitable and friendly,' Sol went on. 'When we have time to notice it, that is.'

Vassia leapt on this titbit of information from him. 'Where else have you...' She paused, searching for the right word, not finding it, and eventually settling for 'visited?' It was a euphemism, for sure, because could you really call turning up in the dead of night to rout German troops and cause devastation 'visiting'? But it was the best she could do.

'Leros, Chalki, Rhodes,' replied Sol, grimacing. 'Before that we were in Sardinia, then Crete. We trained mostly in Palestine.' He halted and looked at Vassia, smiling. 'So we've been around a bit. Beats sitting in a trench, anyway.'

Vassia shook her head. She couldn't imagine any of it. She thought of her father, or Andreas, having to do what Sol was doing, taking on the enemy on islands where they were so heavily outnumbered. The thought was awful.

'But why Santorini?' she asked. Her homeland was so small and, as the southernmost of the Cyclades islands, a long distance from the mainland and Athens. It was extraordinary that the Italians and the Germans had bothered to make such a voyage, and just as extraordinary that the SBS had followed them. 'How do you choose what to target?'

Sol gave a languid smile. 'We had a German prisoner, one Obergefreiter Adolf Lang,' he explained, wryly. 'He proved to be very obliging. He'd been stationed here in '43 and he told us everything he knew about the garrison, and the radio station, which has the long-range capacity necessary to relay messages between Crete and Athens. That's why we need to take it out.' He stopped and lit a cigarette, first offering the packet to Vassia, who declined. 'Andersen carried out a recce a little while ago, just sussing out the access, what we'd need, how many men et cetera, and hey presto. Here we are.'

Vassia silently absorbed this information. So the formidable Captain Andersen had been among the islanders at some unspecified previous time, unbeknownst to all. She shivered as goosebumps rose on her arms. So much intrigue and subterfuge, and she had had no idea. Neither, as far as she knew, had anyone else.

'When did you join up?' she asked Sol, not wanting to find out anything else about the mission right then. If she were captured and she knew nothing, then she couldn't give anything away, could she? And anyway, she really wanted to know more about Sol. He seemed to have seen and done so much, been to places Vassia couldn't even imagine, experienced things that were incomprehensible to her. She wanted to hear all his stories, to know everything about him. First of all, she'd like to ask how old he was, because his face looked young but his eyes much older, as if they had seen too much. And he was wise, and everyone knew that wisdom comes with age. But of course it was rude to directly ask the question.

Sol took his sketching pencil out of his pocket and surveyed it intently for a few moments. 'Well, you don't usually go straight into the SBS,' he replied, slowly. 'You start in another service and then you volunteer, or you're recruited, and, if you pass the tests and your face fits, then you become one of the gang. It's not for the fainthearted. And you have to be a good sailor; seasickness is not helpful. You will know how rough the water can be when the wind gets up.'

She certainly did. The meltemi, the strong dry wind of summer, could ground ships and keep ferries in harbour for days on end. A flash of memory took her back to that terrible storm she, Andreas and Kostas had endured. It would be tragic if the SBS men were lost to the sea, after all they had been through, all they had achieved.

'And what about you, Vassia?' asked Sol, his voice full of gentle enquiry. 'What do you do with your days?'

Vassia smiled a little awkwardly. 'At the moment, I'm mostly helping my mother about the house,' she said. 'My father, you know, the mayor – he's not too well, with diabetes and his heart, so Mama has a lot on her plate. Both of us work in the vineyards around Vourvoulos at various points in the year, assisting with the pruning and harvesting, and occasionally I help out at the restaurant in Fira where my brother works.' Saying it aloud made her aware of how trivial her life was, how insignificant the mundane tasks that occupied her. 'We grow vegetables, and Santorini cherry tomatoes – they are the tastiest you'll ever eat!' she went on, as if trying to prove that at least some of her pursuits were worthwhile. 'I always have lots to do,' she emphasised, lest Sol should think her idle. 'But what I'd really like is to be a primary school teacher, so when the schools start up again in September I'll begin my training.'

As she finished speaking, she felt herself blush again. She'd said too much; she shouldn't have mentioned Ianos' health. She didn't want Sol to think her father was weak. And as for telling Sol about her dreams and ambitions – why would he want to know about those, when soon they'd part and never see each other again?

And yet, somehow, seeing how he was observing her, and listening so intently to her every word, she knew that he did want to hear what she had to say. Just as she wanted to listen to him.

'A teacher,' Sol echoed. 'That's fabulous. I can imagine all the children adoring you. And if you cook for them as well, they'll be yours for life.'

Now Vassia couldn't help but laugh. 'I'll stick to teaching them their letters,' she protested. 'I like cooking but being stuck in the kitchen all day isn't my idea of fun.' She shifted position to get more comfortable on the cave's rough floor. 'What about you? Did you work, before the war? What did you do?'

Sol snorted disparagingly and waved his hand in a dismissive gesture. 'Oh, you don't want to hear about that. A banker, that was me. Boring, predictable, monotonous. I don't know if I'll be able to go back to it, after this.'

A loud clang rang out across the cave. Someone had dropped their gun on the floor. Vassia became aware that the other men were shuffling around, busying themselves with cleaning and preparing their weapons. She ought to let Sol concentrate on getting ready for the night's mission.

She turned back to tell him she should go, and just caught his last few words.

'If there is an after, that is,' he murmured, his voice barely audible.

The impact was immediate, and physical, a shock of horror running through her like lightning.

'You will be fine,' she replied, breathlessly, hastily, assuring herself as much as him. 'I know it.'

And then Captain Andersen was instructing his men, calling them together for a final briefing before the evening's work began, and Vassia made her exit.

Back home, she checked on Nico's little fledgling on its shelf in the kitchen and was relieved to find it still alive. It chirped feebly as she dripped a drop of water from her finger into its gaping beak. At least one thing had survived. Perhaps that was a good omen for the commandos. She hoped so.

Ianos had decided that Kostas, along with Andreas and three local boys named Elias, Helios and Lefteris, would be the ones to accompany the SBS men. Ianos was adamant that each family should provide only one man. He didn't need to explain the reason for his decision – it was obvious. At around midnight the five would rendezvous at the cave, ready for the mission to begin.

Vassia sat on her bed, unable to concentrate on anything. She pulled her scrapbook out from under her mattress. She had been documenting the war in it, right from the beginning, sticking in newspaper articles and describing what was happening. It felt important to her, to have a written record. But as she gazed down at the book, she knew she was too tense and over-wrought to add to it now. Instead, she pushed it back into its hiding place and lay down. There was no point in actually getting undressed as she knew there was no way she would sleep. All she could do was lie there, her eyes closed so that she could more vividly picture Sol, and pray.

But Vassia must have drifted off because when her door opened, she jumped awake, immediately on full alert. Her father came in, and sank down onto her bedroom chair. He was panting and sweating, although it was no longer hot. Behind him hovered Nico. Was this about the bird? Surely Papa wouldn't seem so panicked about an animal, however cute and helpless. And what was Nico doing up anyway? He should have been in bed hours ago.

'Vassia,' wheezed her father, once he'd got his breath back. 'Your cousin has come with a message. He heard screams and yells next door and went to see what was happening. Athena is in labour at last, but it's not going well. The village women who are assisting her think she should go to the doctor in Fira. Of course, Andreas can't leave her.'

Vassia stared at her father, wide-eyed with terror. Surely nothing could go wrong with the baby? That was too dreadful to contemplate. They were lucky on Santorini to have a resident doctor who had returned from Athens when war broke out; many islands had no one with such expertise. But even so, it was no guarantee of survival. A sick feeling rose in her stomach. Please God the baby was all right, and Athena too of course. This longed-for, much-anticipated infant had seemed like a beacon of hope amidst the mayhem of war. He or she had to be safe.

Her thoughts entirely on her brother, Vassia had not yet thought about the implications of Ianos' message.

'Vassia,' her father said now, looking utterly appalled. 'That means Andreas can't go with the commandos.'

'So who will?' she whispered, her eyes darting between her father and Nico. 'You can't go, nor can Nico, he's far too young. It's too late to find anyone else. So who?'

But even as the words were spoken, with a thrill of sheer terror it dawned on her.

# CHAPTER 10

CARRIE, 2024

Next morning, Carrie was up early. After going for a short run, down through the village and along the dusty roads that surrounded it, she was back home, drinking coffee on the balcony and leafing through Sol's sketchbook once more. As always, her heart skipped a beat when she turned to the portrait of the beautiful young woman. It was so lifelike, so vivid, drawn so skilfully by someone who seemed to know his subject so well. Carrie had discovered that the raid on the island had taken place over two days in April 1944; exactly as Harriet had suggested, far too short a time for Sol to have struck up a romance on the island. But everything about the portrait suggested a much greater acquaintance than that of a few fleeting hours interspersed with a bout of fierce fighting.

For herself, and for her mother and the book, Carrie fervently needed to uncover more details about Sol's experiences. She hoped that the local guide Xanthe had identified might be the perfect person to help. The island was the kind of place where everybody knew everybody, so she hadn't been surprised that Xanthe had someone in mind – even if there had been something rather odd about her demeanour when she'd mentioned it the night before. Carrie hoped she wasn't going to be landed with some boring old fart – but surely Xanthe wouldn't do that to her.

Once she'd managed to get Nell out of bed and coated in a layer of sun cream Carrie deemed thick enough to ward off any possibility of sunburn, they set off, the teenager complaining loudly that 11 a.m. was far too early to be going anywhere.

The bus deposited them on the main road that ran through Megalochori, and from there they clambered steeply upwards, along cobbled pathways through clusters of jumbled white houses with pale blue shutters and pots of jaunty geraniums beside immaculate front doors. Little lanes opened out suddenly to tranquil squares watched over by ancient church towers. A tabby cat basked atop a sun-drenched wall while tiny lizards darted to and fro, emerging from and disappearing back into the thinnest of crevices. The ascent took them longer than it might as Carrie was continually stopping to exclaim rapturously at the beauty of it all, and to take numerous photos. At the summit of the hill, Carrie and Nell paused to feast their eyes on the view spread out below them, the deep blue of the sea and the gentle purplish rises of the surrounding islets.

They ate their packed lunch in a shady spot beside a giant prickly pear and then made their way to the Lost Atlantis museum. As they walked, the sun beating down on their heads, Carrie's thoughts drifted back once more to that long, hot summer of the past, when she had been so young, just nineteen. She recalled the smell of salty, sun-baked skin, the smoky aroma of the campfire on the beach, the taste of cold beer and succulent grilled cheese and prawns, the plaintive tones of the guitar music filling the sultry evening. Kyriakos had put his arm round her and she had laid her head against his shoulder and shut her eyes, relishing the feeling of being cherished and wanted.

She wondered what he was doing these days. Was he still on the island? Obviously he'd be bound to have a wife and family by now, wherever he had settled. He was a few years older than her, so he'd probably be nearing forty by now. Gosh. Carrie knew it was ridiculous – it was only a number, after all – but she was dreading reaching that milestone. So many years gone by and what had she achieved? Not much, or that was how it often felt.

Glancing over her shoulder, she saw that Nell had fallen some way behind and was looking very hot and disgruntled, dragging her feet along the dusty roadside. Carrie paused for her to catch up, hoping that the museum was air-conditioned and that there was a café where they could get a cold drink.

'You OK, poppet?' she asked, once Nell was alongside her.

'No,' retorted Nell, looking thoroughly pissed off. 'I'm boiling and my shoes are rubbing.'

Carrie grimaced. Of course she didn't say that she'd advised Nell that sliders were not appropriate footwear for a day out and that she should wear her trainers. No good ever came from 'I told you so'.

'We're nearly there,' she encouraged instead. 'Look, it's right here.' She pointed a little way ahead of them, hoping to encourage Nell that their goal was in sight.

With a scowl, Nell limped on, moving slightly faster now as if determined to stay in front of Carrie so that her mother could witness her suffering. A stab of guilt assailed Carrie. She should have given Nell the option of staying at the house and lounging on the balcony. But on the other hand, there was no point coming all this way and not actually getting out and about and seeing things.

They were a few minutes early and there was no sign of Xanthe yet. It was baking hot and Carrie was wilting as fast as Nell. As she stepped in front of the doors, they opened to release a rush of deliciously cool air.

'Let's stand inside while we wait for her,' suggested Carrie. 'Get out of the sun.'

Dragging her feet, Nell joined her. Carrie pulled her phone out of her pocket and checked it.

'Oh!' she said, 'Xanthe can't make it after all. She's saying for us to go round the museum and she'll meet us at three – with the potential guide.'

Nell raised her eyebrows disinterestedly. 'I need a drink,' she grumbled.

Carrie fumbled in her bag and produced a bottle of water, now lukewarm rather than fridge-cold, which she handed to Nell. Grudgingly, Nell took it and drank a long slug.

'Yuck,' she spluttered. 'Hot water. Lovely.'

Rolling her eyes, Carrie stowed the bottle back in her bag.

The museum was much better than Carrie had expected, with a 9D experience of living through the volcanic eruption, holograms and a diorama, as well as lots of information about the utopian kingdom that was fascinating even if it was no longer going to be the subject of Carrie's book. Even Nell perked up a bit as they went round the exhibits.

As they left, Carrie had her nose in a pamphlet she'd picked up, and almost walked straight into a man who was lingering in the entrance.

'Mum!' hissed Nell. 'Careful.'

Oh God, I've embarrassed her again, thought Carrie, at the same time as she turned to the man to say sorry. As she stuttered her way through her apology, she had a sudden feeling that he was familiar somehow, that she'd met him before. She studied his face, the close-cropped beard and hair, dark brown eyes and Grecian nose, trying to work out where she knew him from. From the way he was regarding her, a crease of puzzlement across his brow, it seemed that he was thinking the same thing. But they were outside now, in the full glare of the sun, and Carrie felt her brain frying under its onslaught, preventing her from thinking clearly.

'It's fine, don't worry about it.' The man responded to her

apology in perfect English that had a tinge of an American accent. 'But it's Carrie, isn't it? I'd have recognised you anywhere – you've hardly changed!'

Stunned, Carrie opened and shut her mouth like a goldfish. 'What do you... I mean, who...' she spluttered, and then abruptly came to halt as recognition dawned. 'Kyriakos? I don't believe it. Wow. Fancy meeting you here!' She laughed a little hysterically. 'You don't look any different either. Well, you do actually, I mean the beard, that's new isn't it, but other than that, certainly no older, ha ha...' She tailed off, aware of sounding like an idiot, but still astounded by the coincidence of meeting the very person she'd been thinking about ever since Xanthe's postcard from Santorini had arrived.

A silence fell as both Carrie and Kyriakos seemed to contemplate the weight of all the years that lay between them. It was broken by a cheery shout of, 'Hiya!'

Xanthe.

'So you two have already met!' she gushed. 'Fabulous.'

Carrie gazed at her, and then at Kyriakos, nonplussed. Xanthe didn't seem at all surprised that Kyriakos was here.

'Wasn't it a brilliant idea of mine?' Xanthe continued, and as she spoke Carrie understood that meeting Kyriakos was no chance encounter but instead entirely intentional. 'As soon as you asked me for help finding a local guide I realised Kris would be the perfect person!' Xanthe exclaimed as she beamed at the pair of them, obviously delighted with what she saw as a stroke of genius.

Then, taking in their still dumbfounded expressions, her smile slowly faded. 'What's the matter?' she demanded. 'Is everything OK?'

Acutely embarrassed, Carrie hastily waved her arms in a gesture of dismissal, nearly whacking a passing tourist in the face as she did so. 'Of course, it's er, a brilliant plan. I was just – a bit, well, surprised.'

'Oh right.' Xanthe laughed, clearly relieved. 'I thought I'd put my size 39s in it there. Trust me to cause an upset. Ha ha.'

At this moment, Kyriakos – who now seemed to go by the name Kris – stepped forward and planted two kisses of greeting on Carrie's cheeks, wafting a delicious scent of manliness and subtle aftershave towards her, which made her even more self-conscious of her own overheated, sweaty and bedraggled state.

'It's an absolute pleasure to be reacquainted,' he said, with an understated charm and elegance that must have developed, over the last fifteen or so years, from the easy-going magnetism he had displayed as a much younger man. 'And I'll be delighted to help you with your – er, project,' he continued. 'Xanthe hasn't told me much but what she has revealed makes it sound most intriguing.'

Carrie blinked, her eyes almost blinded by the light and heat of the sun-scorched car park. 'Thank you,' she muttered, overwhelmed by the unexpectedness of the entire situation. 'I—'

But whatever she was about to say was interrupted by Nell, uttering a plaintive, 'Mum!', followed by a pleading, 'Can we leave now? I'm too hot standing here.'

Carrie had almost forgotten about her daughter for a moment, lost in the surprise of coming face to face with a man who so firmly belonged to the past. She coughed to clear her throat and then gestured towards Nell. 'Kyriakos – Kris – this is my daughter Nell. Say hello, Nell,' she added, as if Nell were six, not sixteen. Why was she behaving like this, like a bashful teenager? It wasn't as if she and Kyriakos really had a history, when it came down to it, other than a few snogs under the stars. They'd only known each other for a few days, many years ago. It simply wasn't that deep, as Nell would put it. There was no reason for the frisson of excitement that had thrilled through her on realising who this handsome man was.

'Well,' cut in Xanthe, briskly. 'As Nell has already pointed out, it's absolutely boiling, so I think we should go somewhere a

bit more conducive to chatting through Carrie's plans.' She eyed
Carrie and Kris expectantly. 'Yes?'

'Do you have a car?' asked Kris, scanning the car park as if
to seek out a likely vehicle.

'Oh no!' Carrie laughed. 'We walked, didn't we Nell?'

Nell, who of course had her phone out, did not oblige with
an answer.

'That's fine,' replied Kris, who remained utterly cool, calm
and collected, while Carrie still felt gobsmacked by Xanthe's
subterfuge in arranging this meeting. 'We'll go in mine. I just
dropped off some guests staying at my hotel – Americans – so
there's plenty of room.' He winked at Carrie in an unexpected
act of complicity. 'You know the sort, worried about being
fleeced by a taxi driver or abandoned by the side of the road to
die... it was easier to bring them here myself than try to assuage
their fears.'

'How kind of you,' responded Carrie. 'To you know, provide
a taxi service.'

They all surged toward Kris's very smart and sleek black
Mercedes – it must be a successful hotel, Carrie thought – and
he leapt forward to open the passenger door.

'You go in the front,' Xanthe said, already clambering into
the back.

The interior of the car was like an oven until Kris switched
on the ignition and the engine purred into life. Within
moments, cool air began to pour from multiple vents. Carrie
breathed a sigh of relief.

'Oh, that's good,' she enthused, surreptitiously trying to
smooth out the strands of her hair that were stuck to her forehead by perspiration. 'How did humankind survive before air
con?'

Kris smiled. 'No idea.' He pulled out of the car park onto
the dusty white ribbon of road, then glanced at Carrie. 'I was
going to suggest that you all come back to my hotel and cool off

in the pool. Then we can talk properly with some drinks and snacks.'

'Sounds perfect!' Xanthe turned to Nell. 'Yes? You up for a swim?'

Carrie didn't hear Nell's reply as she was already answering Kris, saying apologetically, 'That would be lovely but we don't have our swimming stuff with us.'

'We can swing by your place and collect it,' he replied, without missing a beat. 'No problem at all. I'm sure Nell would like it.' He flicked his eyes up to the rear-view mirror as if to silently acknowledge the importance of pleasing capricious teenagers, then flashed Carrie a conspiratorial smile. 'I love seeing people enjoy the hotel, sharing the facilities with my friends.'

'Thank you,' Carrie replied. 'As long as you're sure it's not an inconvenience.' She paused, suddenly tongue-tied. So she and Nell were friends already, were they? It was an inexplicably nice feeling.

'Not at all.' Kris's absolute composure threw her own complete disorientation into sharper relief.

'It's so nice to see you,' Carrie continued, remodulating her voice to something lower than the high-pitched tone that meeting Kris had induced, and trying her best to sound normal. 'I didn't know if you'd still be on the island.' As soon as she'd said the words, she wanted to bite them back. They made it sound as if she'd been thinking about him, a lot, perhaps wondering if they'd bump into each other... And she had been doing exactly that, but only in passing, obviously. Panic returned and she dried up, leaving an impenetrable silence.

Which Kris gracefully broke. 'Yes, I'm still here.' He smiled. 'I moved to Athens, then to the US for almost eight years, but I came back to help my parents with the running of the hotel. They'd extended and improved it over the years, which was great, but involved a lot more work, so they really needed another pair of hands to pitch in. Both of my sisters are settled with families of their own on the mainland and couldn't uproot themselves, but I was happy to do so. It's hard to live anywhere else when you're used to paradise.' He laughed and his eyes sparkled attractively.

Carrie felt herself relax slightly. She nodded in agreement that Santorini was paradisiacal; that was incontrovertible. As the countryside flashed by, an enticing blur of villas and villages and vineyards, Carrie settled back into her seat. Suddenly, for all sorts of reasons, at least one of which was to do with the surprise reunion with Kris, the holiday in Santorini had got a whole lot more interesting.

Half an hour later, they were in Oia. Carrie had a quick dip and then got out and dried herself off, leaving Nell still luxuriating in the glittering turquoise pool. Xanthe had some emails to send, so Carrie was on her own when she joined Kris at a table under a shady pergola. A waiter brought ice-cold bottles of water and Coca-Cola, and a tray of delicious Greek snacks: little spinach pastries, grilled cheese, *koulouria* and slices of glistening watermelon.

The pair chatted about this and that for a while, and then Carrie elaborated on the scant information Xanthe had given Kris about Sol's connection to the island, and explained how she hoped he might be able to help with her research. She had thought ahead and, along with her bikini and towel, had also fetched the sketchbook from the house.

Now seemed to be the perfect moment to bring the subject up.

'I'm hoping I might be able to find out more about the Special Boat Squadron raid that Sol was involved in, visit some of the locations he would have gone to,' she explained. 'There's a huge mystery surrounding his past and what he did in the war, and my mother and I are desperate to get to the bottom of it. We're so regretful we didn't delve deeper when he was alive, but I'm hoping that while I'm here I might be able to unravel the story and lay some ghosts to rest.' Carrie halted, wondering whether to mention the book she wanted to write and the mysterious objects, the ring and the shirt, but decided not to just yet. One thing at a time. 'All I've really got to go on is what's in Wikipedia,' she concluded, 'and this.'

She proffered the sketchbook and Kris took it, opened its battered but still stiff covers and gazed at it with furrowed brow. Sitting eagerly forward in her chair, Carrie observed him as he turned the pages, pausing to closely scrutinise the sketches of what were presumably Sol's fellow SBS combatants.

'They're incredible pictures,' said Kris, still staring intently at the book. 'So well drawn and lifelike. He had a real talent.'

Carrie sighed. 'I know. And we had no idea, while he was alive. No one knew he was an artist.'

Kris shook his head. 'Maybe he put that part of himself to one side after the war, along with the guns and the memories.'

Carrie flicked her eyes up towards him. Kris was remarkably perceptive. She didn't remember that about him. But how would she have done? She'd hardly known him.

She looked back down at the book, and watched as he turned the pages until he reached the drawing of the woman. A gentle breeze ruffled the paper napkins on the table and Carrie grabbed them and secured them under a plate to stop them blowing away. When her gaze returned to Kris, she was shocked to see the change in his demeanour. His skin beneath the dark tan had blanched to a much paler shade and his eyes were full of shock.

Perplexed, Carrie stared at him, tongue-tied, wondering what on earth had gone wrong. Suddenly, Kris closed the book, thrust it back towards Carrie, then noisily pushed back his chair, stood up and walked away.

Carrie was utterly bewildered, and her eyes followed him as he disappeared along the path that led to the hotel building.

What on earth was going on? Why had he been so affected by a simple line drawing in an old sketchbook?

'Kris?' she called out, cautiously. 'What's the matter?' And then again, louder and with more urgency, 'Kris!'

But Kris did not reply.

# CHAPTER 11

## VASSIA, 1944

'Father,' asked Vassia again. 'Who will go if not Andreas?'

Ianos raised his eyes to hers and answered simply, as she had known he would, 'You, Vasiliki. You must go.'

If Vassia hadn't already known the gravity of the situation, her father's rare use of her full name would have made it obvious.

And so it was that, not long after midnight, the band of commandos and their Greek guides, including Vassia, were ready to move off from the cave. Captain Andersen had split them into two patrols; Z patrol, led by Lieutenant Patterson, would head for the radio station at Imerovigli, while P patrol, led by Andersen, would head for Fira. Once they arrived at the capital, P patrol would split into two. One section would attack the barracks and the other, a smaller group, would target Lieutenant Schwarz's residence.

Vassia concentrated hard on Captain Andersen's final instructions, barely able to breathe. He was speaking English and she couldn't understand a word, but that was not the point. Whatever he was saying, it was serious. More than serious; it was life and death.

Someone asked a question, which was met by a hollow laugh and a shaking of Andersen's head. He pulled a packet from his pocket and handed each of the men a couple of tablets, which were swallowed and washed down with a swig of water. What on earth were they taking? As her puzzled gaze landed on Sol's, he leant towards her.

'Benzedrine,' he explained in a whisper. 'To make sure we are wide awake.'

Vassia nodded dumbly. She was dizzy and giddy with the madness of the whole surreal escapade.

Andersen made a gesture with his hand, and in an instant all of the men had fallen in behind him, Vassia among them. Her mouth and tongue were bone dry and her palms clammy with nervous perspiration. But despite her terror, there was no way she would not go through with it. It was her duty to do whatever she could to aid these brave men, and, if their actions tonight helped in any way at all to bring this terrible war to an end, then she would have achieved something in her life. Even if she died in the process.

One by one, stealthy and ever-vigilant, the troop left the cave, Kostas and Lefteris with Z group, and Elias, Helios and Vassia with P. Vassia was sorry to part from Kostas; he was so reliable, so steadfast and level-headed. The other three lads were also trustworthy and dependable, but Vassia didn't know them as well. Either way, once they got to Fira and split up she would be on her own with the sub-group going to the commander's residence, a level of responsibility above and beyond any that she had experienced before.

Captain Andersen, armed with the same pistol and knife he'd had earlier, walked level with Elias, with Helios bringing up the rear, while Vassia stayed in the middle. She fell into step with Sol, round whose neck hung another kind of gun, a machine gun, Vassia thought. Various weapons of various types adorned all the men and Vassia shuddered to think about all this firepower, how much damage could be done. She wished she could protect Sol, and all the commandos, from harm, but all she could do was silently pray for them as they made their advance.

At first, she and Sol talked in hushed tones, picking up the conversation where they'd left it earlier. Sol told Vassia a little more about his job in the bank, his family and his brother Anthony, who had been killed early on in the war.

'I'm so sorry to hear that,' Vassia said.

'That's why I have to do this,' Sol responded. 'I have to do whatever is in my power to make sure he didn't die in vain. If the Nazis win...'

He didn't need to finish the sentence. The idea of a German victory was too much to articulate.

A thought occurred to Vassia. 'What will you do with any soldiers you capture tonight?' she asked.

Sol didn't answer immediately and, in the pale moonlight, Vassia saw a strange expression descend upon his handsome features.

'Any captives will immediately become POWs and will leave with us for incarceration in one of our camps in the Middle East. But we do not expect to take many prisoners. It's not Andersen's way.'

For a moment, as the words sank in, Vassia struggled to detect their meaning. And then it dawned on her and, with it, a flood of alarm that sent shockwaves tingling down her spine. The aim was, purely and simply, to kill.

Changing the subject to lighten the mood, for her own benefit as much as Sol's, Vassia told Sol about Chicky, the baby bird Nico had rescued, how it seemed to be thriving under their care.

'Hopefully it will try to fly again soon,' she told him. 'And then it will be free, like a bird should be.'

'Like the world should be,' added Sol. And then he uttered

a small chuckle and smiled at Vassia, his eyes looking suddenly less tired, and younger. He wasn't wearing his glasses and she wondered if perhaps he only needed them when he was drawing or reading, and her early worries about what would happen if he lost or broke them were unfounded. That was a relief.

'But how kind of you and your cousin to look after a helpless creature – and to do so successfully,' Sol concluded.

'Well, it's more by good luck than judgement,' answered Vassia. 'But it does feel good to save a life, even if it's only a little wild bird.'

Her words had not been uttered with any double meaning but, as soon as they were out, it was obvious what both she and Sol were thinking of. Was the taking of lives that would inevitably happen that night justified, because it was war? Vassia shuddered involuntarily and tried to block such thoughts from her mind. Doubts were not going to be helpful right now.

They had been climbing steadily since they left the cave, and Sol halted momentarily to gulp some water from the flask in his pocket, which he then offered to Vassia. She took the flask from his grasp, tentatively raised it to her lips and took a sip. It felt intimate, too intimate for such a short acquaintance, to drink from the same vessel, but Vassia's mouth was desiccated from a mixture of apprehension and dread and she was glad of the moisture on her tongue.

They resumed their ascent only seconds later. It wasn't only the climb that made Vassia's heart beat at double its normal speed, it was also the fear pounding in her veins at the thought that, at any moment, they might come face to face with a Nazi patrol. And, she had to admit it, the proximity to Sol was also causing her pulse to race. The more she spoke with him, the more that first feeling of having known him for an aeon, rather than just a few hours, grew within her. Merely walking by his side, as she was now, gave her a sense of completion, as if he made her whole. Vassia had never been sure whether she believed in destiny before, but now she was starting to think that she did. It had been her destiny to meet Sol in such an unexpected, emotion-filled way. And it was her destiny to make sure he and the other men got away safely that night.

However much she did not want to let him go.

They reached the outskirts of the town, and the ever-present peril ratcheted up a few more notches. The two patrols split apart. It was up to Vassia now. Slinking down narrow alley-ways more commonly frequented by the neighbourhood cats, sheltering in the shadow of buildings in case of a passer-by, Vassia got the men to within spitting distance of Schwarz's residence.

'There it is,' she managed to mutter, desperately trying to keep her voice from breaking. She pointed, but her finger trembled so violently that she quickly withdrew her arm, for fear of being thought weak. The men had seen the house anyway; they knew which one it was.

Vassia wanted to stay, to make sure that they achieved their goals and that they were able to find their way back out of the town and down to the cave, where they would hole up until the following night, when they would be picked up by the same schooners that had brought them to Santorini. But she had been told by Spyros before they left, under the strict instruction of Captain Andersen, that she had to make herself scarce as soon as they reached their destination.

'We can't help you if you get caught,' Spyros had told her. 'And we don't want that responsibility, or your death, on our conscience. Once we are outside Schwarz's place, you must go.'

Now, quaking with fear, Vassia was motionless, unable to make her legs work to carry her away. Into the silence suddenly came the distant sound of grenades detonating in dull, explosive roars, followed by the staccato rattling of machine-gun fire. The attack on the barracks above the bank on the other side of town had begun.

In this moment, it all became real, and the adrenaline released by the danger ratcheted up to its highest level. Vassia's mind flitted, unbidden, to her brother and Athena. She'd almost forgotten about the baby, Athena's precarious position, perhaps still labouring, in the surgery behind the doctor's house in a town now overrun with combatants. Perhaps she should go there, rather than back to Vourvoulos, find out what had happened.

'Go!' shouted one of the commandos, gesturing frantically to her to leave. She didn't understand the word, but she perfectly comprehended the meaning.

The men were ready, guns primed to fire, while Vassia was still stuck to the spot, paralysed.

Sol appeared beside her. 'It's time now,' he said, simply. And then, as Vassia finally regained the power of movement and was about to turn on her heel, he pulled her towards him, brushed her lips with the lightest of kisses and then pushed her gently away, back in the direction from which they had come.

Faint with surprise and panic and fear and desire, Vassia stumbled away, just managing to put one foot in front of the other, dazed and overwhelmed.

She walked and walked, through deserted streets and alleys, past boarded-up shops and houses with their shutters firmly closed. It was dark, the faint moonlight of earlier now obscured by cloud, and she almost had to feel her way over the well-worn cobblestones.

*I'll go to the doctor's house*, she thought, finally. It was impossible to imagine going back home without knowing about the baby. Or Sol.

Sporadic bursts of gunfire from the barracks rang out across the town, and Vassia smelt the cordite in the air, and the smoke from something burning. It was faint and hard to discern, just like the sulphur from the ancient volcano on Nea Kameni island, but unmistakably there.

Nausea turned her stomach upside down and bile rose in her throat. She was sure she was about to be sick. She halted and placed a hand on the cool wall of the building beside her, using it to steady herself. She was standing this way, oblivious to her surroundings, when she heard them.

Footsteps, belonging to at least two or three people. Footsteps, clicking over the cobbles with rhythmic regularity. What kind of footwear made such a sound? Boots. The polished boots of high-ranking Nazis.

With a terrible sense of impending doom, Vassia froze for the second time that night.

The footsteps drew closer. Vassia came to her senses. She bent down, took her own shoe off, turned it upside down and then put it back on, hoping that her little pantomime of emptying out a stone would have been convincing. Then she forced herself to stand upright, and to turn to face whoever was approaching her.

For a few moments she could not make out the faces of the men. And then she did, and immediately her heart skipped several beats and sweat broke out on her forehead and under her arms.

'Well, well, well.' Lieutenant Schwarz's tone was amused, as if he'd come across something quite peculiar but, nevertheless, diverting. 'I recognise you, do I not?'

Vassia's hands were shaking so badly she hid them behind her back. This was the worst thing that could possibly have happened, for so many reasons she could hardly process them but most of all because, if Schwarz was here, he wasn't at home, which rendered Sol's mission inevitably unsuccessful.

'I d-d-don't know,' stammered Vassia, unable to keep her voice steady. 'Sometimes I work at Loucas's restaurant. Perhaps you've seen me there.'

Schwarz smiled, an arctic smile that held not a shred of warmth, humanity or compassion. 'Ah yes,' he replied. 'That'll be it. You're that handsome waiter's sister, aren't you?' His voice sounded odd and his words were slurred. Vassia realised he must be drunk. Her eyes flickered towards his companions. Were they also inebriated? Was that a good thing, or a bad one? Did it make them more, or less, dangerous? More, or less, volatile?

As Vassia was considering how to respond, Schwarz continued. 'He wasn't in tonight – day off, I suppose. Ah well, no one can work seven days a week, least of all a Greek.' At this, he roared with laughter, and his two companions followed suit. 'Though that boy is certainly not as lazy as most of his compatriots.'

Something snapped in Vassia as she regarded them, chortling away, making a joke at her country's expense. How dare they? They thought themselves the conquerors of the world, and they nearly were. But not quite. Not yet. If Sol and all the others like him fighting across half the globe were successful, Schwarz and his ilk would one day, sooner or later, be mincemeat. At this image, Vassia almost laughed herself. Schwarz, turned into a moussaka. Well, that was a revolting idea, but still...

Sol. It occurred to Vassia, with a force like a lightning bolt, that she must somehow get away from Schwarz and go to warn Sol and the others of the danger they were in. Schwarz would arrive back at his residence in just a few minutes and, if he found the men there, they'd be cornered and all hell would break loose.

As far as Vassia could tell, Schwarz didn't seem to be aware of the attack on the barracks. The restaurant, which was only a short distance away from where they now were, was carved out of the black, volcanic rock, and inside Schwarz wouldn't have heard, or seen, the earlier explosions, nor the gunfire. Everything had been quiet for the last few minutes, when he must have been out on the streets. Perhaps the raid was over. But the peril certainly was not.

'And so what is a pretty girl like you doing out on the streets so late?' enquired Schwarz, moving a little bit closer to Vassia than was necessary. She could feel his hot breath on her cheek, smell the alcohol.

But she was fired up now. Vassia Kourakis, nobody's pushover.

'I'm on my way to the doctor's house,' she answered, boldly. 'My brother, Andreas, the waiter – his wife is in labour but she needs medical attention. They had to take her to him on a mule cart. She might need help to get the baby out... I'm going there to be with her, and Andreas.' She stared defiantly right into Schwarz's emotionless eyes. 'There's no curfew in Santorini. I'm within my rights.'

As soon as the words were out, she regretted them. What was she doing? There was absolutely no need to antagonise this brute. The urge to run to Sol was stronger than ever now. She had to let him know that Schwarz was on his way.

'Well, who's a little firebrand,' said Schwarz, shaking his head from side to side as he looked Vassia up and down. 'No curfew, indeed.' That set the two wingmen off into more hearty chortles.

Vassia's legs wobbled beneath her. She'd done it now.

'But that's troubling news about the child,' Schwarz went on. 'The doctor lives that way, doesn't he?' He pointed vaguely off to the right, the direction in which Vassia should have been heading. 'The thing is, though, a young lady like you can't be left to wander around at this hour unprotected.' It was a nonsensical thing to say, as the only dangerous people on Santorini were the Nazis themselves, but perhaps Schwarz thought Fira was like Berlin or Hamburg, two cities so huge and incomprehensibly foreign-sounding that Vassia could only imagine what depravities lurked there. 'So my two deputies here will accompany you right to the door. And once you are safely there, they can bring me news of how my protégé's wife and child are doing. How about that?'

Schwarz smiled that awful smile again, that was more like an evil sneer. The two men beside him clicked their heels, saluted and then moved to stand next to Vassia, one on either side. Dread subsumed her. There was something terrifying about Schwarz's devotion to her brother and, not for the first time, an awful sensation of foreboding gripped her about where it might lead. In addition, Vassia had to give up all hope of warning Sol.

There was nothing further she could do to help him.

# CHAPTER 12

## CARRIE, 2024

When Xanthe returned to the table, Carrie eyed her despondently.

'Where's Kris?' asked Xanthe, predictably.

Carrie shook her head. 'I don't know. I showed him Sol's sketchbook, he came over all peculiar, and then he got up and left without so much as a goodbye.'

Frowning, Xanthe picked up the book and leafed through it. 'That's odd,' she said eventually, clearly as perplexed as Carrie was.

'Just a bit,' replied Carrie. 'And I feel dreadful now. We'd only just got reacquainted after all this time and I seem to have upset him already.' Of course she didn't add what else she felt; that strange, unaccustomed fizzing in her stomach that had accompanied their meeting, the niggle of disappointment now that she had, in some incomprehensible way, annoyed or distressed him.

Xanthe waved her arm in a dismissive gesture. 'No, it won't be you,' she reassured Carrie. 'Why would it be? There must be something else. Perhaps there's a problem with the hotel and he had to rush off. You know what guests are like. Unreasonably demanding and never satisfied, as far as I can make out.'

Carrie smiled wanly. 'If it was the hotel, he must be telepathic,' she countered. 'Because nobody spoke to him or called him or messaged him, as far as I could see.'

'I don't think you should worry about it.' Xanthe reached out her hand and patted Carrie's. 'It'll be nothing, I promise you.' She turned to look at the kidney-shaped pool, sparkling in the afternoon light. 'How about another swim before you go?' She pulled an apologetic face. 'I'm sorry I can't be with you this evening or tomorrow. I had thought you might do something with Kris...'

'Oh it's fine,' interjected Carrie hastily. She didn't want to be a burden to Xanthe, or to seem helpless and in need of constant input from her. 'Nell and I will be fine on our own.'

'You know what you could do tomorrow,' Xanthe declared, immediately brightening as inspiration came to her. 'A boat trip to the volcano island, the hot springs and Thirassia! Let's get online now and we can book it for you. I'll do it; my friend Dimitrios who owns and captains the ship will give me a nice discount for you.'

'Well,' answered Carrie. 'That would be great. If you're sure it's not too much trouble.'

'No trouble at all.' Xanthe was already tapping away at her phone. 'What's your email address again? I'll send the confirmation there and you can pay in cash on the boat.'


The next day saw Carrie and Nell up early for their trip. It was already hot, so once in Fira they took the funicular down to the port, rather than the 588 steps that also led there. They arrived to find the small quay thronged with tourists getting onto every type of vessel, from traditional wooden ships to modern catamarans. Two cruise ships were at anchor in the bay and tenders buzzed back and forth, depositing yet more people into the tiny area. The noise and crush were overwhelming and finding the right boat while not losing sight of Nell quite the challenge, but eventually they were both safely on board. Carrie gazed back towards the harbour, behind which the austere cliffs rose up sheer from the sea, topped by a sprinkling of whitewashed houses like the icing on a cake. The stepped path cut across the cliffs in a wide, extravagant zigzag and Carrie imagined the years gone by when all imported or exported goods would have had to take this laborious route up and down.

She turned her attention to Dimitrios the captain's introductory spiel, glancing at Nell to see if she was listening. To Carrie's amazement, she was, and not half-heartedly either but with all her attention. She had got quite interested in the whole lost-Atlantis myth since yesterday's museum visit and was eagerly absorbing facts and information wherever she found them, and also asking about Sol and the SBS, explaining to Carrie that history was 'cool'.

Carrie, on the other hand, could not stop worrying about Kris. After he'd left the night before, he'd sent a message via the barman that, whenever they wanted to go home, a taxi would be called for them, but Carrie had not wanted to impose any further on his generosity. Instead, they had taken the bus. She'd been delighted to think that Kris might be able to bring his local knowledge to bear on the mystery of Sol and the SBS. But, she thought with a sigh, that was a non-starter now. Clearly Kris did not want to be involved in her research; he'd made that only too obvious by his actions, if not his words. This would have been a blow to Carrie's plans whoever the prospective guide had been, but the fact that it was Kris made it much more painful.

Trying to put it out of her mind, she attempted to concentrate on the boat trip. The vertical caldera walls were stunning in their height, making it possible to imagine the enormous strength of the volcano that had formed them. There was a path from Fira to Oia that apparently had spectacular views, which Carrie would love to walk, but she knew that Nell would not. It would have been ideal to install Nell beside Kris's pool so that Carrie was free to do the hike alone, but never mind. It wouldn't be the end of the world if she didn't manage it.

Dimitrios resumed his commentary, accompanying his words with gestures towards the landmarks. 'These cliffs are three hundred metres high,' he explained. 'Beneath the sea, they are four hundred metres deep. Many of the houses you can see are built right into the cliff, something the islanders historically undertook to provide protection from the heat of summer and the cold winds of winter. On the other side of the island, there are also caves along the shoreline.'

Carrie's ears pricked up at this. She'd read that, after landing on the island, the SBS men had sheltered in a cave until the time came to launch their raid. This afternoon, she'd have a look to see if it was possible to get there by bus. If not, perhaps she could squeeze her budget to allow for a short car hire to enable her to cover more ground. She'd originally thought about going to the tourist office to see if there were any guides who knew about the Second World War, and she could resurrect that plan.

Despite the disappointment about Kris, and whatever had gone wrong, the day was glorious. Carrie lifted her face to the sun and felt its rays warm her skin as a gentle breeze rippled through her hair. The weather and the island's beauty were proving to be exactly the tonic she had needed, enabling her to temporarily forget the mundanity of her life and the dismal summer they were having – again – at home. She'd even put to the back of her mind her money worries and the dread about the mortgage, promising herself that she'd do her best to enjoy the holiday while it lasted. It was a rare chance to spend quality time with Nell and reset their relationship after the stress of the exams and the clashes over some of Nell's recent behaviour.

They visited the hot springs and the last surviving remnants of the volcano, and then the boat took them to the only other inhabited island in the Santorini archipelago, Thirassia. As always, Carrie had brought a picnic lunch with them to save money, and she and Nell ate this on the pebbly beach. Then Carrie decided to leave Nell sunbathing while she trekked up to the hilltop town of Manolas.

'Taxi,' an old man with a weather-beaten face called out to her as she passed. Surprised, Carrie looked around. She hadn't seen any cars, and the steeply stepped path that snaked up the hillside certainly wasn't drivable. Seeing her confusion, the old man pointed beneath a makeshift lean-to. There, waiting patiently, was a line of donkeys, ears twitching, tails flicking away the flies.

Carrie laughed. So this was a taxi, Thirassia-style. Eat your heart out, Uber. She stopped to pat the nearest animal, but declined the offer of a ride. She could perfectly well walk, and, while these donkeys looked happy and healthy, she was worried about them being overworked in the heat, carrying heavy tourists up such a steep hill. She had read that, in the olden days, recalcitrant beasts of burden from other parts of Greece would be threatened with being sent to Santorini if they didn't buck their ideas up, and thinking of this path, and the one from the port up to Fira, she could see why.

Carrie set off upwards, pausing every now and again to turn to face the sea while she caught her breath. White-sailed yachts criss-crossed the deep waters of the caldera, as fleet and quick as fireflies. As she watched, a ferry nosed its way around the headland, leaving deep furrows of foamy white waves in its wake.

When Carrie finally made it to the top, she found the settlement of Manolas delightful and well worth the effort; a jumble of ancient houses clustered around cobbled streets, perched on a cliff high above the sea and with spectacular views back towards Santorini. The main island, with all its hustle and bustle, seemed far removed from this tranquil spot; Carrie was almost the only tourist here. A pretty little church she came across had the familiar, iconic blue-domed roof, but the colours were augmented by touches of red and amber. At the heart of the town was the commercial centre, consisting of a couple of old-fashioned grocery stores and a café where wooden tables adorned with pots of fragrant herbs stood waiting for customers.

Wandering up and down, Carrie imagined living here, on this tiny island with fewer than three hundred inhabitants. How simple life would be, up with the sun and to bed with the sun, none of the stresses and strains of life in the UK. Of course it was silly, she knew that – there was probably just as much to fret about here as back home, but somehow the sunshine and general herb-scented gorgeousness of everything seemed to take the edge off.

Carrie thought about Sol, too, and what his experience of Santorini would have been like. How different would the island have seemed, visited in wartime when your mission was to kill and destroy, when achieving your aims was essential to restoring peace to the world? Seen through that prism, everything would be distorted. And yet somehow Sol had had the time to draw the mystery woman and to do so with what very much looked to the outside observer's eyes like love. What, exactly, had gone on between him and the woman, all those years ago? Carrie longed to know.

More memories of Sol rose up in her mind as she strolled. When Carrie had been very young, he'd owned an enormous, shaggy Pyrenean Mountain Dog called Snowy. How Carrie and her sister Jenny had adored that dog, vying to be its favourite 'cousin', fighting over who held its lead on walks through the Wiltshire countryside. On one occasion, some wild deer had unexpectedly burst out of the undergrowth and run across their path.

As Snowy gave chase, Carrie had desperately tried to keep

her grip on the lead in the way Sol had taught her to do. She clearly remembered being dragged along behind the dog, her little legs going like the clappers, her heart pounding. Eventually, unable to keep going, she'd let go of the lead and fallen to the ground. Sol had caught up with her to find her in floods of tears, not because of her sore, grazed knees but due to her failure to follow his instruction.

'It's all right,' Sol had comforted her, giving her a big hug. 'You did your very best – I saw how brave and strong you were.' He'd fumbled in his pocket and brought out a somewhat squashed toffee wrapped in pink cellophane, which he'd slipped to Carrie by way of consolation, in secret because he knew Harriet didn't approve of sweets. Only when Snowy had reappeared, presumably having realised that catching deer was not in his skillset, had Carrie surreptitiously unwrapped her bounty and put it into her mouth. She could still recall the syrupy deliciousness of that illicit treat, the way it had stuck to her teeth, how she had tried to suck it slowly to make it last all the way home.

That evening, she had brushed Snowy as he lay dozing in front of the coal fire and then written a story about the dog engaging in an epic fight to save his flock from a wolf, which after all may well have been an accurate portrayal of Snowy's life had he been a working dog in the French mountains rather than a somewhat overindulged pet in the Home Counties. Sol had asked to read the story and, reluctantly, Carrie had agreed, hoping he wouldn't think it babyish and stupid. On the contrary, he told her how good it was, and, because it was Sol and Carrie trusted him implicitly, she had dared to believe him. Buoyed up by his praise, she had entered the story into a writing competition run by the local newspaper and had won first place. Perhaps that was when she'd been bitten by the writing bug; thanks to Sol, and Snowy, and that wonderful chunk of sticky toffee.

She had so much to be grateful to Sol for; not just all the wonderful memories and the money that had enabled her to purchase the now threatened house, but also her writing. If only she could pull off something as good as the Snowy story now, she might be able to save her home after all.

Carrie had been lost in daydreams, and was cutting it fine as she descended the same steep path back down to the water's edge; she got there just as the tour boat was gearing up to leave. By the time she and Nell arrived back in Pyrgos it was mid-afternoon, and the sun was still high in the sky and beating down. Trudging up the steep hill, Carrie saw a silhouetted figure lingering by the gate that led into the property. A tourist taking photos of the abundance of picturesqueness, she assumed. It was only once they were nearly there that she recognised who the person was.

Kris.

Her heart jolted into her throat.

'You go on in,' she said to Nell, hurriedly. 'Put the kettle on for a cuppa. I'll join you shortly.'

It had all ended so oddly the day before that she wanted Nell out of the way before speaking to Kris. She willed Nell to follow her instruction and not start wailing about spiders and, for once, her prayers were answered. Nell opened the front door and disappeared inside, leaving Carrie alone and face to face with Kris.

'Carrie,' he began. He looked cool and collected but there was an anxious note to his voice. 'I hope you don't mind me coming here. I wanted to apologise about what happened yesterday, my odd behaviour.'

Flustered, Carrie ran her hand through her hair, which was windblown and filled with salt. *I must look like a scarecrow*, she thought, distractedly.

'Oh no, it's fine, don't worry about it,' she replied breezily, waving her arms around as if to dismiss all awkwardness.

'Well, it's not fine actually,' continued Kris. 'I was very rude. You must have wondered what was up.'

Carrie gave up trying to be diplomatic. 'I was a bit taken aback,' she admitted. 'I couldn't work out what was going on.'

'Is there somewhere we can sit down?' Kris asked her. 'I've got something to show you.'

'Of course,' answered Carrie, leading him into the tiny house and up the stairs towards the balcony, mentally trying to picture her bedroom and whether she'd left her knickers lying on the floor. Thankfully, as they entered she saw that it was actually passably tidy. She ushered him through, opened the balcony door and gestured to him to take a seat.

As soon as she herself was settled, Kris pulled a large matchbox from his pocket.

Nell called up from downstairs, something about teabags, but Carrie ignored her. All she could focus on was Kris. Slowly, he opened the box. Carrie became aware of Nell stepping onto the balcony, still muttering about tea but then suddenly falling silent as Kris extracted from the box a necklace, that perhaps had originally been silver or some other metal but was now tarnished with age. Narrowing her eyes, Carrie watched as Kris revealed the pendant that dangled from the wire. She still had not worked it out when she heard Nell take a sharp intake of breath.

'It's the same one,' she called out excitedly. 'The one the beautiful woman is wearing in the sketchbook! Look, Mum, it's got the same boat on it.'

All at once, it hit Carrie like a hammer blow. Nell was right. It *was* the necklace in the picture.

'Wh-what the hell—' She broke off, momentarily unable to finish her sentence. 'Where did you get this? What the...' Her words tailed off in disbelief. Yesterday, it had been Kris who was stunned. Now it was Carrie's turn.

Kris gave a thoughtful smile. 'I don't think it's the same one,

I know it,' he replied. 'The woman that Sol drew – she was my grandmother, Vassia Kourakis. It's unmistakably her in the picture. That's why I was so overcome, and behaved so rudely. She only died a couple of years ago and it still feels raw, the loss of her. Apologies again.' He paused for a moment, collecting himself, before resuming. 'When she died, this was in the little collection of her most treasured possessions that she said in her will must never be disposed of. Where she got it, or how, we've never known.'

Carrie continued to stare at the aged, battered necklace. It was a tangible link to Sol, more real and palpable even than the sketchbook. It occurred to Carrie that Sol must have made this necklace from a halfpenny piece buried in a pocket somewhere about his person, and gifted it to Vassia. How else would she have got hold of British money in the middle of a war?

'How would Sol and Vassia have met, though?' breathed Carrie, softly, more to herself than to Kris. 'The SBS men were on the island for such a short amount of time, according to the historical records I've read. I don't understand how Sol would have got to know your grandmother so well, to make her a necklace and draw her with so much love.'

Kris shook his head. 'I don't know.' His brow was still furrowed in concentration as he reached out and put the necklace back into the box. He caught Carrie's eye as he did so. 'I don't know,' he repeated. 'But I think we should try to find out. Don't you?'

'Absolutely!' agreed Carrie, instantly. 'Where to start though? It's all so long ago now. Nearly everyone from that time is gone.'

'It's a long shot,' Kris replied, slowly, 'but I've got an idea. Are you and Nell up for a short drive?'

# CHAPTER 13

## VASSIA, 1944

The explosion that rent the air was apocalyptic, its sonic boom resounding off the surrounding buildings. The noise was accompanied by a luminous red glow that coloured the night sky in shades of vermilion, illuminating the faces of Vassia's Nazi companions, making them seem evil, vampiric. Vassia's legs shook, either from the aftershocks running through the ground beneath her feet or from the terror that gripped her soul.

The radio station at Imerovigli. The bombs must have gone off.

'Mein Gott!' The Germans halted abruptly and looked at each other for a moment as if unsure what to do or how to react. And then they began to shout, words that Vassia couldn't understand but that she could tell were angry, confused – and full of vengeance.

For a moment the soldiers seemed to have forgotten her presence, and then, suddenly, one of them turned to her. 'Go home,' he ordered. 'Do not go to the doctor's house. Get out of Fira.'

And with that, the pair strode off down the narrow street, leaving Vassia alone, heart racing, breath coming in uneven pants as her panic ebbed and flowed. Unable to think straight, she wavered, wondering whether to obey their commands. And then she heard the sound of running feet, and more shouts uttered in German, and she realised that there were troops everywhere and that going home was indeed the only sensible thing to do. Desperate as she was to see her brother and his wife, who hopefully would now have their new baby safe in their arms, it would be utter foolishness to ignore the express instructions of a Nazi.

Heart pounding, she stole through Fira towards home, hiding behind doorways and ducking beneath walls whenever she feared the enemy was near, taking the way she thought safest rather than the fastest route. Moving this way, it took her nearly an hour to reach Vourvoulos and, when she finally arrived back at her house, she found her father wide awake and pacing up and down. Her mother was in the kitchen, distracting herself by making bread.

'Vassia! Oh thank God, thank God you're back.' Thalia flung floury arms round her daughter as Ianos sank down heavily onto a chair and put his head in his hands.

'What happened, my child?' asked her father, when he had recovered from the relief enough to speak. 'Do you know how it went?'

Vassia sighed. 'I don't,' she replied. 'I heard a lot of noise from the direction of the barracks, so there was definitely a battle there. And I'm sure they got the radio station, as we saw and heard the explosion – it was massive. But Schwarz – he wasn't at home. And I've no idea what has happened to any of the SBS men, if all have survived, or none.'

In the fear and worry of it all, Ianos didn't seem to pick up on how Vassia could possibly have known about Schwarz, and Vassia wasn't about to tell him and give him the heart attack he looked to be on the verge of.

'I thought about going to the doctor's,' she ventured, not

sure if this would bring her father's wrath down on her shoulders. 'But then I realised it was too dangerous.'

Thalia let out a long, low moan. 'The baby,' she keened, 'the baby. When will we find out about the poor mite?' She picked up her ball of dough, slammed it down on the wooden counter and began pummelling it as if her life depended on it. It was probably a good way to relieve stress, thought Vassia, but right then she felt as if she herself hardly had the strength to lift a feather. A moment later she remembered Chicky. She should check on him.

Summoning all her remaining energy, she hauled herself to her feet and went to look. In the box, the fledging was so still that for a moment she thought it must be dead. But then she ran a gentle finger over its tiny head and it woke and chirped loudly. Despite everything, Vassia smiled. She dropped some water into its beak and, in the darkest hours that come before the dawn, went outside with a lantern to find some insects. She remembered telling Sol about the bird, how interested he had been, how hopeful that poor Chicky should live. That conversation felt as if it had taken place a hundred years ago.

Once the bird was fed, Vassia resolved to give it back to Nico. It was time. She was pretty sure it was on track to survive, and he would be so proud that he had played a part in that. She'd take it to his house the following day. She lay down on her bed and dozed off for a while, exhausted from the events of the last day and night.

Not long after, just as dawn was breaking, the smell of burning woke her. Leaping out of bed, she rushed to the kitchen, where she found Thalia's bread still in the oven. That was how stressed they all were; her mother had forgotten about her baking for the first time in her life.

Vassia was in the process of cutting off the burnt bits when a knock at the door disturbed her. It was Kostas, hair dishevelled, face blackened, eyes sunk deep in his skull with exhaustion. Vassia recalled that massive explosion, the fiery red sky, and shuddered. She sat Kostas down with a glass of water and went to wake her father. Her mother got up too, and was soon in the kitchen, plying Kostas with slices of hot bread and honey.

'You need the sugar,' she explained as she fussed around their next-door neighbour, just as she would have done when he was five years old. 'It's good for...' Her voice tailed off. She didn't know what word to use. 'Shock' seemed inadequate for what had transpired that night on the normally tranquil, quiet island of Santorini.

Eventually, still pale and shaken, Kostas wiped his mouth with the back of his hand and began to speak.

'Z patrol was successful,' he said. 'The radio station – it's gone. At the barracks – I heard that at least twenty were killed, and many injured, but the Nazis are already trying to cover up what really happened to save face. Two of the commandos also died.'

At this Vassia took a sharp intake of breath as horror rippled through her body. But it could not be Sol, she reassured herself. He had not been at the garrison. It surely could not be him.

'Were any – captured?' she asked falteringly, wanting and not wanting to know the answer in equal measure.

'I've told you all I know,' responded Kostas, bleakly. 'There's nothing else.' It seemed that the danger he had been in, the mortal peril, was only now truly sinking in.

He left, saying he needed to sleep. Vassia wondered if he would be able to drop off.

Thalia and Ianos disappeared to their bedroom to get properly dressed; they had flung on any old thing when Kostas had arrived. Vassia picked up Kostas's plate and glass, and carried them over to the sink to wash. Before she got there, the kitchen door burst open and another young man stood on the threshold.

This time it was her brother.

'The baby's here,' Andreas reported, his voice cracking with emotion. 'A little boy. We named him Atlas.'

Vassia's legs almost collapsed underneath her as relief subsumed her. She leant on the sink for stability. 'Thank goodness,' she breathed.

Andreas called out, 'Mother! Father!' and the siblings' parents came running. Once they were seated, Andreas repeated his news. Thalia immediately began to weep, happy tears of joy.

'And all is well?' Vassia spoke softly. 'How's Athena? When will they be coming home?'

Andreas shook his head, his earlier elation fading already. 'The doctor had to use forceps to get him out. She's in quite a bad way. And – Atlas – well, the doctor thinks there might be something wrong with his heart.'

After the hope came the body blow of catastrophe. Vassia felt the world ending, everything collapsing around her. Surely not. His *heart*. Please not that. Of all the organs of the body, this was the one that nobody could do without. Her eyes flitted involuntarily towards her father. His heart was failing him and look how unwell he was, however much he tried to hide it. Babies should have strong hearts, strong lungs, strong kidneys, strong everything.

'Oh no,' she muttered, inadequately. 'No, no. Surely not. Is the doctor certain? What has he told you?'

Andreas ran his hands through his hair and then held them out in a gesture of despair. 'Nothing much. He just listened with his stethoscope and said he'd have to keep an eye on it. Atlas might need surgery, but it's not possible here. We'd have to go to Athens, but he might not be strong enough to make the journey.'

Thalia's weeping intensified. Other than her sobs, she was silent, as if incapable of speech.

'Go back to Fira.' Ianos' voice was firm and authoritative. 'Go and be with your wife and child. They need you.'

Andreas nodded. Vassia caught the stricken expression on his face and her heart went out to him. She'd gift it to baby Atlas if she could. If that would make him better.

Ianos went out without saying where he was going, but Vassia was sure he would be consulting with the other wise old men of the village. Thalia took her knitting to the courtyard but the needles did not move, their habitual gentle click-clacking silenced by the news from both Kostas and Andreas.

Vassia tried to busy herself with chores; there was always laundry to be done, and the kitchen floor needed washing. On her hands and knees, scrubbing with a heavy bristle brush, her mind constantly ran back over the night's events; stealing into Fira under the cover of darkness, having to leave the men to their fate, the terrible encounter with Schwarz, the desperate anxiety over newborn Atlas... What had happened to Sol? Had he got away? If so, where was he now? Already speeding across the sea in a white-sailed schooner, getting further from danger – and from Vassia – every moment? Or had he been captured? In which case, Vassia dreaded to think what might be happening to him.

Desperate for any distraction, she headed for the family's vegetable garden. She hadn't been there since before Ianos' name day, and the young plants needed to be watered, the beds weeded. Bent double over the tomato vines, at first the sound was like the distant drone of a bee. And then, as it got louder and louder, she realised that it was no insect. Standing slowly upright, using her hand to shield her eyes, she gazed into the cloudless blue sky.

There, flying low, was a single German Ju 88 reconnaissance plane, slowly sweeping across the breadth of the island, then executing a skilful turn over the sea and returning. As she watched, the plane grew closer and closer, the ear-splitting roar of the engines filling the air, until it was so near that Vassia thought she could reach out and touch it, so close that she felt the pilot's eyes upon her, scrutinising her. Could he see her guilt in the way she stood, read her mind, know that she had been involved? Vassia shuddered violently. Far away, at the other end of the island, she could make out other black dots moving through the heavens.

More planes.

More searching.

The Germans were seeking out their attackers. They wanted revenge, and Vassia knew they would not cease until they had got it. If Sol and any of the others were out there, it would surely only be a matter of time before they found them. And God only knew what fate would befall them then.

# CHAPTER 14

## CARRIE, 2024

The huge iron key Kris held in his hand looked far too medieval and rudimentary to fit in an actual lock but, as he inserted it into the keyhole and jiggled it around a bit, the pale blue front door slowly swung open. Kris had brought them to the village of Vourvoulos, nestled amidst the contours of the hills, looking out over the sea. He led them along narrow streets, past a church with multiple blue domes, each one topped with a simple cross, and through the village square, where the intensity of the light reflecting off the whitewashed walls hurt Carrie's eyes. They passed low-slung houses with the characteristic blue doors and window frames, small front gardens overflowing with bright geraniums, statuesque prickly pears and decorative olive trees in pots. Eventually, they arrived at the house at the end of a pedestrian lane where his grandmother Vassia had lived.

Stooping under the low lintel, Kris ushered Carrie and Nell into the cool interior. It was not dissimilar to the cottage where they were staying but, rather than feeling used and lived in, it smelt dusty and fusty, the ceiling adorned with spiders' webs that hung like delicate, faded old lace.

'My mother keeps meaning to clear it out and fix it up for

tourists,' said Kris, as he followed them inside. With the three of them in there, the room felt crowded. 'But she hasn't got round to it yet. In any case, there's no air con and no vehicle access, so it wouldn't be the most popular rental. I think the reality is that she still can't quite face it. Ya-ya Vassia was a ripe old age when she died but Mum hasn't come to terms with it yet. She was much loved by all of us.'

Carrie pulled a sympathetic face and briefly reached out to touch Kris's arm. 'I'm sorry,' she murmured. 'It's always hard to lose a parent or grandparent.'

Kris nodded. 'I'm not sure what we're looking for here, if I'm honest. It just occurred to me that it was worth a try. But maybe it wasn't such a good idea.' He gazed around him somewhat helplessly, at the heavy, old-fashioned furniture that crowded the small room, at the walls, upon which hung a few crooked pictures, and then stepped towards the window and threw open the shutters, letting in a welcome shaft of light.

'If you don't want to be here, we can go,' said Carrie hastily. 'It's fine by me...' It really wasn't; she was desperate to see if Vassia's house yielded anything, but it had to be Kris's decision.

'No, it's fine,' insisted Kris. 'Let's have a look in that old sideboard first,' he went on, pointing to an ancient-looking piece that stood against the back wall. 'Grandma used to polish it until you could see your face in it,' he added, as he and Carrie moved towards it. 'It's a shame to see it neglected.'

'Perhaps we can polish it when we finish,' said Carrie. 'Nell can do it. Can't you, Nell?'

Nell, earphones firmly pushed into her ears, raised an eyebrow by means of reply.

'Do you want to go and get a drink somewhere, leave this to us?' Carrie asked her. 'I'll give you some cash.'

This time, Nell looked up. 'Noooo!' she responded, sounding horrified. 'I can't sit in a café on my own, I'll look like an idiot.'

Carrie suppressed a giggle at the self-consciousness of the young. When did one get to the age of realising that other people were far more interested in themselves than anyone else?

'Anyway,' Nell continued, 'I want to help. You know I like history, I'm going to do it for A level. This is like history for real. It's even better than all that Atlantis stuff. I know I never met Sol, but he's still my relation. I want to be involved.'

'Great!' exclaimed Carrie, somewhat taken aback by Nell's enthusiasm. 'That reminds me, though,' she added. 'You were going to do sketches for your art project while we're here, weren't you? Have you started that yet? It's just occurred to me that perhaps you got your artistic talent from Sol. It certainly isn't from me.'

Nell rolled her eyes. 'Yeah, probably,' she rejoined. 'But I don't think Kris wants to hear about all that. We should get on.'

Carrie made a mock salute with her right hand. It was funny when Nell suddenly became the one issuing instructions.

Kris smiled too. He seemed to have cheered up a bit, which was good to see. Nell had that effect on people when she was in charming mode. 'Right, I'll take the left-hand set of drawers and you take the right-hand ones,' he said to Carrie.

'And I'll look in the kitchen,' Nell interjected. 'People always keep important documents in kitchen drawers, because then they know where they are.'

Carrie exchanged a look with Kris and he grinned back at her. The capacity of the young to know it all was amusing, when it wasn't irritating.

Carrie and Kris maintained a companionable silence as they sorted through Vassia's sideboard. It was rather a futile exercise on Carrie's part, as obviously anything written in Greek was completely incomprehensible to her. But some things were clearly of no interest; instruction manuals for a lamp or the TV, letters that seemed to be from the local council and suchlike. Anything handwritten she passed to

Kris, and he would run his eyes over it before putting it to one side.

'It's so lucky that in previous generations letters were the means of communication,' mused Carrie, as they worked. 'What will future generations do, when everything's on inaccessible email or, even worse, disappearing messages like Snapchat?'

Kris shook his head. 'I know. It might be harder, I guess. But on the other hand, perhaps also less hard. So much more is actually published these days, isn't it, online in blogs and vlogs and all the rest. There'll probably be far too much information, not too little.'

'True enough.' Carrie sat back on her heels with a handful of postcards she'd pulled out of a drawer. She leafed through them, pausing to study the faded pictures that adorned them; the Acropolis and the Parthenon, a donkey wearing a hat and a long-suffering expression, and then further-flung destinations, the Colosseum in Rome and the Eiffel Tower. The trips and holidays that punctuate a life, now nothing more than footnotes. A feeling of melancholy briefly troubled her as she passed the cards to Kris for him to check. There was nothing of any interest to their search.

Half an hour later, they'd emptied every drawer and were wondering where to look next. There was no sound from Nell in the kitchen. She'd probably got bored and started going through her phone again, Carrie suspected.

'Perhaps it's time to go and get a cool drink,' suggested Kris. 'All this dust... it's sticking in my throat.'

Carrie felt a stab of guilt. She was the one who had initiated this. 'Of course,' she agreed. She stood up too quickly and her head spun with the rush of blood. Putting her hand out to steady herself, she rested it more heavily than she meant to onto a little side table, which wobbled and then fell to the floor.

'Sorry,' mumbled Carrie, leaning down to pick it up. The top seemed to have become detached from the legs. 'Oh gosh,' she exclaimed, as soon as she saw the damage. I'm so sorry, I've broken it.'

Kris, frowning, picked up the table and examined it. 'I don't think it's broken. I think it's supposed to move – look, it opens right up.' He put his hand, spread to its widest span, onto the table and applied some gentle pressure. Slowly at first, and then more quickly, the tabletop revolved to reveal a hidden storage compartment beneath.

Inside, there were a couple of photographs, blurred with age, a few tiny off-white things that Carrie at first thought were stones, and some papers. She reached in, picked up one of the stones and scrutinised it, then suddenly dropped it in shock and surprise.

'It's a tooth!' she exclaimed, the unexpected and slightly toe-curling nature of her find making her laugh.

Kris, also chuckling, reached out to pick the tooth up. 'It must have belonged to my mother or one of my uncles,' he said, examining it. 'In Greece in those days we didn't have your American and British tooth fairy. Children threw their lost teeth onto the roof. Grandma Vassia must have gone up and collected them.'

'How cute!' exclaimed Carrie. 'I kept some of Nell's due to sentimentality but I found them a little while ago and they really grossed me out, so I chucked them out.' As soon as she finished speaking she clapped her hand over her mouth and glanced anxiously towards the door, worried that Nell might have heard her being disparaging about her baby teeth. But fortunately there was no sign of Nell, just the sound of cupboard doors opening and shutting in the kitchen.

'I know what you mean.' Kris laughed. 'I'm not sure that these go in the "must keep" pile.' As he spoke, he was examining the papers from the compartment. He laid them down on the floor, and picked out one that was folded into a small, tight square.

'I've got a feeling about this one,' he said, his voice suddenly low and serious. 'You have a look. I'm too nervous.'

Carrie nodded, then tentatively reached out and picked it up. She opened up the folds and, as she did so, something caught her eye. She looked again, scarcely believing it, then screwed up her eyes and brought the paper closer to her face to scrutinise it more closely.

Kris was right. The letter was signed: *Sol x*

'Kris!' she almost shouted. 'Look!'

Kris took the sheet and examined the signature, then ran his eyes over the short paragraph above.

'He's writing in Greek, so he must have known the language quite well,' suggested Carrie. 'The only bit in English is his signature.'

Kris shook his head. 'He is using Greek, but most of the ink is so faded I can't make it out at all.'

'Really? Nothing?' asked Carrie, trying to hide her disappointment.

Studying the paper carefully with narrowed eyes, Kris stared at it for a few more moments. 'There's something here about remembering... perhaps he's saying he'll remember her?' He sighed. 'But it's not clear enough to know for sure,' he concluded.

'Oh no,' groaned Carrie. 'That's so disappointing. But it proves that they had some kind of relationship, doesn't it? And gives us a bit more of a picture of what may have happened. Did Vassia ever talk about Sol? Does your mother know about him?'

Kris ran his hand through his close-cropped hair. 'Certainly not my mother. I asked her last night; she had no idea.'

They remained in silence for a while, Carrie leaning against the cool stone wall, Kris kneeling on the floor next to the table.

'It must have been precious to keep it for so long,' insisted Carrie, as if trying to convince herself that they had made a good find.

'Yes,' agreed Kris. 'I guess so.'

He studied the letter again. 'Wait a minute,' he said. 'Here are some words I can read. Faith, hope... and love, I think. I wonder what that means?'

At that moment, Nell burst into the room from the kitchen. 'Look!' she cried excitedly, an echo of Carrie earlier. 'I found this photo. Of a woman who looks just like the picture in the sketchbook, and a man. Do you think it's Vassia and Sol? It's got some writing on the back, see, Kris!'

Kris took the picture and studied it in the dim light, frowning deeply, then took it closer to the window. 'It's not Sol,' he said eventually. 'It says, "Me and my brother Andreas, 1943".' He handed it to Carrie, continuing, 'Which is really strange.'

'Why?' questioned Carrie, wondering what could be odd about a photo of two siblings.

'I grew up with my grandmother Vassia,' continued Kris. 'She was always there, with love and care and *koulouria*. But I've never heard of this Andreas. Ya-ya never mentioned him. And neither did my mother.'

He shook his head and took the picture back from Carrie. 'So how on earth can it be that neither I, nor anyone else as far as I'm aware, had any idea that she had a brother?'

# CHAPTER 15

## VASSIA, 1944

The planes droned above Santorini the entire day after the SBS raids. Vassia felt sick to her stomach at the thought that two of the SBS men had lost their lives, and that the rest – including Sol – were being hunted down like an eagle hunted a mouse. During the afternoon, Elias brought more bad news. He had heard from friends in Imerovigli that, after the attack on the radio station, thirteen villagers had entered the damaged building, intending to take advantage of supplies kept there by the Germans. They had been blown up when time bombs left by the commandos detonated.

This was awful news.

Vassia climbed up to the highest part of the village, where she sat on a wall and gazed out at the cerulean blue of the Aegean Sea. It was as beautiful as ever, the water calm and placid, sparkling under the April sunshine, the island greening as the vineyards came to life. It was hard to imagine the horrific events of the night before, the death and carnage. Before the war, she had had plans – nothing enormous, nothing adventurous. But plans all the same, the one she had told Sol about becoming a teacher, and others such as visiting some of the neighbouring islands and seeing how they compared with her adored Santorini. All this seemed so trivial now, so banal and unimportant. The only thing that mattered, apart from her family and the newborn Atlas, was Sol. And she had no idea where he was.

Eventually, Vassia left. She went to the church, its walls freshly painted for the new season. Inside, she lit a candle and murmured a few prayers for all those who had died. Most of all she prayed for the English man who had appeared out of nowhere and captivated her from her very first sight of him.

Later, in the early hours of the next morning, finding herself unable to sleep, Vassia crept out of the house and down to the beach. She advanced slowly towards the cave, anxious that, if the men were there, the lookout would have the opportunity to see who it was. Everyone would be jittery, their nerves on edge, and she did not want to be mistaken for the enemy.

But as she drew nearer, she got the sense that there was no one else around. She had brought a lantern to light her way, and she lit it now, shielding it as much as she could just in case there were still German patrols out searching for the men. Pausing for a moment, she strained her ears to listen, but could not hear the slightest sound. Cautiously, she slunk forward, close to the sheltering overhang of the cliffs. At the cave's entrance, she halted once more, holding the lantern as far in front of herself as she could, shining its light inside.

It was immediately obvious that there was no one there.

All that remained inside were empty tin cans and cigarette stubs. So they had gone. Vassia had expected to be relieved to find the men safely spirited away from this island where they had caused so much destruction, and where death sentences now hung over all of their heads. But instead she felt a deep sense of disappointment, a crushing sensation of hopelessness.

Back out on the beach, she sank down onto the gravelly sand and cried. In some hazy way that she couldn't have put into words, what had happened over the last twenty-four hours had changed her life. The arrival of the SBS, the fact that she, simple Vassia Kourakis, had been called upon to help them out, had expanded the narrow horizons of her life immeasurably. With the commandos had come the fresh breeze of another world, where people travelled and spoke many languages and did heroic things as a matter of course. Merely being acquainted with Sol, even so briefly, had turned upside down everything she had ever known, and now her horizons had shrunk again, back to where they had been before, and she felt stifled by them. She cried and cried, weeping for all of the commandos, for broken dreams and for Sol, because they had not had a chance to say goodbye.

Vassia wasn't sure how much time had passed when she suddenly became aware of a shadowy figure approaching her through the darkness. She glanced at the lantern, still glowing in front of her. Her nostalgia and grief disappeared in an instant. Stupid girl! Why had she not put it out? Once she'd stared at the light, her eyes took time to readjust to the pitch black that surrounded her, and the person was almost upon her before she realised who it was.

Not a German soldier.

Andreas.

'What on earth are you doing here?' she snapped, fear making her jumpy. 'Creeping up on me like that!' Hurriedly, she wiped her eyes with the back of her hand and fumbled in her pocket for a handkerchief to blow her nose. She didn't want Andreas to know that she had been crying.

'I could ask you the same thing,' rejoined Andreas. Despite her disgruntlement, Vassia was happy to hear some of his old bantering tone in his voice.

'You scared me,' she went on. 'How are Athena and Atlas? What's going on?'

Andreas allowed a brief smile to break across his face. 'A bit better. The doctor still doesn't know if there is something wrong with his heart, but he said the pair of them can come home tomorrow. I've tidied the whole house, got it ready for them.'

'That's a huge relief,' breathed Vassia, 'thank goodness.' Then she frowned and glared at Andreas anew. 'But why are you down here on the beach? You should be getting some rest. You won't have much sleep once you've got a newborn in the house.'

Andreas shrugged. 'I know. But I don't care. I'd never sleep again to protect Atlas.'

Vassia nodded. 'I understand. But still – what are you doing?'

'I came to find you,' Andreas replied. 'I went to the house and looked in your bedroom. When I saw that you weren't there, I was worried about you. You feel things so deeply, I've always known that. I wanted to make sure you were all right.'

Vassia's heart turned over. In the midst of so much worry about his own family, her lovely brother was still thinking about her.

'I'm fine,' she lied. 'Absolutely fine.'

Andreas listened to this response in silence. Then he sank down onto the sand beside her.

'It's not that simple actually, is it?' He picked up a handful of the stony sand and let it dribble slowly through his fingers. Vassia watched the pieces drop. Her eyes were gritty and sore from weeping.

She let her head drop between her knees. 'No,' she answered, her voice muffled by her skirt. 'It's not.' Lifting her head, she gazed at Andreas imploringly. 'But it has to be, hasn't it? The commandos have gone now, they're never coming back, and the rest of us just have to get on with our lives.' As she spoke, yet more tears were gathering at the corners of her eyes.

Andreas shuffled closer to her and put his arm round her shoulder in a brotherly embrace. 'Come on,' he said. 'You've got me, and Mum and Dad. And now you're an auntie, too, and Atlas needs his Theia Vassia.'

Attempting a smile, Vassia nodded. Andreas handed her a handkerchief to wipe her eyes, and then stood, pulling her up with him. Together, they trudged back to the village. Once Andreas had seen Vassia safely home, he continued on to his own house. Reluctantly, Vassia went to bed, and fell into a fitful sleep. She wasn't sure how long she'd been drowsing when the noise woke her.

Gunshot? The noise came again, a flurry of bullets against the window.

Terrified, Vassia cowered under the covers. There was silence for a few moments, and then the same noise. Gradually it occurred to her that it wasn't gunfire at all, but pebbles being thrown against the glass of her windowpane. Mustering all her courage, she got out of bed and inched towards it. Peering out, her eyes searched the courtyard, lit by the pale light of the morning sun.

And then she saw the figure and immediately her legs went weak as shock jolted right through to her core.

# CHAPTER 16

CARRIE, 2024

It was evening time, and the famous Oia sunset was about to paint the sky in colours of red, orange, gold and amber. Nell had been disconsolate at first, her excitement about finding the photo dimmed by Kris's inability to come up with any instant answers to the Andreas enigma. Like most teenagers, she was pathologically impatient. As they'd travelled to Oia, Carrie had been aware of her tapping away at her phone, but when she'd enquired into who she was so assiduously communicating with, Nell had simply answered, 'Dad,' and failed to elaborate.

Much as Carrie burned to know what her daughter was telling him, she could not ask. However much she acknowledged her mother's wisdom in advising her to let Jack have contact with his daughter, she didn't like their closeness. It was base and awful of her, but she would prefer Jack to suffer the consequences of his actions all those years ago.

Once at the hotel, Nell cheered up at the sight of the swimming pool. She soon fell into a conversation with another girl of the same age whose family were guests and before long the two of them were happily splashing around in the pool. Carrie was glad to see her make a friend; this holiday was supposed to be a lovely treat for Nell after her GCSEs and Carrie was always conscious that she might find it dull just being with her mum, especially after the dissatisfaction Nell had expressed the evening they arrived. It struck her with a thud of realisation that perhaps that was what Nell had been telling her father – that she was bored and fed up. Carrie didn't want Nell expressing that sentiment to anyone, including Jack. Especially Jack.

Xanthe rocked up, busy as always but able to spare the time for a drink, and also seated at a table beneath the pergola was Elena, Kris's mother. She managed the chefs at the hotel, and often took a lead role in the cooking herself. Today was her day off, though, so she'd come to discuss the family history with her son and Carrie.

'I'm completely baffled,' Elena admitted. 'I always thought my mother was an only child – she never gave the slightest hint of having a brother. And my grandmother, Vassia's mother, never mentioned she had a son as well as a daughter.'

'How did her husband, your grandfather, die, if you don't mind me asking?' Carrie ventured, apprehensively. It was never easy to gauge how sensitive such topics were.

Elena grimaced and pursed her lips. 'It was during the war. I was never told the full story. It was one of those topics, you know, that you are aware from an early age not to go near.'

Carrie frowned. 'I'm sorry.'

'Don't be. It's good to be talking now. We should know these stories, learn from them. But the world doesn't seem to, does it, when it comes to war...'

'I guess not,' agreed Carrie.

'You know,' intervened Kris, pensively, 'despite living through those dark times, all my memories of Grandma Vassia are happy ones – she was so kind and loving, so endlessly patient, always eager to hear about all of our childish triumphs and grievance. We spent so much time with her – my sisters and I – while Mum and Dad were working. She indulged us constantly – but she also made us do the chores. I'll never forget the afternoons spent scrubbing those stone steps that lead up to her house – they had to be clean as a whistle or she'd make us do them again! I devised a plan where I fetched the water while the girls put in the elbow grease – I convinced them I had the hardest job as water is heavy, but it was much easier really.' He paused before concluding, 'I've never confessed that one before. I guess that makes me a bit of a cheat.'

Everyone laughed. In Carrie's mind an image formed, of a little Kris sniggering impudently behind his hand while his two sisters diligently scrubbed away.

'And she wanted to keep up with the old Santorini traditions,' Elena added, smiling nostalgically at the memory. 'She was so proud of the island and its history of seafaring and quarrying, along with wine-making and agriculture. During her childhood, there were hardly any visitors – not like the millions who come today. She told me that, if someone important was due to arrive by ferry, the townspeople would greet them by using small mirrors to reflect the sun, so that whole side of the caldera would be lit up with bursts of light.'

'That's so lovely,' enthused Carrie. 'Santorini really is a special place.'

'Agreed,' said Kris. 'Exactly why I came back.' His gaze fell on Carrie and lingered there just a few seconds longer than necessary, and she felt a tingling sensation in her tummy. For a moment, the two of them were the only people there.

'I'm glad you can see all the lovely aspects of the island, despite the over-tourism and the crowds.' Kris smiled and then added, 'But enough idle chit-chat – we need to find out about this Andreas, as well as trying to get to the bottom of the relationship between Sol and Vassia.'

Xanthe sighed exaggeratedly. 'Here I was, thinking I'd invited Carrie to Santorini to have a bit of a rest, and instead the detective work is mounting up on a daily basis!'

'It'll be a "change is as good as a rest" type of holiday,' asserted Carrie, firmly.

Elena handed around a bowl of olives and then took one for herself, ate it contemplatively and discreetly disposed of the stone. 'I've got an idea,' she said. 'Some of the old ladies in the village – well, they're old enough that they knew Vassia. And a couple of them definitely remember the old days; they might recall Andreas, too. I'll have a word with them, see if they'd agree to talk to you.'

'That would be marvellous,' enthused Carrie. 'Thank you so much.'

They'd been watching the sun in its final flare of the day as they spoke, and now it dipped below the sea and the evening noticeably darkened.

'Let's go to the restaurant to eat,' said Kris. 'You guys are my guests, and Nell's friend too, if she likes. They can sit at their own table and discuss teenage-girl stuff.'

Carrie laughed. 'Yes, we certainly won't want to be part of that. They talk utter nonsense most of the time at that age.' It occurred to her as she spoke that Kris was so thoughtful and considerate of Nell, which he really had no need to be. Just as her mother had puzzled over Sol's lack of a wife and family, Carrie pondered the same about Kris. He was so handsome, and so nice, there must be no shortage of potential partners. Maybe he'd had some terrible disappointment that he'd never got over—

Carrie stopped herself continuing with this line of thought before she got carried away. Her overactive imagination might make her a good writer, but it sometimes led to her leaping to unjustified conclusions. The reality was that she had no idea why Kris was single. She'd have to wait and see if, at some point during the holiday, she found out the reason.

It turned out that the parents of Nell's friend, whose name was Amy, were only too happy for their daughter to join Carrie, Xanthe, Kris and Elena for dinner, saying they'd enjoy the opportunity to have dinner by themselves. Amy's mother explained that Amy's brother and sister were much older, already at university and no longer coming on family holidays, which left Amy having to amuse herself most of the time. Amy making a friend was as much as a boon for them as it was for Carrie.

Carrie felt a familiar stab of regret as she watched Nell and Amy disappear to the pool changing room, giggling and chatting as they went. That could have been Nell and her sister Jenny's girls, if things had been different. She and Jenny could be here together, undertaking this voyage of discovery as a partnership, like they had been when they were younger and so close. Sometimes missing Jenny felt even more painful than missing Jack, and the absence of her sister in her life certainly left a gaping hole that no one else could fill. Hearing about Kris's idyllic childhood with his siblings had sensitised Carrie even more than she already was to the solitary nature of Nell's family circumstances, and to the huge shadow that hung over her own life. But after what Jenny had done, how could they possibly have remained friends?

She rubbed a tired hand over her forehead. So much had happened today already. She'd almost forgotten that, earlier, she and Nell had spent six hours on a boat trip, before the surprise meeting with Kris, the visit to Vassia's house in Vourvoulos and now this dinner in Oia. Carrie was starving, but also exhausted, and was already looking forward to getting back home and into bed.


The next day dawned as sunny and glorious as the one before. Carrie had slept soundly until nearly 10 a.m., something she hadn't done for years. When she woke up she felt full of trepidation, but couldn't at first work out why. And then she remembered. Elena was going to get the old ladies of Vourvoulos together today, to see if they could shed any light on her mother's vanishing brother. Maybe they remembered the SBS men too. Could one of them have met Sol?

Nell was still slumbering and there was no hurry, so Carrie let her sleep. She made coffee and took it onto the balcony, where she gazed over the broad sweep of the hills that led down to the sea, dotted with picturesque white windmills and small vegetable patches. Here and there, blue swimming pools sparkled in the sun like so many sapphires scattered haphazardly across the landscape.

As Carrie feasted on the view, a herd of goats wandered onto the scrubland at the edge of the village and the gentle tinkling of their bells mingled with the intermittent buzzing of bees feeding on the jasmine that grew up a trellis in a neighbour's garden down below. The air was filled with the flowers' heady, intoxicating scent and Carrie shut her eyes, feeling the sun on her face. Her shoulders relaxed and she breathed in deep and slow. Whatever else was not going right in her life, she was so lucky to be here, enjoying this beautiful island, working on a book idea, uncovering (hopefully!) a family mystery.

She jumped out of her skin when Nell suddenly materialised on the threshold, holding her phone in front of her face. 'I've changed my mind,' she was saying to her interlocutor. 'This island is pretty lit, actually. And the place we're staying – well, it's not luxury but it's OK. This is the view from the balcony...' As she held out the phone, she turned her head towards Carrie. 'I'm talking to Dad,' she mouthed.

For a moment Carrie had a dreadful feeling that Nell was going to place the phone in front of her and she would have to say something polite to Jack. But thankfully, Nell was soon retreating back into the house, chatting away now about her new friend Amy.

Breathing a sigh of relief, Carrie clenched her fists as she waited for her heart to stop pounding. It was ridiculous that

Jack still had such an effect on her after all these years, that the memories were still such painful stab wounds. Just thinking about him set the same old questions revolving around her mind. She had loved him more than she thought it was possible to love anyone. When he walked in the room, he had made her feel complete, like he was the other half of her, and she had believed he felt the same way.

What he had done had torn her apart; but it was not only that he clearly didn't, in fact, love her the same way she did him. It was the fact that she had got it so wrong, misjudged it so thoroughly. She had misread the signs, misunderstood what their relationship was. This had led to Carrie feeling that she could no longer trust anybody ever again. Almost subconsciously, she had also come to the conclusion that loving someone was not worth the pain and possible hurt. Better to stay single, focus on her baby, take no further risks.

And that was how it had been for the last sixteen years.

'Mum?'

Nell's voice roused Carrie from her reverie. Her phone call must have ended.

'Yes,' Carrie called back. 'What is it?'

Nell bounded onto the balcony and gave her mother a goofy grin. 'I finished all of that juice in the fridge,' she said. 'I hope you didn't want any.'

Carrie shook her head. 'No, I'm fine with my coffee.'

'Good. I didn't want to deprive you.' Nell yawned and stretched, her lithe teenage body like a cat's, so sleek and smooth. 'Did you bring a nail file?' she asked, contemplating her fingers. 'I need one.'

Carrie gestured to the bathroom. 'In my washbag,' she replied, checking her watch. Kris had arranged to pick her and Nell up for the meeting with the old ladies. Xanthe couldn't make it but would hopefully be free by evening time. 'And we'll be going out to meet Kris in ten,' she called after Nell's

disappearing figure. She'd offered Nell the opportunity to
hang out with Amy at the pool but, ever contrary, both the
girls wanted to come so Kris was kindly bringing Amy
with him.

After Carrie had spent some time urging Nell to hurry up,
mother and daughter set off through the village and down to the
main road, which was the closest Kris could get in the car. As
soon as he'd pulled up, he leapt out, came round to the
passenger side and held the door open. Nell climbed in next to
Amy and immediately the two girls fell into a deep conversation. Kris leant forward and kissed Carrie on each cheek. He
smelt as delicious as ever, and Carrie felt a little frisson of
delight at his proximity and the calm firmness of his hands on
her shoulders.

As they drove, Kris pointed out the vineyards they passed
through. Carrie had already noticed the dearth of wild trees on
the island, and the fact that the vines grew at ground level,
rather than on wire trellises as they did in France and Italy.

'It is called the Santorini kouloura,' explained Kris. 'The
vines are woven into the shape of a large basket that rests on the
volcanic soil. It protects the grapes as they develop, sheltering
them from the wind, the sun and the lack of moisture.'

'Very ingenious,' commented Carrie. 'And the wine is delicious.' They'd had a lovely bottle of Santorini Assyrtiko the
evening before, so good that Carrie had been tempted to have
more than she should. Probably why she had slept so long that
night. But if you can't overindulge on holiday, then when could
you, she'd thought to herself on accepting her third glass. She
couldn't really afford to drink alcohol at home and she'd
forgotten how nice it could be.

In one of the vineyards she spotted a group of tourists gathered around a tour guide. She'd read about the wine tours you
could do; most of the island's wineries offered them. If Nell was
occupied with Amy one day, she could book onto one. She

knew nothing whatsoever about wine, but perhaps now was the time to learn.

Before too long they arrived in the outskirts of Vourvoulos. They parked up and, once again, Kris led the way through the maze of lanes and alleyways, where cats slunk in the shadows and the frothing pink fronds of bougainvillea spilled over walls and doorways. In a tiny square next to a minute chapel with four oversized iron bells, two old ladies sat on ancient brown kitchen chairs in the shade. While Kris was introducing them as Maria and Daphne, Elena emerged from a shadowed doorway with a tray of cold water and glasses of Greek coffee, which she passed around to everyone before disappearing back inside to fetch Coca-Cola for Nell and Amy and a huge plate of sticky, tooth-achingly sweet honey and nut pastries.

Mindful of the conventions of Greek hospitality, Carrie held back from asking any questions for Kris to translate until the drinks had been sipped and the treats partaken of. Only once the niceties had been dealt with did she begin to gently probe the old ladies about life in Vourvoulos in the 1940s.

'We were just small children then, if you can believe it,' reminisced Maria, with a toothless smile. 'Knee-high to a grasshopper. Life was hard – so much harder than the young ones now can even imagine. But it was good, too, as I remember it. The sun shone, the wind blew, the sea was warm in summer and the vineyards prolific. We didn't have much, but we had what we needed. When you have your family around you, that's enough, isn't it?'

Carrie shifted awkwardly in her chair as she nodded her agreement. She was sure Maria would not approve of Carrie's decision to go it alone as a single mother. But times had been different then, hadn't they?

'What about the war itself?' Kris asked. 'Do you remember that time? The SBS raid?'

Maria shook her head, while Daphne's brow furrowed in

contemplation. 'We were too young,' she answered eventually. 'I have some vague memories, scary men in uniforms, the noise of aircraft, guns and explosions.' She paused, screwing her face up in concentration. 'I believe that something terrible happened at some point, something the village didn't get over for a long time. People died. Islanders, I mean. But more than that, I don't know...'

Damn, thought Carrie as Daphne's voice tailed away, lost in that dark past. These two, delightful as they were, did not remember far back enough. Kris, however, carried on prompting.

'What about my grandmother, Vassia Kourakis?' he questioned. 'She was a friend of yours, I think?'

'We were all friends, all of us girls,' replied Maria. 'There were not so many children in a small village like this. We stuck together, even though we were different ages. Vassia was about four or five years older than us but we all got along so well. She was such a kind, caring person. Brave, too. Well, she had to be...'

Carrie held her breath. Now they were getting closer to real information. That Vassia had been kind and caring was evident from everything she'd already learnt. But the fact that she'd been brave, had had to be so... that was news.

Frustratingly, Kris chatted to the old ladies for a few more minutes without stopping to translate for Carrie. Champing at the bit, she had to stop herself from intervening and demanding to know what they were saying. Amy and Nell were sitting just behind her, on the chapel steps as there were no more chairs, and only seemed to be half listening; they had their phones in their hands as always, like an extension of their own arms.

Kris turned to Carrie. 'I asked what Maria meant about Grandma being brave but she was really vague, unable to clarify herself. They never met any of the commandos either, which isn't surprising as presumably it would have been a very secretive operation. Now I'm going to ask them about whether they remember Andreas.'

He faced the two women again, and began to talk. Carrie noticed how his voice was quieter and softer now, as if gently cajoling and coaxing their memories. Clenching her fists, Carrie listened intently, even though she could make no sense at all of what was being said. All she recognised were the names Vassia and Andreas, and that told her nothing. She fixed her eyes on the women, trying to read their expressions and work out what they were saying. What she saw was not encouraging.

Blank faces and eyes without a single spark of recognition.

After a few agonising moments, Kris sat back and looked at Carrie. She knew what he was going to say even before he uttered the words.

'I'm sorry, Carrie. We still don't have any answers.' He shrugged resignedly. 'They don't remember anything at all about Vassia having a brother.'

# CHAPTER 17

VASSIA, 1944

Sol.

His eyes gleamed in the moonlight as he gestured to her to let him into the house. Stunned, Vassia hastily pulled on some clothes and rushed to the kitchen door to open it. As Sol stepped inside, they fell into each other's arms in a tight embrace. Only after they had reluctantly pulled apart did Vassia see how he wore his exhaustion on his pale, drawn face. He had a rudimentary bandage round one wrist and his hair was tousled and streaked with dirt. She wanted to reach out and smooth it down, then soothe his furrowed brow with her cool hand.

Instead she bustled around, putting the kettle on the stove, spooning coffee into a pot, pouring water for Sol, which he guzzled down so quickly she realised that he had been parched with thirst.

Only when the coffee was made and they were sitting across the kitchen table facing each other did Vassia venture to ask him what on earth he was doing still on the island. Weren't the commandos all supposed to have left already? Why was Sol still here?

'We didn't get Schwarz,' he explained, his voice full of regret. 'Once the barracks were ransacked, there were soldiers everywhere and our patrol got split up. I was determined to find the man, track him down. I wanted to capture him, not kill him. He would have been a trophy for us, proof of our worth. Because there are those in London who don't like what we do, Vassia. It's too unconventional for them, too unorthodox.'

Vassia blinked and gulped. She hadn't considered for a moment how the SBS were regarded by the powers that be. But all she really cared about was Sol, and that he was alive, here in her kitchen, drinking coffee.

The surreal nature of the past forty-eight hours was intensifying by the minute.

'But you didn't find him?' suggested Vassia.

Sol shook his head sorrowfully. 'No.' He took a sip of his coffee. 'That's so good. Thank you.'

He pulled a packet of cigarettes out of his pocket, tapped one out of the box, lit it and took a long drag. 'I spent too long hunting Schwarz down. By the time I realised I must get out of the town, it was almost daybreak. I holed up in an abandoned shed until the coast was clear, but then I couldn't leave as the whole place was crawling with patrols. The sun was already rising when I finally reached the rendezvous point on Vourvoulos beach, and it was too late. The others had already been picked up.'

Vassia gripped her coffee cup and chewed at the inside of her cheek. Sol had been in so much jeopardy, and still was, stuck on enemy territory, his chance of escape long gone. She couldn't begin to think what he was going to do. Could she keep him here, hide him here? But the mayor's house would be the first place to be searched...

'So what will you do now?' she asked, anxiety making it hard for her to speak. 'How will you...' She paused, not wanting to articulate what was going through her mind. '...escape?' she concluded, her voice barely audible.

'We hid a field radio near where we first holed up,' Sol replied. 'I used it this morning and I'll fetch it when it's dark – then I can keep in contact with base. I'll be all right.'

Vassia couldn't believe that was in the slightest bit true. Sol was in the gravest danger, that much was obvious.

'I'll help you,' she whispered. 'I'll do whatever I can.'

Sol's eyes fell upon her, his expression full of thanks and appreciation and something else that Vassia couldn't identify.

'It's not me I'm concerned about,' he responded. He paused and took a deep breath before continuing. 'Vassia, I've got to tell you something really important. You're going to have to pass the message on to your father, so that he can inform the rest of the community, the mayors of all the other towns and villages.'

Vassia's blood ran cold in her veins. It was clear that this was something of great consequence, momentous, even. She could hardly bear the suspense as she waited for Sol to continue.

'The Germans are sending reinforcements from Milos. They'll be here in a few days. Any commando found on Santorini faces instant death.' He stubbed out his cigarette into his saucer, then rubbed his forehead as if he could erase the strain etched into the deep lines across his brow. 'Well, that's all right because the only one left is me.' He gave a hollow laugh before continuing. 'But I don't know what it will mean for everyone else, most particularly for those who helped us.' He looked up, straight into Vassia's eyes, and held her gaze. 'What it will mean for you.'

For a few moments, Vassia could neither move nor speak. The whole island community would be suspects, her friends and neighbours, her parents, everyone. And on top of that, Schwarz was still alive and he had seen her in Fira last night.

How long would it be before he put two and two together and made four?

With a scraping of the chair legs against the tiled floor, Sol stood up.

'I need to find somewhere to hide,' he said. 'Until I can arrange to get off the island.'

Vassia leapt up and stood facing him. 'I know a place,' she replied, her voice still low, but urgent now. 'Another cave. But not on the beach, this one is inland, overlooking the village. Andreas and I found it when we were children, but I don't think many people know about it. Not the Germans, in any case. Come, let's go now before it gets any lighter.'

After throwing together a simple package of provisions, Vassia and Sol left the house and stole away through the village, seen only by a couple of cats returning from their night-hunting. Once they had passed the last house, they trekked across rocky, stony, steep ground, broken up only by the odd clump of tussocky grass, a few squat shrubs and some statuesque prickly pears, for about ten or fifteen minutes, until they reached the cave. Years ago, a goatherd must have used it to shelter from the sun; someone had carved a series of steep, rudimentary steps into the rock that led into the bowels of the earth.

Sol looked around him, appraising his new temporary home.

'This is perfect,' he said.

It was far from perfect, Vassia thought. Dank and airless, it smelt musty and fetid and, as little daylight penetrated this deep, it was miserably dark. But it was the safest place she could think of, and it would have to do.

She wanted to stay, sit down with Sol, talk some more, reassure him that all would be well, but he was impatient for her to be off before the sun came up.

'You must go home and spread the news about the arrival of

fresh German troops,' he said. 'Once a few people know, the rumour mill will do the rest.'

'I'll be back though,' Vassia promised him. 'I'll bring you more food and water. Tell me where the radio is and I'll fetch that, too. It's not safe for you to go out. I'll look after you for as long as it takes, no matter the danger.'

Sol smiled his lovely, sweet, sad smile. 'Thank you.' He had no choice but to accept her offer, however much he'd rather she didn't have to take such risks.

Vassia hesitated for a few moments. She thought of Chicky. The fledgling's survival had been down to her, and she had succeeded. But a soldier? That was completely different. Overcome with a terrible sensation of doom, she threw her arms round Sol, desperate for the touch of him, for the reassurance of his warm embrace.

'Just hold me for a minute or two,' she whispered in his ear. 'Before I leave.'

Sol drew her into a tight hug, pressing her close, so close she could hardly tell the difference between what was her and what was him. He bent down, his mouth seeking out hers, and then the kiss that Vassia had longed for since that brief brush of his lips when they had parted the night before was happening. Hungrily, she kissed him back; she'd never kissed a man before but somehow she knew what to do. The kiss continued for long, heart-rending moments, until finally Sol broke away. Vassia stood, dazed by the unfamiliar feelings of longing and desire assailing her.

'Go,' Sol whispered. 'Do what I told you.' But even as he instructed her to leave, his hand still held hers.

Eventually, Vassia turned and, slowly and reluctantly, he let her fingers go.

As Vassia scrambled out of the cave she could still feel the imprint of his grasp. When she reached the outside world, she paused for a moment to regain her breath. It was a beautiful spring day with a dusting of light, fluffy clouds in the sky, pink-tinged by the sunrise, a sensuous breeze blowing gently from the south. Looking around her, Vassia took in the glorious landscape, so familiar but always lovely, the rocky, volcanic land sloping away to the sea, the water stretching to the far horizon.

Out there somewhere were Sol's comrades-in-arms, sailing towards safety in their Turkish lair. She was glad the others had got away. Sol should be with them, planning the next assault, enjoying the times when he and the band could laugh and joke together, turning serious when seriousness was required. Vassia understood that they had not been able to wait for him, had had to leave. They would be confident that Sol was well-trained, resilient and resourceful, that if anyone could survive abandonment amidst hostile forces it was an SBS man.

She knew all of this and yet at the same time was torn in two. She wanted him to have got away and so to be safe. But she was also glad that he hadn't, glad that they would, by dint of circumstance, be able to spend more time together.

It was wrong and it was crazy, she knew. Sol would not be here for ever; the call of duty would ensure that he escaped Santorini as soon as he could. But despite all the reasons that it was a bad idea, she couldn't help herself. She was developing feelings for Sol that were far more than friendship, far deeper than her desire to help rid the island of the Nazis.

Raising the hand that Sol had so recently held in his to her lips, she breathed in deeply, as if the scent of him still permeated her skin. And then she turned and marched purposely back to the quiet village that had no idea what was in store for it. As she strode, her befuddled mind was clear on only one thing.

For the immediate future, Sol's life depended on her – and she would not let him down.

# CHAPTER 18

CARRIE, 2024

'Well, it was worth a try, wasn't it?' Carrie said despondently, more to herself than anyone else. Did the old ladies really not know about Sol, or Andreas? Or had the need for silence been imposed on them so many years ago that they had quashed the memories? Whatever the truth, it was clear there was no more information to be had from either Maria or Daphne. She got up and went over to them, taking their hands and saying *efharisto*, thank you, for giving up so much of their time. Elena rushed back inside to bring more refreshments and Carrie wondered what they could do next. She was still mulling this over when she looked up to see another lady, bent almost double and seeming even older than the first two, coming up the lane. Her progress was agonisingly slow and, as soon as Kris saw her, he rushed off to offer the woman his arm.

When they finally reached the shady square, Kris stood by as the woman lowered herself into his vacated chair. There was a flurry of excitable Greek between the new arrival, Maria and Daphne, and then, when it had subsided, Kris performed the introductions.

'This is Penelope,' he said, 'and she's proudly informed me

that she's the oldest person in Vourvoulos, one of the oldest on the whole island.'

'Gosh, that's some achievement.' Carrie smiled at Penelope in awe. 'Nice to meet you,' she said, reaching out to shake the old lady's hand. Her skin was cool despite the strength of the sun, her skin soft and papery.

'My mother didn't ask Penelope to come,' explained Kris. 'She thought it would be too much for her. But apparently word got out and Penelope was somewhat displeased not to be included! Hence making her own way here.'

Carrie inclined her head in a gesture of deference to Penelope's determination. 'I'm very grateful,' she murmured, and Kris translated.

Elena came back outside with more water and coffee and, after benignly scolding Penelope for defying her instructions and walking here on her own, brought out an extra chair. Carrie wondered what was going through Elena's mind. After all, Andreas would be her uncle and it must be very strange and possibly upsetting to discover she had such a close relative she'd never known about, especially as everything about their family life seemed otherwise so idyllic.

'So how old are you, Penelope?' asked Carrie, unable to keep her curiosity at bay. *Old enough to remember the war years?* she secretly added to herself.

'I'm ninety-five,' responded Penelope. 'I was born in 1929.' Her voice quavered as she spoke but there was no hesitation and no confusion about her age. She obviously had all her marbles. Carrie hoped that she would be so switched on if she made it to such a ripe old age.

'So you must have been fifteen in 1944,' Carrie suggested.

'That's right,' Penelope said, her eyes taking on a distant look. 'After such a long time, I don't remember everything about those days, but some things are still as clear as day.'

Maria and Daphne shuffled their chairs a little closer to

hear better and the entire assembled company waited for Penelope's next words.

'When those men came, the special ones, they needed local people to help them, to bring them food and water and take them to the locations they were to attack. Anyone would have done it, of course, if they had asked. But the mayor, Ianos Kourakis, Vassia's father, took control. Well, that was only right and proper. He was the most important man in the village.' She paused, drank some water, placed the glass back on the tray with trembling hands. 'I don't know any of the details about what happened, I never did. It was kept between the adults. But of course we all heard things, we picked up on tail ends of conversations.' Another pause, as Penelope's gaze fixed on some invisible point on the other side of the square, where perhaps she saw herself as a young girl, eavesdropping on the adults' words, barely comprehending them. Carrie waited with bated breath for her to continue.

'There were consequences, afterwards. The Italians, even the Nazis, they didn't bother us much at the beginning. But after the raid, things changed. Of course they did.' Shuddering, Penelope spread her gnarled brown hands across her lap and contemplated them for a moment, as if imagining the damage hands could do, Nazi hands. 'Blood was spilled. People died.'

A profound silence greeted this last remark, broken only by Kris speaking to Penelope again. Carrie heard the names of his grandmother Vassia and the man who, if he existed, would have been his great-uncle. This time it was a long while before Penelope answered.

'Yes,' she began, very slowly and cautiously. She glanced over at Elena and frowned, as if fearful of the younger woman hearing what she had to say. 'Yes, Vassia had a brother. Of that I am certain.'

Carrie guessed what Penelope had said even before Kris

had translated, due to the sharp intake of breath her words elicited from Elena.

'He was called Andreas, you are right. He was a fine young man. Tall. Very handsome.' She smiled and fixed her gaze on Kris. 'You resemble him, you know.'

Carrie almost giggled as she saw Kris blush beneath his tan. And then as soon as the flush of colour had come, it was gone, and Carrie's mirth subsided. This was no laughing matter. It was of huge significance to Carrie, in her quest for Sol's history, but just as much if not more so for Kris and Elena. On such a small island where the community was so close-knit, it was virtually unimaginable that someone would not know about a relative's existence.

Penelope's demeanour darkened as she continued her recollections, her eyelids half-closed as if the weight of memory was dragging them down. 'Andreas was respected and admired by all. I didn't know him well, but I know that about him. And I've no idea what happened to him. One day he was there and the next, gone.'

Kris, listening intently, ran his hand through his hair. Elena sat silent and still as a statue, as if scarcely breathing.

'Gone where?' she asked, softly.

'It was during the war. So it must have been something to do with the Nazis,' Penelope said, slowly. 'But what, I don't know.' She gazed into the distance as if she could still see them there, Vassia's big brother and a German soldier. 'Whatever happened, Andreas was neither seen nor heard of again and we youngsters learnt never to mention his name for fear of upsetting his mother.'

'Right.' Carrie slumped forward in her chair. Penelope's recollections had only really confirmed what they already knew or had surmised.

Kris looked exhausted, as did Elena, and in that moment Carrie recognised what a big deal this was for him. What a shame the conversation hadn't yielded all the answers; but then that would probably have been too much to hope for.

At this moment, Nell came to stand beside Carrie, took a strand of her hair and twisted it round her finger. Carrie put an arm round her.

'You haven't asked how Vassia knew Sol,' said Nell. 'Why he drew the picture of her. You've got to ask that.'

Kris and Carrie smiled simultaneously. Nell was right, there were a lot more questions; but Carrie was worried about whether Penelope was up to it. Elena stood up and whispered something in Penelope's ear, but the older lady flapped her arm at her in a dismissive gesture and responded with a forceful, 'Ochi!' No.

'She says she's fine to carry on talking,' said Elena, with a grimace. 'She won't hear about going home to rest.'

She was certainly a redoubtable old stick, thought Carrie. Good for her.

'The men hid in caves,' Penelope reminisced. 'The ones down by the shore. There are several there, and some more above the cliffs a short way back from the sea. Before the war we used to play in them but afterwards we were told to stay away. The adults said the entrances had become unstable, that mines had been planted.'

'Oh goodness,' exclaimed Carrie. 'That sounds dangerous.'

Penelope didn't respond, seemingly lost in the world of the past, of the war and the awful things people do to each other.

'There were stories that the SBS men left things behind when they fled, radios and supplies and whatever.' She paused, shaking her head as if to deny such rumours. 'Some even say that one of the men didn't manage to escape, or perhaps he was too wounded to move. He died in a cave, and his skeleton lies there still among the sand and the damp.'

Carrie raised her eyebrows and grimaced in horror. This

was a terrible prospect, but it also seemed very far-fetched. The product of years of whispers and gossip, she was sure.

Penelope chatted on a little more, about what life had been like before the war, how families eked out a living, surviving on barley, fava beans and Santorini's famous cherry tomatoes, as well as the fish and seafood that the waters offered up.

Eventually, Elena put her foot down. It was clear that Penelope was flagging and must rest. Her own granddaughter would be back from work soon and would be most perturbed to discover her grandmother entirely worn out. Kris offered to escort Penelope home and Carrie, Nell and Amy waited in the shade for his return, when he would take them to Oia.

Lost in thought, Carrie was aware of the girls burbling away beside her.

'Those old ladies *ate*,' said Amy, emphatically.

'They so ate,' agreed Nell, 'and left no crumbs.' At this, both of them burst into gales of laughter, as Carrie listened in bewilderment.

'They ate a banquet and left no crumbs whatsoever.' Amy giggled. 'Not a single one.'

'But they hardly touched Elena's snacks,' countered Carrie, still perplexed. 'What are you talking about?'

This elicited even greater mirth from the two teenagers.

'Oh Mum,' sighed Nell, when she could speak again, 'it's just what you say. When someone absolutely smashes something, owns it. When they ate, literally.' With that, she began laughing again, as hard as before.

'Well,' mused Carrie, 'I don't think it is a literal expression because as I said, they didn't eat, so I think you're talking metaphorically.' She paused, eyeing Nell with a sharp look. 'And don't even consider saying, "OK, boomer" because, as I have told you many, many times, I am NOT a boomer, nowhere near.'

Nell and Amy held their sides as their laughter redoubled

and Carrie smiled indulgently at them. Weird teenage lingo aside, it was so good to see Nell enjoying herself.

Kris returned and, as the four of them walked together to his car, Carrie pondered upon the fact that Maria, Daphne and Penelope had, in fact, most definitely eaten.

'I've taken a liberty,' Kris said, when they reached his hotel in Oia and the girls had gone off to change into their bikinis. 'I've booked a table for dinner at my favourite restaurant in town. Nell and Amy are welcome to come too, but it's our pool party night here and I thought they might prefer to attend that, and have burgers and chips with the other young people. I've mentioned it to Amy's parents and they're more than happy for Amy to join in.'

Carrie had a moment of panic. Was it a good idea to leave two young girls on their own at a pool party? Nell had been behaving a bit better recently, but it was hard to know if she'd completely turned over a new leaf.

As if reading her mind, Kris spoke again. 'Don't worry, there won't be any alcohol – all the staff know who is underage. And it's only for a couple of hours, a chance for our young guests to let their hair down – in carefully monitored conditions.' He smiled reassuringly at Carrie as her insides turned to liquid at his care and consideration.

'Thank you, Kris,' she responded. 'I'm wondering about Xanthe... we said we'd see each other this evening and I haven't contacted her to—'

'I have.' Kris's gentle tones cut across Carrie's slightly flustered ones. 'She's got a transatlantic call to make, so she's not going to make it.'

'Oh, right, that's OK then,' said Carrie. 'I mean, more than OK,' she continued hastily, lest Kris misinterpret her response. 'I'd love to have dinner with you, that would be... nice,' she ended, lamely. Because dinner alone with Kris would be fabulous, but she didn't want to come across as overly enthusiastic and terrify the poor man. There had been a couple of moments – certain looks he had given her, the times when his hand in greeting lingered on hers a little longer than necessary – when Carrie had had a sudden feeling that perhaps she and Kris could be more than friends, that perhaps they could rekindle the spark that had so briefly ignited between them all that time ago. She had laughed it off when Xanthe had suggested such a thing all those weeks ago when the trip had been mooted. But now – was the idea still so far-fetched?

But immediately on having these thoughts, she jumped away from them. She was hallucinating, making it up, creating a deeper meaning than really existed. Which was hardly surprising when she was so out of practice, but had the potential for utter embarrassment if she got it wrong.

As expected, Nell and Amy were delighted to be left without parental supervision for a while. Carrie and Kris strolled into town, Carrie exclaiming repeatedly about the views.

'Gosh, imagine staying there,' she exclaimed, pointing downwards to the layers of exquisite and exclusive hotel rooms, many with tiny plunge pools smaller than bathtubs, that lined the caldera walls as they plummeted down into the sea. 'What a view to wake up to. What luxury!'

She stood and gazed out at the spectacular vista, the unbelievable blues of sea and sky and, in the distance, the first flares of colour from the setting sun. The air was still treacly-warm from the heat of the day and expectation hung there, though quite what she was anticipating Carrie wasn't sure.

Kris smiled. 'You haven't seen that part of my hotel, have you?' he said. 'We have caldera rooms, as well as the ones on the other side of the road where the pool is. One gets used to it when one lives with it all day long, but I appreciate it must seem pretty special to the newcomer.'

Carrie watched him closely as he spoke. He obviously loved

Santorini, loved his hotel, loved his work. But there was something missing, she was sure of it. Perhaps Kris's life wasn't as picture perfect as it seemed on the outside.

'It does,' she rejoined. 'It's just so lovely. All of it.' She made an expansive gesture with her arm, indicating the gorgeous town of Oia and the whole island.

'Like—' began Kris, and then stopped abruptly, as if he'd been about to say something and then thought better of it. Carrie regarded him, puzzled. But the moment passed and he was indicating to her to continue walking.

'I'll show you our caldera side tomorrow,' he promised, as they ambled through immaculate lanes lined with shops selling everything from fridge magnets and tea-towels to high-end designer-label clothes and hand-crafted ceramics. 'We have some guests leaving, so we can see inside the rooms, too.'

'Sounds great,' replied Carrie. 'I'll look forward to that. Thank you.'

The narrow streets were thronged with tourists wielding cameras and selfie sticks, chattering excitedly in a cacophony of different languages, and at times there was so little room to move that it was hard to make any forward progress. Carrie marvelled at the unfailing good humour of the Greek shopkeepers, restaurateurs and residents, who didn't seem to hold any ill will towards this annual invasion. She'd read that the permanent population of the island was only 15,500 and that over two million visitors arrived by plane and boat every year. Most of them seemed to be here right now, making for the far end of Oia ahead of the much-vaunted sunset.

They reached a bottleneck where a number of lanes intersected and the milling crowds impeded their progress. Carrie hesitated, unsure of how to weave through the rabble. As she dithered, Kris reached out, put a protective hand on her back and expertly steered her in the direction they were to take. At his touch, a shiver ran down Carrie's spine and, far from finding it awkward, she relished the contact. She had another of those feelings of something happening between her and Kris, some-thing that had happened, albeit so briefly, all those years ago. The feeling was far from unwelcome and, as she strolled beside him, she had a sudden realisation of how lonely she was, how lonely she had been for many years.

Kris had dropped his hand now, and Carrie could feel its absence almost as deeply as she had its presence. He paused beside some steep steps and indicated to Carrie to go ahead. She climbed the stairs and came to a rooftop terrace adorned with flourishing pots of brightly flowering plants. The walls were strung with a myriad soft white fairy lights that sparkled like stars in the balmy evening air. It was so beautiful. And – Carrie couldn't help thinking it – so romantic. All the other cosy couples already ensconced there obviously thought so too; they all looked thoroughly loved up, leaning intimately in towards each other as they chatted and tried morsels of each other's food.

Kris arrived beside her and, as he smiled at Carrie, she searched his face for clues that there was something more than friendliness in his expression, in his choice of restaurant to take her to, but found nothing. *Stupid*, she hissed silently to herself. She was undoubtedly seeing things where they didn't exist. Why on earth would Kris have any romantic interest at all in a washed-up, insolvent, soon-to-be-homeless single mother of a demanding teenager? It was a nonsensical notion from begin-ning to end.

Sitting down at the table, Carrie resolved to pull herself together and concentrate on what she was really here for – her book, Sol and Nell. And of course, since this afternoon, the mystery of what had happened to Vassia's secret brother, Andreas.

She and Kris discussed this latter issue as they ate their meal of braised sea bream with tomatoes. They talked and talked, throwing around this theory and that but coming up with nothing that seemed remotely plausible.

'Perhaps he had enough of the war and the occupation and just upped and left,' suggested Carrie. 'Or he could have run away to join the Allied army somewhere. I think some Greeks did that, didn't they?'

Kris nodded. 'I believe so. But wouldn't that be something the rest of the family would celebrate and be proud of, not hide away and treat as some kind of disgrace? And if he'd died fighting, he'd be a war hero, and always remembered as such.' He shook his head. 'No, it just doesn't add up.'

Carrie had to agree. There just didn't seem to be any possible reason for a much-loved son and brother to simply disappear.

Eventually, having run that subject dry, she switched to another. 'Tell me more about Vassia, about your life growing up,' she asked Kris.

He smiled. 'She was a wonderful lady,' he said, wistfully. 'Life to her was about family first and foremost. Which is what makes the missing Andreas even odder.' He shook his head. 'I hope we can get to the bottom of what on earth went on. But in answer to your question, I already mentioned the step-scrubbing! Hard work was second nature to that generation, whether in chores around the home or on the land. She used to talk about the vedema – the harvest of tomatoes and grapes. The donkeys would arrive from the fields bearing hand-woven baskets of grapes that were spread out on the terraces in the sun. Then, with bare feet, the villagers would press them, accompanied by much singing and dancing. These were the rituals she really enjoyed.'

'She sounds amazing,' said Carrie. 'That way of life has completely gone now, hasn't it?'

'It has,' agreed Kris. 'She used to tell us about her grandmother and mother, who ate live crabs, straight out of the sea, and were grateful for the food!'

'Eugh.' Carrie screwed up her face in disgust. 'I'm not sorry we've moved on from that, I must say.'

'My mother told me that Vassia trained to be a teacher after the war,' Kris continued, 'and worked in the local school for a while. But she gave it up when she got married, as all women did in those days.'

Carrie nodded. 'It was the same in the UK. I don't think the marriage bar ended entirely until the 1975 Sex Discrimination Act. Vassia sounds like she'd have been an amazing teacher though – so kind and patient.'

Kris continued reminiscing, with Carrie hanging on every word, until eventually she looked at her watch and saw that it was gone ten thirty.

'Gosh!' she exclaimed. 'I should be getting back. Nell will be wondering where I am.' Nell wouldn't be wondering anything of the sort. Far from it – she'd be having a whale of a time at the pool shindig – but, as a caring mother, Carrie had to at least pretend that her presence was important to her child.

Kris smiled. 'She'll be getting a taste of her own medicine then, won't she? Worrying about you instead of you worrying about her.'

Laughing, Carrie nodded her agreement. 'Well, now you put it like that,' she chortled, 'perhaps I shouldn't hurry back.'

'Time for a nightcap then,' suggested Kris, then called the waiter over and put in a rapid order in Greek.

The decision made, Carrie sat back in her chair and relished, for an entire minute at least, the feeling of someone else taking responsibility, and of being taken care of. It was rather a nice feeling. She could get used to it.

'So,' said Kris, as they waited for the drinks to be brought. 'About Nell. Forgive me if I'm talking out of turn, but she seems like an amazing girl and the two of you are so close.'

Carrie, on high alert as soon as Nell's name was mentioned, thought about this. Was it how they came across? That was reassuring when she spent so much of her time worrying that Nell didn't listen to a word she said and was itching to cut the apron strings.

'That's nice of you to say so,' she ventured cautiously.

'It can't be easy, though,' Kris mused. 'Working, being a mum, coping with everything on your own.'

It was a statement, rather than a question, but Carrie answered anyway. 'To be honest, it's not,' she agreed. 'I mean of course I'd do anything for Nell, anything in the world. But when I stop and think about it, sometimes I feel so exhausted. She had a heart condition when she was born, which was incredibly tough, and though it was successfully treated we do still have to be careful. She doesn't cope well with the cold, which isn't great when you live in England, and she'll always be under medical supervision.' Carrie sighed and then added hastily, 'I mean don't get me wrong, I'm not complaining. So many families have it so much worse, so many children are far, far sicker than Nell ever was.'

Kris smiled sympathetically and looked into Carrie's eyes. 'You don't have to apologise,' he assured her. 'You've had a hard time and I, for one, salute you for the brilliant job you've done. Nell would make any parent proud.'

Carrie smiled, her heart swelling with love for Nell and appreciation of Kris's comment. Then her natural self-deprecation got the better of her. 'I guess I've tried to do my best,' she said, modestly. 'But we've had some difficult times, especially recently. It's so easy to doubt yourself and your decisions about child-rearing when there's no one to bounce them off. I feel the weight of the responsibility sometimes.' She paused, then corrected herself. 'Always.'

Kris smiled sympathetically. 'As I said, it seems to me that you've done a great job.'

Embarrassment flooded over Carrie. She was being a bore, forcing Kris to repeat himself. Time to move the conversation on. Thank goodness she hadn't got started on the house or, God forbid, Nell's father. That really would be oversharing.

Fortunately, at that very moment the waiter returned, bringing two small shot glasses of a clear liquid, which he set on the table, one in front of Kris and one for Carrie.

'Tsipouro,' Kris informed her, in answer to her enquiring look. 'It's commonly drunk here as a digestif.'

'Oh well, when in Greece and all that,' replied Carrie, picking up one of the glasses, glad of the distraction. Kris did the same, and touched his lightly against hers.

'Wait,' Carrie said, carefully regarding the drink. 'Is the etiquette to sip, or down in one?'

Kris laughed. 'You can do either,' he answered, 'but I recommend a sip of tsipouro, followed by a couple of water.'

Obediently, Carrie raised her glass to her lips and took a tiny taste. 'Cripes!' she exclaimed, as the alcohol burned down her throat. 'That is strong.'

'But good, no?' said Kris, taking a rather bigger slug of his.

'I guess.' Carrie drank some more. 'If you like having your socks knocked off.'

Kris peered elaborately down at her feet, making Carrie very glad she had painted her toenails and was wearing a nice pair of sandals she'd got in the sales last year. 'Well, I see no socks, so I can only assume you do like it.'

For some reason, which could possibly have been something to do with the 50 per cent proof concoction she was imbibing, this struck Carrie as hilariously funny and she burst out into gales of laughter. Seeing her hilarity, Kris joined in and they laughed and laughed.

Finally, Kris forced himself to stop. 'Come on,' he said, 'it probably is time to go home now.'

As they left, he paused to bid farewell to the waiter and

another man who'd appeared who seemed to be the manager, and Carrie waited until the back-slapping and hugging had ended. Courteously, Kris held her arm as they descended the steep staircase back to street level, and somehow was still holding it when they were halfway back to the hotel. Carrie became acutely aware of how close they were to each other, of the intoxicating scent of him, of the reassurance his presence gave her, so strong and firm, as they made their way through the darkened streets, the souvenir shops closed now and the chatter of the crowded alleyways replaced by faint sounds of music filling the night air from the many bars they passed.

When they reached a junction on the outskirts of the old town, Kris halted and pointed upwards. 'Look at the full moon,' he said, 'and how it's reflected in the sea. It always gets me, that sight.'

Carrie looked, and, as she did so, emotion tugged at her heart. It was beautiful, and the fact that Kris appreciated its beauty and loved this island so much that he wanted her to appreciate it too suddenly felt very profound.

Her lack of confidence in relationships since the split from Jack meant that she didn't trust herself to spot the signs of attraction. But was she really wrong about Kris? Somewhere deep inside herself something was telling her she wasn't but that, up to now, she hadn't been quite ready to believe it.

As these thoughts swirled through her pleasantly alcohol-fuddled mind, she felt Kris drawing her closer. Looking back down from the moon to him, she was aware for one blissful, exquisite moment of what was to come, and then it was happening.

Kris was kissing her, and all she could think, once she'd remembered how to kiss him back, was that she wanted it to go on for ever.

# CHAPTER 19

## VASSIA, 1944

Down by the seashore, everything was quiet, just the rhythmic suck and pull of the gentle waves against the shore. For a moment, Vassia drank in the tranquillity, so different from the terrible scenes she had left behind in the village. The Nazis were going door to door, demanding entry, ransacking kitchens and bedrooms, throwing crockery and bedding and mattresses out into yards, savagely carrying out their hunt for any commando who might still be on the island.

Vassia had taken a huge risk in coming out, but she'd had no choice. She had to do everything she could for Sol, no matter the peril that put her in. Sol had described in detail where she would find the radio. She'd brought a sack to carry it in, and in her basket she also had food for him. It was twenty-four hours since she'd taken him to the cave; he'd be starving by now. But what with Andreas and the baby, and her father with his failing health, Vassia had struggled to find time to get away. She hadn't breathed a word about him to anyone, but from now on Sol would be her priority.

The radio was easy to find, exactly where Sol had said it would be. It was bigger and heavier than Vassia had imagined and she wasn't quite sure how she was going to manage both it and the basket. She got it into the sack and stood looking at it for a moment, planning how she was going to get it up the hill to Sol's new hiding place. With a great effort, arm muscles straining, she managed to get the end of the sack over her shoulder, and to pick up the basket with her other hand.

Taking a deep breath, she struck out, back across the small, sifting stones of the beach. It was hard going and she was soon sweating profusely. Her arms ached and she longed to stop for a rest, but the thought of manipulating her load back up again once she'd put it down was too much.

Stumbling along, wincing with pain every time the radio banged against her legs, she didn't notice the people walking towards her until they were almost upon her.

'Vassia!'

When someone shouted out her name, a bolt of pure terror travelled like lightning through her body. It must be German soldiers, out on patrol, watching out for anyone acting subversively. That was it. She'd failed before she'd even begun.

It took her a moment to come to her senses and realise that nobody among the occupying troops knew her name. And then she saw that it was two fishermen from the village, Christophoros and Charalambos, heading towards the harbour.

'What are you doing?' asked Christophoros, not unreasonably. His brow was furrowed as he stared at her, laden down with the sack and basket. Vassia's heart pounded.

'Er, just... collecting... er... stones.' She couldn't think of anything else that would be heavy enough to account for what she was carrying.

'Stones?' echoed Charalambos, incredulously. 'Why?'

It was a good question, and one Vassia didn't have a ready answer to. 'Um, well, I thought I'd use them in the vegetable garden,' she improvised. 'You know, to make a path!' Her voice got suddenly louder as inspiration struck.

Charalambos and Christophoros exchanged looks that indicated that they'd never heard anything so bizarre.

'Can we help?' asked Christophoros, doubtingly. 'It looks far too heavy for a woman. Here, let me...'

He reached out his hand to take the sack, but Vassia whipped it away before he could touch it, stumbling backwards and almost falling in her haste and confusion.

'Oh, no, it's fine, thank you, no need to help. I can manage.' A silence greeted this, in which Vassia could hear the fishermen's bewilderment.

'Well, if you're sure,' said Charalambos, eventually. 'Let us know when you've finished your – er, path. We'd like to see it.'

Vassia gripped her load ever tighter. This was a nightmare, but she'd have to deal with the non-existent path another time. Right now, she needed to get going.

Determinedly, she took a step forward. 'Of course,' she said, 'I'll make sure to tell you.' And then she walked away, praying that the men would not follow her. They clearly thought she'd lost her mind, but rather that than knowing what she was really up to. Not because they would betray her but the less anyone knew, the better.

It was a steep uphill walk, every inch of which was torture. By the time she reached the cave, her arms felt as if they were breaking. But get there she did, and experienced a short, sharp burst of triumph at a task accomplished. She had no choice but to leave the radio outside the hole while she descended. Immediately, Sol went up to bring it in.

When he, Vassia and the radio were safely inside, Vassia finally allowed herself to breathe more easily. The encounter with the fishermen had been a warning – of how dangerous her mission was, how easily it could all go wrong.

She thought about telling Sol what had happened, but didn't. He might try to stop her coming and that was the last thing she wanted. Instead, surreptitiously flexing her shoulders and arms to try to ease the strain out of them, she unpacked the basket. She knew Sol was hungry, starving in fact, by the way his stomach gurgled as soon as he smelt the *fasolatha*, white bean and vegetable stew, that she had made. It pleased her to watch him devour it, scraping every last morsel out of the pan.

'That was really good,' he complimented her, leaning back against the cool wall of the cave. 'Thank you.'

'I'm glad you liked it,' she replied, smiling.

There was a pause. It flitted across Vassia's mind how strange this was, talking about food as if they were sitting round the table in her kitchen having just had a perfectly normal meal, not hiding out as enraged enemy troops conducted random searches among defiant but terrified islanders.

She pulled a paper-wrapped package out of the basket, opened it and offered it to Sol.

'*Loukoumades*,' she said.

Sol took one of the tiny doughnuts drenched in honey and sprinkled with cinnamon and crushed walnuts. He put it into his mouth in one go and spent a long time chewing, savouring every morsel.

'Delicious,' he pronounced, when he had finally swallowed it down. 'That honey is the best I've ever tasted. It must be local. It tastes of the island, the sunshine and the summer.'

Bashfully, Vassia grinned. 'It's from our own hives,' she told him. 'Lots of people keep bees on Santorini. I suppose they do on other islands, too,' she added a little doubtfully, as if the habits and customs of such 'foreigners' might not be as she thought.

With a chuckle, Sol reached out and took another *loukoumade*.

'Tell me more about everywhere you've been,' Vassia urged him, trying to disguise her eagerness, not just to know more about him but also about all the places he had experienced and she had not. Sol had brought into her mind a consciousness of the vastness of the world and, though she couldn't go and travel it for herself, she could experience it vicariously, through him.

'In the war, do you mean?' Sol replied. 'Or before?'

Vassia spread out her arms in an expansive gesture that said, *everything*.

Sol chuckled again. 'Well, let me see,' he mused, screwing up his eyes as if having to look far back in his memory. 'Before the war, when I was a child, we used to go on holidays to France. Well, it's the easiest place to get to, from England.' He paused for a moment, surveying Vassia with a scrutinising gaze. 'I suppose that's something we have in common,' he went on, 'we're both island people. Your island is small and full of grape and tomato vines. On mine, we have fields of billowing wheat, and orchards of apples and pears. But we both understand what it's like to be surrounded by the sea.'

Vassia nodded but didn't speak, not wanting to break the spell of Sol's reminiscences.

'We'd drive to Dover and onto the ferry,' Sol continued. 'My sister and I would rush up on deck and spend the entire voyage hanging on to the railings, gazing into the distance. The first one to spot France got the prize, you see.'

'What was the prize?' asked Vassia, too curious not to interrupt.

'There wasn't one!' exclaimed Sol, laughing. 'It was just the glory and one-upmanship of being the most sharp-eyed.'

Vassia joined in with his laughter. She and Andreas had had jokes and japes like that, too. The similarities between her and Sol's relationships with their respective siblings made her feel even closer to him.

'When you reach Calais, you have to remember to drive on the other side of the road,' Sol explained. 'My mother always used to get very worried about that and she'd keep reminding my father until he got rather exasperated. Sometimes he'd say, "Why don't you drive then?" But he was only joking, because

she didn't have a driving licence, so she couldn't take over even
if she had really wanted to.'

Sol's expression changed a little at the memory, softening
somehow. Vassia wondered whether his parents were alive –
surely they must be, as he was very young. But she didn't like to
ask. Maybe another time, when they'd got to know each other
better.

'We'd drive all the way to the south,' Sol went on. 'It was a
long journey, with one or two overnight stops along the way.
Finally, we'd arrive in Nice. We always stayed in the same hotel
by the Promenade des Anglais. My sister and I thought it so
funny that we'd come all that way only to end up somewhere
built by the English and named after them.'

Vassia saw that Sol's gaze was directed somewhere in the far
distance, beyond the walls of the cave, on something that
belonged to a past life.

'I never imagined that, when I grew up, I'd return to France
as a soldier,' he concluded. 'We thought we'd done with all that,
after the First World War. But sadly not.'

'Why did you join up in the first place?' she asked.

'Ha!' expostulated Sol, so loudly Vassia jumped. 'If I'm
honest, I'm not entirely sure. Perhaps it was some kind of self-
aggrandisement, wanting to be a hero. Perhaps it was pure ignorance, not knowing how hard it was going to be. I don't know.
Or perhaps it was the inevitability of it – I would have been
called up at some point anyway.'

He fell silent and Vassia waited, also silent. She felt that
there was more, something Sol wasn't telling her. She had found
in the past that saying nothing is sometimes what encourages
others to talk. And so it was with Sol.

'I think I mentioned my brother died. It was at Dunkirk in
1940. I try to take comfort from the fact that he would have
preferred to have been dead than a prisoner-of-war but that's
crazy, isn't it? Everyone would rather the chance to live.'

Vassia didn't know what to say. It was awful. To lose your brother... she couldn't imagine not having Andreas in her life. She loved him so much; as her only sibling he was part of her, part of her history and her future. To be without him was unthinkable.

'I'm so sorry,' she said, eventually. It was inadequate, she knew, but what other words were there?

Sol shook his head. 'It's all right,' he replied. 'Nothing to be done about it now. Except do everything I can to rid the world of those Nazi bastards.'

Swearing was not something Sol often did, and it took Vassia by surprise. But his anger was understandable; she shared it.

'You have learnt so much Greek,' she said, to change the subject. 'And more every day.'

Sol smiled. 'I was always good at languages,' he said. 'At my school, we learnt Latin and Ancient Greek from eight years of age, as well as French and German. I'm lucky, I think. I have the ear for it.'

'Perhaps you should teach me English,' Vassia murmured. 'We used to get tourists from England, and America, before the war. Just a few, now and then. Andreas and I thought they were so funny, with their pale skins and loud voices.'

At this, Sol burst out into a gale of laughter. 'Loud voices! That's rich, coming from a Greek. You people are so loud. There can't be much call for megaphones in this country – no need for them.'

That wasn't true, was it? Vassia opened her mouth to protest, but then just as quickly shut it again as she conjured up a picture of the menfolk in the market place, all talking at the tops of their voices, interrupting and speaking over each other with total abandon. She'd never thought about it before, never seen her own community through an outsider's eyes.

'Well, maybe,' she reluctantly agreed.

Sol was still laughing. He prodded her in the side. 'You were going to get all indignant then, weren't you? Tell me I was talking balderdash, stick up for your compatriots. Go on, admit it.'

He held Vassia's gaze with his as if daring her to contradict him.

'All right, I was,' she admitted finally, trying and failing to keep a straight face. 'You can see straight through me.'

When they'd got over their hilarity, a silence fell. It was if both became suddenly aware of their situation, that this terrible, dangerous hiatus in Sol's wartime activities was no laughing matter. Tension descended like a heavy blanket, squeezing the air out of Vassia's lungs, threatening to suffocate her.

'Here,' she said, a little desperately. 'Have another *loukoumade*. They're best when they're fresh.'

Soberly, Sol reached out and took one, then ate it, but didn't savour it as he had the last time, just gulped it down as if he were in a hurry.

'You oughtn't to stay much longer.' His voice was gravelly with worry, as if he'd got wind of trouble, as if he'd heard the boots of advancing Nazis thudding on the cave roof.

Suddenly, he reached towards her and grabbed her hands. 'Vassia, I don't know if you should keep coming here. It puts you in incredible danger. I couldn't bear it—' He broke off, released her hands and rubbed his face with his own. When he dropped them again, Vassia could make out in the dimness that he'd left streaks of black volcanic soil across his cheeks, and that moisture had gathered around his eyes. Was he crying? Her breath caught in her throat. She couldn't think of the danger, the peril she put herself in every time she left the village with a basket full of food, every time she returned with empty pots and plates.

How on earth would she explain that away, if she were stopped? If she were in the village, she could claim she had been to her grandmother's house or something similar – but if they found her tramping across the rocky wasteland into the middle of nowhere carrying all that stuff, there was nothing she'd be able to say to prove her innocence.

For a moment, helplessness vied with hopelessness in her heart. This was doomed to failure, this plan of hers to protect Sol. She had no chance. It was bad enough now, when the troops on the island were still depleted from the attack. When the reinforcements arrived from Milos... She shuddered, suddenly intensely cold.

Sol was watching her. 'Hey, what's up?' he said, so gently that tears welled in Vassia's eyes.

She shook her head. 'Nothing. Just... nothing.' She tried to smile, pursing her lips and forcing the corners of her mouth outwards, but she knew it must look more like a grimace.

'Vassia, don't,' remonstrated Sol, his voice deep with concern. They were already sitting close together, but he moved closer, then reached out and took her in his arms. 'Don't cry. I can't bear to see you cry, and on my account, too. You've done so much for me, you're so incredibly brave. I can never repay you.'

Vassia let him hold her for a while, then she pushed him slightly away. 'You can repay me,' she countered. 'Absolutely you can.'

Sol put his head on one side enquiringly.

'You can repay me by stopping telling me to stay away,' she answered, more forcefully than she intended, but she was incapable of being moderate on this subject. 'Yes, I'll admit to being afraid. Terrified, actually.' She wiped away her tears and challenged him with her eyes. 'But I'll keep my promise and look after you, whatever happens.'

Sol's kind, tired eyes stared back at her. Finally, he nodded his tacit agreement. Vassia let her head drop onto his chest and allowed fresh tears to fall as he gently stroked her hair. She wept and wept until she was spent and then, at last, they kissed, again

and again, until the tension and stress and strain were
temporarily erased.


It was late when Vassia exited the cave. Twilight had fallen and
a crescent moon hung in the velvet sky. Vassia was glad of the
semi-darkness that gave her cover. As she trudged back to the
village, she felt a strange mixture of light-headed happiness
mingled with leaden dread.

However much they pretended, the reality was that Sol was
in mortal danger, and so was she. But at the same time, incredible though it was, unimagined and unimaginable, Vassia knew
it now. Knew that something had happened to her that she had
never experienced before.

She was falling in love.

# CHAPTER 20

## CARRIE, 2024

Next day Kris messaged Carrie early, thanking her for a lovely evening, but going on to say that there was a crisis at the hotel – a blocked drain and something with the electricity as well – and so he couldn't show her the rooms that morning as he'd intended. Could they reschedule for later? And of course if she and Nell would like to come and use the pool, they were more than welcome.

This set Carrie into a predictable spiral of self-doubt. Was he regretting the night before? But that would be very teenage behaviour, wouldn't it? To avoid someone you were having second thoughts about? She'd arranged to have an early brunch with Xanthe in the village that morning; perhaps she should ask her friend what she thought, if she were brave enough to broach the matter.

As she was mulling this over, Nell came into the kitchen.

'Amy's messaged. She says can I come over?'

Carrie considered this for a moment. 'When?' she asked. 'Because I'm meeting Xanthe later, so I can't take you to Oia.'

'Kind of like now,' answered Nell, with a slight edge to her voice that indicated this was really important.

'Right,' said Carrie. 'So would you be able to get there by
bus on your own?'

'Yeah, I can do that,' agreed Nell, her agitation immediately
diminished by Carrie's ready acceptance of her plan.

'Great! It's so easy at the terminal, isn't it?' added Carrie, for
her own reassurance rather than Nell's. 'They shout out where
each bus is going and all you've got to do is get on, and then get
off at that stop that's right outside Kris's hotel.'

'Mum,' answered Nell, rolling her eyes. 'I'm not
completely incompetent. I can get on a *bus* by myself.' The
emphasis on the word bus seemed to suggest that other modes
of transport – space rocket, submarine, aircraft carrier – might
be tricky, but a simple wheeled road vehicle was within her
ability range.

'All right, sorry. Mothers always worry, you know that. It's
in our DNA.' Carrie handed Nell another glass of the orange
and mango juice she liked, anxious for her to stay hydrated in
the heat. 'Remember, plenty of water and lashings of sun cream
– keep reapplying, especially after you've been in the pool,' she
added, strictly.

'Yes, of course.' Nell's thumbs were flying over her phone,
presumably confirming arrangements to meet Amy.

'What will you do all day, other than swim?' enquired
Carrie, hoping Nell wouldn't take this as too intrusive. It was so
hard to tell what would cause umbrage with a teenager.

Nell shrugged. 'You know, hang out. And,' she continued,
looking suddenly more animated, 'we thought we might try to
find out more about Vassia and Andreas after what the old lady
told us.'

Frowning, Carrie eyed her daughter quizzically. 'How will
you do that?'

'Oh, online and – stuff,' answered Nell airily. 'I literally love
history. Amy does too. And this is about Kris's family, and our
family, and nothing's more important than family, is it?' She

looked back down at her phone. 'Anyway, I've told Amy I'll be there soon, so I better get going.'

Clearly there was absolutely no reason for such urgency, but Carrie showed admirable restraint by refraining from pointing that out.

'That's fine,' she said instead. 'Of course you can go. I hope you have a lovely time together.' She handed Nell some euros. 'Please make sure you pay for anything you have from the pool bar,' she added. 'I don't want Kris to think we're taking advantage of his generosity.'

Without moving her eyes from her phone, Nell took the money and shoved it in her shorts pocket.

'Look after it!' wailed Carrie. 'Is that a safe enough place? Will it fall out? Haven't you got a purse, and a bag?'

Silently, Nell removed the notes from her pocket and shoved them inside her bikini top, which she was wearing under her T-shirt, barely breaking the flow of her typing. Carrie had to laugh.

'OK, OK, I'll back off,' she conceded. 'Final word. Words. Be careful. Be good. Love you.'

Having seen Nell off, imploring her to message when she got there, Carrie got ready to meet Xanthe. Wending her way down the cobbled alleyways to the café, she mulled over Nell's assertion that family trumped everything. It was so true, but she'd never heard her daughter express such a sentiment before. Was this a sign that Nell was growing up, maturing? What a relief that would be!

By the time Carrie reached the café in the village, she'd changed her mind about telling Xanthe about Kris. Xanthe was wonderful but she was sometimes a little over the top about things. Carrie was worried that, at the slightest hint of a romance, Xanthe would be planning a double wedding with her and Spencer within seconds. She was unlikely to understand Carrie's doubts and fears about whether Kris was regretting making his first move the night before. Which, Carrie thought as she reflected on it, probably meant her doubts and fears were unfounded.

While she waited for her friend, Carrie ordered coffee and opened her notebook to read through the scant notes she had made so far on her findings about Sol. On her phone, she scrutinised anew the picture she'd taken of the ring he'd left with her mother. This was a ring you gave to someone you loved; carefully chosen, expensive: jewellery to treasure. The inscription emphasised that even more. It suddenly occurred to her to ask Xanthe what the words meant. Why Sol had never given it away, though, Xanthe wouldn't be able to answer. Carrie was the one who had to find that out.

As she was pondering this, Xanthe arrived in a whirlwind of apologies for being late, complicated explanations about work that Carrie couldn't quite follow, and suggestions of what they must eat. Soon after, the table was laden with dishes; yoghurt with local honey, *koulouria*, olive bread and *strapatsada*, scrambled eggs cooked with tomatoes and feta.

Carrie tucked in, and had just taken a mouthful of the delicious egg concoction when Xanthe, with customary lack of reticence, leapt straight into an interrogation.

'So,' she began, with purpose in her tone, 'what's the deal with dreamboat Kris?'

'What do you mean?' answered Carrie, affecting a faux innocence that she knew would not put Xanthe off for one moment.

It didn't.

'Don't pretend, Carrie,' she hooted. 'I can read your face like a book. You like him, don't you? And he clearly likes you, so I can't personally see what the problem is.'

Carrie sighed. If only it were that simple. 'I guess there isn't a problem,' she ventured, cautiously. 'But you know, I'm not a free agent, I've got Nell to consider and—'

'And nothing,' interrupted Xanthe. 'You've sacrificed enough for Nell – your degree for one, and a love life for the past sixteen years. I know you don't regret it, and nor should you. But you and she are old enough now for you to follow your own desires for once.' With that, she gave a satisfied smile and popped a morsel of bread into her mouth. When she'd finished chewing, she fixed Carrie with a steely eye and added, 'So tell me – has anything actually happened? I swear he must have kissed you by now.'

Try as she might, Carrie could not prevent a small smirk from breaking out on her face. 'Well, OK, I confess – he has.'

'And?' demanded Xanthe.

'It was lovely,' replied Carrie, still grinning.

Xanthe threw her napkin onto the table. 'I rest my case! I *knew* you two were going to get together. It was written in the stars.' She sighed and rolled her eyes dramatically. 'Now that's sorted,' she continued, 'fill me in on the Sol mystery.'

Sadly, there wasn't that much to tell yet. Carrie relayed the few details she had, and then got out her phone to show Xanthe the pictures of the ring and the inscription that she'd copied down. She hoped her attempts at Greek script were good enough.

'Right,' said Xanthe purposefully as she studied the photos. 'Your Greek handwriting's not that bad, you know,' she pronounced, after a second or two. And then, 'The words are *faith, hope, love.*' She looked triumphantly at Carrie. 'That's so adorable, isn't it? A bit like *eat, pray, love* but with more heft and gravitas. Whoever Sol intended this ring for, he must have really loved her.'

Carrie hastily scrawled down the translation onto the piece of paper. 'It seems that way.' She took a gulp of coffee and stared pensively at the three words. 'I'm so sure that Sol bought it for Vassia, the girl in the picture, but I can't understand why he would have done that and then not given it to her. I'm desperate to know what happened between them, how it came about, what brought them together and tore them apart.'

Xanthe nodded thoughtfully. 'If only the dead could talk, huh,' she answered.

'I so want to solve the mystery,' said Carrie, forehead furrowed in concentration. 'For Sol, and my mum, and for Kris's family, too.' Not to mention for her book, so that she could get it written and published and somehow alleviate all the problems that were waiting for her back in Wiltshire.

'Look, I really want you to solve it too,' replied Xanthe. 'But I'm afraid I'll be out of the picture for a few days. My grandmother on my father's side, who lives in Thessaloniki, has fallen ill and I need to go and give her a hand. It's not serious, in that she'll recover, but she needs some help in the short term. I'll be gone a week at most, so I should get back before you go home. I hope so, anyway. But I'm not going to be able to help with your investigations while I'm away.'

'I'm so sorry to hear about your grandma,' commiserated Carrie. 'I'll miss you of course, but I totally understand that you need to go and I'll be fine getting on with things here. It's good of you to leap to her aid. I hope she's OK.'

'She's a tough old stick; she'll be fine. And I'm sure that, in my absence, Kris will be more than happy to take care of you.' Xanthe accompanied this statement with an exaggerated wink and leering smile. 'Make sure you tell all, and I mean *all*, on my return.'

'Honestly, you have got an overactive imagination!' protested Carrie. 'There'll be nothing much more to tell, I'm sure.' But secretly she hoped there would be.

Strolling back to the little house, she remembered that Nell had not messaged to say she had arrived safely. Carrie tapped out a text to her and anxiously waited for her response, which came, eventually, once Carrie was ensconced in her bedroom at her laptop, with the doors open to the sunshine. Nell informed her that she'd been invited to have lunch with Amy and her parents. Happy that Nell was being fed and watered and was in safe hands, Carrie absorbed herself again in her developing manuscript. Even if there were still so many unanswered questions, she had the information about the SBS that she had gleaned from the internet and could work with that in the meanwhile. As she wrote, her mind returned once more to her memories of Sol. He'd been such a close part of their family, Carrie supposed now because he didn't have his own.

She recalled playing rounders and French cricket, which Sol assiduously allowed either herself or Jenny to win, and card games of Racing Demon or Twenty-One that he just as assiduously cheated his way through so that he would be the victor. It was such a shame he hadn't lived to meet the next generation – Nell, and Jenny's two girls, Zoe and Elsie. Thinking this brought Carrie round to contemplating her sister and how close they had been as children, sharing everything – clothes, sweets, secrets. How she had wanted that for Nell, if not with a sibling of her own then with her cousins. But Jenny had ruined it all.

Over the years, Carrie's mother had tried on numerous occasions to bring her daughters back together, encouraging Carrie to bury the hatchet and make peace, but Carrie had simply not been able to forgive and forget.

Now, in this idyllic place, Carrie experienced a strange sensation. Was it regret? Or was it a creeping sense that exoneration should be offered? That Carrie should drop her grudge of over a decade and a half? But she was not ready to go there yet. Shaking off these difficult thoughts, she set her mind back to her work.

She soon got into a rhythm. It had been a long time since she'd felt the words flowing out of her as naturally and easily as they were now. At first, she worried about that – did it mean the writing was too simplistic? Wasn't good writing supposed to be hard, torturous even? Every syllable sweated over? Perhaps she was penning a load of rubbish, that her publisher would return to her with a one-line email – *sorry, not suitable.*

Resting her head on the cool tabletop, Carrie groaned. Why did she always second-guess herself like this? She fetched some snacks and ate them contemplatively, trying to reason with herself. What she was writing might not be good enough to be published. But if she didn't write anything, it *definitely* wouldn't be published.

There was no other option than to keep going.

By late afternoon, Carrie's shoulders ached from being hunched over the little table. Good or bad, she had got a lot done. It was a hot day and she'd been gently perspiring for hours. The thought of a refreshing swim in Kris's gorgeous pool, and perhaps a nice glass of cold Santorini wine under the pergola, was very enticing.

She checked the bus times on the app, and saw there was one in forty-five minutes that she could make if she got a move on. She rang Nell as she gathered together her essentials – swimming costume, book, sunglasses, hairbrush, sunscreen. The call went straight to voicemail. That was strange. Could they still be out at lunch somewhere, out of range of a signal? Carrie had no idea how good coverage was on the island, but it was such a small place she would be surprised if there were many black spots. Nell must have run out of battery. She'd likely borrowed Amy's charger and left the phone plugged in somewhere, Amy's room probably. That would be it.

Half an hour or so later, Carrie was at the main bus terminal in Fira. It was its usual scene of organised chaos, huge vehicles leaving and entering continuously, moving a few feet forward or reversing noisily in a kind of oversized, balletic choreography. The drivers were exceptionally skilful, manoeuvring into the smallest of spaces and coping, in varying degrees of good or ill temper, with the crowds of clueless tourists swarming around the place.

When she arrived at Kris's hotel, Carrie followed the sounds drifting up from the pool; the music coming from the speakers, the cries of children playing, the breeze flapping the numerous brightly coloured parasols. Expecting Nell and Amy to be among the swimmers and sunbathers, she confidently descended the path, jumping down the last couple of shallow steps. Standing on the poolside, she surveyed the scene. To her surprise, there was no sign of either of the girls, nor of Amy's parents.

Perhaps they'd gone for a drive around the island, she thought, decided to visit one of the archaeological sites or a beach somewhere. They'd be back soon. Settling down with her book, she stared at the pages for half an hour or so, without taking in much of what she was reading. Her eyes kept flitting up, hoping to see Nell and Amy approaching, bikini-clad, carrying swim towels, ready to leap in and cool off.

But the girls did not materialise.

Carrie tried Nell's phone. Straight to voicemail again. If she'd had Amy's number, she could have called her, but she didn't. Nor Amy's parents' numbers. How stupid of her. Why had she not got Nell to write them down or send them to her? What was she thinking, letting her daughter, her only, precious child, go off with people she barely knew without any means to contact them in an emergency?

*It's not an emergency*, she told herself sternly, *you are being melodramatic*. It was the sort of thing she accused Nell of, when being told that not having the right shoes/coat/packed lunch or whatever would ruin Nell's life.

At what point should she go to the hotel reception and see if they could contact Amy's mum and dad? Glancing at her watch, she saw that it was five p.m. What time did they reopen after the siesta? Around now, surely. Standing up, she wandered round the pool towards the wall beyond which lay the car park, hoping to catch a glimpse of the family returning.

A jeep stood by itself in the furthest parking space. Carrie studied it with a sinking heart. It was Amy's parents' hire car, wasn't it? She'd seen them in it the other day. Was it the same one? She looked at the number plate, but of course she hadn't memorised it. Why on earth would she? But the more she stared, the more she was sure it was their car.

Trying desperately to suppress the incipient panic that was making her throat ache and her head pound, Carrie hastened to the reception area. The familiar face of one of the receptionists, who Carrie had seen around the hotel several times, greeted her with a smile.

'How can I help you?' Sofia said.

'I'm not sure where my daughter Nell is,' replied Carrie, forcing herself to say the words carefully, to enunciate them properly, and to keep to a measured tone, when all she really wanted to do was shout at the top of her voice, WHERE IS SHE?

'She was having lunch with that family, Amy's parents... I thought they'd be back by now, but there's no sign of them, so I just wondered...'

Sofia nodded. 'Mr and Mrs Edmead have been on their private terrace since the four of them got back from lunch,' she stated, calmly. 'I'm not sure about your daughter, or theirs. I haven't seen them this afternoon.'

A lump of dread, heavy as a ton of bricks, crushed down on Carrie's heart. Had they gone swimming somewhere, drowned... Had they gone for a walk, been knocked down, were they lying by the side of the road, scorched by the sun, bleeding out—

*Stop it*, she told herself. This isn't helping.

Squeezing back the tears that were pricking behind her eyes, she clenched her fists. 'Do you know where Kris is?' she asked Sofia, as calmly as she could possibly manage. 'I'd like to speak to him.' The absence of Nell had dissipated any embarrassment Carrie had been feeling about the events of the previous evening. Now the only person she wanted to see, apart from Nell, was Kris. He would know what to do, wouldn't he?

The wait for him to arrive was around ten minutes that felt like a lifetime. As soon as he materialised, an enquiring expression on his face, Carrie explained the situation, and immediately he attempted to reassure her.

'They'll be somewhere nearby,' he said, confidently. 'Amy's parents might know where they are. Sofia, could you pop across to their room and ask them?'

As soon as Sofia had left, Kris stepped closer to Carrie. He drew her into a tight hug, planted a kiss on her forehead, let her rest her head on his shoulder and then smoothed her hair with his hand. In normal circumstances, his actions would have assuaged Carrie's worries that he was having second thoughts. But she'd forgotten all about her earlier doubts, faced as she was with the fear induced by Nell's absence.

'It'll be all right,' he soothed. 'Please don't worry.'

As he spoke, Carrie felt her heart rate reduce and her breathing return to normal in the safety of his embrace. But that changed the moment Sofia returned, saying that Amy's parents had no news and were coming over to reception as soon as they had changed out of their beachwear.

'Oh God, oh God,' groaned Carrie. 'Where can they be? Where could they have gone? I don't understand!'

'Perhaps they've gone shopping, or taken a walk along the caldera path to watch the sunset,' Kris said, still trying to put her at ease. 'You know what young people are like – they've just got carried away, lost track of time and forgotten to let you know.'

'Yes but Nell always has her phone with her, she always answers eventually,' wailed Carrie, feeling herself losing control. 'I've heard nothing from her for hours.' She swiped her hand across her eyes, where tears were welling. 'I should never have let her go. I should never have let her out of my sight. What was I thinking of?'

Her outpouring of emotion ended abruptly with the arrival in the room of Amy's parents, Jim and Debbie. Amy's phone was also going straight to voicemail.

'Her phone is constantly running out of charge or whatever,' Debbie said. She seemed remarkably sanguine about the situation. Carrie wondered how she and her husband could remain so calm. Perhaps she was overreacting. But she had a bad feeling, deep in her bowels, that there was something really wrong about the girls' absence.

'We'll walk into town and see if we can find them,' Jim declared. 'They might just have lost track of time looking round the shops.'

'Great,' replied Kris. He turned to Carrie. 'We can check out the caldera path,' he pronounced. He reached out to take her hand and then led her off in that direction.

As they marched, Carrie could not take in the beauty of the spectacular view. She'd wanted to walk this path, but not in these circumstances. It was all she could do to stop herself from breaking down by the roadside and sobbing. Kris's face was set firm, his eyes constantly scanning the landscape. They came to a gap in the path, where the cliff fell dramatically away. Carrie saw Kris falter and try to peer discreetly over the edge.

At this, she could hold in the tears no longer. As they streamed down her face, she watched helplessly as Kris got out binoculars and studied the sea far below. Then he turned away.

'They haven't fallen,' he said, with more confidence than he probably felt. 'We'll find them, don't worry. We won't rest until we have.'

He came to Carrie's side and put an arm round her shoulders. 'Come on, let's go a bit further. There's a church not far from here – they might have sat down by it and we'll find them there, chatting.'

Still sobbing, intermittently dabbing at her eyes with a ragged bit of tissue she'd found in her pocket, Carrie stumbled along the uneven path beside him. They walked and walked, far further than the girls were likely to have ventured, past a tiny church, where there was no sign of life, and further still. But by ten p.m., there was no sign of them.

Back at the hotel, Carrie barely holding it together, Kris called the police, who said it was too early to do anything but to call again if they remained missing after twenty-four hours.

At one a.m., the girls had still not reappeared. It had been too dark for a while to carry on without torches or vehicles. Carrie sat in the reception at Kris's hotel while he phoned around to muster a search party of locals. The pictures on the wall, of gleaming whitewashed buildings under cloudless skies, of white-sailed yachts on an azure sea, of whitewashed churches with blue-domed roofs, stared down at her.

But suddenly, this beautiful island wasn't so idyllic any more.

# CHAPTER 21

## VASSIA, 1944

The next couple of days passed in a blur. Vassia spent hours in the kitchen, preparing nourishing meals for her family – but mainly for Sol. For the first time in her life, she enjoyed cooking; making sure that he was well fed during his enforced period of confinement in the cave was so important to his health and future, and the meals broke up the monotony of his days. Vassia was glad that he had his sketchbook and pencils as it gave him something to do when he was alone, along with trying to make contact on the field radio. That was risky as he had to come to the surface to get a signal and, though the planes were no longer out searching, foot patrols continued.

Equally risky, if not more so, were Vassia's daily journeys to the cave. Every time she left her house, carrying provisions for Sol, her heart pounded with fear. Vourvoulos had been barely visited by the occupying troops during their entire sojourn on the island but now, since the raid, there was always the chance of rounding a corner and coming face to face with a German soldier, eyes scouring his surroundings, looking for renegade commandos or rebellious civilians. Vassia hoped that, by virtue of being a woman, she would not arouse suspicion. But she didn't know for sure.

Despite the ever-present danger, the love she felt for Sol permeated every pore of Vassia's body and when, on the odd occasion that she could momentarily forget about the war and just think about him, it was as if the already bright, sparkling springtime world around her was painted in technicolour. All she wanted was to be with him, and the time she spent in the dim, dark cave seemed magical, gilded by its unexpectedness, although underneath always lay the fear that at any moment it might end, through capture or Sol's departure.

Vassia refused to think about either of those possibilities. She was centred in the now, focused on the present. Everything else was noise and distraction. Nothing mattered but her and Sol, and the precious hours they could spend together.

She embroidered a sampler for him, and took it to the cave.

'I made this for you,' she told him, a little bashfully, suddenly self-conscious, wondering whether a soldier would think such a thing trivial or foolish.

He unfolded the cloth and studied it, his brow furrowed as he translated the Greek.

'Faith, hope and love; but the greatest of these is love,' he read. And then read it again more slowly, as if savouring each word, lingering especially on 'love'.

'It's from the Bible,' explained Vassia hastily, lest he think it was just a village saying, nothing important. She was always worried about her humble origins, when Sol was so worldly, had seen and done so much.

'Yes, I know,' said Sol. He smiled and shook his head, then looked at directly at her. 'It's beautiful. Thank you so much.'

Flooded with relief, Vassia took the embroidery and hung it on a spike of rock on a part of the wall that caught the light shining down the shaft. When she had done so, Sol kissed her gently and then pulled her down to sit in front of him, her back against his chest.

'Tell me about your childhood,' he said. 'You've heard so much about me – now I want to hear about you.'

Vassia snuggled herself deeper against him. She loved the feel of him, his solidity and strength. He was lean and muscular from years of fighting and physical exertion, every part of his body taut and alert, ready to spring into action at any moment. But when they sat together like this he was relaxed and easy, and, with his arms round her, she felt grounded and secure, even though the reality was that her world was less safe than it had ever been in her life before.

'It was good,' she replied, dreamily, her eyes misty with memories of the past. 'Andreas and I were not like some siblings, forever quarrelling and squabbling. We always got along well, and we were surrounded by family and friends who cocooned us in their love. Our parents, grandparents, great-grandparents – we saw all of them almost every day, and each of them was special in their own way.'

Vassia sighed as she recalled those halcyon days. They seemed a million years ago now.

'My brother is named after our Pappou Andreas; it's the tradition for the first son to be given the same name as the paternal grandfather. He had a huge black dog with the most gentle temperament imaginable. It didn't even mind when we pulled its ears.'

'I love dogs,' Sol said, tightening his arms round her. 'I'll definitely be a dog-owner as soon as I get the chance. I'd like a Pyrenean Mountain Dog, or an Alsatian. One that's big enough for a child to ride like a horse,' he concluded, laughing.

Vassia giggled too, and then abruptly stopped. Whose child would this be? The thought of Sol's future offspring gave rise to an uncomfortable mix of emotions that she couldn't disentangle or identify. She paused, wondering if he would elaborate, but he didn't. Of course he didn't. Having children was the last thing on his mind, in the middle of a terrible war, hiding from a ferocious enemy, his life hanging in the balance. Vassia scolded herself internally for having expectations that could not possibly be met.

'And Ya-ya Olympia made the best honey pie imaginable.' Determinedly, she returned to her childhood reminiscences. 'No visit to her house was complete without us being served up a huge slice.'

'My mouth is watering at the thought,' murmured Sol dreamily, and then quickly added, 'but I'm sure it wasn't better than the amazing desserts you've been bringing me. I'll get fat if I stay here too long.'

They both laughed, but behind her mirth Vassia felt a shock of disappointment run through her. The words 'too long' were not ones she wanted to hear. She wanted Sol to stay for ever and, however much she knew this wasn't possible, she couldn't stop herself from fantasising.

'But snacks aside, it must be wonderful to grow up in such a close community,' continued Sol. 'My mother's and my father's parents were from London, but they moved out of the city when they retired, to Dorset and west Wales, and I rarely saw them. I wish we'd been closer, and that we'd spent more time together.'

Vassia nodded. 'I'm sorry for you not to have had that,' she sympathised. 'I'm lucky, I know it. But apart from family, there were lots of other good things about growing up on Santorini. We had complete freedom to roam over the island, and the sea. Once Andreas and I were old enough to sail our own boat – well, we would spend days doing nothing else.' She didn't tell him about the incident in the storm; nothing would spoil these golden memories.

'Just messing about on the water...' said Sol, and then sighed heavily, as if he were nostalgic for a similar experience. Perhaps he was thinking of his fellow SBS commandos, thought Vassia, who even now might be afloat, heading for another idyllic Greek island tainted by the presence of Nazi soldiers to perform some piratical feat of derring-do.

'And then of course,' Vassia continued, 'we had all the events that occur in the Orthodox year; Christmas and Easter, of course, but also carnival, the day of the Holy Spirit and, for individuals, name days – those are always celebrated with a feast and festivities that everyone's invited to. We'd just had my father's name day when you arrived.'

'Wonderful,' enthused Sol. 'I don't think the British are as good at fiestas as you Mediterranean types are. It's not so much dancing with abandon to the bouzouki as tiptoeing quietly around, observing etiquette.'

'Oh, Sol, you are always putting your own country down!' remonstrated Vassia. 'It's too cold, too grey, too rainy, too reserved. I don't believe it's half as bad as that, or why wouldn't everyone leave?'

Sol chuckled. 'You're right, as you always are,' he agreed. 'I don't really mean what I say. But sometimes – I don't know, perhaps it's this ghastly war, and the fact I've been away so long – but sometimes I wonder what there will be for me in England when I do finally go home.'

Vassia had squirmed around in his embrace so that she could see his face and, as he said these words, a flutter of hope, a momentary feeling that maybe their future was not already mapped out but could be altered, ruffled her heart. The whole conversation had ebbed and flowed between light and dark, possibility and disappointment, and now had landed here...

'So do you think,' she began, tentatively, not sure whether she should put her thoughts into words, 'would you consider...' And then her voice petered out as she lost her nerve. If she asked him to stay and he said no, how would she feel then? And anyway, it was impossible, ridiculous. She knew that, really.

'What?' asked Sol. 'What were you going to ask?'

Vassia managed a small smile and waved her hand in a care-free gesture. 'It was nothing,' she lied. 'Nothing important.' With a huge internal effort, she forced herself to put such daydreams to one side.

Sol looked at her a little strangely for a moment, before saying, 'I have something to ask you, then.' He paused for a moment. Vassia waited to find out what it was, expecting a request for a particular food, more meat or more bread, perhaps. When he resumed, what he said took her totally by surprise.

'Would you mind if I drew you?' he asked, softly. 'I'm not so good at portraits, and I'd like to be better and you would be such a...' He paused as if struggling to find the right words. 'Such a perfect model, or muse perhaps I should say,' he concluded, more animated now. He was already getting to his feet, causing Vassia to move too as they disentangled from each other.

Vassia smiled at him, her melancholy banished. Enjoy the moment. That was all anyone could do in wartime.

'Of course, I'd love that. And it's not true that you're not good at portraits; I've seen your sketchbook with the pictures of the other men. I think that's another one of your self-deprecating... er, how shall I put it... untruths,' she added, playfully.

Laughing once more, Sol got out his sketchbook and pencils. It was midday, and sunshine poured down through the cave shaft like a spotlight in a theatre. Sol arranged Vassia in it, seating her on his folded jacket, and then he paused, considering her closely, a doubtful look in his eyes.

'What's wrong?' she asked. 'Don't I look right?'

Sol smiled a little ruefully and shook his head. 'No, of course not. You look—' He stopped and seemed for a moment to be having trouble breathing. 'Beautiful,' he murmured, eventually.

He knelt down beside her and fumbled in his pocket for something. As he pulled it out, his expression changed once more, to one of uncertainty and indecision.

Vassia said nothing, just regarded him quizzically. She had a sense of something important coming, but had no idea what.

'I—' began Sol, before breaking off, coughing, and then starting again. 'I've made something for you, too. I thought you might like it – and I don't have anything much to give you, to thank you for all you've done for me.'

He handed her something, but she couldn't at first see what it was as it was entirely enclosed in his palm. When she had taken it, she held it up to the light and examined it closely. It was a necklace made of thin, flexible wire, and attached to it was a small bronze pendant, on one side of which was the profile of a man's head and on the other, a picture of an old-fashioned sailing ship and the letters *HALF PENNY*.

'It's a coin,' explained Sol. 'Just a ha'penny, hardly worth anything. I punched a hole in it and strung it on some radio wire.' He regarded her for a moment before going on, 'I know it's not much. But it's all I have.'

As Sol stared concernedly at her, waiting for her reaction, a few drops of water moistened the thin layer of sand that covered the cave's hard, rocky floor. Eventually, Vassia raised her head. Her cheeks were streaked with tears but she was smiling. A gift for a gift, she thought, and was gladder than ever that she had been brave enough to give Sol the embroidered sampler. 'It's gorgeous,' she whispered. 'I love it. Thank you. Thank you so much.'

Sol gave a great guffaw of laughter that seemed to explode within the confined space of the cave, ricocheting off the walls and echoing all around. Vassia understood that he was laughing like that because he'd been so tense, so apprehensive about her reaction. It had been really important to him that she like his present. And she did. She was telling the absolute truth when she said that she loved it.

She leant towards him. 'Please, help me to put it on,' she said, gently.

He did so and then, having admired it for a few moments, put his arms round her. They hugged and kissed and a long time passed before they were ready to get back to the portrait. Once they did, Sol began to draw with quick, definite strokes of his pencil. It took only minutes.

'Let me see!' Vassia begged him, full of curiosity. She'd never been drawn before by anyone, let alone a man with whom she was desperately in love.

Sol showed her the sketch. It was simple, but so lifelike that Vassia gasped in wonder as she gazed upon it. 'It's so good,' she breathed. 'And so – I don't know, so accurate. Anyone who knew me would recognise it.' Sol had even drawn the pendant, with the tiny boat in the centre of the coin's reverse.

'You need to go,' Sol said, his voice deep with reluctance. The light had moved away from the shaft, indicating how much time had passed. Vassia should be on her way. 'And take the necklace off. If the Germans see it – well, they'll know it's British. It could give you away.'

Vassia's hand shot to her throat and closed round the precious thing. 'I will. But I'll keep it with me always in my pocket, and beneath my pillow at night, and I'll wear it when I come here.'

Sol smiled his beautiful, kind smile, that always seemed permeated with something that Vassia couldn't quite define. Was it regret? Was it sorrow? She didn't know.

She was still puzzling over it as she slipped across the hillside, hoping to get home without seeing anyone who might question where she'd been. But as soon as she reached the outskirts of the village, a terrible sight met her eyes. There were German soldiers everywhere.

Her heart pounding, she faltered. Had they seen her? She didn't think so. Taking an abrupt turn, she ducked for cover behind a wall, and waited until she'd recovered some equilibrium. When her legs had steadied, she crept out, slinking through the streets that wound between the house walls until she was nearly home. She took a short cut across someone's courtyard and reached her house – just in time to see the most appalling sight she could ever have imagined.

Two Nazis, eyes blazing with anger and hostility, were strong-arming her father, the mayor of Vourvoulos, Ianos Kourakis, out of the house. She watched, struck dumb and paralysed by fear, as the pair of brutes manhandled her father along the street that led to the village square.

'Please allow me to walk by myself,' she could hear her father saying, with a politeness that seemed incomprehensible. 'It is a matter of my position. The villagers won't like to see me treated like this.'

'What the good-for-nothing residents of this traitorous place think of us is not our concern,' barked one of the soldiers, pulling her father so hard that he jolted forward and almost lost his footing.

Finally, Vassia came to her senses. Running after them, she soon caught up.

'Papa,' she shouted, unable to stop herself. 'What's happening? Where are they taking you?'

The soldiers stopped abruptly and one of them demanded, 'Who are you?'

Clenching her fists and willing herself to be strong, Vassia replied, 'I am Vassia Kourakis. That is my father. You have to tell me what you are doing with him.'

The first soldier sneered at her. 'We don't have to tell you any such thing. But we will.' He glanced at his companion, who gripped Ianos even more tightly.

'We are going to the square. The whole village will be there. And we will find out who was involved.' He turned and began marching her father forward again. 'You must come too,' he called back over his shoulder.

Panic swept over Vassia.

Where was her mother? Andreas, Athena and the baby? Her grandparents, and great-grandparents? She stood in the street, her head turning wildly in all directions, with no idea what she should do.

And then another word, one that could not be argued with, rang out in the whitewashed street. '*Schnell.*'

Without waiting another moment, Vassia followed her father and the two soldiers, knowing something dreadful was about to happen that she was powerless to stop.

As she entered the square and saw the ranks of villagers already there, with more arriving from every side road and alleyway, their shuffling gait and downturned faces indicating their fear and trepidation, bile rose in her throat. She had been telling Sol about all the joyous occasions of celebration the island community enjoyed. And now here they were, gathered together again, but not for happiness and revelry. The very opposite. Men and women, old people and young people, huddled nervously against one another, while children buried their faces in their mother's skirts, all conscious of the ominous atmosphere, all aware that nothing good was going to come of this summons to the square.

Silently, Vassia scanned the crowd for her mother and the rest of her family. As she did so, it came to her. She knew what that look in Sol's eyes was, what imbued his smile with something that was more than happiness.

Longing.

Longing tinged with desire.

Why was she thinking this now? Angrily, she pushed the thought away. Sighting Thalia, she moved towards her, pushing her way through the crowd. Reaching her, she felt for her hand and squeezed it. Her mother was already weeping. Her father had been let go by the soldiers and was just standing there, helplessly surveying this awful collection of his family, friends and neighbours.

An army jeep drew up, noisily belching fumes, tyres rumbling across the ancient cobblestones. A door opened and the entire crowd drew a collective intake of breath as Lieutenant Schwarz stepped out, eyed them all disdainfully, and then walked to the side of the square already lined by German soldiers.

No one had been saying much before, but now a terrible, and absolute, silence descended. It was as if the entire village had stopped breathing. It was obvious what was happening. Of course they should have known, should have expected it. There was no way the Nazis were going to ignore the blow to their pride the SBS raid had inflicted, not to mention the loss of their troops. There had always only been one possible outcome, and now here it was.

Reprisals.

# CHAPTER 22

## CARRIE, 2024

At three o'clock in the morning, Kris insisted that Carrie get some sleep.

'There are lots of people out looking,' he told her. 'You'll be no good to anyone if you're exhausted.'

Carrie disagreed. She wanted to carry on searching until she literally couldn't move another muscle. Anything could be happening to Nell and Amy; she couldn't rest until she'd found them.

'They won't have been abducted,' Kris told her, firmly. 'That simply doesn't happen on Santorini. Abducted to where? We are surrounded by sea.'

'These things can happen anywhere,' she raged back at him. 'Anyone could bundle them into a car, take them to an isolated beach, shove them onto a boat...' Even as she spoke, she realised how improbable it sounded. 'Their drinks could have been spiked, it happens all the time at home, someone could have them somewhere, locked up in a cellar, I don't know. They'll both be terrified, Nell could be calling for me and I'm not there, helping her, rescuing her.'

Kris took hold of her hands. 'You need to calm down,' he

instructed her. 'Getting yourself all worked up will only make things worse. If you can't sleep, fine, just sit by the phone, but at least have a hot drink and some rest.'

Reluctantly, Carrie agreed. Kris took her to an empty room in the hotel. It was one of the expensive ones on the caldera side, but the magnificence of the view was lost on her. Who cared about scenery when two young women, one of them her own priceless daughter, were missing? Somehow, she managed to wait until seven a.m., drifting in and out of a fitful sleep, before calling her mother, forgetting that Greece was two hours ahead so it would still be only five back home.

Nevertheless, Harriet answered after the third ring. Carrie could hardly get the words out to tell her that Nell, her beloved granddaughter, was missing. After listening in silence, Harriet told her, if there was no news by the afternoon, to let her know and she and Bill would fly straight out there. She'd look up the flights now, so as to be ready.

A shadow passed in front of the window, momentarily darkening the room, and then came a knock. Carrie hastily said goodbye to her mother and rushed to open the door. Was this someone coming with good news?

As soon as she caught sight of the dark uniform of the police officer, her heart seemed to stop beating.

'Wh-what is it?' she asked desperately, her breath catching in her throat. They'd been told nothing would be done until the girls had been missing for twenty-four hours, and it wasn't that long yet. So this must mean... the thought was too terrible for her to allow it to form.

The police officer gave her a kindly smile at the same time as shaking his head.

'We have no news. I need to take a full description, please. When exactly you last saw your daughter, where she was, her hair and eye colour, her clothes. Everything.'

Carrie tried desperately to drag herself back from the

terrible hole down which her thoughts were descending. She thought back to the day before, which now seemed light years ago. Nell, in her shorts and T-shirt, shoving the euros into her bikini top. Which shorts had she been wearing? Which tee? *Think*, Carrie, *think*.

Somehow she managed to speak coherently enough to answer the officer's questions, describing Nell, her dark brown hair and eyes, the laddered scar on her chest from her heart surgery. When she got to this last bit, Carrie's words stuck in her throat, choking her. Oh God, how had it come to this? Telling a police officer in a foreign land about her daughter's distinguishing marks that might be used to identify her—

No! She must stop.

Somehow managing to get the words out, she stumbled to the end of what she needed to say. As they were finishing up, Kris appeared on the threshold. He looked exhausted, his eyes sunken, his lips pale and thin. Carrie realised immediately that, far from sleeping as he'd instructed her to do, he'd clearly been up all night looking for the girls.

Kris and the police officer had a rapid conversation in Greek and then Kris turned to Carrie.

'They still think that they had too much to drink and are sleeping it off somewhere. Even if they're outside, they won't come to any harm – it's not cold at night. They'll just be tired, hungry and thirsty when they do eventually turn up.'

Carrie shook her head. 'I don't think that's what has happened,' she mumbled. 'But...' She shrugged despairingly, and left the sentence hanging, not knowing how to finish it. Could she really be so sure that Nell hadn't been dabbling in alcohol and, God forbid, drugs, given her daughter's past history? Nell had been remarkably well behaved of late, but teenagers were notoriously inconsistent, unpredictable and erratic.

'We're searching everywhere in town,' Kris continued.

'Every church, every side street, every garden and terrace. We're asking all the bar staff and waiters and shopkeepers.' He spoke to the police officer again briefly.

'Have you got a picture of Nell for the police to use in their enquiries?' he asked.

'Of course,' replied Carrie, falling over herself to unlock her phone and scroll through it to find a suitable photograph.

The police officer left, and Carrie slumped back into the chair.

'I've asked room service to bring coffee,' Kris said, 'and something to eat.'

Carrie shook her head and wrapped her arms round herself. 'I can't eat anything, I'd be sick,' she mumbled, biting her lip to try to hold back a fresh onslaught of tears. 'I need to keep busy. Can we go somewhere?' And then she paused, clapping her hand to her mouth. 'I'm so sorry,' she blurted out. 'You must have things to do – the hotel... I'm sure you don't have time to spare for all of this.'

Kris waved his arm to dismiss such suggestions. 'No, no, it's fine. The team can handle everything in the short term. Let's go out for a drive, see if we spot anything.'

Carrie had the sense that Kris was picking an activity to keep her occupied, rather than one that had real purpose, but right then she didn't care. She wanted to keep on the move, be doing something, anything.

They drove for hours, along the dusty white roads that wound up and down the steep volcanic hills, between villages and hamlets, past tiny churches standing in solitary isolation and large villas with turquoise swimming pools, through vine-yards where the distinctive Santorini kouloura baked under the strong sunshine. It was beautiful and Carrie hated all of it.

They stopped off at the cottage, in case Nell had gone there, but it was empty, as Carrie had known it would be. By the time they returned to Oia, it was just after three o'clock – twenty-four hours since the girls were last seen.

Kris parked up, cut the car engine and put in another call to the police. Carrie sat beside him, feeling the heat rise inside the stationary vehicle but not having the energy or will to open the door, let alone get out. She listened to Kris speaking in rapid Greek, recognising only Nell and Amy's names. Overwhelmed, she let her head fall into her hands. How could this be happening? Carrie had devoted all of her love to her daughter from the moment she'd found out she was pregnant, and she and Nell had been through so much together, not least that dreadful day when she'd been told about her daughter's heart defect. She had thought then that, if Nell's life was over, then so was her own.

When Nell's condition had turned out to be operable and curable, Carrie had done everything she could to bring her baby up healthy and strong enough to withstand the operation and to recuperate quickly. She'd never forget going to the recovery room after the procedure, where little Nell, so pale and vulnerable, lay in a hospital gown, crying for her mum.

She'd willed Nell to live then, and she willed it again now.

Kris's call to the police ended. 'They're getting moving.' He grimaced. 'At last.' He leant back into the car seat and ran his hands through his hair. Beads of perspiration had formed on his forehead and he looked utterly wrung out. 'It's boiling in here,' he said, as if he'd suddenly realised that he was sweating. He got out of the car and came round to Carrie's side to open her door, just as another vehicle passed them, driving far too fast for the small car park and throwing up a cloud of dust.

'Slow down,' barked Carrie angrily at the errant car as it came to a squealing halt. Even though the driver couldn't possibly hear her, it felt good to let out some of her pent-up fury. But no sooner had she said the words than she was overcome by terror and trepidation. Her legs were barely able to support her weight and she grabbed onto the nearest form of support: Kris.

She flung her arms round him and held on to him as if her life depended on it. Kris responded, drawing her close and holding her tight. They stayed like that for many moments, despite the intensity of the afternoon sun, ignoring the other driver as he approached. Out of the corner of her eye, Carrie saw the man pause, rather than walk on by. Annoyed, she manoeuvred herself away from his gaze, using Kris's body as a shield between him and her.

Eventually, Kris released his hold on her. 'Let's get inside, out of the heat,' he said.

Carrie didn't want to let him go. She needed him, his strength and support, his calm, reassuring presence tempering her terror, helping her to rein in her wild, desperate imaginings. She'd left him once before, all those years ago, a decision that seemed inconceivable now. Why had she done that? To fit in with her friends, for fear of being left behind. Had it also been from fear of finding out that Kris wasn't serious? Whatever the reason, it seemed to her now that she'd been totally wrong in every respect.

Kris took her by the hand, slipping his fingers between hers. It had been such a long time since Carrie had had this kind of casual physical intimacy, but it felt like the most natural – and necessary – of gestures. She leant into him as they began to make their way to the hotel buildings, and saw at the same time that the man was still there.

A jolt of recognition seared through her, but at first she didn't believe it. It couldn't be; her eyes were deceiving her, her distress making her hallucinate. She stared, and squinted, trying to work out whether what she was seeing was true.

It was.

This time, the shock was too much. Carrie's legs buckled beneath her and she fell to the ground.

# CHAPTER 23

VASSIA, 1944

The sound of a wailing infant filtered across to Vassia through the crowd. She turned towards it and there was her brother and his family. Athena had the newborn Atlas wrapped in a shawl and tied to her chest, while she leant on Andreas's arm so that he could support her as she walked. She had still not recovered from the birth and Atlas' thin, wavering cry, far from the robust howls of a healthy baby, indicated that he was also not strong. Fear sent icy shockwaves through Vassia's veins, which were soon replaced by anger towards the Nazis for forcing everyone out when it was clear that Athena and Atlas should be tucked up in bed. But it was also clear that they did not intend anyone under the age of eighty to be spared from whatever collective punishment they were about to dish out.

The square, usually disturbed by nothing more than a competitive game of *tavli*, was filled with palpable tension. Everyone was there; Kostas and Evangelos, Elias, Lefteris and Helios with their families, Vassia's grandparents on her father's side standing near their other son. Her maternal grandparents had moved in with their eldest child at the beginning of the war, over the other side of the island, thank goodness, so were not

involved in whatever horror was about to unfold. Vassia closed
her hand over the necklace Sol had given her in her pocket.
Please God the Nazis didn't start searching people. That would
be the end for her.

Feeling nauseous with worry and apprehension, she caught
sight of Nico, proudly carrying Chicky's box. Despite his best
efforts, Chicky didn't seem to want to leave. The little boy took
the bird everywhere with him, hoping that one day he'd decide
to fly off and join his brothers and sisters. Or at least that was
what he said he hoped for. Vassia suspected that he had some of
the same feelings for the bird that she did for Sol. Wanting them
to be free, but simultaneously wishing they would stay for ever.

Vassia shifted her gaze over the rest of the crowd. People
were still arriving, but there couldn't be many still left to come.
The square was already packed. A movement by her side
caused her to look down. It was Nico, squirming his way to the
front, not understanding what was going on but curious to find
out. She hoped Schwarz would not notice him. Nico was only
ten; too young to be involved.

But Schwarz, who had been prowling up and down like a
lion stalking its prey, stopped right in front of the child. His
hand found the gun in its holster and his fingers trailed over it.
Vassia couldn't breathe. What was happening? Schwarz wasn't
going to shoot, was he? A young boy? She was about to scream,
to run and grab her cousin, throw herself in front of the pistol
instead of him.

Schwarz smiled at Nico, and reached out his other hand to
ruffle the boy's hair, like a kindly relative who hasn't seen a
child for a while and cannot believe how much they've grown.
Then Schwarz looked at the bird in the box, gestured towards it,
and seemed to ask Nico a question. Relief flooded over Vassia,
making her feel weak and tremulous. Who knew the
commander was a bird-lover? Nico was beaming back at
Schwarz while chattering away; Vassia could imagine him

telling the man all about Chicky's rescue and rehabilitation. She wondered how much of the Greek Schwarz could actually understand.

Schwarz, bent forward with his arms crossed behind his back, nodded as if interested in what he was hearing. Nico lifted the box higher, as if to invite him to take a closer look. And then, in a trice, Schwarz seized the diminutive bird in his two hands, wrung its tiny neck and, with a smile that mixed utter cruelty with grim satisfaction, casually tossed its dead body to the ground.

All the air seemed to leave the atmosphere as the entire village of Vourvoulos took a collective breath of horrified bewilderment and tried to take in what they had seen, the level of brutality meted out on a defenceless creature.

The silence was broken only when Nico began to cry, great heaving, howling sobs as he stared helplessly at his dead Chicky. In that moment, the little boy seemed as broken as the little bird. For a moment, no one reacted, too stunned to move, and then the child's mother defiantly shoved her way through the crowd to comfort her son, to try to kiss away his pain and anguish.

It was not long after that realisation dawned. The killing of the bird had been act one.

Now the real horror was to begin.

# CHAPTER 24

CARRIE, 2024

The man ran to pick Carrie up but Kris, already right next to her, was there first.

'It's OK,' Kris said, in a tone of marked hostility. Presumably he was wondering why this person was hanging around. 'I've got her.'

Once upright, Carrie ran her hands down her dress a couple of times, in a futile effort to banish the dust as well as buy herself some time to think of what to say. The last person she had expected to see in a car park on Santorini was Jack. Because that was who this person was who'd been driving far too fast.

'How did you get here?' she ended up muttering, tentatively and somewhat meaninglessly. Obviously he'd come on a plane. What she meant was *why* was he here. How did he know he should come, where Carrie was, what was going on? But even as her mind whirred with all these confusing thoughts, she understood that her mother must have told him. It was the only explanation. She didn't have the time or the headspace to be cross with Harriet, and she knew what her argument would be,

anyway – that Jack had a right to know about Nell's disappearance.

Carrie's heart lurched anew as she mentally said the word.
The situation was becoming more of a nightmare with every
hour that passed.

'I got an easyJet flight from Gatwick,' Jack replied. Carrie
remembered how literal he always was. 'Thankfully there are
lots of flights a day at this time of year. I booked the first one I
could. Obviously. I had to come.'

There was an awkward silence, that seemed to be filled by
the silent throbbing of the pulsating sun.

Carrie broke it. 'Um, Kris, this is Jack, Nell's dad.' She
waved her hand vaguely in Jack's direction. 'I guess he's here
to...' Her voice tailed off, overcome by fear and grief, and her
legs wobbled again. Hunger gnawed at her stomach; this,
together with the unfolding tragedy, was making her weak.

'Nice to meet you.' The tone of Kris's voice indicated that it
was anything but. It was the first time Carrie had heard him be
anything but unfailingly polite. The tension was getting to all of
them.

'Carrie, you don't look well at all,' said Jack, his eyes
narrowed with concern. 'Neither do you, mate, if I'm honest.'

Carrie cast an anxious glance at Kris, wondering how he'd
take being referred to as 'mate' by a total stranger, but he didn't
flinch.

'We're tired,' she interjected hastily. 'As you'd expect.'
Vaguely, somewhere in her subconscious, she understood the
men were acting in a rather hostile way to each other, but couldn't
for the life of her think why. Her concern for Nell and Amy had
eradicated anything else from her mind. 'Kris has been searching
for the girls all last night and today. He's gone above and beyond.'

Kris drew his shoulders up and suddenly seemed a foot
taller, almost the same height as Jack. 'I think we should have

something to eat,' he said, in a voice that brooked no argument. 'And work out what to do next.'

He escorted Carrie and Jack to his office, which was located behind the reception area, so that they could eat in private rather than in the busy restaurant. Once he'd flicked the air-conditioning on, the room became instantly cooler. The room housed a huge desk, impeccably tidy, and a small round table, where Kris indicated for them to sit. The obligatory photos of spectacular Santorini sunsets and views adorned the walls. Carrie saw Jack surveying them, but averted her own eyes; the island's incredible beauty felt like an insult at this terrible time.

While Kris went to sort out the food, Carrie filled Jack in with what was going on. She swung from expressing the bald facts, to defensively explaining that she'd had no reason not to let Nell hang out with Amy, to sobbing with fear and anguish. And through it all she had to forget how much she hated Jack, how he had hurt her so irredeemably, how his actions before Nell had even been born were the reason Carrie was a single mother and Nell an only child— But no, she couldn't go there. It would not help. Just try to stick to the now, the dreadful situation they were in, and how to fix it.

Because it must be fixable, mustn't it?

Once Carrie had told Jack everything, a hush descended on the office, broken only by the mechanical whirring of the a/c unit.

'And this bloke,' Jack piped up suddenly, his voice brittle and sharp. 'This...'

'Kris,' said Carrie. 'His name is Kris.'

'Right, Kris,' repeated Jack. 'What... why... who is he, exactly?'

'You know who he is,' replied Carrie, irritatedly. *What the f\*\*\* does it matter who he is,* she wanted to say, *he's helping find my daughter.* The possessive pronoun was definitely 'my', not 'our'. 'He runs this hotel, my friend Xanthe introduced us –

well, reintroduced as we first met years ago, that uni holiday I spent island-hopping – she thought he might be able to help me with my family research... Look, it's too complicated to explain everything now, it'll have to wait for a better time. Suffice to say we're friends – and I couldn't have got through the last day and a half without him.'

Jack frowned. 'And you're—'

The door opened, interrupting Jack and revealing Kris carrying a tray piled high with dishes of meze, followed by an employee with another of drinks. Jack shifted his chair so that Kris had to sit opposite Carrie rather than next to her.

Carrie stared at the food, salivating, her stomach grumbling, but at the same time sure that the tiniest morsel would make her gag. How could she eat when Nell might be starving? When Nell might be... She couldn't finish the sentence.

'Come on,' Kris said coaxingly, pushing a small plate towards her. 'Try to have something. You'll be no good to anyone, least of all Nell, if you pass out from hunger.'

Reluctantly, Carrie took the pastry parcel he handed to her, aware as she did so of Jack glaring at them both. What was wrong with him?

She ate the parcel, which was mouth-wateringly delicious, while doggedly ignoring Jack. She didn't eat another one. Instead she chose the dolmades, which she'd never really liked, as she found the rice too greasy and the vine leaves too tough and stringy. It was bad enough to be eating at all. Having food she actually enjoyed felt like a crime.

Just as the meal was being cleared away, Kris's phone rang, loud and insistent. Carrie's heart skipped a beat as she watched him answer it, scrutinising his face for any clue as to who it was and what was being said. As the conversation continued, the expression on his face grew grim and his skin paled beneath the tan.

'Efharisto,' he said eventually. 'Thank you. Bye.'

He put the phone down and stared at it for a second that
seemed to last for millennia.

'What?' snapped Carrie. 'Was that the police? What's
going on?'

For one moment a look of despair clouded Kris's face, and
then, almost instantaneously, he corrected it and plastered on a
smile.

'OK, so it seems that the girls hired a moped yesterday afternoon,' he explained. 'Amy had fake ID declaring her to be
eighteen.'

Carrie's mouth fell open in disbelief. She'd thought Amy
was so nice, so reliable. That she'd be good for Nell, unlike her
undesirable friends back home. She'd thought that they couldn't
get into trouble in such a small place, just the two of them. How
could she have got it so wrong?

'The police are therefore now working on the theory that
they've had an accident.'

He didn't need to say the rest. On a tiny island like this,
wherever they had come off the bike they wouldn't have been
far from civilisation and someone to help them. The fact that
they hadn't sought such help indicated that they were injured,
or worse. A terrible vision of Nell and Amy, bruised, battered
and broken, hidden from view on some side road or goat track,
filled Carrie's mind.

'Nooo...' The jagged cry burst from the depths of her being,
guttural and animal. 'It was my one job!' she screeched, out of
control, unable to stop, jumping to her feet. 'A mother's *one* job
is to keep her child safe. And I couldn't, I didn't, I haven't... I
don't know what to do. I don't know how to do this.' She was
tearing at her hair and staring wildly around her, frantic, beside
herself.

Kris reached out and took her hand. He looked inexpress-
ibly tired and sad. Jack stared at the table.

Carrie lunged for the door, disentangling herself from Kris's grip. 'Kris, I need a car. Or perhaps a moped, so I can go off-road, go where they might have gone. I'm going to comb the island. You can't stop me. No one can.'

She opened the door, teetering on the threshold, then faltered. She'd need documents to hire a vehicle, her driving glasses, a map—

'Whoa,' interjected Jack, suddenly leaping into life. 'Steady on, Carrie. We need to do this properly, make a plan.' He glanced at Kris. 'The police must be searching, no? A coordinated search, so all parts are covered and everyone knows where everyone else is looking. That's how it works, isn't it?' He flicked his gaze between Kris and Carrie as if daring them to dispute the accuracy of his understanding.

Carrie glared defiantly back at him. 'Whatever. The police can do whatever they think is right, but I can't just sit around waiting. I'm going out to find my daughter.'

Jack leapt out of his chair. 'OK, OK. Let's go together. I've got my hire car. We'll go in that.'

He marched over to where Carrie stood between the table and the door. She didn't want to go with Jack, she wanted to stay with Kris. But he had done enough already, and looked about to drop; he probably shouldn't be driving until he'd had a rest.

'Will you try to get some sleep?' she asked him, trying to modulate her voice so it sounded like a suggestion rather than an order. 'You've done so much.'

'I think I will,' Kris agreed. 'But just a couple of hours. I'll be back on the case soon, I promise, once I've recharged my batteries.'

'Thanks for everything,' Carrie added, as Jack opened the door to leave. 'I can't thank you enough.'

'For sure,' answered Kris, with a sweet but tired smile.

In the car, Jack handed Carrie his phone. 'We should work in squares,' he said. 'Keep a record of everywhere we've been so we don't end up going over and over the same ground.' He started the engine. 'Is there anywhere you can think of that they might have gone to on this scooter? Anywhere Nell wanted to visit but you couldn't get to because you don't have your own vehicle?'

Carrie racked her brains. 'I can't think.' Nell hadn't mentioned anything she particularly wanted to do, had she? 'I don't know.'

And then something came to her, filtering into her consciousness through the fug of dread, fear and distress. 'It's a long shot,' she muttered, 'it might be stupid. But...' She couldn't be bothered to explain the whole story of Sol, and Vassia, and Vassia's lost brother, Andreas; it seemed to belong to another age, to be part of another life. Carrie could hardly remember it. But Nell had been interested in the mystery, much more so than Carrie had imagined she would be. Penelope had spoken of the caves near Vourvoulos, the legend of the dead SBS man, the missing artefacts. What had Nell's last words to her been? That she and Amy wanted to follow up on what the old ladies had told them? Could Nell and Amy have tried to find the caves? It was possible. In fact, the more Carrie thought about it, the more likely it appeared.

'Let's go to Vourvoulos,' she told Jack. She programmed it into Google Maps on his phone and hit 'Go'.

'Take a right out of here and then next right,' she instructed.

The one-way street outside the hotel was busy with cars, motorbikes and tourists sauntering along, not looking where they were going, wandering into the middle of the road, seemingly heedless of vehicles. Jack made slow progress and Carrie clenched her fists and chewed the inside of her cheek, willing all these idiots to get out of the way.

By the time they'd pulled clear of the crowds, Carrie was so wound up she felt nauseous. She opened the window and watched the now familiar scenery flashing by. The gleaming buildings, the verdant vineyards, the pristine hamlets glistening in the sun seemed like a personal affront. How could they be so cheerful when Carrie was so broken?

Instead of the gorgeousness that surrounded her, all Carrie could see was her precious daughter through all her ages and stages.

Nell, so small, in hospital wrapped in that standard-issue, flimsy gown, about to have her breastbone broken, her heart exposed and operated on. Holding the anaesthetic mask over her face, watching her flail and kick and then, all of a sudden, stop. The hours the operation had taken had seemed like years, but these hours now seemed even longer, because then she had known Nell was in good hands, that everyone was working for her, gunning for her. Now, she could be anywhere. With anyone. Or all alone. It was unbearable to contemplate.

Nell, on her first day at primary school, her beaming smile and red cardigan, the belief that emanated from her that this was the start of a whole new life.

Nell, on her twelfth birthday, at the riding school party that Carrie had spent six months saving up for.

Nell's words as she had set out to meet Amy echoed in Carrie's mind: there's nothing more important than family. But without Nell, there was no family.

Letting out a sob, Carrie buried her face in her hands, trying to block out the memories. They were not all she had. There would be more. Nell would be found and all would be well. She had to believe it.

They reached Vourvoulos.

'What do you think?' asked Jack, paused at a junction. 'Which direction?'

'We need to find the caves,' said Carrie. 'Try down there.' She indicated a track that led towards the sea.

Jack obeyed. The car rumbled down the uneven road and they soon arrived at the marina. The wind was up and choppy

waves topped by white horses buffeted the concrete quay.
Carrie looked despondently out of the windscreen.

'I don't know exactly where these caves are,' she said,
sounding as defeated as she felt. 'Or even approximately.'

Jack sighed. 'We'll have to seek them out then, won't we.'

They got out of the car. On the hills behind them stood
several ancient windmills converted to luxury holiday homes. It
would have been so picturesque, in any other circumstances.
They trudged along the seafront and eventually came to some
fisherman's caves carved into the cliff. They were deserted, only
a scattering of litter, squashed drinks cans, plastic bags and
cigarette butts to indicate that anyone had ever been there, but
nothing that pointed to Nell and Amy's presence.

After they'd been searching for over an hour, Carrie sank to
the ground.

'I don't think they're here. I'm not feeling it.'

Jack shoved his hands into his jeans pockets. He must be
hot, wearing that heavy denim, thought Carrie.

'OK, let's get back in the car, drive around a bit. We can go
off-road if the suspension will take it. If it gets knackered, who
cares? The important thing is finding Nell.'

Carrie hauled herself to her feet.

'Yup,' she answered.

They drove and drove, down every little lane and track they
could find. It was getting late, seven o'clock, when they found it.
Carrie screamed so loudly that Jack, applying the brakes too
quickly, stalled the engine.

'There!' she shouted. 'Just there, behind that bush. I saw
metal, I know I did.'

She was out of the car in seconds, and flying across the
rough scrubland studded with stunted, windblown bushes. As
soon as she got closer, she saw that she was right. It was a
moped, propped up behind a giant prickly pear. There was no
one in sight who could have put it there. Carrie realised she

didn't know the registration number of the one the girls had hired. But surely this was it.

She surveyed the surrounding landscape, barren and bare under the darkening sky. If it was theirs, then where on earth were they? Carrie might have found the moped, but there was still no sign of either Nell or Amy.

# CHAPTER 25

VASSIA, 1944

Schwarz stepped forward to speak. For a moment, the thrumming of blood in Vassia's ears was so loud she couldn't hear what he was saying. And then the words started to make sense, but also didn't, because they were too appalling, too awful.

'All males over fourteen years of age must come forward.' Schwarz's stentorian tones filled the square and bounced back off the whitewashed buildings.

A murmur, quickly suppressed, rose up from the crowd and the tension, which had already felt unbearable, ratcheted up another couple of notches. The pendant bit into the flesh of Vassia's palm as her grip tightened round it.

At first, nobody moved. Schwarz stood, his mean, disparaging eyes roving over the untidy ranks of villagers like he was examining a particularly motley bunch of raw recruits. He wrinkled his nose as if he'd smelt something bad.

And then, very slowly, as if being drawn by a puppet-master gently but expertly pulling the strings, Ianos stepped forward.

Schwarz went right up to him, their noses almost touching, and stared the mayor up and down in a way designed to intimidate. Vassia watched on, unable to truly comprehend what was happening. She wanted to shut her eyes but knew that, if she did, she'd lose her balance and fall over. Her mother's grip on her arm tightened and Vassia moved her feet a little to plant herself more firmly on the ground.

Following Ianos' example, Andreas also stepped forward and then, one by one, all the village men joined them.

'Good,' snapped Schwarz. 'We can begin.'

Despite her best efforts, Vassia's legs shook. She could feel her mother quivering also. An utter and deathly silence had descended on the square, and now the sun went in and it suddenly felt cold. Vassia pulled her mother closer to her, to shelter her in her own warmth.

'Those who were responsible for helping the enemy must confess,' Schwarz continued, his harsh, grating voice filling the air like a thundercloud. 'Or every one of you will suffer the consequences.' At this, the soldiers flanking him on either side cocked their rifles as if to emphasise the message.

'They burn villages that don't cooperate,' someone close to Vassia whispered. 'All the houses destroyed, everything razed to the ground.' Within moments, the words were winging their way from one person to another and people were looking anxiously at each other and at Schwarz.

He had all the power. He could do anything he liked. And he knew it.

A dreadful sensation of light-headedness washed over Vassia. She had helped. She should be standing up there with the men. It wasn't fair, it wasn't right, that she should be spared. Spared from what, she wasn't sure. Torture? Imprisonment? Either way, it would be better if it were her than Andreas, a new father with a worn-out wife and a poorly baby.

She made as if to join the men, but found she couldn't move. Her mother was anchored to her arm, holding her back with all her strength. 'You are not going up there,' she hissed under her breath at Vassia. 'I will die before I let you go.'

Vassia faltered, torn between her ingrained sense of justice and her mother's desperate exhortations. As she watched help-lessly on, overwhelmed by terror, but also by anger at the humil-iation Schwarz was so vindictively dishing out to the villagers, her father put up his hand.

'I was one.' His voice was firm and steady, with no hint of fear.

Without a second's pause, two of the soldiers took hold of his shoulders and wrenched him towards them. As Ianos stum-bled in their grip, Vassia saw how pronounced his limp had become. A huge sweat stain covered his back and his salt-and-pepper hair was plastered to his scalp. His diabetes and bad heart made him sweat profusely when put under any pressure or strain. Vassia put her head in her hands. This would exacer-bate his condition, perhaps irrevocably. Her kind, generous father, so wise and level-headed, was being treated like an animal.

When she looked up again, she could hardly believe her eyes. Next to her father, being roughly held by more Nazis, were Kostas and Elias, and then Helios and Lefteris. Vassia met Andreas's gaze. His eyes were wild and desperate. He had helped by taking the commandos food, but how could he jeop-ardise his wife and son's future by confessing? On the other hand, how could he let others take a punishment that he would not?

Vassia saw him picking up his foot to make a move. Oh God, her father and her brother, both taken...

Casually, Schwarz strolled up and down the line of those men who had not moved out of the larger group. He drew level with Andreas and, without pausing, pushed him backwards. Vassia gasped. Surreptitiously, she tried to see if anyone else had noticed what Schwarz had done, but it was impossible to tell. Everyone was immobile with fear, quite literally petrified.

Had Schwarz's action been motivated by his fondness for Andreas, his favourite waiter at his favourite restaurant? Vassia couldn't think of any other explanation.

Schwarz scrutinised the five men who now stood separated from their community, from their mothers and fathers, wives, sons and daughters. The silence was loaded with fear and hatred. It seemed to last for ever.

Schwarz snapped his fingers and the henchmen bundled the men into a corner of the square. Ianos was speaking; his words floated towards Vassia as if from a nightmare.

'It was me,' he said. 'Just me. I was the one who organised the help. I should take the punishment.'

Schwarz considered this for a moment.

'It was all of you,' he declared, his voice a dull monotone. And then, with one deft movement, he whipped his pistol from its holster and fired.

Five shots, in rapid succession, rang out across the village square.

# CHAPTER 26

## CARRIE, 2024

Jack arrived by Carrie's side, jiggling the car keys anxiously in his hand. Momentarily, he placed a restraining hand on Carrie's arm, then retracted it almost immediately as if conscious of overstepping a boundary.

'Don't touch it,' he instructed her. 'Just in case...'

Carrie didn't even want to think in case of what. Distractedly, she waved away his words and strode across the rocky ground, with no real idea where she was going. Jack caught up with her and blocked her way.

'Carrie, we need to think this through,' he said. 'First of all, we should call the police, inform them, check whether this is the moped the girls hired. And then – well, we might need an ambulance, paramedics, I don't know.'

Perhaps he was right, but Carrie didn't care. She refused to be put off. It might take ages for the police to get there, it might take just minutes. Either way, she wasn't prepared to wait when time was of the essence. She pulled her phone out of her bag and called Kris. He answered on the fifth ring, his voice bleary and thick with sleep. She felt awful for waking him, but she had a profound sense of needing him there. He knew the island, knew the terrain, even after such a short time knew *her*. At that moment, Carrie needed him more than anything or anyone she'd ever needed in her life before.

As she explained their discovery of the moped, Kris listened in silence. When Carrie had finished, he got her to tell him exactly where the scooter was, and the number plate, and told her he would call the police straight away, as well as the other emergency services. And he'd be there as soon as he could: twenty minutes or so.

Carrie turned to Jack. 'Kris is coming,' she said, tersely. 'He'll be here soon. You and I should spread out in the meanwhile, keep calling the girls' names. Surely they wouldn't have walked that far from the scooter.' Gazing around her, eyes narrowed against the brisk wind that was sweeping down the hillside, bringing dust and fine grit with it, she pointed to the right. 'You go that way. I'll try here.' She gestured in the opposite direction.

Jack opened his mouth to say something but then obviously thought better of it. 'OK,' he agreed.

Carrie began to walk forward, calling out every other step. 'Nell! Amy! Nell!'

Her calls yielded nothing. No sign of Nell, or of Amy. She searched on until, on high alert for the slightest sound, she heard Kris's car. He was driving fast down the stony track, bouncing over the uneven surface. Carrie had a fleeting thought about Amy's parents' jeep; it would be a better vehicle for these conditions. And they should be here, shouldn't they? They'd want to know...

The police would tell them, Carrie told herself. She could only focus on the here and now.

Kris was out of the door almost before the car had halted. He ran over to Carrie and threw his arms round her in a spontaneous embrace. It felt good to be held by him, and his presence gave her renewed energy and hope for the search. Amy and

Nell were young, and even with Nell's heart issues, they had the resilience youth brought. They would be able to survive a lot.

The three of them continued to search in an ever-widening area around the moped. Time passed and Carrie wondered where the police were. She had been right to insist they conduct their own exploration. But it was getting darker, making it harder to see and get their bearings.

She carried on looking, and calling. Her cries sounded thin, reedy and insubstantial, each one swallowed up by the wind. Kris and Jack's voices were louder and deeper, and seemed to carry much further. As she watched them, the latent animosity between them suddenly became obvious to her; the two men were keeping twenty metres or so apart, as if separated by an invisible force field. She dismissed the notion as soon as it occurred to her – she couldn't be bothered with anybody else's feelings. Managing her own was difficult enough.

They didn't seem to be getting anywhere though, any of them. Carrie strode purposefully over to Kris, hoping he might have some more or better ideas of what to do. As she drew level with him, she saw in the half-light his taut, tense expression. Her heart went out to him. He had taken on the stress of a search for two teenagers he barely knew, and Carrie felt so guilty. If it hadn't been for her need for a guide, and Xanthe's bright idea that Kris would perfectly fit the bill, he'd never have got involved in any of this, would not have had his life turned upside down in this way. It was all her fault, in the end.

She reached out and rested her hand on his arm. 'Are you all right?' she asked. 'I'm sorry for all this trouble; please don't feel you have to stay. Jack's here now – we can sort it out together.'

Kris's expression as he regarded her was full of sympathy and affection – and something else that she couldn't quite define.

'It's fine,' he replied. 'Please stop apologising. When we find the girls, *they* can say sorry.' He attempted a small laugh, but it petered out before it had really begun. There was no way to lighten the mood.

They stared at each other for a moment, both seeming lost for words.

And then they heard it. Jack shouting. His voice came to them in fits and starts, snatched and toyed with by the wind. Both strained their ears to listen harder and then, the moment it was clear that it really was a cry of alarm, or summons, they turned and looked wildly around. Jack was out of sight and they had to work out where his voice was coming from. Just as they did so, his tall figure appeared from behind a rocky outcrop. He was waving frantically, arms as wide as the windmills on the hill behind them. There was no sign of anyone with him. No one else moved on those barren, volcanic slopes. For a heart-stopping moment Carrie was paralysed. And then she and Kris ran, haring towards Jack, awkwardly tripping and stumbling as they went.

Jack's eyes were bright in the dusk. 'Over here,' he said, breathlessly. 'Quickly. I can't work out exactly where it's coming from but I heard someone returning my call.'

Kris held up a warning hand. 'Be careful. This is where the caves are, the ones Penelope told us about, that they used to play in but were told to avoid. I thought they had all been filled in once the shafts became unstable but perhaps not, or perhaps one has opened up again.'

Fleetingly, Carrie recalled Penelope talking about landmines, but she dismissed such thoughts immediately. It was just a tall story, told to make the children stay away from somewhere potentially dangerous. There was no way on such a small island that mines could have lain undisturbed for eighty years. She had to believe that was the case.

Creeping along, feeling the way with tentative hands, the

three of them inched over the stony, dusty ground. Jack continued calling, his voice rhythmic and regular. At first there was no response. And then suddenly they all heard it. A faint cry, a whisper of sound, floating upwards as if from the bowels of the earth.

At first the calls were hardly discernible, but then came another, louder and stronger.

'Help! Help us! Down here. We're down here.'

Neither Vassia nor her mother saw the bodies being carried away. Thalia collapsed to the ground in a dead faint as her beloved husband of twenty-five years, along with four of the village's young men, lads who were four mothers' and fathers' pride and joy, were executed for their part in helping the SBS commandos. Crouched down beside her mother to tend to her, fanning her gently with her hands and trying to coax her back to consciousness, Vassia struggled to process what she had just witnessed.

The commandos had come to Santorini with the dual purpose of disrupting the Nazis' hold on the island and their communication network in the southern Mediterranean, and in that they had succeeded. But they had failed to assassinate Schwarz. And the result of that failure was the terrible vengeance that had been wrought upon Vourvoulos that day.

It could have been any village, Vassia couldn't stop thinking, Agios Georgios, Perissa, Kamari, anywhere on the accessible coastline of the island. And if it had been another village, it would have been another mayor, other young men.

But it had been Vourvoulos.

If only Sol and his group had been lucky, found Schwarz at home, captured him... But then she remembered Sol's words that night, which seemed a million years ago but was in fact less than a week. 'We do not expect to take many prisoners. It's not Andersen's way.'

What was the phrase? *Live by the sword, die by the sword.* This wasn't a game, this was war. And in war, people got hurt, and often those people had done nothing wrong except try to protect their communities or fight for their freedom.

Her father had been noble, honourable, honest and, above all else, courageous. His many good qualities would live on in people's memories. But knowing that wasn't helpful right now. He was still dead.

At this, Vassia found herself weeping, huge salty tears flowing down her cheeks and dropping onto the dusty cobblestones beneath her feet. Her mother opened her eyes, saw Vassia crying and promptly closed them again, before slowly managing to sit up and take in the world around her, a stunned expression on her face.

A couple of friends helped Vassia to get Thalia to her feet and escort her back to the house. Vassia took her mother to her bedroom and encouraged her to get into bed, where she lay staring at the ceiling with unseeing eyes. In the courtyard, Vassia plucked some fresh mint leaves from a terracotta pot and made tea, going through the motions of filling the kettle, putting it on the stove and pouring the boiling water into the glass as if she were a machine working automatically.

Every now and again, the grief bubbling inside her threatened to well up and overflow, erupting like the terrible volcano that had rent the ancient landmass apart all those centuries ago. She herself felt split open, eviscerated by raw and extreme emotion, so intense she did not know what to do with it.

Somehow, Vassia got through the night, and the next day. She knew she must go to Sol, must take him the food and water without which he would not survive, must tell him what had happened. But for the first twenty-four hours after the nightmare of the executions, she was incapable of doing so. The simple acts of cooking, loading up her basket, walking to the cave, were simply too much to contemplate.

And then there were her feelings to contend with, a bewildering, writhing, seething mess of conflicting emotions, that started with whether it was Sol's fault, at least in part, that her father was dead, for coming to Santorini in the first place, and ended with the stark fact that, despite everything, the love she felt for him was undiminished.

When she went to the cave Sol did his best to comfort her. His kindness and empathy was always in Vassia's mind as she and Andreas helped their mother to plan Ianos' funeral. The day came and went, and then more days, and somehow they got through them, though nobody really knew how. To make matters worse, in the weeks that followed the raid and the reprisals, concerns for baby Atlas resurfaced. It was around mid-May, when he was less than a month old, that Atlas' health seemed to deteriorate further. Vassia arrived at the house one afternoon to find Athena in bed, clutching her baby to her. The windows were tightly shuttered and the room was stuffy and hot. Vassia longed to throw them open and let in the sunshine and fresh air, but draughts were bad for infants. Bending over Atlas and peering at his tiny, pale face wrapped up in a sheet, Vassia could not help but notice his blue-tinged lips and the way every breath seemed to be a struggle.

'He's not feeding well,' murmured Athena, her eyes moist with tears. 'The doctor will come tomorrow, to check his heart again.'

Vassia held on to the bedhead in an attempt to steady herself. She thought of the toll Ianos' heart problems had taken on him, how he had been sapped of energy but tried so hard to hide his struggles so as not to worry the family. She had hoped against hope that Atlas was not similarly afflicted. But it seemed that her wishes and prayers had been in vain.

'Wh-what can the doctor do?' she managed to say, trying not to cry. It was important that Athena didn't see other people panic.

Athena shrugged as her tears fell, and Atlas gave a weak, pathetic wail as the movement rocked his tiny frame. 'There is a medicine that could help,' she said through sobs, 'but only the Germans have supplies of it. So...'

She left the sentence trailing and Vassia didn't need help filling in the gaps. There was no way the Nazis would share their drugs with the traitorous islanders, least of all anyone from Vourvoulos.

'Would you like to hold him?' Athena asked. It was a generous offer, as Vassia could imagine that she didn't want to let him go, and normally she would have been only too eager to give a newborn a cuddle. But Atlas seemed so delicate that she was scared to touch him, let alone pick him up, and had not yet done so.

Athena was already securing the sheet round the baby in readiness for Vassia to take him, so she couldn't voice her concerns. Instead, she allowed Athena to place the infant in her arms. He was light as a feather, seeming hardly heavier than Chicky, although of course he must be. Vassia pushed the memory of the bird from her mind; that way only more floods of tears lay.

'He's so sweet,' she whispered to Athena, without taking her eyes off the sleeping baby, keeping her voice low so as not to disturb him. 'So absolutely adorable.' Infinitely carefully, she lifted him a little closer and bent to kiss his forehead.

Athena nodded. 'I know. And I can't bear it if... I wouldn't be able to carry on if...'

Immediately Andreas, who had just come into the bedroom, was by her side, soothing her with a calm hand on her shoulder.

'Shush, shush,' he said, 'don't fret. It will be all right. I'll make sure of that, I promise you.'

Vassia understood why he was saying such things but at the same time she worried that her brother's promise was a hollow one. How could he make it all right? If the Nazis had the medicine and the islanders didn't, what on earth could, or would, a humble waiter be able to do about it?

Half-reluctant and half-relieved, Vassia gave Atlas back to Athena. He was so frail and delicate, she was terrified of harming him by holding him too tight or loving him too much. Because even though he wasn't hers, Vassia felt a visceral, fierce adoration for the infant; she couldn't imagine her feelings being stronger even for her own child.

In the kitchen on her way out, she tried to say something consolatory to Andreas, but the words stuck in her throat. Andreas was sloshing muslin cloths around in a bowl of water that stood on the kitchen counter. As Vassia watched, struck dumb with concern for her brother and his baby, he began wringing the cloths out, doing it so violently that the veins stood out on his hands. Vassia could see the tension in them, and the worry.

'He vomits a lot,' Andreas said, answering a question that Vassia hadn't asked. 'I think it's because of what's wrong with him... it makes him weak and he can't swallow the milk down or something. The doctor – he said so many different things and it gets confusing.'

Joining him at the sink, Vassia picked up a muslin and squeezed the water out of it.

'We're getting through a lot of these!' Andreas went on, trying, and failing, to make it sound like a joke.

Vassia put the muslin down. On the kitchen table sat Athena's knitting, the needles stabbed into the wool and standing upright, as if ready and waiting to be picked up again. Andreas saw the direction of her gaze.

'Athena was making him a shawl,' he said. 'For winter.' He stopped and the air was suddenly leaden with pessimism. 'If he ma-makes...' Her brother was unable to finish the sentence but Vassia knew what he'd been going to say. *If he makes it. If he survives that long.*

Andreas was crying and Vassia went to him and put an arm round his shoulders. They had always stuck by each other; a perceived unfairness from one of their parents or grandparents, a squabble with a friend, a telling-off by a teacher. Minor stuff, when looked back at, but seeming serious at the time.

'He'll be all right,' she reassured her brother. 'Try not to fret. You need to stay strong for them both.'

Through his tears, Andreas nodded, then wiped his nose with the back of his hand and stood up taller, throwing his shoulders back. He turned a quizzical gaze on his sister.

'There's something different about you,' he said abruptly. 'I'm not sure what it is. You seem on edge. Are you hiding something?'

On the one hand, Vassia was surprised at his perceptiveness, but on the other, not at all. They knew each other so well. She took a deep breath and explained about Sol.

Andreas looked stunned. 'I didn't realise there were any commandos left on the island,' he murmured in disbelief.

'Well, there are,' replied Vassia. 'Or rather there is. One. I took him to that old cave that used to be a shepherd's shelter, you know, the one we found years ago. And it's my job to take care of him.' She halted, holding up her hand to stop Andreas from saying anything. 'And you are not even going to think about helping out. All your energy and attention is for your wife and son. So don't even suggest—'

'I won't,' interrupted Andreas. 'You're right, I can't.'

'Leave it to me,' Vassia stressed once more. And then she picked up the bowl with the wrung-out muslins. 'I'll hang these up,' she told him. 'And then I must go. But I'll be back tomorrow. Try to get some sleep.'

As she left, she shuddered at the thought that tiny Atlas might follow their father to the grave... It couldn't happen, wouldn't happen. Surely God would not be that cruel?

Once back at her house and having checked on her mother, who since the funeral spent most of her time in an almost catatonic state in bed, Vassia put on her apron and began to cook. She had mouths to feed, including herself. She'd barely been able to manage a morsel since the executions, but she knew she needed to keep her strength up so that she could support her mother – and Sol.

In the end, it was gone ten p.m. by the time she set off for the cave. She was surprised that the Nazis had not imposed a curfew on the islanders, but perhaps they realised there was no need. With the arrival of the extra troops from Milos, and the reprisals in the village square, they would have known that everyone was too terrified to dabble in collaborating again.

Except that Vassia wasn't. Or at least, she was but it was irrelevant. However great her fear, she must look after Sol; she had a duty to do so, and that was that.

At the cave, she hesitated for a moment before descending, looking around her carefully, scanning the open countryside that led down to the sea, night-dark and ominous. Listening intently, she used her ears as well as her eyes to detect any signs of a threat.

Nothing.

Without further ado, she scrambled down the steps, giving Sol a low call of warning as she did so to alert him to her presence. When she got to the bottom, he was waiting, his handsome face upturned, his arms outstretched before him.

With a huge great gulping sob, Vassia fell into his embrace, put her head against his warm, solid chest and cried and cried.

'I'm so sorry,' he groaned, holding her tightly. 'All of this is my fault, our fault, the SBS, Andersen, all of us... The reprisals, the danger you're in... I'm so sorry.'

'No!' Vassia's tone was commanding. 'It's nobody's fault but the Nazis'. They caused this, all of it.' She flung an arm out wide to encompass the island, Europe, the world. 'They are the only ones to blame.'

Sol hardly seemed to be listening. 'Can you ever forgive me?' He turned to look at her, grabbed her wrists and held them, forcing her to return his gaze. 'You and your brother have lost a father, your mother has lost her husband.' He paused and gulped as if holding back tears. And then he continued, in the softest, saddest tone imaginable, 'I've said it so many times already, but every time I see you so upset I need you to know that I'm sorry. So very sorry.'

Now it was Vassia's turn to take him in her arms. 'It's not your fault,' she repeated over and over again as they clung to each other. 'I know my father would not want you to think that.' She sniffed loudly, wiping her eyes with the back of her hand. 'I'm upset today about baby Atlas as much as anything else. After all, he's the future. Or at least he should be...' With that, her sobs redoubled, until eventually she managed to stem them enough to explain to Sol about the renewed worries over the baby's ailment.

'Oh, Vassia, that is terrible for you all,' exclaimed Sol. 'Poor Athena, poor Andreas. Poor little Atlas.' He raised his arms in a gesture of helplessness and then drew Vassia close, rocking her gently in shared grief.

Eventually, knowing she shouldn't stay too long, Vassia disentangled herself from Sol and laid out the food. He ate hungrily while she watched on, hugging her knees and, despite everything, enjoying the sight of him relishing what she had prepared.

'I wish you could teach me to cook all these dishes you bring,' said Sol, once his appetite was sated. He was clearly trying to take Vassia's mind off all the bad news. 'Everything is so tasty.'

Vassia chuckled. 'Men don't usually cook on Santorini,' she explained. 'It's women's work. Is that different in your country?'

Sol lit a cigarette and thought about it for a moment. 'Not really. Women do the cooking at home. But in all the great restaurants, the chefs are mostly men. Harumph.' He snorted derisively. 'So I suppose I deduce from that that cooking is a man's job when people are paying to eat the food and a woman's when they're not.'

Vassia had never really looked at the issue this way before. It had never occurred to her that it mattered who did what chores. On Santorini, everyone worked hard, no matter what they were actually doing. Though the men did heavy work like quarrying the pumice stone, when it came to harvest time for the grapes and tomatoes everyone pitched in, males and females alike.

Sol's words caused Vassia to once again blush at her own ignorance. She had no idea how the rest of the world operated.

'Penny for them,' said Sol, teasingly.

Vassia looked at him quizzically.

'It looks like you're thinking of something important,' he explained. 'I was wondering what it was.'

Smiling, Vassia waved her arm in a dismissive gesture. 'I was imagining a British woman being head of a bank or some great enterprise,' she explained. 'Can women over there do things like that?'

Sol shrugged. 'I'm sure they could. I don't see why not. Someone told me not long ago that back home they've learnt to fly planes so that they can deliver them from one airfield to another. And they're doing intelligence work, too, deciphering codes and whatnot.'

'Gosh.' Vassia sat back, absorbing this information. It struck her with a stab of horror that her ambition of being a teacher was tiny and insignificant compared to what the bold, brave, well-educated women of northern Europe were doing. Sol would probably much prefer this other breed of female who was strong, capable and intelligent—

'They're no better than you, though,' Sol continued, interrupting Vassia's thoughts, reading her mind. 'No braver than you. What you're doing is incomparable.'

His eyes were on Vassia, assessing her, seeing how she would react. Heat rose in her cheeks.

'I don't think so,' she mumbled, dropping her gaze.

'Well I do.' He moved over to be closer to her, taking her in his arms. 'I think you're amazing. The very best, and bravest. Don't ever think differently.'

Vassia still wasn't entirely convinced. But the proximity to him, the touch of him, made all other doubts and uncertainties melt away. She banished her mental images of those English women, with their fair skins and blonde hair, who had ten times more knowledge and confidence than her, and focused on the here and now, on Sol's arms round her, his mouth on hers. As darkness descended outside and a myriad stars came out to adorn the night sky, she forgot about the outside world and focused only on Sol, and her love for him.

Who knew how much longer they'd have together?

# CHAPTER 28

## CARRIE, 2024

Carrie's heart stood still.

'Nell,' she shouted. 'Nell! It's Mum. I'm here, you're OK, we're coming to get you.' Frantically, she flicked her gaze between Kris and Jack. 'Where are they?' she hissed, not wanting the girls to hear that despite her assurance they still didn't know exactly where to find them.

Jack fell to his hands and knees and began to crawl forward, in between large boulders and tussocky clumps of wild grasses. He was silent now, listening intently, trying to follow the sound of the girls' responses. Kris and Carrie followed.

And then Jack stopped, abruptly. 'Down here,' he said. 'There's a hole, look, you can see marks here where they must have slipped...'

As she craned her neck and tried to make out what Jack had uncovered, Carrie's blood stilled in her veins in desperate anticipation. Jack called out again. 'Nell, Amy. We're here. Don't move. We're coming to get you.'

Jack lay down on his front and shone the torch on his phone down into the hole. When he sat back up his face was ashen, his eyes sunken with relief and fear. 'They're there,' he reported.

'They're both – I saw them both. Now we've got to get them out.'

'I've got a rope in the car that I use for my boat,' Kris said. 'I'll go and get it, and some water, too. You two stay here and keep them talking. I'll call the police again as well. They should have been here ages ago, and the fire service and paramedics. And Amy's parents...' He disappeared into the darkness.

'Thanks,' said Carrie distractedly. She couldn't care less about the emergency services. She just wanted to get the girls out. 'Let me see them,' she went on, almost shoving Jack out of the way so that she could peer down the hole. By the wavering light of her phone, gripped in her shaking hand, she could make out, a long way down, Nell and Amy huddled together, clutching each other and staring upwards, desperate to be rescued.

Carrie did not realise she was crying until she smelt the dusty ground beneath her becoming damp. Trying to stifle the tears, she spoke to them. 'It's all right now, girls, you'll be out soon. Everything's going to be OK. Hold tight. We love you.'

Despite the distance that separated them, Carrie saw and heard Nell begin to cry. Amy made no sound and Carrie had a sudden, dreadful feeling that she was really hurt.

It seemed like an age before Kris came back. He handed Carrie two plastic bottles of water.

'Here, let me take them,' Jack said. 'We need to drop them carefully.'

Carrie gave the bottles to him. For some strange reason, she wasn't even annoyed with what he'd said, in fact was glad to give him the responsibility of getting the water to the girls. For the first time since he'd arrived she felt a loosening of the tension, the small release from the dead weight of the terror she'd been carrying around since she'd realised Nell was missing. She and Jack could share the burden between them, the burden that, being Nell's parents, only they could really feel.

Kris had a coiled rope draped round his shoulders and, the water successfully dropped down to the girls, Jack reached out for it.

'We could tie it round that rock,' he suggested, forehead creased as he tried to work out the best plan of action. 'And then I could lower myself down.'

'But how does that help get the girls out?' asked Carrie.

'Then I'll attach the rope to one of them and you two can pull them up.'

Carrie looked down at her arms. Did they have the strength to haul a teenage girl out of a hole in the ground? But it was too late to protest. Jack had secured the rope and in a matter of moments was lowering himself down.

Something caught Carrie's eye and she saw flashing lights on the main road, some distance away.

'The fire brigade,' said Kris. 'We should leave it to them.'

'No.' Carrie's response was immediate and forceful. 'There'll be a huge fuss, endless talking, more delays. I want them out, now. We'll do as Jack said.'

The rope was lying on the ground next to her and suddenly it tautened and tightened.

'We're ready to go.' Jack's voice floated up from the depths below. 'Amy first. Pull, now!'

Kris and Carrie gripped the rope and leant back into it, heaving and hauling with all their might. The harsh fibres rubbed against Carrie's flesh and the pain was intense, but she took no notice.

Suddenly, Amy's head emerged from the cave entrance. 'Help her,' hissed Kris from between pursed lips. He used all his weight to keep Amy's position stable while Carrie grabbed her under the arms and heaved her upwards. With a final surge of effort, the two of them fell to the ground, Amy on top of Carrie. Despite Carrie's earlier worries, Amy seemed unharmed, but she still didn't say anything, as if the awfulness of their ordeal had rendered her speechless.

Trying not to be too brusque, Carrie freed herself from Amy, picked up the rope again and unfurled the slack into the hole. Once again, it tautened, and Jack shouted to them to pull again. This time, it was even harder. Blisters had already formed on Carrie's palms, and they screamed out in pain as she heaved on the rope. How come Nell was so much heavier than Amy?

It was so dark now that she could not see more than a few feet ahead of her, but she heard the pounding footsteps of the firefighters as they approached. Nevertheless, she took no notice. Nell was surely nearly out now; there was no way Carrie was going to stop.

A hand emerged, scrabbling around on the stony soil, trying to get a hold of something. Carrie stared at the hand. It was large, with huge knuckles and nails cut down to the quick – nothing like Nell's small, pale hand with her bright nail varnish and many rings.

Where was Nell? Why wasn't she climbing out? Was it because she was really badly hurt, perhaps even—Carrie stopped herself from thinking the worst. And in the same instant, realisation dawned and her jaw dropped in disbelief.

Was Jack getting *himself* out before his child?

# CHAPTER 29

## VASSIA, 1944

Vassia's eyes ached as she painstakingly stitched the rough brown cloth, straining to see in the flickering light from the oil lamp. She had noticed how ragged and torn Sol's clothes were, not to mention filthy, and had resolved to remedy the situation. She had already altered a pair of her father's trousers so that they would fit the much slimmer Sol, although she couldn't do much about the length – Sol was taller than her father by at least four inches – but she let the hems down as much as she could. Then she had started on two new shirts for him, sitting up late into the evening and rising early in the morning to get them finished.

'Are you still working, Vassia?' her mother asked, as she came into the kitchen for a glass of water.

Vassia nodded, concentrating too hard to speak. There was a pause, during which Vassia could feel her mother's eyes upon her.

'I'm worried about you,' Thalia said, eventually. 'I don't like you being involved. After what happened... you know.'

'I must finish what Papa started,' Vassia told her, simply but insistently. 'I'm not afraid.' She laid the sewing to one side and shifted her gaze to her mother, challenging her to point out that this was a blatant lie. Thalia opened her mouth to say something but shut it again without speaking. She shrugged her resigned acceptance. Like father, like daughter; Vassia was as stubborn and strong-willed as Ianos had been.

It was June now; over six weeks had passed since the raid and Sol was still here. Vassia had almost stopped thinking about when he would leave. Or perhaps she just refused to let herself contemplate the inevitable. When every visit to the cave drew to its end, she found it harder and harder to tear herself away. All she wanted was to be close to Sol, next to him, touching him.

At the same time, and despite the bravado she wore superficially, the fear of being caught lurked deep within Vassia's being. The island was crawling with additional troops, and she was continually worried that walls had eyes; that she was being watched. She had no evidence for this apart from an uncanny sensation that crept over her each time she stole out of the village, sending a shiver down her spine and causing goosebumps on her arms. When her fear threatened to get the better of her, she would tell herself sternly that she was imagining it. And that even if she wasn't, as she continually protested to her mother, she could not leave Sol to fend for himself.

One evening, Vassia packed her bag with particular care. She not only had food to take to Sol but also the clothes she'd made and altered, water for him to wash with, a bar of green olive soap, her embroidery scissors and a mirror; the basket was laden down with so many things. Sol's hair had grown and, as well as washing it as she often did, he had asked her to cut it for him. She was a bit nervous as she had never cut anyone's hair before, least of all that of a man she loved, but how hard could it be?

As she sidled through the narrow alleys while the sun sank in the sky and the shadows lengthened, she longed for Sol to be able to come out of the cave to watch the sunset with her. But of course that was impossible. The only time Sol could leave his hideout to stretch his legs, and use the latrine he had dug and camouflaged, was under cover of complete darkness.

Reaching the edge of the village, Vassia cast a few nervous glances over her shoulder. Thankfully, there was no one about. No one to notice her, no one to question her. But wait. Was that odd? Why were there no villagers going about their business? Why no fishermen coming back from the harbour, no quarrymen returning from site, no farmers arriving home with dirt beneath their fingernails and soil on their calloused hands? Pausing, Vassia pretended to fiddle with her shoe while she attempted to calm her racing heart and think rationally. She had left a little later than usual, that was all. All the men were already in their houses, their womenfolk serving up a hearty evening meal.

Straightening up, she pushed a strand of loose hair behind her ear. She took a deep breath and forced her legs into a walk. She could not give in to her overactive imagination. Somehow, she managed to continue, but when she arrived at the cave entrance her palms were moist with the sweat of fear. She stood for a moment, pushing all worries and doubts out of her mind. Sol lived with enough of those things on a daily, hourly basis. Her visits should provide relief, should lift his spirits, not depress them.

Forcing away her underlying feeling of unease, and plastering a cheery smile onto her face, Vassia cautiously and carefully descended the steep, uneven steps into the cave. Sol was waiting for her, eyes upturned in anticipation. As soon as she was in front of him, he wrapped her in his arms and held her close, then showered her with kisses.

Laughing, all her apprehension dispelled by the joy of seeing him, Vassia eventually pushed him away.

'There's no time for this,' she joked. 'I've got work to do.' She placed her bag on the floor and pulled out the package of food, and the clothes. 'I've brought you these,' she explained, holding out the shirts and the trousers. 'Yours are so tattered and torn.'

Sol looked at her in amazement. 'That's incredible!' he enthused. 'Thank you so much.' He made as if to tear off his own shirt and replace it with one of the new ones, but Vassia intervened.

'Don't get changed yet,' she said. 'I've brought the stuff to cut your hair as well, like you wanted. Let's do that first.' She took out the mirror she had brought with her, propped it on a natural ledge on the cave wall and sat Sol down in front of it. Sol settled into place and sat up straight, eyeing her reflection solemnly.

'So, sir, how would you like your hair today?' Vassia asked him, smiling bashfully. 'I can do short, quite short or very short.'

Sol's grinning face reflected back at her from the mirror. 'I'll have short then, please,' he replied, shifting a little on the cave floor to make himself more comfortable.

'Of course.' Vassia knelt down behind him so as to be the right height. Pursing her lips, she considered Sol's head with its liberal shock of sandy-brown hair. Should she start at the top or the bottom? She really had no idea.

Sol picked up on her hesitation. 'It doesn't have to be a style fit for a king,' he joked. 'I just need it to stay out of my eyes!'

'Right then,' answered Vassia. And then she said, 'Right,' again because it made her sound determined and assured, even though she wasn't in the slightest. She picked up a few strands of Sol's hair and snipped tentatively at them with the small, sharp scissors. Sol was watching her intently in the mirror and she felt suddenly self-conscious in a way she never had before.

'You look so beautiful,' he said, the words blurting forth as if he were unable to keep them inside. 'Iridescent with loveliness.'

A flush crept up Vassia's cheeks. 'Thank you,' she mumbled, not knowing how to react.

'I wish I could capture all of your beauty in my drawings,' he went on, a wistful edge to his voice.

Vassia had resumed her snipping and clumps of hair fell away onto the cave floor.

'To remember you by,' Sol concluded.

Vassia's stomach turned over. In the corner, just discernible in the dimness, was the all-important radio, Sol's only means of communication with the outside world. His means of escape.

She did not want to think of this. Of course she wanted him to survive, to get away. But the thought of him leaving made her impossibly sad, as it always did, like someone was gripping her heart in their fist and squeezing it.

There was a pause, then Sol continued, 'I don't like thinking about it either.'

Vassia blinked in confusion. Had he read her mind again?

'But I'll have to go some day. In fact, on the radio last night I learnt that a boat will be on its way soon. It'll be here in less than a week, all going well.'

A loud clang rang out, echoing back from the rock walls. The scissors had slipped from Vassia's hand as she clutched at the halfpenny pendant that adorned her neck. She always wore it when she visited Sol. A silence descended, deep and absolute.

*All going well.* There was nothing 'well' about it, as far as Vassia was concerned. Frozen, she could not move.

At last, Sol reached out to retrieve the scissors and passed them to her, and she plunged them haphazardly into the next section of hair, chattering away meaninglessly as she struggled to control her anticipatory grief. She had lost her father and would lose Sol, and she wasn't sure that she could bear the pain.

'I'll be helping in the vineyards for a few days soon,' she

burbled, 'you know, checking up on the grapes, a bit of light pruning, fixing the kouloura. They think it's going to be a good year for wine, though it seems too early to tell that yet, but perhaps everyone just wants a reason to be cheerful...' She wittered on, aware that she was probably boring Sol rigid but not caring. She didn't want to talk about him going, couldn't talk about it. The fact that she knew it would happen some day didn't mean that she had to face that fact quite yet.

Eventually, she finished cutting. Sol peered forward to see better; the candles were burning out now. He turned his head from side to side and pulled comical faces as he pretended to admire himself. Despite herself, Vassia had to laugh.

'Do you like it?' she asked, eagerly.

Sol nodded solemnly. 'I think it's most fine,' he replied. 'As good as my barber in Fenchurch Street could do.'

'High praise indeed!' Vassia affected enthusiasm and smiled wanly as she wiped the blades of the scissors on a clean cloth. She had no idea what or where Fenchurch Street was, but knew it must be part of Sol's other life. His real life. The life where she didn't feature.

The news about the impending arrival of the boat added to her pain. Sadly, she cleared up the hair, sweeping it into the cloth and tying the corners to take home and dispose of. 'Come into the far corner,' she instructed. 'And I'll wash it for you.'

She fetched a towel, the olive soap and a jug of water, and they both retreated to a little antechamber for the ablutions. The soap's delicate aroma, redolent with comfort and homeliness, mingled with the heady, masculine scent of Sol himself, making Vassia feel light-headed with love and desire. As she gently massaged his head she sang, a Santorini song of the sea and the land, of love and loss, its lilting melody as old as time itself. Sol closed his eyes as the rhythm ran through Vassia's fingers and the water and into him.

When his hair was washed and towel-dried, they stood up

and faced each other. Vassia appraised her handiwork. The close-cropped style made Sol look older, more serious. And, if this were possible, more handsome than ever. Observing her observing him, Sol smiled. 'Come here,' he said, gruffly, then stepped forward and pulled Vassia into his arms. He bent down towards her. Their mouths met and his kisses sent her heart rate soaring. She knew it was dangerous to be here. She knew it was dangerous to love him so much, a foreigner and a soldier, a man she could never really have.

But there was no way she could stop. No way she could pull back from the brink. She had fallen over the edge of love, head over heels, and she was drunk on it, intoxicated.

It was a long while later that Vassia gathered up her things to leave. She had stayed too late; they both knew it, but had been unable to part. The knowledge that he would be gone soon made them desperate. Passion and longing had won out over fear and dread. But now, she had to go.

At the bottom of the cave shaft, she looked upwards. A profound darkness stared down at her. There was no one there. It was safe to head out.

As quietly and quickly as she could, Vassia ascended the roughly hewn steps. Outside, the air was warmer than in the cave, treacly with the rising temperatures of summer. She paused briefly to look back down and wave goodbye, though she doubted that Sol could see her.

Pushing back her shoulders and straightening her back, she resolutely set off for home, every pore in her body wishing she could stay the night here, with Sol, could curl up in his arms and remain with him.

There was no moon that night; the clouds obscured it and the stars so that the sky was pitch black. Vassia could hardly see her hand in front of her face. All of her senses were on high alert, hearing, smell, taste and touch working twice as hard to make up for the lack of vision.

She smelt it first. The smell of boot polish and hair oil, of leather and gun grease. Then she heard it. Footsteps. The crackle of starched uniforms. The cocking of pistols.

And then her eyes made out figures in the distance.

Watching.

Waiting.

# CHAPTER 30

## CARRIE, 2024

Jack hadn't left Nell behind and climbed out by himself. On the contrary, he was piggybacking Nell out of the cave. The muscles in his arms and the veins on his forehead bulged with the effort and, even by the pale light of the rising moon, Carrie could see the sweat pouring down his face.

With a final, Herculean effort, he managed to get his upper body onto the ground outside the hole, Nell still hanging on like a monkey, eyes closed as if she could not bear to witness what was happening. Kris and Carrie dropped the rope and rushed forward. Together, they lifted Nell off Jack's back and placed her down on a patch of grass. Carrie bent over her, clasping her head to her chest, covering her hair with kisses. Looking down, she saw that Nell's feet were bare and that her right ankle was bent at an unnatural angle and extremely swollen.

'Mum,' croaked Nell. 'I'm so sorry. I didn't mean... my ankle... broken. Sorry. Sor—'

Carrie interjected, shushing Nell and continuing to caress her. 'It doesn't matter, darling, nothing matters except that you're alive, I love you so much, thank God, thank God...' And then, because she had to know, 'What were you doing here? Why didn't you say where you were going?'

Nell closed her eyes and uttered a small, desperate sob. 'I'm s-sorry,' she whispered between heaving breaths. 'We wanted to find the cave, see if the rumours were true. And we did, Mum, they are... some, anyway... we found this... a letter... look inside.' She thrust a rusty tin, the type that might once have held tobacco, at her mother. Gingerly, Carrie opened it, to reveal a piece of paper, wafer-thin and brown with age, that did indeed seem to be a letter, written in Greek, much of the ink so badly faded as to be almost invisible.

'Wh...' Carrie tried to digest this information, but it was too much, too soon, too confusing and before she could ask Nell more her daughter was gazing around with glazed, puzzled eyes. 'What's Dad doing here?' she whispered. 'He got me out, Mum, he picked me up and got me out. We tried to climb up ourselves, Amy did, but she couldn't make it and my ankle hurt too much.'

There was a flurry of activity all around them, firefighters and other looming figures in dark uniforms. Carrie ignored them all. She glanced over at Jack. He'd managed to get into a sitting position and was breathing heavily, his body bent forward, his hands clasping his knees. He looked like someone who'd just run a marathon. No, several marathons on consecutive days. No wonder. He'd carried Nell out of her subterranean prison and brought her to safety. OK, so the fire brigade would have got the girls out eventually. But Jack had done it.

All the pent-up hatred and resentment, the years of hurt, seemed to suddenly dissolve away and Carrie saw Jack with fresh eyes. He really cared about Nell, and perhaps about Carrie, too. After all, he'd been there when they both needed him.

She opened her mouth to say something to him but before

she could get the words out the paramedics were beside them with a stretcher and, within moments, they'd loaded Nell onto it and were bearing her away to a waiting ambulance. Carrie loped along beside them, desperate not to let Nell out of her sight ever again. Suddenly, Jack was by her side, expression grim and determined.

'Wherever they're taking her, I'm coming too,' he panted, still out of breath from his earlier exertion.

Nell tried to sit up on the stretcher. 'Mum, Dad,' she cried out. 'Don't leave me.'

Carrie's heart broke in two. 'No, of course we won't,' she assured her, as Nell disappeared inside the ambulance.

'We go to clinic Fira,' one of the paramedics said. 'Get in please.'

Jack, ahead of Carrie now, leapt aboard. His body blocked Carrie's view of Nell but she could still hear her.

'Mum,' she was saying, her voice wavering, full of incipient tears, 'there's other stuff in that cave, not just the letter, from the war, like the old lady said...'

Carrie's head whirled with everything that was going on, the finding of Nell and Amy, Nell's injury, the news that Penelope's story was, according to Nell, correct... it was too much. She couldn't absorb any of it.

She stepped onto the ramp to enter the ambulance.

'Sorry,' said one of the paramedics, emerging from inside. 'One person only.'

Carrie had no choice but to step off again, to let the man past. In a flash, he'd pressed a button to retract the ramp.

'Wait a minute,' pleaded Carrie. 'What are you doing? I have to be with her, I'm her mother, she needs me...'

'Sorry but it is one person only,' reiterated the man, slamming the doors shut with a resounding clang. 'She has dad. All OK.'

He jumped into the driver's cab and almost instantaneously the engine sprang to life, the wheels began to turn and the ambulance moved off, swaying over the uneven, bumpy ground.

Carrie gazed after it in despair, the wafer-thin piece of paper in her hand fluttering wildly in the wind.

# CHAPTER 31

## VASSIA, 1944

She had known that there were soldiers everywhere. That everyone, especially in Vourvoulos, the traitor village as the Nazis would call it, was under suspicion. She had felt the prickles on her skin when a subconscious sense told her that she, along with everyone else, was under surveillance. And now all her worst fears had been realised.

About two hundred metres ahead of her, a line of uniformed troops formed an impenetrable barrier between her and the village. Were they lying in wait for her? Did they know about the cave, about her movements? About Sol? Her breath caught in her throat as her heart pounded wildly. Desperately, she crouched down behind the inadequate cover of a prickly pear. She wanted to shut her eyes and hide her face in her hands like a child who believes she cannot be seen if she can't see herself. But at the same time, she could not tear her gaze away from the assembled rank of soldiers.

As she stared, she noticed that they were not moving. Perhaps they hadn't spotted her after all. If they had, surely they would have advanced immediately towards her, grabbed her with their iron grips, dragged her away to their prison or execution chamber. Vassia shuddered, then forced herself to stop imagining what may lie in store for her. She couldn't predict or change the future. She could only deal with the now.

And the now involved coming up with a plausible story in case she was apprehended. How could she explain away being out at gone midnight, all on her own, wandering the country-side? Her mind frantically tried to sift through the possible excuses – visiting a sick relative? Out of the question; the direction she was coming from was devoid of housing of any kind and did not lead to another village. Wanting some fresh air? That was a non-starter – who would choose to stray so far away from home, in the pitch black, even if they were feeling stifled by the warm summer night? Needing to stretch her legs? See above; equally unbelievable.

As she crouched, her legs quickly becoming stiff and numb, Vassia's basket slipped from her shoulder and hit the ground with a soft thud. The sound was low and muffled by the under-growth, but nevertheless it sent a thrill of sharp fear searing through her veins. Vassia tensed, waiting for a reaction from the troops positioned so close to her.

Nothing happened. What were they doing? Had they received intelligence about someone's nocturnal movements that had brought them here? Or was this a routine exercise with no particular victim in mind? It was impossible to tell. What-ever the situation, Vassia was in a perilous position right now.

The basket lay beside her, accusing her. It was full of incriminating objects. The bowl in which she had transported the food. The scissors and the hair clippings, wrapped up in the cloth. Sol's old clothes, which she had intended to add to the compost heap, where they would decompose along with the other organic matter. It suddenly struck her that she needed to get rid of these items. Now.

Vassia cast furtive glances around her, barely able to discern anything in the obscurity, as her hands crept towards the rough woven straps to pull them towards her. Conscious of even the slightest noise, she managed to retrieve the cloth and scissors. To lose the latter would be a calamity; a new pair would be almost impossible to find in wartime, as well as to afford. But there was nothing else to be done.

Quietly, but with as much force as she could muster, Vassia drove the blades into the hard, black volcanic soil beneath her feet. If she buried them, perhaps she could retrieve them at some point. Even as she thought this, she had to suppress an ironic burst of laughter. The possibility of being reunited with her needlework tools was not the priority right now. It was unlikely that it ever would be.

What to do with the clothes, and bowl? If she left them here, it would be easy for the soldiers to find them – once they'd found her. Oh God, she couldn't think straight, couldn't form her wild ramblings into any kind of coherent plan of action.

A noise, dreadful and ear-splitting, rent the night. Vassia's blood stilled in her veins as the frenzied baying of hunting dogs filled the air. Narrowing her eyes, she tried and failed to locate them in the obscurity. In her imagination, huge, fierce hounds, desperate for the thrill of the chase, strained at the leash.

A sudden flurry of movement from a different direction sent her pulse racing and her heart pounding once more. There was a momentary pause, and then the barking diminished as the ground beneath her vibrated with the thump of many footsteps. The soldiers were marching forward, still in line, as if searching for something.

For her.

Flashes of torchlight lit up the landscape, sweeping from right to left, momentarily blinding Vassia as her pupils struggled with the repeated changes from light to dark. She was dreadfully exposed, just the huge jutting pads of the prickly pear shielding her from view. As she struggled to make herself as small as possible she accidentally brushed against the two-inch thorns, and gasped in pain as the tip of one ripped through her thin skirt and pierced her skin, oozing an immediate trickle of hot blood.

Looking up to check the soldier's progress, in a burst of a flashlight she saw one of the dogs, massive and fearsome, pulling at its lead. Along with the others it had fallen quiet, but now suddenly began to bark once more, loudly and ferociously, as if it had scented Vassia's blood and was out to get her.

Clenching her fists and ramming them against her face, Vassia held her breath. Once the dogs were let loose, it would be game over. A few horrific moments passed, each one feeling as long as a millennium. Almost crying with terror, Vassia wished it over with. She even contemplated giving in, standing up and facing the men, hands held high in a gesture of surrender, feeling the futility of holding out. If she was going to die, let it happen, painlessly and quickly.

And then in an instant everything changed.

The soldiers began to cheer, and surged as one body towards something that Vassia couldn't see. Released, the dogs careered off at top speed. But not towards Vassia; in the opposite direction, only to abruptly halt somewhere in the middle distance. The men congregated around the pack and Vassia heard cheers and shouts of congratulations.

Straining her eyes, she tried to make out what was happening. One of the men raised his arm, and Vassia saw something dangling from his outstretched hand. What was it? She waited, frozen to the spot. A torch beam rested on the object.

A marten. One of the few mammals that lived on Santorini, a sweet, shy animal that had never done those soldiers any harm. But they obviously enjoyed hunting down innocent creatures. Despite the warmth of the evening, Vassia shivered with a sudden chill as relief flooded through her.

The hunt was over and she had not been the prey.

Gradually, the troops retreated up the hill and over the

brow, back towards Fira and their garrison. Many minutes later, when she finally judged that they were gone and she was safe – for the moment at least – Vassia stood, legs trembling, stiff and unwieldy after being motionless for so long. When she had regained control over her limbs, she emerged from the cover of the prickly pear, once again tearing her skirt as she did so. Looking around her, she double-checked that there were no lingering members of the hunting brigade still on the hillside.

It was completely empty, haunted and lonely under the moonless sky.

Wasting no further time, Vassia headed towards the village and ran. She ran and ran until she reached the courtyard of her little house, where she slowed, catching her breath and attempting to appear composed. Her mother didn't sleep well these days, not since Ianos had been killed, and the smallest noise was apt to wake her. If Thalia got out of bed, Vassia did not want her to have the slightest idea of what had happened that night.

It would more than likely be the death of her.

Slowly and with infinite caution, she entered through the kitchen door, scarcely daring to breathe lest her mother hear. Thalia did not stir. In bed, Vassia was unable to drop off. The events of the evening, the beauty and passion of the time she had spent with Sol ran through her mind, all jumbled up with the horror of what had occurred afterwards. She had been lucky that night. It was unlikely she would be so again.

Every minute of every day, the danger increased.

# CHAPTER 32

## CARRIE, 2024

Two days after the dramatic rescue, Nell sat on the terrace overlooking the caldera with her injured leg resting on a chair, looking pale and wan, but otherwise almost back to normal. Jack and Carrie sat either side of her, handing her cold drinks, checking she'd taken her painkillers, making sure she wasn't getting too much sun, generally fussing over her and tending to her every need.

Kris had sped with Carrie to the hospital that fateful night the girls had been discovered, following the ambulance. Amy's parents, who'd arrived as the ambulance was departing, followed in their hire car. Once there, the doctors had declared that Nell had suffered nothing worse than a badly sprained ankle and dehydration, but they kept her in for twenty-four hours, just to be cautious. Amy had been allowed out straight away.

Once Nell had also been discharged. Kris had insisted that Carrie and Nell come back to his hotel for the remainder of their stay and have one of the best rooms, with a sea view, for which he flatly refused to take any money. Carrie had made a long phone call to Xanthe, explaining the drama that had unfolded since her departure from Santorini, and Xanthe had said that of course Jack could stay in her grandparents' house, he was more than welcome. With the hire car, he could easily travel to Oia whenever he wanted or needed to. And so the matter had been settled.

To Carrie, the fact that Nell was there, alive and well, seemed miraculous. She kept remembering her worst imaginings as the search continued to yield no sign of the girls, and then almost hyperventilating at the horror of what might have been. Stories of people who had succumbed to heat exhaustion on Tenerife, Symi, Corfu rattled around her head, driving her mad. She reined in her anger and resisted shouting at Nell all the things she really wanted to say: '*What were you thinking of, using fake ID, going off without telling anyone, not taking charged phones and water with you, are you both halfwits, do you realise what you've put us all through...*'

The time for the serious conversation would come, but it wasn't now.

The day after the girls had been found, Carrie and Nell were so exhausted that they had spent most of the time napping. Now, finally, both felt somewhat revived.

On Carrie's bedside table sat the tin containing the letter that Nell and Amy had quite literally stumbled across. At first, Carrie had been far too distracted by Nell's health and recovery to even look at it and, once she had done so, it had revealed nothing. The ink was so old and faded that most of the writing was indecipherable, and what could be made out was in Greek. Carrie had put it to one side to deal with when everything had settled down a bit. On the night of the rescue, Nell had mentioned other items in the cave, but she had not said anything about it since and Carrie didn't want to risk PTSD by questioning her. The full story would come out in due course, when Nell was ready, and not before.

Jack had asked, as he and Nell spent so little time together, if he could take her out for the day. Both of them wanted to do the boat trip to see Santorini's famous black, red and white beaches, and the lighthouse. There wouldn't be much walking so it would be achievable for Nell, even with her ankle boot and crutches. Still high on relief and absolutely not feeling that she had the energy to go on another excursion herself, Carrie had agreed.

Shortly, father and daughter would be off, and Carrie had planned to spend the day working on her book, with a break to have lunch with Kris. She still hadn't had the chance to thank him properly for everything that he had done – not just the room, but his part in the rescue effort and all the rest of his generosity.

'I'm not planning on leaving the hotel,' Carrie said to Jack and Nell as they got ready to leave. 'So call me if you need me.'

It was a pointless thing to say – why would they need her and what would she be able to do that Jack couldn't? But it made her feel better to think she was endlessly available to Nell.

'What are you doing for lunch,' Jack asked. 'Room service?'

Carrie shifted awkwardly from one foot to the other. 'Kris invited me to eat with him,' she replied. 'So I'll still be on site.'

'Oh.' Jack narrowed his eyes and pursed his lips. 'Right. Well, have a good one.'

He climbed into the car, threw his daypack onto the back seat and started the engine. Carrie suppressed a sigh as she waved them off as cheerfully as she could. She didn't like to let Nell out of her sight, but she had to be reasonable and Jack was perfectly capable of looking after her. It was more Jack's weird attitude towards Kris that was bothering her; Carrie really didn't have time for it.

As she got back to their gorgeous room with its spectacular view, her phone was ringing. She ran to pick it up from her bedside table and saw that it was her mother calling.

'Hi, Mum,' she said as she answered. 'Are you OK?'

There was a slight delay and then her mother said, 'I'm fine! Just checking on the invalid. How is she today?'

Carrie reported in detail on Nell's state of health and the fact that she had gone out with Jack. Her mother's silent approval of this plan came winging down the line. Harriet never openly judged Carrie or any of her decisions, but Carrie knew what her mother thought about her relationship – or lack of it – with Nell's father.

'That all sounds very good,' Harriet replied when Carrie had finished. 'But I've actually got some other news for you.'

'Oh, right, what's that then?' asked Carrie. Absent-mindedly, she picked up the letter Nell had brought from the cave. She'd barely had the time or headspace to think about it up to that point, but now its possible true importance suddenly dawned on her. Could this frail, thin sheet hold the key to the secrets she and Kris had been trying to uncover?

'I remembered that,' began Harriet, 'when we moved, I put a whole lot of books that belonged to Sol on the bookshelf in the attic bedroom. I don't go up there very often, but Jenny's girls are coming when the school holidays begin, so I needed to put fresh sheets on the beds.'

'Umm,' said Carrie, impatient for her mother to get to the point and not wanting to dwell on the visit by the nieces she barely knew.

'Anyway,' Harriet continued, 'I had a quick flick through them all and I found a little book on the SBS. I think it must have been self-published by one of the men in the 1950s – it looks a bit home-made, if you know what I mean, not very slick.'

'Right,' said Carrie, still wondering where this was going.

'So I've only had time to skim through it,' Harriet said. 'But – it's very interesting. I can't believe we never knew any of this. It seems that Sol didn't get off the island with all the others. He was left behind and relied on—'

Her voice cut off abruptly and Carrie could hear her talking to someone else.

'Carrie,' she said eventually, 'I've got to go. Dad's taken the week off work, thinking we might be needed out there – thank heavens we weren't! – but he's suddenly remembered a hospital appointment. We'll have to leave right away if we're not to be late.'

Carrie tried to hide her disappointment at not getting to the end of the story. 'OK, no problem,' she replied. 'Off you go. Ring me later to tell me more.'

She put her phone down and wandered over to the doors to survey the glorious vista. Now that Nell and Amy were safe, her mind was free once more to worry at the mystery of what had happened to Sol, the nature of his relationship with Kris's grandmother Vassia and, of course, what on earth had happened to Vassia's enigmatic brother, Andreas. She was desperate to solve the puzzle once and for all.

# CHAPTER 33

VASSIA, 1944

After the terrifying encounter with the soldiers, Vassia avoided going to the cave every day, though it broke her heart to leave Sol for so long. She knew that whenever she left the house she could come face to face with the enemy – and that this time she wouldn't get away unscathed. The not knowing, the imagining, what they might have in store for her if they caught her was a crushing weight that she carried everywhere with her.

Nevertheless, there was no question of stopping her visits to Sol entirely. All she could do was to vary the times she went and the route she took. One morning a week after she'd played hairdresser, she got up before dawn so as to arrive earlier than ever before.

As usual, it was quiet as she approached the cave's hidden entrance. There was no one anywhere in sight; everything was just as normal. Before descending the steps she called out softly to Sol, to alert him to her arrival and therefore not alarm him. Without waiting for a response, she entered the cave and in a few seconds was standing on the rocky floor. As her eyes adjusted to the darkness, she peered around anxiously for Sol. It was unusual for him not to hear her approach and be waiting in the small circle of light cast by the sun shining down the shaft.

But today he was not there.

Was he asleep? Vassia fumbled around for the stash of candles, lit one and shone it around the gloomy space, then walked around the cave's full extent.

Nothing.

With a rising sense of panic, Vassia was forced to acknowledge that Sol had said a boat was coming, that he could be collected any time, that it might not be long... Sternly telling herself that if he'd been summoned to go he would have to obey those orders, no matter what, she searched the cave again. Because surely, if that were the case, he'd have left a note. Wouldn't he?

The field radio was tucked into a natural fissure in the rock, where it was impossible to see unless you knew it was there. Did the fact that it was still there mean anything? Wouldn't Sol have taken it with him when he left? But maybe he'd had to travel light, carry nothing. If he'd had to swim out to the boat he wouldn't have been able to carry a radio and, even if he had, it would have got so wet it would be useless ever after.

Vassia climbed out of the cave and began to frantically search the surrounding area. Perhaps he'd fallen and hurt himself, or been struck down by some terrible illness, or been shot— She forced herself to put such terrible scenarios to one side.

'Calm,' she told herself. 'You must stay calm.'

But there was no sign of Sol anywhere she looked. Eventually, she reached the beach. The first place the men had sheltered was as empty as it had been last time she was here. Standing on the rough black sand, she gazed out to sea, scanning the horizon as if she might make out, somewhere far in the distance, Sol standing on the deck of a sailing boat, waving goodbye.

There was nothing there. Just the expanse of water, grey in the dawn light.

Reeling with sorrow and deep disappointment that she knew she had no right to feel – if Sol had got away, that was only a good thing for him – Vassia made her way to her brother's house. She couldn't face going back home quite yet and spending another day bolstering her mother, trying to get her to eat, to wash, to get out of bed. She would do anything for Thalia and was desperate to find a way to make her see the purpose of living again, but at the same time it was exhausting. And how could she alleviate her mother's despair when she was feeling a similar emotion, not only because of Ianos' loss but because of Sol's, too?

In Andreas's courtyard, she found Athena sitting in the shade of the bougainvillea tree, nursing Atlas. From the even rhythm of the baby's sucking, it appeared that Atlas was getting stronger.

'Sit down,' said Athena, gesturing to Vassia to bring a chair from the kitchen. She seemed brighter, too, her eyes no longer creased with worry, her skin regaining its normal healthy glow.

Vassia entered the house to fetch the chair. Her eyes took a moment to adjust to the low light after the bright sunshine outside. The room smelt as it always did, of tomatoes and spices, and on the table under the shelf Athena's knitting still sat, untouched, as she lacked the time to pick it up with a newborn to care for. Vassia's gaze lingered for a moment, and then a few moments more.

'Vassia!' Athena called to her from outside. 'Would you bring me some water? I get so thirsty when I'm feeding the baby.'

Pensively, Vassia picked up a glass, filled it and reached for the chair with the other hand. Back outside, pupils contracting painfully, she handed her sister-in-law the water and sat down.

'You look better,' she commented. 'And Atlas does, too. That's a relief.'

Athena nodded and smiled beatifically down at her son. 'Yes. He's on the mend. The doctor – well, he...' She hesitated before resuming. 'Doctors don't know everything, do they?'

Vassia's interaction with doctors had been limited to say the least; she'd never had any kind of illness other than the normal childhood ailments that get better by themselves in a few days, and there hadn't even been a medic on the island until 1940.

'I suppose not,' she agreed. Atlas' recovery seemed magical and extraordinary. *God gives with one hand*, she thought, *and takes away with the other*. But that was only right. Ianos was dead, Sol was somewhere out at sea. The hope lay with Atlas now; he was the future.

'I've got the pram ready,' Athena continued, proudly. 'I'll be taking him for his first stroll through the village soon, in the next couple of days. Will you come with me, as doting auntie?'

'Of course!' replied Vassia. 'As long as you let me have a cuddle when he's had enough milk.' Now that Atlas seemed so much stronger, less frail and breakable, Vassia was eager to reap the auntie bonus of lots of hugs with the little one.

Athena laughed and gently detached the baby from her nipple, then handed him to Vassia. 'He's drunk on milk,' she said. 'He keeps doing that. Guzzling so much that he conks out.'

Smiling down indulgently at her nephew, Vassia felt a tug of deep adoration as Atlas folded his minute fingers round one of hers.

Andreas came into the courtyard, carrying a carefully wrapped package.

'Red mullet,' he announced, proffering the fish as if it were some kind of offering. 'Fresh in this morning.'

Athena leapt up from her chair and took it into the kitchen. 'I'll prepare it today and we'll eat it tomorrow, on your day off,' she promised him when she returned. Everyone knew that red mullet was Andreas's favourite. It gave Vassia a cosy feeling to see her brother and Athena together, the easiness of their relationship, the mutual respect and love they had for each other. A bit like her and Sol—

A sudden, renewed fear that Sol pitied the smallness of her life, of all their lives on Santorini, the mundane domestic tasks that occupied their days, the limits on their ambitions and futures, struck her once more. He'd be glad to have got away from this backward island, where a proposed dish of red mullet was something to look forward to.

London, where Sol had lived before the war, was a great city with universities and theatres, cathedrals and newspaper offices, huge banks and businesses where deals were done and money made. It was so much bigger and more important than the tomatoes, grapes, fishing and volcanic stone that provided people with a livelihood here. No one on Santorini would never be as cosmopolitan as Sol, as worldly wise, let alone herself.

She did not have time to ponder this truth any further. Andreas was preparing to leave for lunch service at the restaurant in Fira, but then the thrumming sound of running footsteps became audible from the street outside. It was quite unusual for anyone in Santorini to hurry anywhere, especially when the sun was at its highest. No sooner had Vassia thought this than Nico burst through the courtyard door and halted abruptly, bent double and panting for breath.

Laughing, Andreas patted his heaving shoulders. 'What's the matter?' he asked. 'Why such a rush?' But his smile quickly faded as he took in Nico's demeanour.

When the boy could finally speak, he stood upright and practically shouted, 'The Germans are out again, looking for a commando! One who didn't get away with the others. They say he's hiding somewhere and they're going to find him; they're going to cover every square inch of Santorini in their hunt. Everyone in town is talking about it!'

Vassia's stomach fell through the floor and bile rose instantly in her throat. It could only be Sol. How could they know? Since she had discovered the cave empty, she had no idea whether Sol was on or off the island, and therefore how much danger he was in.

Dizzy with shock, she somehow managed to bundle Atlas back into his mother's arms, casting a sharp glance at Athena she tried to read her face. Had Andreas told her that Vassia was sheltering and caring for a commando stranded on the island? Did Athena know anything? From what Vassia could see, her sister-in-law was ignorant of the saga.

While Athena was distracted with the baby, Vassia signalled to her brother with her eyes. Andreas bent over his wife and kissed her, and then his son, on their foreheads.

'I must go,' he said. 'See you later.' He turned to Nico. 'There's honey cake in the kitchen,' he said. 'Have some before you leave.'

The child grinned and rushed straight into the house, forgetting the drama at the mention of a sweet treat. Vassia followed Andreas out onto the cobbled lane that twisted and turned between the low-slung buildings.

'It must be Sol they're hunting,' she whispered, casting fearful glances around her to check whether anyone else was around. But the village was quiet, the roads deserted. 'I went to the cave this morning and he wasn't there. He was so close to getting away; he told me the boat was on its way. But how could the Germans have found him? How would they have known about him, that someone got left behind, where he was?'

Andreas shook his head, his brow creased in puzzlement and concern. 'I don't know,' he answered. 'I've got no idea. Maybe he was spotted outside the cave, or... I just don't know.'

Suddenly overcome with dread, Vassia halted, reaching out her hand and resting it on the cool, whitewashed house wall for support. She looked up into her brother's eyes. 'What do we do?' she breathed. 'How can I protect him now?'

# CHAPTER 34

CARRIE, 2024

Clutching the letter that Nell had found in the cave, Carrie made her way to the restaurant. Kris arrived at exactly the same moment. He reached out his hand, put it to the side of her face and lifted up her chin for a kiss. It was as delightful as ever; more so, in fact, enhanced by the absence of the terrible worry and tension that had so recently prevailed. After the kiss, he put both arms round her. Despite the heat and the public place they were in, Carrie felt herself melt into him. Every time they touched, she remembered again how long it had been since she had been held by anyone, and how much she missed it, and how lonely she had been without it.

After a couple of minutes, Kris stepped back and gently led Carrie to a free table under the pergola. He'd already ordered, which Carrie was more than grateful for, as her brain was still so frazzled that she was finding the simplest decision quite beyond her. Once they'd eaten, she presented the letter to Kris and asked him if he could make anything out. After scrutinising it closely, he shook his head.

'It's so faded and the writing is tiny. Let's go to my office – I've got a magnifying glass there.'

At his desk, as they huddled together under a strong lamp, Kris directed the lens over the paper. Carrie held her breath as he moved it very slowly along the lines. Looking up, he met her eyes.

'I love you,' he said.

Carrie stared at him, speechless, as if she'd been winded by a blow to the diaphragm. She was beginning to think that she could feel the same, but surely it was too early for such declarations?

And then Kris returned his gaze to the paper and continued speaking. 'For ever and always, come what may.'

Carrie's heart missed several beats. Kris hadn't been addressing her, he'd just been reading the words on the page. What an idiot she was. Clenching her fists, she hoped he hadn't noticed her reaction. But Kris was entirely focused on the letter. He paused and then resumed, slower and more hesitant now as if working hard to decipher each sentence.

'Thank you for everything. See you when all of this is over.'

They both sat in a stunned silence for a moment.

'It doesn't say who it's to, or from?' asked Carrie, anxiously. 'This could be anybody's billet-doux... there was nothing to say it was anything to do with Sol, or Vassia, or the Second World War, except that it seemed quite old and "all of this is over" could relate to the war. But then again, it might not.'

Kris grimaced in a way that said he didn't have the answers either. He sat back in his chair and put his hands behind his head, closing his eyes for a moment. Then he opened them again and looked straight into hers. And this time Carrie definitely felt something stir between them, something that had been lingering in the background but, now the panic and distress was over, could come to the fore. She moved a little closer to him. Kris opened his mouth to say something, then, at that precise moment, a sharp rap sounded on the door.

Carrie and Kris sprang apart as if they'd been caught doing something illicit. Sofia entered.

'Sorry to disturb,' she said, 'but I need a signature on these invoices, please.' She placed a sheaf of papers on the desk.

Had she picked up on the atmosphere, the palpable tension? If she had, she gave no sign of it.

A lingering sense of disappointment settled upon Carrie as Kris dealt with the paperwork. He'd been about to say something important, she was sure of it. But the moment had gone. When the admin was completed, Kris turned to her.

'I think we need to go back to the cave,' he said. 'You said that Nell indicated there was other stuff there, which fits in with the rumours we heard as children, that the caves were used to hide things in. Let's go and take a look.'

Startled, Carrie gaped at him in open-mouthed surprise. 'Really?' she said. 'Do you think so? Do you have time?'

Nodding, Kris gathered up his phone and car keys and made for the door.

'How will we get down there?' Carrie asked, remembering the effort it had taken to get the girls out.

'Trust me,' was all Kris said. He left her waiting in the car park while he went to fetch something, which turned out to be a big black case. Carrie had no idea what it was but accepted that Kris knew what he was doing.

Back at the dramatic scene of a few days before, now they knew where it was, Kris drove right up to the cave entrance. Other than some tyre tracks on the rocky ground, there was nothing to show what had taken place there so recently. Kris lugged the black case out of the boot and unzipped it.

'A rope ladder,' he said, as he pulled and tugged at the case's contents. 'The kind the fire service use. We have it in the hotel – health and safety, you know, even though most of the building is only one storey so we're never going to use it. But just so we can tick the box.'

There was a tow bar for his boat on the back of his car and he fastened the top of the rope ladder round it, then let its length descend down the hole. Carrie stared at the cave entrance. It all felt rather surreal and dreamlike. Was she actually going to climb down there and potentially make some seismic discovery to do with both of their relatives? Could today be the day they finally found out the truth?

# CHAPTER 35

VASSIA, 1944

The hours after Sol's disappearance passed torturously slowly. That night, Vassia tossed and turned in bed, unable to sleep at the thought of what might be happening to him. She tried to sort it all out in her fervid mind. The cave had been undisturbed. It was impossible to imagine that the German soldiers would have left the field radio there if they'd been inside, so perhaps they hadn't discovered the cave. In that case, they must have seen Sol outside. She knew that sometimes, in the dead of night, he went down to the sea to swim and exercise. He needed to keep fit, for when the escape boat came, and he craved fresh air because he was spending so long underground.

That must be it. They'd seen him in the water, or on his way there. But on the other hand, if Sol were captured the news would be all over the island within minutes – and Nico had said that they were searching for a commando, not that they had found one. So that meant that, more than likely, he was still here, in this hot, dry rocky place, all alone and in mortal danger. Where would he have gone? Vassia knew him, she knew so much about him. She should be able to guess what actions he might take in this situation. Scouring her mind, she tried desperately to get inside his and work out what he might be doing, where he might be hiding.

Gradually, piece by piece, she sorted out her knowledge of Sol. He would stay away from the islanders, not through fear of being informed upon but to avoid anyone else facing the same fate that had befallen her father and the others involved in the raid. His conscience would not allow his presence to bring horror to any more families. His familiarity with Santorini was very limited; he had arrived on the beach in Vourvoulos, been led to Fira by night, and then Vassia had taken him to the cave. He didn't know anywhere else on the island and he had no map to guide him. If a boat really was on its way to collect him, how would he know where to meet it? Would he dare to go back to the cave to retrieve the radio for further communications? Vassia doubted it.

A shiver went down her spine at the thought that, blissfully unaware of anything amiss, she had gone there that morning. The feeling of being watched had come and gone over the last few days, but lately she'd convinced herself it was all in her mind. If it were more than that, if she really were under surveillance, then the Nazis would have picked her up by now.

Wouldn't they?

It struck Vassia with a terrible hammer blow that perhaps they were waiting for her to lead them to Sol. Perhaps they had found out that she had been harbouring him and were relying on her to give him away. She wished she could ask Andreas for advice, but she didn't want to say another word about Sol to him. The less he knew, the better. Then he couldn't incriminate himself. Even if Atlas was getting better, he needed his dad and always would.

Where would Sol have gone?

The next day, Vassia was exhausted from lack of sleep and the mental anguish of not knowing where Sol was or what was happening to him. She went about her chores mechanically, avoiding talking to her mother more than was absolutely necessary in case the huge weight of worry inside her burst out in a revelation of what was going on. Just as she didn't want Andreas to know anything that could put him at risk, she felt the same for Thalia.

In the late afternoon, she could bear it no longer. She needed to get out of the house and be alone for a while. She set out with a determined stride and made her way to the small harbour, where the fishing boats bobbed lazily on their moorings and a few seagulls pecked at the remains of the day's catch strewn across the pebbles. Vassia sat down on the wall, drew her knees up to her chest and hugged them, sometimes resting her face upon them and sometimes lifting her eyes to gaze at the impossibly blue sea. How could it all seem so normal here, when life right now was anything but?

It made no sense. Nothing made sense.

Vassia stayed at the harbour for several hours. Only when the sun began to drop in the sky, streaking the clouds with rose-pink and gold, did she stir. It was chilly now and she wished she had a shawl. She thought of Athena's knitting, the cosy blanket she was making for her child. And then she remembered the other thing that had caught her eye when she had been in their kitchen that day. She furrowed her brow and was trying to picture it when her attention was distracted by a high-pitched voice calling her name.

'Vassi!'

It was Nico, astride his pony Apollo, and they were coming towards her.

Getting up gingerly, as her legs were stiff from sitting in one position, Vassia waved at her cousin. 'Where have you been?' she asked. 'It's getting late – won't you be wanted at home?'

Nico grinned. 'I know, and yes,' he replied. 'But we had a good ride. Do you know I'm going to be a showjumper when I grow up?' he told her eagerly.

Laughing despite herself, Vassia fell into step beside him and the pony. 'Last week it was a fisherman like your dad,' she joked. 'And the week before that, if I remember aright, a train driver on the mainland... I can't keep up with all your career ambitions.'

They chatted away until they reached the paddock at the edge of the village where Nico's pony lived. There was a wooden shelter so Apollo could find refuge from the searing sun of summer, and a collection of other outbuildings that were barely used now and had become a repository of various broken and obsolete tools. Something that was still well used was the steaming pile of rotting manure, which was eagerly coveted by the entire extended family for its soil-enhancing properties.

Once Apollo had been fed and watered Nico ran back home, where his dinner would be waiting. Vassia stayed a while, listening to the comforting sound of the pony munching on his hay, patting his smooth neck and breathing in the sweet, earthy smell of him. Every now and again he nickered softly as if in acknowledgement of her presence, and turned to nuzzle at her outstretched palm. She would bring him some carrots next time she came, she promised him, and watermelon once the first ones were ripe. Apollo adored watermelon.

Even though she knew that Nico was exceptionally conscientious in looking after his animals – look how he'd tended poor Chicky – Vassia still decided to check Apollo's water before she left. Horses needed many litres a day and Nico might have forgotten to top up the bucket far enough.

She soon found that her fears were unfounded – the bucket was full to the brim, easily enough to last Apollo until the morning. As Vassia was turning to go, with one last pat and stroke of his soft, gentle nose, she heard a noise, a sound of metal clanging against stone. It came from the tool shed. For a moment Vassia froze stock-still, but she quickly pulled herself together. It was just a mouse in there, or perhaps a cat that had found itself a little corner to sleep in. She had begun to walk away, across the paddock to the gate, when she heard it again.

The same noise.

She turned around. If it was a cat, maybe it couldn't get out... She marched back towards the shed and opened the door, saying, 'Come on kitty, kitty, come...' Her words came to an abrupt halt and she stared, open-mouthed in amazement at the sight that greeted her eyes.

Sol.

At first, she couldn't believe it.

But it really was him and he was gesturing frantically to her to shut the door. Even in her bewilderment, Vassia found herself thinking, of course. The pony's paddock. She'd told Sol about it – he must have remembered it as a possible hiding place.

Once inside with the door closed, Sol gave her a brief hug. 'You can't stay,' he whispered. 'I'm sorry for going missing but I had to leave the cave. The boat that's coming back to get me is hiding out on Christiani island; they picked up radio messages that the Germans are on to me and my presence on Santorini.'

Listening, Vassia was speechless with fear for him, and filled with dread.

'I don't think they actually know about the cave,' Sol continued urgently, 'but they know about me all right. I've got to keep moving now until I leave.'

Vassia swallowed twice, trying to summon her voice from somewhere. 'We need a plan,' she squeaked. And then, having resumed full control of her vocal cords, 'A strategy. How to outwit them.'

Sol nodded. 'I have to get back to the cave to pick up a final message about exactly when and where they'll collect me. I know it's going to be tomorrow, but I need the time and place. The only way to do that is by diverting the Nazis' attention elsewhere, making them think I'm somewhere else.' He paused, brow furrowed as if considering how this could be done.

'I've got an idea,' pitched in Vassia, her brain working at extra speed. 'I'll write a letter – an anonymous one, of course, giving information that you've been seen – in Oia, perhaps. I'll have it delivered to the HQ in Fira and then they'll have to go and search that place. That'll buy you some time.'

Sol's face lit up with a wonderful smile. 'Brilliant plan! Do it tomorrow, in the morning,' he instructed her. 'I'll go back to the cave tomorrow night, use the radio at exactly midnight. That's when I'll get the final information I need in order to escape.'

As he said the last word, his voice faltered. He sounded close to tears, and so was Vassia. In fact her heart was breaking, but she couldn't tell him that. Not now, when his chances of getting out of Santorini alive had become so vanishingly slim.

'Vassia.' Sol's voice was firm again now, unwavering. 'I need to ask one more thing of you. A dangerous thing, that I wish I didn't need to involve you in.' He paused, let out a long sigh and rubbed his hand across his forehead, leaving behind a streak of dust on his roughened skin. 'There are many isolated beaches on this island and the routes to get to them are difficult and hard to find. I need your services as a guide one more time.' He broke off and made an odd sound, a kind of strangled sob combined with a low wail. Vassia reached out her hand to him and he grasped it in both of his before continuing. 'If you do this, you will be putting yourself in more danger than ever before. But I need someone to guide me to the pick-up location tomorrow. Will you meet me at the cave at quarter past midnight to take me there?'

A cold shiver ran through Vassia's entire body at these words. Only her hand, held in his, remained warm. There were so many reasons she didn't want to do what Sol asked. She was frightened witless, of course, but more than that there was her desperate desire to hold on to him, to keep him on Santorini... But that was impossible, she knew. He was a wanted man; he had no future on this island. Back with the rest of the SBS, on future missions, he could hope to change the course of the war. Here, whether living underground in a cave or as a fugitive trying to evade capture on a small island, he was not able to help defeat the Nazis at all.

'Yes,' she replied simply. 'I will be there.'

Sol dropped her hand and pulled her into his arms for a brief embrace, before urging her to go.

Walking back into the village, her legs shaking beneath her, Vassia thought long and hard about whether what she had proposed to Sol was the best thing to do. She'd had another idea. It wasn't exactly what they had discussed, but she was pretty sure it would work.

Instead of going straight home, she headed for Andreas's house. He would be there now, probably about to enjoy the red mullet Athena had prepared. She'd drop in on them for an hour or so. She wasn't absolutely sure that she was right, but she was sure enough. If she were right, it was a terrible kind of rightness that she wouldn't have wished on her worst enemy; she needed to see Andreas to be certain.

If it saved Sol, that was the only thing that mattered.

# CHAPTER 36

## CARRIE, 2024

'I'll go first,' said Kris. 'Test that the ropes will hold. When I'm at the bottom I'll shout up and give three tugs, and then you know it's your turn.'

Gritting her teeth, Carrie nodded.

Kris's descent was rapid and straightforward. Gingerly, Carrie half-walked, half-crawled to the hole, placed her feet on the first rungs and, holding her breath, began to climb down.

Unbelievably, she reached solid ground safely. Looking around her, she could just make out a large cavern with jagged rock walls.

'Gosh,' she breathed. 'I don't know what I expected, but it wasn't this.'

Kris turned on a torch and the full extent of the underground space, much bigger than Carrie had imagined, became apparent. She thought of the girls being stuck down here with no way of knowing if they would ever be found. What a terrible ordeal they had been through.

'Look, over here,' said Kris excitedly. He sank to his knees where a dark brown wooden box sat next to a pile of recently dug up sand and stones, evidence of the girls' discovery of it.

Carrie joined him, heart pounding. Kris lifted the lid, the front edge of which splintered into fragments as he did so. Beneath it was an array of knobs and dials, rusted and blotched with damp, together with some twisted wires and plugs.

'A radio set,' declared Carrie in awestruck tones. 'Wow. It must have belonged to the SBS men.' She hadn't told Kris what her mother had discovered in the old book on the attic shelves, and quickly did so now.

'So Sol got left behind,' mused Kris. 'And someone looked after him. Which was more than likely Grandma Vassia...'

He had the beam of the torch inside the box now, searching it. Attached to the remains of the lid was a metal plate with the words 'PA Tune Chart' embossed upon it. Three rusty screws held the plate in place; the fourth was missing. As Kris ran his fingers over it, another screw was dislodged, causing the plate to fall forward and revealing, tucked behind it, another piece of paper. With extreme care, Kris pulled it out, biting his lip with concentration as he tried not to damage it.

He opened the paper and shone the torch onto the Greek writing that covered almost half the page, muttering to himself under his breath.

After a few minutes, he let the frail paper drop and put the torch down. He ran his hands through his hair, then turned to Carrie.

'We were right!' he said, exaltedly. 'It's from Vassia, to Sol,' he went on. 'And it's dated June, which is weeks after the raid in April.'

'Gosh,' breathed Carrie. 'So it's really true, what we suspected, what the portrait indicates – that they knew each other for a lot longer than just forty-eight hours and...' She let the sentence dangle, unable to finish it. What had passed between these two in that far-off time when mere survival was a fight to the last – and never guaranteed?

Kris frowned and continued reading. 'I can't read all of it,' he said, squinting to see the faded writing. 'I think it might be the first part of the letter that Nell found. She's telling him that both of their lives will be on the line tonight.'

'Oh God.' Carrie's breath caught in her throat as if the jeopardy was real and now, not from eighty years ago. 'Why? Why this night more than any other?'

Kris studied the words intently as Carrie waited in painful suspense.

'She says—' Kris began in a faltering voice, and then broke off, unable to continue.

'What? What is it?' Carrie's questioning was urgent, frantic.

Kris looked up, shock written across his expression. 'She's saying she knows who gave him away, who told the Nazis about him.'

The two of them sat in silence, looking at each other, absorbing the revelation.

'So he was betrayed?' asked Carrie, scarcely able to comprehend it. 'I don't believe it.'

Kris shook his head sorrowfully. 'Neither do I. But it's what it says.' He was still studying the letter intently, eyes narrowed in concentration. 'There are a few more words,' he said, eventually. 'Faith, hope I think, and love – and the greatest of these is love.'

'Oh my God!' Carrie could hardly breathe with excitement. 'That's the engraving on the ring – part of it, anyway. Here, look!' She fumbled in her pocket for her phone and showed Kris the pictures.

'It must have been their special saying,' Kris suggested, his voice wavering. Carrie put her hand over his. The emotion of it all was getting to both of them. In the midst of war, Sol and Vassia had been desperately in love, but someone had betrayed them. It was incomprehensible. Who, on an island of people who wanted nothing more than to see the Allies successful and the hated Nazis ousted, could possibly have done such a thing?

# CHAPTER 37

VASSIA, 1944

The next day, Vassia sat at the table in her room and wrote the letter. When it was finished, she went out. The first person she bumped into was Evangelos. She didn't want to stop and talk but how could she not, when he was so kind, asking solicitously after her mother, expressing his concern over her health. Vassia thanked him for his consideration. Neither of them mentioned those who had been murdered in such violence and horror. Instead they stood for a few moments, awkwardly, lost for words in this time of terrible grief.

Eventually, Vassia took her leave. As she went, she glanced back over her shoulder and saw Evangelos gazing after her, a wistful look in his eye. She gave him a wave and carried on her way. In each of the village shops, the news was the same. The Nazis were searching for a fugitive British SBS man, and they believed him to be in Oia. Residents of that town were huddling indoors, terrified to come out and face the Nazi troops who were combing through each nook and cranny in their efforts to unearth the commando.

It was as bad as Vassia had expected. Clearly the Germans would leave no stone unturned in their search. She set off again to look for Nico. In the past he'd have been with his little friends, playing under the fig trees in the village square, but they never went there now. It would be forever tainted by the horrific events of that day in April. Instead, they were outside the church, kicking a ball around in the shadow of the bell tower.

She gave him the letter and told him where to take it.

Nico nodded with huge, solemn eyes. 'I will,' he answered. He took hold of the precious envelope and pocketed it, before turning on his heel and running off along the dusty street.

All Vassia could do for the rest of the day was wait. It was agonising. She tried to sew, but without her scissors she had to break the thread with her hands, and this was too hard and left the ends too frayed to put through the needle… and anyway, thinking of her scissors reminded her of cutting Sol's hair, of holding him and touching him, smelling him and tasting him. It made her heart physically ache, and her stomach feel leaden and full. She could neither eat nor drink, despite the warmth of the day and the long hours.

At some point she managed to entice her mother to sit outside for a while and enjoy the fresh air. In the courtyard, all was quiet and tranquil, luscious pots of fragrant herbs scenting the atmosphere around them. But Vassia could not settle; she kept jumping up and sweeping away an imaginary leaf on the tiled floor, or plucking an invisible weed from a pot.

'You've got ants in your pants today,' her mother said, attempting a half-hearted joke. At least she was out of bed for half an hour; that was something.

Vassia tried to laugh in response, but it dried up and died in her throat.

'I'll make mint tea!' she exclaimed. Anything to calm her nerves. Once the tea had been made, however, Vassia was once again at a loss. There was nothing to do now but wait.

The minutes ticked by torturously slowly.

Thalia went inside for a siesta. Vassia, left alone, wished she had the courage to go out and see where the German troops were searching, check on their progress. But she didn't dare. She didn't want to be seen, just in case. She needed to lie low, stay out of trouble until the evening came. It was absolutely essential that she was able to meet Sol at the designated time.

The day was perfect, the June sunshine strong and bright, the soaring blue sky streaked with a scattering of cirrus clouds. But the shocking-pink blooms of the bougainvillea were almost garish in their unashamed profusion, seeming to mock Vassia as she paced up and down, unable to settle to anything.

Eventually, evening came. Vassia served some food for her mother and herself but could hardly swallow a mouthful.

'Are you unwell?' Thalia asked anxiously, watching Vassia pushing the baked aubergine around on her plate. 'You look so sad. Oh, those hellish Nazis, to do what they did...' At that, she broke down, her weeping drowning out the rest of her words.

Anxiety gnawing away at her insides, Vassia struggled to offer her mother the consolatory and reassuring words that she knew she needed. If only she could unburden herself to her mum, to whom she had always entrusted her secrets. But she couldn't tell her this. Thalia had not mentioned Sol for days now. Vassia wondered if she were trying to block him from her mind, along with everything associated with her husband's death, pretend Sol didn't exist so that she didn't have to think about him or worry about him – or her daughter's role in tending to him.

Fortunately, despite her siesta, Thalia was tired and went to bed at ten p.m. Breathing a sigh of relief, Vassia decided to pass the time by cleaning the kitchen floor again. On her hands and knees, a large wooden brush in her hands, she scoured the aged tiles for all she was worth. The result was sore, blistered palms and a floor that sparkled with cleanliness – and still it was not time to leave.

After what felt like several lifetimes, the clock in the hallway struck quarter to twelve. Vassia let herself out of the house, slipped along the sleeping streets and then struck out across the rough ground towards the cave. It occurred to her that this might be the last time she ever walked this way. The thought struck her in the solar plexus like a body blow, winding her.

Yet, as if in a trance, her legs carried her forward to her fate.

# CHAPTER 38

CARRIE, 2024

Back in Oia, Carrie got a message to say that Nell and Jack had finished their boat trip but were going to stay out a bit longer and have dinner in one of the beach restaurants in Perissa.

'Let's go for a stroll, watch the sunset and have a drink at my friend's place,' Kris suggested.

Ambling through the town's perfect streets, dodging the young tourists with their selfie sticks and the oldies with their walking poles, Carrie had again that dreamlike sense, as if she'd been here for twenty years, not less than ten days.

Right at the very end of the island, when she was thinking there could be no further to go, they reached a door in a wall. As they entered, Carrie gasped at the scene before her eyes. The restaurant consisted of numerous terraces carved into the rock, each one big enough to accommodate a table for two, with an unimpeded view of the flat, calm sea all the way to the horizon, which would soon become vivid with the reds and pinks of sunset.

'Wow!' she breathed. 'This is incredible!'

Kris's friend whisked them through to what must have been the best table in the best location in town, where they sat side by side so that both could gaze out at the perfect tableau before them.

'I'm struggling to imagine who would have betrayed Vassia and Sol,' said Carrie with a sigh as the waiter poured them glasses of pale amber Santorini wine.

Kris shook his head. 'Me too. What an awful thing to do. We've learnt so much, but there's still so much we don't know.'

Carrie grimaced. 'Indeed.' She gulped a slug of her wine. It was going down far too easily but she had a sudden sense of abandonment, as if she needed to drink too much to rid herself of the terrible tension and agony of the last few days.

They ordered their food and chatted a bit more about Vassia and Sol and what could possibly have happened to them. Their meal arrived and, as they ate, emboldened by alcohol Carrie suddenly found herself asking Kris why he was single, why there wasn't a special someone in his life.

He shrugged. 'I've just never met anyone I felt that committed to,' he replied. 'Or at least, when I say never... perhaps that's not true. And things can change, can't they? I haven't given up hope.' Their two hands were lying close together on the table and Kris's crept towards hers and then was holding it. A sizzle of electricity seared through Carrie.

'It's difficult though, isn't it?' he continued. 'My life is on Santorini and, though it's beautiful, it's very small and the weather isn't perfect all year round. It can be windy and cold in the winter and there isn't much to do. Lots of people ship out to Athens or somewhere livelier in the off-season, whereas I prefer to stay. I like it when everything's quiet and relaxed, but it's not to everyone's taste. Those with children worry about their education, questioning whether what the island provides is good enough... you can imagine—' Abruptly he stopped.

His fingers closed slightly round Carrie's and his eyes held hers in a meaningful gaze. 'And what about you?' he asked her. 'You haven't really told me anything about you – and Jack.' His nose wrinkled as he said the name, as if he'd smelt something off.

Carrie let out a long sigh that seemed to emanate from the depths of her being. 'Well, the short version is that he broke my heart,' she said, and stopped, overwhelmed with emotion. Though she knew she shouldn't, she drank more of her wine. She was already on her second, or was it third glass, and it was making her feel light-headed, as well as loquacious. But what the hell.

'And the long version?' Kris had tilted his head to one side and was smiling at her in a way that made her insides turn over. 'Do I get to hear that, too?'

Carrie rolled her eyes, took another glug of wine. 'OK, if you really want the ugly truth, I'll tell you,' she replied. And then promptly burst into tears.

Dabbing at her eyes with her napkin, she managed to stem the tears enough to allow her to speak. 'What happened is this,' she began. 'Jack and I met and we fell in love. So far, so good. I thought he was my soulmate, that we'd be together for ever, that nothing would ever part us. Whenever we were together, it felt so good it hurt. When we were apart, I thought of nothing but him. Crazy, I know. But when you're young, you feel things so much more deeply, don't you? I mean, relationships. They matter so much.'

Kris indicated to the waiter to bring more wine and Carrie faltered, knowing she should resist drinking anything else and knowing equally well that she wouldn't.

'Honestly, everything was so perfect I should have known it could never last, that it was too good to be true. I actually met Jack through my sister Jenny. She was already at Nottingham Uni, and I followed her there – I was only the year behind her in school. We were so close, we always did everything together; that's why I chose the same university as her, and the same course! Honestly, that's how unoriginal I am.'

Carrie gave an ironic laugh before continuing.

'Anyway, she'd made friends with Jack and she introduced him to me and hey presto. Love's young dream. I always had this lingering feeling that perhaps she liked Jack too, but I didn't give it much thought, I was so swept up in the relationship. Then one day there was a house party and I didn't drink anything but the others all did, and we started playing hide-and-seek. It was pitch dark and everyone was hyped up and a bit hysterical. I ran off to find somewhere to hide, went into a bedroom, opened the wardrobe door – and discovered Jack and Jenny entwined with each other, kissing passionately.'

At this, another small sob erupted from Carrie's throat. Determined not to dissolve again, she choked it back.

'I was devastated,' she continued. 'Beyond upset. I felt so humiliated; I didn't know how many others had seen them, who else knew – because I assumed it wasn't a one-off but had been going on for some time. I was convinced that everybody was laughing at me, pitying me. It was unbearable.'

She paused for a moment, realigning the cutlery at her place setting so that the knife and fork were perfectly parallel. 'And that was it. I vowed never to speak to Jack or Jenny again. If it hadn't been for finding out, two weeks later, that I was pregnant, I never would have done. But my mother made me tell Jack I was keeping the baby and she made me let him have contact with Nell.'

Kris frowned and nodded. 'You don't seem too happy about that?' he said.

'Well, I wasn't,' railed Carrie. 'Would you have been? I didn't see that he had the right, after behaving like such a shit, pardon my language. I thought that I would keep my baby all to myself and that would serve him right. But Mum told me that fighting him in court for access would be really damaging, not to mention expensive, and persuaded me to meet him halfway.

And I did!' Carrie's voice had risen to a high pitch of indignation now. 'He should be grateful for that.'

Kris's expression was of shock and concern. 'I'm so sorry to hear all of this,' he said, eventually. 'It must have been awful. And all these years, looking after Nell single-handed...' He looked away, far out to sea, as if Nell were out there somewhere, being demanding, as children are. 'You must be so proud of her though. She's amazing.'

Carrie burst out laughing with the release of all that pent-up emotion. 'When she's not using fake ID to illegally hire a moped, falling into caves, putting twenty years on me with all the stress and worry, distracting you from your job when we hardly even know you...'

Kris conceded a smile. 'OK, well, she's a teenager. They all have their moments. But in general, as I've said before, she's wonderful.'

Suddenly serious again, in those mercurial mood swings that alcohol engenders, Carrie felt fresh tears welling up in her eyes. 'She is. And I love her so, so much,' she blubbered, burying her face in the now-drenched and ragged napkin. 'And the worst thing is that she loves her dad and I can never, ever tell her what he did because she might see it as me trying to turn her against him, and I can't tell her why she can't know her auntie and cousins and it's all so *shit*.' She paused for another slug of wine.

Suddenly she felt that, having revealed so much to Kris already, she could bare even more of her soul to him, confess something that she had never told anyone before, something that she had only really understood since she had been on this holiday. 'And it's only since I've been here that I've realised, really realised, how lonely I am, and how much I'd like to have a relationship, even though I've always denied myself that, but of course I would, I've just always felt I can't because what if it goes wrong, Nell would be affected too and anyway, I never meet anyone, where would I, I'm not going to go online, swipe right, or is it left, and oh, I don't know, I...' Suddenly her uncontrolled ramblings ceased, as if she'd run out of words. She had a fleeting, crippling sensation of having said too much. Far too much.

But Kris was all sympathy. He let go of her hand, put his arm round her shoulders and pulled her towards him. 'I'm sorry,' he said, 'that you're lonely. I am too, sometimes.'

There was a long, expectant pause, broken by the arrival of the waiter coming to clear away the plates and offer them dessert, which neither of them wanted.

Before they left, Carrie drank three glasses of water to try to eliminate the alcohol swishing around in her system. They strolled back to the hotel, Carrie with no idea where she was going, just letting Kris lead her. His hand felt so cool despite the heat, and strong. She rested her head against his shoulder.

'Let's walk up the crater path a bit,' she suggested, when they reached the hotel. 'I can't go to bed, I'm not tired yet.' She laughed again, knowing she was drunk but not caring. She hadn't let her hair down for over sixteen years. Seventeen, really, if you counted the nine months of pregnancy.

They stopped by the tiny, freshly painted chapel that they'd passed when they started the search for Nell and Amy, and sat down on the low wall that surrounded it, looking out to sea.

'Do people still worship here?' Carrie asked, fingering the rough texture of the limewashed wall.

'Not often,' replied Kris. 'But Greeks never abandon a church. They are always looked after, never neglected and left to crumble.'

'Amazing,' whispered Carrie. Greeks were so lovely. So welcoming and hospitable and tolerant of all the hordes of tourists that they had to put up with every year. Wonderful people. A wonderful country. Perhaps she could stay here. Throw everything in and move to Santorini, live with Kris, forge a whole new life for herself and Nell. She'd be lying if she said that possibility hadn't crossed her mind over the last few days. She could study Greek and become a tour guide, or learn to sail and become a sailor, or perhaps wine-making would be more fun...

She turned to Kris and then, before she really knew what was happening, she was in his arms and they were kissing, and, however good all the previous kisses had been, this was better than them all, the best possible. It was like a long drink after being parched in the desert; the woody, spicy scent of him, his strong arms holding her, the passion in his lips, which held all the promise of the sun and the sea and this idyllic island.

Carrie lost all track of time. Had they been there for minutes or hours? She had no idea. At some point they moved onto the ground and kissed some more.

Eventually, Kris pulled gently away from her. 'We should go back now,' he said. 'It's getting late.' He hesitated. 'Would you come to my room? Spend the night with me? Only if you want to. No pressure.' The last words were spoken hastily, as if he was anxious that he'd overstepped the mark.

Carrie smiled at him. Of course she wanted to go to his room. Who wouldn't? He was gorgeous, delectable, edible. And why shouldn't she? She was a grown woman, she could do what she wanted.

In a tipsy haze, she nodded her agreement. 'That sounds lovely,' she replied, as Kris pulled her to her feet. They headed back down the path, Carrie tripping and stumbling, dreamy with love and alcohol and that constant feeling she'd had ever since Nell had been found of being so lucky, so very very lucky, that Nell was all right and the worst hadn't happened and here she was with this adorable man, which was another bit of unbe-lievable luck—

'Carrie? Carrie, what are you doing? Where have you been?'

Jack's voice startled her into alertness.

'Er, oh, nowhere,' stuttered Carrie, trying to surreptitiously brush down the back of her skirt, hoping it wasn't covered in incriminating leaves and soil. 'I mean, obviously somewhere, we had dinner and then a walk and...' She looked wildly around her. 'Where's Nell? What's happened?'

Jack jingled his car keys in his pocket. 'Nothing's happened. She's fine. We had a fabulous day but she was understandably exhausted, so she's gone to bed.' He paused and looked pointedly between Carrie and Kris and back again. 'She's probably wondering where *you* are.' The accusation in his voice was unmistakable.

Kris detected the awkwardness. 'Well, Carrie, you can see yourself to your room, can't you? I better be off.' With that, he turned and left.

Carrie watched him leave, wondering. Would she have done it? Would she actually have gone back with him, slept with him? Her head told her no, she would have come to her senses, realised that she couldn't leave Nell, remembered that she had no idea how to even do sex any more, it had been so long. But her heart would have wanted to. Definitely it would have wanted to.

Once Kris was out of earshot, Jack took a step towards Carrie.

'Carrie, we need to talk,' he intoned, his voice firm and emphatic. 'We've needed to talk for years, but enough is enough. I need to put the record straight. After everything we've been through these last few days, the least you can do is let me say my piece, and listen. Agreed?'

Carrie's eyelids flickered up and down. All she wanted to do was lie down, right here on the hard pavement, in the dust and sultry heat, and sleep. But Jack was right. This had been a long time coming and now it needed to be done.

'Agreed,' she murmured.

# CHAPTER 39

## VASSIA, 1944

The waning moon cast little light but the stars were bright and, her eyes accustomed to the night, Vassia easily traced the route to the cave. It was what came after that concerned her more; some of the beaches could only be accessed by steep clambers down volcanic cliffs; but of course the rescue boat had to pick somewhere as secluded and hard to get to as possible, to minimise the chance of being detected.

As she neared the cave, a shadowy figure appeared from the undergrowth. For a moment, Vassia's heart stopped. What if it was a trick? What if Sol were captured and she had walked right into a trap?

But within moments she had recognised his form, the body she knew so well. After just a brief kiss of greeting, Sol spoke. 'Let's go,' he said. 'The place is next to the harbour of Pori. Do you know it?'

Vassia nodded. 'It's about five kilometres from here,' she replied. 'It will take around an hour, I think, as there's no path.'

'Even if there was, we'd have to keep away from it,' murmured Sol, scanning the open country ahead of them. 'We need to move at top speed. The rendezvous time is one fifteen a.m. If I'm not there, they won't wait.'

With this grim warning, the pair set off. There was almost no shelter the entire way; trees were largely absent from the island, due to the volcanic activity of the past and the sparse rainfall. It meant that Sol and Vassia were alarmingly exposed as they trudged across scrubby country, the sea to their right, no sign anywhere that other human beings existed on the planet.

They walked in silence, more and more stars filling the sky with each passing minute. If they were not in mortal danger, it would have been beautiful; a midnight hike down to the beach, to swim, perhaps, in the cool, dark water, to sit on the smooth, rounded pebbles and watch the galaxies pass over them.

But this was no stroll in the countryside. It was a march, with a purpose, and fraught with peril.

After forty-five minutes' hard hiking, Vassia pulled up short. Not far below them was a small harbour with a wooden pier and one or two fishing boats tugging at their anchors in the gentle swell of the water.

'This is Pori,' she said. She stared out to the black expanse of the sea. 'I can't see a boat yet though.'

Sol grimaced. 'They'll be here,' he replied, assuredly. 'They'll be waiting until the last minute to make their approach. We need to get down there.'

In five more minutes, they were standing in the lee of the harbour wall. Vassia felt suddenly nauseous. This was it. Time to say the farewell that had been inevitable since the first moment Sol had set foot on Santorini. The fact that it was always going to end this way didn't make it any easier to bear.

They stood looking at each other for a long, tense moment and then, all at once, each fell towards the other and Sol was hugging her so tight she could hardly breathe. He released her a little, lowered his face to hers and kissed her, again and again, until finally he broke away.

'I can hear the engine,' he said, gruffly.

Vassia held out her hands, placed them on his shoulders, ran them down until they were touching his palms. She closed her fingers round his.

'I can't stop touching you,' she murmured. 'I can't let you go.'

The tension between them crackled like electricity, filling the air, crowding out all thought of the peril they were in, the jeopardy.

'I got your letter,' Sol murmured, his lips caressing her neck. 'I left it with the radio set, where no one will find it. It would be ruined by the water as I get to the boat if I took it with me, so I memorised it instead. Every word. And what you put at the end. Faith. Hope. Love. And the greatest of these is love. I've got the sampler in my pocket; I'll do my best not to lose it.'

Vassia listened, her eyes shut, everything concentrated on him, her lover and her friend. She hadn't followed the plan she'd outlined to Sol to write to Nazi HQ. The letter she'd given to Nico had been sent to Sol. The Germans hadn't searched Oia because of an anonymous tip-off they'd received from her. She'd achieved that aim another way.

'The words you wrote meant everything to me,' Sol continued, before kissing her, his mouth strong and firm on hers. It was as if the whole world contained only Vassia and Sol, and the stars, and this moment, that seemed to last for all time and to also be over in a flash.

He broke off and looked straight into her eyes. 'Come with me. Please, Vassia. Come.' His voice was almost normal, save for a tremor in the last syllable. 'You can get away from here, from Santorini, from the danger. Come with me. We'll take you somewhere safe, to our base, you can live there until...'

The word 'until' stretched into an infinite and untold future, as unfathomable as the galaxies above.

*Until the war is won*, thought Vassia, *and all the soldiers can go home, to England or Scotland or America or Australia. Or until you die, perhaps.* Either scenario was possible. Neither scenario was where she belonged. But for a few precious seconds she allowed herself to dream, of a life with Sol in an English country village like the pictures she'd seen in books, thatched cottages with roses round the doors and hollyhocks in neat front gardens edged by white picket fences, the cool, dew-laden damp of an English summer's morning, so different from Santorini's fierce, unrelenting heat—

She stopped herself, cutting the dream off short, forcing herself back to the present.

Sol was asking her to choose between her love for him and her love for her country, and that was an impossible choice. The decision was already made. Her mother needed her here. There was no way on earth that Vassia could leave her.

Squeezing back the tears, she shook her head. 'No,' she replied softly. 'I'm sorry, but I can't do that.'

The look of anguished despair that descended upon Sol's face at her words nearly destroyed her, all her courage and all her resolve nearly gone in an instant. Almost, but not quite. She had meant what she said. It simply wasn't possible.

The engine noise grew stronger. Vassia looked towards the sea, and there was a schooner, sails furled, appearing like a ghostly galleon out of the darkness. It came as close as it could to the harbour wall and, after one last, passionate kiss, Sol was gone, splashing through the dark water, then leaping aboard the boat and immediately helping to set the sails for their swift departure. Vassia watched, her eyes so flooded by tears and the light so poor that she could hardly make anything out. She couldn't really believe they'd made it, that they'd got to Pori, that Sol had evaded the Nazis one more time.

Wiping her eyes, she stared until the boat disappeared, leaving nothing behind but a faint undulation of the water, the hint of green olive soap mingled with the salt tang of the sea, and a hollow chasm in her heart that she knew would never be filled.

Faith, hope and love. And the greatest of these is love. The words spun around her head, time after time, unstoppable.

Lost in memories, Vassia ignored the approaching sound of vehicles. Just as Sol's departure had been unavoidable, so was what was destined to happen next. She was quite calm when the dark shadow loomed up from behind her; she had already made her peace with her inevitable fate.

'Kaliméra,' she said, evenly and serenely, as she turned to meet the approaching figure with a steady gaze. For the next few moments, the world stopped turning as the night waited, full of terrible anticipation.

'I was expecting you earlier, Lieutenant Schwarz. What took you so long?'

# CHAPTER 40

## CARRIE, 2024

After having spent half the evening crying, Carrie was dry-eyed as she and Jack walked through the hotel and down to the pool, where they could sit and talk in privacy without any danger of Nell hearing. Jack, though, was almost tearful as he began to speak.

'What you saw that night, Carrie, it was nothing,' he began. 'That stupid game of hide-and-seek – most of us were drunk, running around that huge, dilapidated student house like a bunch of idiots. Jenny and I ended up fighting with each other to get the space in the wardrobe – I almost fell on top of her and we were giggling and laughing and the next thing, we had a snog. That was it. All it was. One drunken kiss. Stupid, ill-advised, never to be repeated. Once we'd sobered up, we were both appalled by what we'd done. But it was just a kiss, nothing more. And you happened to walk in that very moment and you didn't give us – me – any opportunity to explain. You cut me out of your life in an instant. I heard from your mother about the baby. You didn't even tell me that yourself.'

Now Jack was really crying, tears welling in the corner of his eyes, which he angrily swiped away with his hand. Once he'd composed himself, he continued. 'I've regretted it every moment since, and wished I could make it right. You have never wanted to see me, or speak to me. You've never given me the chance to explain in all these years. Every girlfriend I've had – tried to have –it's not worked out because I didn't want anything to come between me and Nell, didn't want you to have any reason to hate me even more than you do already.'

Carrie squeezed her hands into fists, gripping onto the soft cushion of the seat.

'Did,' she said, almost inaudibly.

'What?' Jack leant forward to try to hear her.

'Did,' repeated Carrie. 'I did hate you, yes. And I'm sorry for that. It's not an excuse, but perhaps you can understand how I felt. It was so humiliating to think that you'd been going out with me, told me you loved me, but could get off with Jenny at the drop of a hat.' She looked at Jack and then waved her hands up and down at him. 'I know, I know, I know, you've explained what really happened. But I'm telling you what I thought, how it landed on me at that time. I was young, and naive, already pregnant though I didn't know it, full of hormones, vulnerable. You remember I was never the most confident of people, over-sensitive and low in self-esteem. University is hard, trying to fit in, always worried that everyone else is having more fun than you and all that sort of stuff. When I met you, it suddenly all made sense, everything fell into place, I began to come out of my shell and flourish. And then you and Jenny crushed me, utterly and completely.'

Carrie halted, holding out her arms in a gesture of supplication, as if imploring Jack to understand.

Then she ran her hands through her hair, which she could feel was frizzy and wild with the heat. 'So yes, I did hate you. And I can see now how wrong that was, and how stupid and ill-judged and damaging to all of us. At least Mum talked some sense into me about you and Nell and not tarnishing your relationship. And, well, the truth is that I don't hate you any longer. It's taken me years, honestly. But I don't know, maybe being here in this beautiful place, almost thinking I'd lost Nell, has helped put things into perspective. The truth is, I've been so lonely these past years. Nell is my favourite person in the world, obviously, and I love her more than I can really say. But I'm ready to start thinking about myself again now. Ready to start living again.'

She reached out and took hold of both of Jack's hands, meeting his gaze. 'Can you forgive me?'

Jack stared at her for a moment as if struggling to let it all sink in. Then he spoke. 'Yes, I forgive you,' he said. 'Of course I do. But it's you who had to forgive, and thank you so much for doing so.' He looked around him, at the pool and the gently swaying palm trees, and a ginger cat slinking along the boundary wall. 'So what happens now?'

The directness of the question took Carrie by surprise. 'What happens with what?' she asked, even though she knew the answer, just to buy herself some time.

'With us.' Jack's response was bald and direct.

Carrie wriggled awkwardly in her chair. She didn't know how to react. She'd gone from being single and unattached for so many years to suddenly having two men in her life. It was incomprehensible.

'What would you like to happen?'

Jack opened and shut his mouth, then shrugged wearily. 'Perhaps now's not the right time. Because there's something else we need to discuss first, isn't there?'

Carrie stared at him blankly, even while the tiniest niggle of understanding worried away at her. She was not surprised by Jack's next words.

'You and K—'

Carrie's phone rang, interrupting Jack and making her jump out of her skin. It was Nell. 'Mum, where are you? I woke up and you're not here.' Her voice over the airwaves was pitiful and woebegone, and Carrie's heart turned over with love.

'I'm coming right now,' she assured Nell, already up and out of her seat, squeezing past the table while waving to Jack and pointing at the phone, mouthing 'got to go.'

'Sorry, darling,' she continued, striding as fast as her unsteady legs would take her across the road to the caldera side and their luxury room. Even while she reassured her daughter, she had a sense of being saved by the bell. It was obvious what Jack had been going to ask, and Carrie did not feel ready to answer. 'I got talking to Kris and then to Dad and the time ran away with me,' she explained to Nell. 'I'm here now.'

She dropped the call as she let herself into the room. Nell was sitting up in bed, phone clamped to her ear, eyes wide and full of fear. Carrie ran over to her and clutched her in a tight embrace.

'Mum,' she said, her voice cracking with impending tears. 'I wanted to say sorry.'

Carrie frowned, puzzled. 'What for?' she answered. 'What have you done now?' She accompanied this with a chuckle to show she was joking. Sort of. You never knew with Nell.

Her daughter shook her head. 'Nothing! But that's the point. I, er, I – well, I've been being an idiot. Getting into trouble and stuff. Not here – that was an accident – well, the fake ID, but honestly, we didn't mean any harm, all we meant to do was help you find out about Sol, so that you can write the book – I know you really want to be a writer again, Mum, and I think you need to do it. It's what you're good it. And I guess I've always wanted a bigger family and Sol feels like he's part of that and...' She paused, wiping her nose with her hand. 'But anyway, I'm talking about back at home as well. Stupid things I've done. Drinking and... all that. And I wanted to say I'm sorry and that I'll do better, try harder. I don't even know why I was doing all those idiotic things. I don't even like smoking, or drugs, or any of it really. I think I was trying to fit in.'

For a moment, she looked unutterably sad, her eyes narrowed, her mouth pulled into a sorrowful grimace. A wave of love and emotion threatened to make Carrie cry. She remembered only too well the hell that is being a teenager – so unsure of yourself beneath whatever front you showed to the world, so anxious to impress, so dependent on the opinions of peers and rivals. She'd still been experiencing lots of the same things at uni when she and Jack broke up. God, she wouldn't want to be that age again for anything. It was genuinely frightful.

She pulled Nell into an even tighter embrace.

'It's OK, my darling,' she crooned. 'I'll always love you, whatever you do. You'll always be my precious girl, you know that, don't you?' She felt Nell's head against her stomach move in a silent nod. 'And thank you for your apology,' she murmured softly. 'It means a lot.'

There was a pause while Carrie let the emotion subside. She knew how much it would have taken for Nell to say sorry. Then she smiled and ran her hand across her forehead. 'Phew,' she sighed, jokingly. 'I'm looking forward to this new life of zero anxiety, I can tell you.'

Nell smirked. 'Well, I wouldn't necessarily go that far. I'm not putting myself forward for sainthood quite yet...'

They both laughed and, once the laughter had subsided, Nell's eyelids flickered shut.

'You're exhausted,' crooned Carrie. 'Time to sleep now.'

She lay down on the bed next to her daughter, stroking her hair, until she dropped off, just as she had done when Nell was only a little girl. There was a bottle of disinfectant on the bedside table that Nell had left with the top off and the faint, medical smell of it took Carrie back to Nell's surgery, to learning how to dress the wound, which she had done with such infinite care as Nell had stared trustingly up at her with her big, brown eyes.

Oh God, she was so lucky that Nell was alive. That was all that mattered. The only thing.


In the morning, Carrie and Nell went to the restaurant to meet Kris for breakfast. Carrie was once again riven with embarrassment. She and Kris had admitted some of their deepest longings to each other – for love and affection and togetherness. They had almost slept together. What was the etiquette here? Would they discuss the next opportunity to get it together? Would there be another opportunity, with Nell and Jack always present? Did she want another opportunity?

It was all too confusing; she had no idea what was going on. She resorted to ordering a large espresso, hoping that strong caffeine might provide the answer.

Kris appeared shortly after the coffee. 'I've got some news,' he announced.

Immediately, Nell pricked up her ears.

'What?' she demanded eagerly. Her brush with death had not diminished her interest in the wartime story she and Amy had set out to investigate. Carrie had filled Nell in on the return journey to the cave that she and Kris had made, including the discovery, and retrieval, of the radio and the letter. She'd also told Nell that, like her and Amy, they'd thankfully found no sign of Penelope's mythical skeleton. But the story did seem to have some basis in reality. Presumably word had got around that one of the SBS men had got left behind and perhaps, from there, it was an understandable extrapolation that he had died and his body had never been recovered, because who on the island, apart from possibly Vassia, would have known if he'd got away?

'I did some digging around on the internet last night, after we got back from our meal,' Kris continued. 'I hadn't had the time before now, but I'm glad I finally got round to it because I think I've found Andreas's son.'

'No way!' shouted Carrie and 'Cool,' cried Nell, at the same time. Sudden dizziness swept over Carrie, a mixture of her hangover and excitement.

'I unearthed an Atlas Kourakis who says on his Facebook page that he was born in Santorini in 1944. Then in one of his pictures, if you really zoom in, you can see some photos on a shelf behind him. One is almost the same as that picture Nell found in Vassia's house, like it was taken at the same time or a copy was made. I sent him an email.' Kris looked up and caught both Nell and Carrie's eyes before continuing. 'But he hasn't replied yet.'

Carrie slumped to the table, head in hands. 'Ooof,' she said, letting out a great slough of air. 'I thought we had some answers then.'

Kris smiled. 'I think we do. Because that's not all. I also picked up a message from my mother. Our visit to Vassia's house galvanised her into action. She says that even if she's not going to rent it to tourists, she should get it cleaned up and let it to a local couple. There's so little housing for those who were born and bred here.'

'Lovely idea,' agreed Carrie.

'And she's found something she wants us to see. When we've finished breakfast, do you fancy a quick visit to Vourvoulos?'

As they weaved through the winding cobbled alleyways, Carrie was struck again by the beauty of the village. Did her beloved Uncle Sol once walk these same streets to this house? At the tiny house surrounded by shocking-pink bougainvillea, Elena let them in with a sombre expression on her face. Once Carrie, Kris and Nell were settled on the sofa, she held up a hard-covered scrapbook before them, about A5 size.

'I think it's something Vassia made during the war,' she explained. 'I started to clear out the bedroom and I took out the mattress – no one's going to want something so old. It's filled with straw I think, it's so ancient! Not a comfortable rest for anyone.'

Carrie gazed at her, on tenterhooks. She could feel Nell squirming beside her, whether at the thought of sleeping on straw or from impatience Carrie didn't know. She nudged her with her elbow to get her to stop.

'And I found this underneath the mattress. It must have been there for years.'

She handed the book to Kris, who opened the stiff cover with a creak. He moved it to his right, dangling over Carrie's knees, so she and Nell could see too. It seemed to consist of newspaper cuttings together with pictures cut out of magazines and short passages of writing. Every few pages there was a heading of a new year: 1940, 1941, 1942, 1943 and, finally, 1944.

'She seems to be documenting the war,' Kris surmised. 'And look what she's put in 1944.'

He, Carrie and Nell all bent forward to see more closely. It was a line drawing, similar to the one in Sol's sketchbook, but simpler, and seeming to have been torn from its pages. The signature beneath it read *Sol Baker*.

'A selfie for her to keep.' Nell sighed. 'That's so romantic.'

Kris turned to the next page. An official document was stuck there, its black typed print bold and ominous.

'It's from the occupying forces,' he murmured as his eyes moved back and forth, trying to establish exactly what it was. 'It says Vassia Kourakis has been arrested and charged with aiding and abetting the enemy.'

'Harumph,' snorted Elena. 'Their enemy maybe. Not ours.'

'So she was right that they'd been betrayed,' whispered Carrie, not entirely sure why she was speaking so quietly. It wasn't as if there were Nazis waiting on the street corners, looking for traitors. But somehow, immersed in Vassia's world, it felt that way.

'Who would do that?' cried Nell, echoing Carrie and Kris's thoughts when they had found out the dreadful fact.

Kris turned the page to where dense writing covered every inch. He read it in silence, then dropped the book down, letting it rest on Carrie's lap.

'I don't believe it,' he croaked, in a voice thick with emotion. 'I simply can't believe it.'

'What?' questioned Carrie, desperately. 'What is it?'

Kris raised his eyes to meet hers.

'It's here. The person who did it. It's incomprehensible.'

Carrie was practically grabbing him by this stage, wanting to shake the discovery out of him. 'Who?' she demanded. 'Just tell us who!' Nell was breathing down her neck, anxious not to miss a word.

'Andreas,' Kris replied, simply. 'Her own brother betrayed Sol.'

# CHAPTER 41

## VASSIA, 1944

### THIRTY-SIX HOURS BEFORE

Entering her brother's house, Vassia felt a lump in her throat at the thought of what she was about to do. She longed more than anything for her suspicions to be unfounded, to be plain wrong. But she was more and more sure that they weren't. The worst thing of all was the involvement of tiny, helpless Atlas in the whole thing. That innocent baby knew nothing of what his father had done, and neither did his mother. But if it ever came out, the shame would engulf all of them.

Vassia did not want this for her nephew and sister-in-law. She didn't want it for her brother, even though he was the one to blame. She still loved him, always would. But there was nothing she could do about it. Whatever she set in motion today would lead irrevocably in one direction only and nobody would be able to stop the roller-coaster once it started moving.

In the kitchen, Andreas was seated at the kitchen table, holding Atlas. Athena, with an apron tied round her waist, was serving the fish. It smelt delicious. Vassia's stomach rumbled and saliva collected in her mouth as she greeted the family.

'You're just in time!' cried Athena, hurriedly fetching a third plate from the dresser. 'You'll eat with us, won't you? This is the first proper cooking I've done since the little one was born. We've been living on kind offerings from our neighbours and leftovers from the restaurant.' She bit her lip regretfully after uttering this statement, as if not quite able to believe how lax she had become.

'None for me, thank you,' Vassia quickly replied. She was hungry – starving in fact – but she couldn't eat anything right now. 'I'll dine with Mama when I get back. Otherwise she won't take anything. She's still in pieces after...' There was no need to finish the sentence. 'I wanted to check on Atlas,' she continued. 'He's improved again, I think?'

Athena made the sign of the cross. 'Thank the Lord,' she uttered, almost breathless with relief.

'You got some medicine for him?' Vassia added. 'That's it there, isn't it?' She pointed to a small bottle that sat on the shelf behind the table, next to Athena's half-knitted shawl.

'Again, praise the Lord,' enthused Athena, and then turned to her husband and lovingly patted his arm that held their child so protectively against him. 'Andreas managed to source it, I don't know how.'

Andreas was playing with a piece of bread from the basket on the table and didn't look up.

'Wonderful news,' Vassia said. It wasn't a lie. Seeing Atlas grow and thrive was a top priority, nobody would disagree with that. It was just a shame what had enabled it to be so.

'I really came to see Andreas about something,' she went on apologetically. She met her brother's gaze and raised her eyebrows in a gesture that told him they needed to be alone.

'I'll be right back,' Andreas said. 'Carry on dishing up. Two minutes.'

Clutching the baby, he followed Vassia out of the house.

'Andreas, I don't k-know what to do,' Vassia began, stuttering slightly with nerves she hoped he would interpret as distress. 'They know about Sol – the Nazis. They know he's on the island, but I don't think they know about the cave. They haven't gone there yet. But they're definitely after him. And surely it won't be long until they find him.'

Andreas stared at her in wide-eyed horror. The baby stirred and he lifted him up, propped him against his broad shoulder and absent-mindedly patted his little back.

'That's terrible,' he mouthed.

'Yes,' agreed Vassia. Of course she didn't add, *they know because I told you and you told them.* 'I think he's gone to Oia to hide out there, in one of the old cave houses dug out of the caldera wall perhaps. And then tomorrow night – I'll meet him and escort him to the pick-up point where he'll be taken off the island.'

Andreas greeted this news with silence.

'I better go now,' Vassia concluded. 'I'll see you soon.'

The next morning, once she'd established that the Nazis were turning Oia upside down in their attempts to unearth Sol, clearly informed by Andreas, she sent Nico to find Sol in the shed by Apollo's paddock and give him the letter. The letter that declared her undying love, the letter in which she assured Sol that she would meet him by the cave to lead him to the rendezvous point as agreed. And the letter that mentioned nothing about the fact that she now knew who had betrayed him. To tell Sol it was her own brother who had done such a terrible thing would drown Vassia in shame. At this time of so much heartbreak, let him remember her and her family well. At least Andreas had not told the Nazis about the cave; if they had known about that, Sol would have had no chance of getting away alive.

Vassia could only guess at exactly how it had played out. Schwarz had had a soft spot for her brother ever since he'd arrived on the island, and was always to be found in Loucas's restaurant, eating and drinking and carousing. Vassia pictured Schwarz congratulating the young waiter on the birth of his baby son – a good, strong, fit boy who could eventually fight for the Reich like Schwarz! And when he'd seen in Andreas's eyes and demeanour that all was not well, he would obviously have enquired as to the problem.

The baby needed medicine for his heart, Andreas would have told Schwarz. It wasn't a particularly unusual drug, or a new one. In fact, it had been around for years. But there was none on Santorini, apart from what the Germans had.

Schwarz had spotted his opportunity, as only a true brute possessed of a certain low cunning could. He had made a deal with Andreas.

Information for medicine.

If Andreas told Schwarz everything he knew about the raid and the commandos, Schwarz would provide for his baby the treatment needed to save his life. Andreas, torn between his love for his people and his adoration for his son, had had to make an impossible choice.

Vassia wasn't surprised that he'd chosen Atlas' life over and above Sol's. His own flesh and blood for a complete stranger? Not much of a contest. But still... To know the truth was devastating. Soul-destroying. She could never had believed her family would be involved in something like this, would be put to the test like this. It was still hard to believe it.

Athena's knitting had given it away. That and Atlas' seemingly miraculous recovery. Vassia had spotted the bottle on the shelf, with the German label and writing in the Roman alphabet that she couldn't read, when she'd been looking at her sister-in-law's half-made baby shawl. She'd known immediately. It had all fallen into place. She'd been sure that no one knew about Sol except herself – and her brother. So it had been odd that the Nazis had found out that Sol was still on the island. That had aroused her suspicion. To test her theory, she'd told

Andreas that Sol had fled to Oia – and straight away, that was where the Germans had gone looking. When she set out to lead Sol to the rendezvous for his departure, she knew Schwarz would find her. Of course he would.

Andreas had told him.

# CHAPTER 42

## CARRIE, 2024

The discovery of the truth about the elusive Andreas shocked them all. Kris read out loud Vassia's scrawling diary entry, which explained a lot more. It described how she had led Sol to an isolated beach, just in time to be picked up by the SBS schooner that had sailed across from Turkey to collect him. As she had turned to leave, she'd come face to face with the island's commanding officer, and been arrested and thrown into a prison cell.

## VASSIA, 1944

Schwarz had really pushed out the boat for this arrest, thought Vassia, as she was bundled into one of only two army jeeps on the island. She'd half expected to be carted away by donkey. As the engine fired up and the tyres rumbled over the stony hillside, she marvelled at how calm she felt. Or maybe it was numbness, the inability to feel pain or fear while her heart was breaking.

Sol had got away; that was all that mattered. But he had gone and that was devastating. And on top of that was the knowledge that she had been betrayed by her own brother. Vassia remembered being worried about Schwarz's frequent visits to the restaurant and his interest in Andreas, how she had fretted that this boded ill for him. Now her fears had been shown to be well-founded, but in a way she could not possibly have envisaged. The shattering revelation of what Andreas had done was still hard to comprehend. Yet when Vassia closed her eyes and saw behind her lids little Atlas' scrunched-up face, his laboured breathing, his pallor, she understood. If the Germans killed her as they had her father and the other men, she would have given her life to save a life. Was that fair enough?

It was hard to think about it rationally.

She tried to judge the distance they had travelled by how long she had been trussed up in the dark, but time distorted, expanding and contracting with every lunging, lurching move-ment of the jeep so that it became impossible to measure the time that had passed. Her limbs ached as she wondered if the driver was deliberately hitting every pothole and rock in the road to torment her. He probably was; she was under no illusion that, to her captors, she was anything but anathema.

Eventually, the vehicle came to an abrupt halt that sent Vassia jolting across the floor. The doors opened and two grim-faced soldiers roughly hauled her out, shaking her unnecessarily as they did so. It was still dark, with not a glimmer of the dawn yet breaking. As the men frogmarched her forward, she tried to make out where she was, but in the obscurity she recognised nothing. The Nazis' barracks in Fira were presumably still out of use after the bombing and the raid, so they must have requisi-tioned another building, but Vassia had no idea where it was.

The heavy wooden door opened as they approached, and Vassia was strong-armed over the threshold, the butt of a rifle against her back. Inside, it was dark and smelt dusty and fusty. She was pushed into a room, so violently that she fell to the floor and, as she cowered on her knees, her hands still tied behind her, she heard the clang of the door closing and a key being turned in the lock.

For a few moments she did not move, as she tried to slow her breathing and calm her racing heart. A couple of times panic threatened to overwhelm her, and she fought it back, willing herself to stay strong. If she was going to get out of this predicament alive, she had to remain in control, keep her wits about her.

Slowly, she somehow managed to clumsily clamber to her feet, despite not having the use of her hands. In the corner of the windowless room, her eyes could just make out a wooden pallet that was the only piece of furniture. She stumbled over to it and sat down on its edge. She needed a plan – what to say when she faced the inevitable interrogation, whether to plead innocence or admit her guilt. To do the former seemed unwise, given that she'd been caught red-handed. To do the latter was plainly a death sentence. Whichever way she looked at it, her future seemed grim.

Vassia thought of her mother, who would not know what had happened to her daughter. She relied so heavily on her since her father's death; how would she cope without Vassia? It was all she could do not to let despair sweep over her at the thought of Thalia, worried and fretful, waiting at the window for her daughter's return.

Hours later, how many Vassia could not estimate, the door of the cell-like room was flung open and a soldier in full uniform entered. He carried a plate in one hand and a tin cup in the other, and he set them down on the floor next to her, doing it so violently that water slopped over the edge of the cup. Despite everything, Vassia's stomach gurgled at the sight and smell of the food and her parched throat cried out for moisture. It was a long time since she had last eaten or drunk.

The soldier made as if to turn and leave. Vassia plucked up her courage, which, in the event, wasn't as hard as she had imagined. After all, if her fate was already sealed because of what she had done, she could hardly make it any worse.

'Please could you untie my hands,' she asked, politely.

The soldier hesitated, pausing for a moment halfway to the door, as if deliberating over her request. Then he turned and stared at her, so intensely that her insides turned over in trepidation. After considering her in a way that felt like a physical assault, he stepped forward, seized the rope that bound her wrists and undid it in one extravagant gesture. He tossed the rope onto the pallet, stood back and surveyed Vassia again, hands on hips.

'Don't even think about trying anything on,' he threatened. 'It'll only make things worse for you.'

Vassia, refusing to be cowed, held his gaze. 'Thank you,' she said, in as neutral a tone of voice as she could manage.

With that, the soldier left.

When Vassia's hands had come back to life and the pins and needles had subsided, she ate the food – tough mutton and bread – and drank the water. She wanted twice as much. After a while she lay down on the pallet, and must have dropped off because the next thing she was aware of was the door opening once more and two soldiers entering. They took an arm each and propelled her through a labyrinth of dimly lit corridors. Vassia tried her best to fix the route in her head so that she would know the way she had come, but it was hard to do when she had so much else clouding her mind.

They ended up in a large room. In the centre stood a desk, behind which sat Vassia's nemesis: Lieutenant Schwarz himself.

'Ah, Miss Kourakis,' said Schwarz, making it sound like a sneer even though he was smiling. 'Thank you for coming to see me.'

Vassia did not reply. He was trying to unnerve her, and she wouldn't let him.

'I think you've got a bit of explaining to do, don't you?'

Schwarz went on. 'I mean, I could just shoot you now, of course. But I thought it might be amusing to hear what you have to say for yourself. We've met before, have we not, and I've noticed a feistiness about you that isn't fitting for a young woman, even a Greek one.'

The two soldiers who had delivered Schwarz his prey laughed smarmily.

'I have never had any complaints about my conduct, Lieutenant Schwarz,' replied Vassia.

Schwarz reached out and picked up a pipe from his desk. He struck a match and the sulphurous fumes momentarily filled the air. For a few moments he appeared to be entirely concentrated on lighting the tobacco, before he took a few puffs and blew out a cloud of smoke.

'So,' he said. 'I find you on a beach in the dead of night, the scent of a British commando still on your skin. I'm not sure what defence you could have for your actions but please, if you think you have one, do share.'

Again, his sidekicks chortled as if this were the funniest quip ever.

Vassia swallowed and forced herself to composure. 'I was on the beach, and I did go there with a British commando. He needed to escape and I helped him.' She fixed her eyes on Schwarz's face, trying to discern his expression behind the wafts of smoke that partially obscured his face. 'You would never have known anything about it if it weren't for my brother, Andreas. I know that he told you about the commando's existence in return for essential medicine for his baby. I'm sorry that, for a German, an infant is only worth saving if there is something in it for the saviour. As a Christian, I don't live my life that way. But there you are; that's the difference between a simple Greek girl and a Nazi officer, I suppose.'

When she finished speaking, all Vassia's blood seemed to drain from her body. She felt weak and dizzy. Why on earth had she been so bold? So provocative? She held on to the sides of the chair with her hands, gripping the wooden seat with all her might, trying to stay upright, keeping her face as impassive as she could.

For a few moments, absolute silence reigned in the room.

Then, with an almighty crash, Schwarz slammed his palms onto the desk. 'Impudent woman,' he shouted. He gestured angrily to the guards. 'Take her away, get her out of my sight.'

Vassia was snatched up roughly and almost lifted bodily from the ground as the two soldiers hastened to remove her from the room.

Back in her cell, she had nothing to do but sit on the pallet and wait. It wouldn't be long, surely. Schwarz would have her shot pretty soon, and then she really would be out of his way for ever. As she sat, she closed her eyes and thought of her family and her childhood, her adored cousin Nico, and finally of Sol, the man she loved. She replayed their precious moments together, over and over, like a speeded-up series of photographs, how she imagined a movie would be, although she had never seen one.

She thought of Sol's arms round her, his weather-beaten lips on her mouth, the tenderness of his touch despite the roughness of his soldier's skin. She pictured the schooner, slipping away in the darkness, sails unfurling, nothing to give it away apart from the slosh of the water around its bow. He would have reached safety now, God willing, have been reunited with his brigade. They'd already be planning their next audacious raid, plotting their course to another Greek island. Would he meet another girl there, like herself? Vassia forced such thoughts from her mind. *Enjoy your beautiful memories*, she told herself.

*They are all you have.*

# CHAPTER 43

## VASSIA, 1944

Over the next few days, Vassia was brought out of the cell and questioned by various other officers, but she never saw Schwarz again. He hadn't been lying when he'd said he didn't want to see her any more. Before the events of the last couple of months, Vassia had never given any thought to whether she would give way under interrogation. It had never occurred to her. Now, she realised it wasn't relevant anyway. She told the Germans everything she knew because the simple fact was that she knew nothing. She had no idea where the SBS were headed next, what their intentions were.

In the hours spent alone, she tried to come to terms with her brother's actions. She imagined her own baby, and how she would feel if the child was very, very sick like Atlas. Gradually, piece by piece, she let go of her anger and, instead of hating her brother, she forgave him and prayed for him.

On what Vassia reckoned was the fourth or fifth day of her imprisonment, the door swung open once more. Expecting another interrogation, she stood up to accompany the guards, neither of whom she recognised. But this time, instead of leading her through the labyrinth of passages, they took her in another direction and, before her disbelieving eyes, the heavy wooden front door appeared. As it opened, her pupils contracted painfully in the bright light and she stood helplessly for a moment, blinking and unable to see. A shove in her back sent her flying, and she struggled to stay on her feet. Recovering from the shock of being pushed, she turned to see the guards preparing to retreat back inside.

'You're free to go,' one of them said, his voice thick with disapproval.

The second guard spoke next. 'I'd get out of here straight away if I were you.' His tone was softer than the other's, with a hint of something that sounded a bit like sympathy.

Needing no further exhortation, Vassia wrapped her arms round herself and began walking purposefully away.

Back in Vourvoulos, she found her mother at the kitchen table, her face worn and tear-stricken. On first laying eyes on her daughter, Thalia stared as if in disbelief. Then she leapt up, threw her arms round Vassia and sobbed into her shoulder.

'I thought you were gone,' she cried, over and over again. 'I thought I'd lost you.'

'There, there, Mama,' soothed Vassia. 'I'm not gone, I'm here, safe and sound. Everything's fine. Everything's going to be all right.'

Later that day, Vassia went out to fetch fava beans for supper. She felt disembodied, unable to truly believe she was free, not sure if her release was another of Schwarz's cruel jokes and that at any moment she might feel a hand on her shoulder and would be hurled back into jail. Buying food seemed simultaneously utterly trivial and completely urgent.

On her way back from the grocer's store, where she had avoided conversation with anyone, she bumped into Evangelos, who greeted her with a cheery smile. As he chatted away, Vassia realised that he knew nothing about her disappearance. Her mother couldn't have told even their closest neighbours.

'Is there anything you need?' Evangelos asked her eagerly. 'Anything at all, you just ask. Any man's job that you can't handle in your house, let me know.'

Vassia's heart melted. Evangelos had lost his brother, and yet still he was thinking of her and her mother making do without her father.

'Thank you,' she replied. 'We're fine at the moment. But if we do need anything, I'll know who to ask.'

Evangelos nodded and smiled. 'Good. That's good, Vassia. We neighbours must look out for each other.' He hesitated for a moment. 'I was thinking,' he went on, 'that it's not long until the feast day of Agioi Anargyroi in Megalochori. Perhaps you'd like to accompany me to the church service that day?'

The question took Vassia by surprise. 'Oh, well, I'm not sure,' she stalled. 'I mean, there's my mother to think of – I can't really leave her at the moment ...' She tailed off, not sure what other excuses to give.

'Well,' replied Evangelos, a little too quickly and a little too off-handedly, as if wanting to make it seem as if it was of no importance. 'If you change your mind, you can just let me know.' He lingered for a moment but then turned and walked briskly off in the direction of the harbour, where his fishing boat lay at anchor.

'I will,' answered Vassia, quietly, her words buffeted and dissipated by the breeze.

In the house, her mother had managed to rouse herself, rein-vigorated by Vassia's release from prison. She seized the beans from Vassia's hands and bustled around the kitchen, busily preparing supper. 'I saw you talking to Evangelos,' she said, as she chopped and fried. 'He's a lovely boy. As was his brother, God rest his soul.' She paused, on the brink of tears. Vassia put a protective arm round her shoulders.

'Don't think of that time,' she urged. 'It will only upset you.'

To take her mother's mind off it, she told her about Evangelos' invitation.

Thalia bit her lip and wiped her eyes. 'You should go,' she said.

By the time the meal was ready she'd brightened up a little more. 'It would be good for you to get to know Evangelos better, don't you think?' she suggested. 'You should definitely attend the feast day service. And then later in July we have our own one for Agios Panteleon. I will invite Evangelos' family over to share a meal. It will be a perfect opportunity.'

Vassia greeted this remark with silence. She pushed her fava beans around her plate as her mother continued.

'I mean to say that it's time for us to think about a marriage partner for you. With your father no longer here, the thing that would bring me the greatest happiness would be to see you settled down, like Andreas.' She stopped and let her fork drop to her plate, before putting her head in her hands. 'The thought of my only daughter's wedding is all that's keeping me going,' she wept, reaching out to clasp Vassia's hand. 'I need to know you're safe, and protected, in case... well, before I go.'

'Oh, Mama,' cried Vassia. 'You're going to be around for years and years. There's plenty of time. I'll always be here for you, and so will Andreas. Don't worry about that.'

But the next day, when Vassia went to call on her brother, the house was still and empty, the windows shuttered and the doors locked. She knocked and knocked, but there was no reply. It was as if the three of them, Andreas, Athena and Atlas, had melted away.

She didn't tell her mother about the family's disappearance, just said they were busy being new parents. After three days, she began to have suspicions about what must have happened. She hitched a ride on a donkey cart to Fira, and when she got there she made her way on foot down the long, snaking staircase of nearly six-hundred steps to the port. In the ferry office, she enquired about recent departures.

'Did you see a young family leave?' she asked. 'A man and his wife, with a small, almost newborn baby?'

The port official's forehead creased as he thought back over the last few days. 'Yes,' he said, eventually. 'They left on Wednesday. They bought tickets for Athens.'

'Thank you,' answered Vassia.

Outside, in the bright light of the scorching sun, she leant against the whitewashed wall and stared out to sea, as if she might still be able to make out the vessel that had taken her brother, Athena and Atlas away. They'd be on the mainland by now. They could be anywhere there. Greece was a big country. There was absolutely no way to find them. If she were a free agent, perhaps she could have got on a boat and followed them, tracked them down, traced them to some other place where they had gone to hide away Andreas's shame. But she couldn't leave Thalia, and anyway she had no money. She wondered where Andreas had got the funds. From Schwarz? Perhaps. Perhaps Schwarz was the one who'd advised him to go. Vassia wouldn't put it past him.

At this, a flame of fury fired up in her body. She would go and ask Schwarz. It was the stupidest thing she could possibly do. He hated her. He'd probably shoot her on sight. She was so enraged that she didn't care.

At his house, she marched straight up to the guards outside. 'I need to see Lieutenant Schwarz,' she demanded. 'It's important.'

Taken aback by her forwardness, one of the men took her inside and seated her in an antechamber of the official residence. As she sat and waited, there was time for her anger to subside and to be replaced by utter dread. What on earth was she doing? She must be mad. But there was no going back now.

In due course, Schwarz arrived. This was becoming more

surreal by the minute. He'd actually come to her summons. Vassia realised she hadn't expected him to do so.

'Miss Kourakis again. I thought I'd seen the last of you.' Schwarz's voice held a whiff of the same sneer, but it was definitely less than before. Vassia wondered what had changed.

'I want to know where my brother is.' She couldn't be bothered being polite.

For a fleeting moment, Schwarz's expression changed, revealing a flicker of doubt behind the ingrained superiority. 'He left.'

Vassia fought to hide her surprise that Schwarz was answering her questions. This encounter was getting stranger and stranger.

'Why?'

'You realise that I should have had you shot straight away, don't you?' Schwarz's question was rhetorical, and he didn't wait for an answer. 'Your brother begged and pleaded with me to have pity on you, to release you. I decided to humour him. But he had to go, before any of my subordinates found out. They might not be so merciful.'

It suddenly struck Vassia what this was about. After the reprisals, horrific though they were, there had always lingered the question of why the rest of the villagers, and the village itself, were spared. Now she and Andreas had also been that fortunate. There could be only one reason. Schwarz knew the war was turning in the Allies' favour, that one day fairly soon he might find himself on the losing side. He wanted to buy himself some good will, cleanse his record, make himself one of the good guys.

She gave Schwarz a look that made clear that she found him despicable. If she had been that kind of person, she would have spat at him. But she wouldn't demean herself in that way.

'You praise yourself very highly, Lieutenant Schwarz,' she replied, her voice smooth and expressionless. 'I'm afraid I can't feel the same way. You could have just offered my brother the medicine he needed for his child. But you would never do that, would you? Something for nothing doesn't exist in your world, does it? And that has cost me my only sibling and my nephew, my mother her only son and grandchild. I hope you're happy with what you've done.'

And with that she left, without a backward glance.

# CHAPTER 44

CARRIE, 2024

'No wonder Andreas left Santorini and never came back,' commented Kris grimly when they had finished reading Vassia's account. 'He wouldn't have been welcome.'

Elena harrumphed again. 'You're right. He would have been too scared. Though as parents we understand the desperate urge to help a poorly infant.' She sighed long and hard before continuing. 'My mother and grandmother obviously managed to keep the real reason for the family's disappearance quiet, as we know from the old ladies' ignorance of it.' Her eyes flicked to the window in a wistful gaze. 'But it was a long time ago now. We should forgive and forget, as Vassia herself did. What a shame she never got the chance to tell her brother she didn't hold it against him.'

They all sat for a while in quiet contemplation of a time in history that had had such momentous consequences for a close-knit island family.

Eventually, Elena got up. 'Well, at least we solved the mystery,' she said, with a heavy air of finality. 'Our mystery, at least.' She sighed. 'It's strange to hear of this huge love affair that no one knew anything about. I always thought my mother and father had only ever had eyes for each other. Whatever else, I do think Vassia managed to make a happy life for herself.' She looked at Carrie. 'But maybe Sol did not, given that he never married. There are some things perhaps we'll never know.' She sighed again, more heavily this time, and shook her head. 'And I've got this place to clear up.' She looked around somewhat hopelessly, as if bewildered by the scale of the task.

Kris said he would stay and help his mother move some of the heavy furniture.

'How are you going to get it down the lanes and out to the dump or wherever it's going?' asked Carrie.

'The old way.' Kris laughed. 'On a donkey.'

'No way!' exclaimed Nell. 'People really still use donkeys to do stuff like that?'

'Of course,' replied Kris. 'Why not?'

Nell laughed and Carrie felt a rush of relief that she seemed entirely back to normal. Or at least, nearly normal. Her contrition at the worry she had put her parents through meant that she was being super-polite and obliging.

It was Amy's last day on the island and Carrie, in the spirit of forgiveness modelled by Vassia, agreed that Nell could hang out with her by the pool, but only in Carrie's full sight and they weren't going anywhere else.

It gave Carrie the excuse to have a lazy day. Jack came over from Fira and they took two sunloungers underneath the palm trees and stretched out together. Like a married couple, thought Carrie, reflecting on how strange it was. She and Jack chatted about this and that, catching up after years of exchanging little more than a few words. Carrie felt so comfortable with him, as if they had slotted back into just how they had been all that time ago.

That evening Nell, Carrie and Jack went out for dinner and it felt completely natural. Carrie kept catching sight of Nell observing her mother and father from under her eyelashes, seeming to be weighing up the way they were reacting to each other. Carrie knew she'd always longed to have a mum and a dad who lived together, and had always felt bad about not delivering that for her. It had always seemed so impossible after what had happened.

Once Nell had gone to bed – or, rather, gone into the room to peruse her phone for a few hours – Jack and Carrie sat on the idyllic terrace. The doors were firmly shut to keep out the heat, so Nell wouldn't be able to hear what they were saying.

'So, Carrie,' began Jack, his tone of voice indicating that he had something important to say. 'I'm not trying to come between you and your...' He hesitated and then said the word. 'Your boyfriend. But I do have a right to know if you're thinking of relocating to Greece or some—'

'No!' Carrie cut in before Jack had a chance to finish. 'No, he's not my boyfriend. I mean, not really. Not at all. God, Jack, with everything that's happened, I've hardly had the time, energy or inclination to think about my love life. And anyway, it's none of your business who's my boyfriend.' The basic rules of grammar deserted her as she tried to formulate her answer.

'Right,' said Jack, abruptly, but then his tone softened. 'Carrie, I'll just cut to the chase. Please can we try again? We were so good together and we can be again. There's never been anyone like you. All these years, trying to be the best dad I could be to Nell – of course I did that for her, but I did it for you, too. Hoping I could prove to you that I wasn't a useless waste of space. I've never given up thinking we could get back together.' He paused, looking suddenly exhausted. 'I've admitted I behaved badly and I've apologised. I've served my penance for it. And now I'm not too proud to tell you that I still love you. I always have. I always will.'

Stunned into silence, Carrie stared at him open-mouthed. She didn't know what to say, how to react. When she came to her senses, she realised what was bizarre about it. That now that

Jack had said it, now that he had used the 'l' word, she knew that she felt that way too.

But earlier that very week, she'd begun to think she loved Kris. It was all too much. She was too bewildered and discombobulated to respond.

'I... er, I-I'm not sure...' she stuttered.

Jack nodded, not waiting for her to finish. 'OK,' he said. 'I've said my piece and now I'll be off. I just needed you to know.'

And with that, he strode away, bounded up the steps to street level and disappeared from view.

Carrie went to bed, but she didn't sleep. She lay for a long time, gazing at the domed ceiling, listening to Nell's soft, rhythmic breathing. Kris wasn't her boyfriend, obviously, they'd only known each other ten minutes. Although maybe he wanted to be. They had that little bit of history that had brought them together in the first place. They had, undeniably, kissed, several times, and even nearly had sex. Jack had read her mind when he'd accused her of wanting to move to Greece. She had thought about it. Seriously considered it, even, swept away by the romance and glamour of it all, drunk on Santorini wine and sunshine.

If things had been different this last ten days, would something more have happened between her and Kris? Something that made such a move more likely? Carrie had to accept that very probably it would have. Did she still want something more to happen, now? Since Jack had arrived? Since their 'clearing the air' conversation? Since Jack's declaration of love?

She wasn't sure. She wasn't sure at all.

# CHAPTER 45

## VASSIA, 1947

'Are you ready?' Thalia had been fussing all morning, and Vassia already felt weary. She understood her mother's excitement, and was happy that she was happy. Since the war had ended, all everyone wanted was to put the horrific past behind them and move on. So many people were absent: her father, her brother, Kostas and all the others who had been so ruthlessly cut down by the Nazis. Those who remained had many pairs of big shoes to fill, and Vassia felt the weight of this on a daily basis. Her engagement had given her mother something to focus on for the past few months and it had been wonderful to see how it had lifted her spirits.

Thalia stood in front of her daughter and carefully arranged the veil round her head, ready to pull down as she entered the church.

'You are so beautiful,' she breathed. 'What a lucky, lucky man he is!'

Vassia smiled. 'Can you check the buttons at the back?' she asked. 'I think one feels a little loose.'

As her mother moved out of sight, Vassia squeezed her eyes closed to try to clear her mind. She wanted to get married, of course she did. Evangelos was a lovely man; safe and solid, caring and adoring. She couldn't want for more.

Except that of course she could. She wanted Sol. But she had long ago accepted that that dream was gone, along with Sol himself. When he'd sailed off into the night on that evening two years ago, she'd known in her heart that she would never see him again. But perhaps she'd always held a kernel of hope that he might return.

Eventually, the pressure to do right by her mother and give Thalia her heart's desire – that is, a ring on her daughter's finger and, with any luck, a baby nine months later – had been insurmountable. She loved Evangelos, she really did. It wasn't his fault he wasn't Sol. Vassia had told herself very sternly that, once she'd accepted his proposal, she had to throw herself into the relationship and the impending nuptials wholeheartedly, and that was what she had done, and intended to go on doing.

'All the buttons look fine to me,' said Thalia. 'The dress fits you perfectly. Oh, I remember when I had a figure like yours.'

Vassia was wearing the dress that had been worn by her mother and grandmother. It was tradition, but also necessity. No one had money or cloth for new clothes, not even for such an important occasion.

'Right, well, I suppose it's time we were off.' Vassia took one last look in the stained and rusted mirror and then swept off towards the door. Outside, her besuited pageboy, cousin Nico, was waiting, sitting straight-backed on a chair, following the instructions he'd been given not to run around and get himself dirty.

'Vassia, you're so pretty!' he called out when Vassia appeared. He jumped up and came to hold her hand. Vassia clasped it tightly and bit back more tears. 'Thank you, Nico,' she murmured. 'You look very handsome yourself.'

Nico laughed and danced along beside her as they made the short journey to the village church. As they took their first steps, the bells began to ring, sounding out along the lanes and alley-ways, drawing the wedding party to their pews. Evangelos' and Vassia's nuptials were the first to be held in Vourvoulos since peace had come and everyone was looking forward to a party.

Walking up the aisle, Vassia's legs trembled as Evangelos turned to watch her. He looked wonderful in his suit, his hair freshly cut and oiled, his kind, familiar face clean-shaven, his smile as broad as his shoulders. A sense of calm serenity descended upon Vassia as the priest began the simple cere-mony. Evangelos and she were of a kind – village people, Santorini people – and their children, of whom Vassia hoped there would be several, would be the same. The British commando would always have a central place in her heart, but this was reality.

Sol had only ever been a dream.

# CHAPTER 46

## CARRIE, 2024

Next day, Kris was in the restaurant when Nell and Carrie got there for breakfast.

'He replied,' he said, as soon as he saw Carrie. 'Atlas. He got my email and he's replied.'

'What! What did he say?' she asked, the words exploding out of her like bullets.

Kris grimaced. 'I haven't had the courage to open it yet,' he said. 'I thought we could do it together.' He had his laptop with him and, the three of them crowded as close together as they could get, he clicked on the message.

Thank you for your mail, which I read with great interest. My name is indeed Atlas Kourakis and my father's name was Andreas. We left Santorini when I was a baby; I have no memories of living there, nor of any of the rest of the family. But as he lay dying, my father told me about what had happened on the island that meant he had to leave and never return. My parents stole away in the dead of night because my father had done something terrible to save my life.

'Wow,' murmured Carrie. 'What a thing to reveal when you're on your way out.'

'But listen to the rest,' said Kris, excitedly.

The SBS commando got away. But my father's sister, Vassia, was arrested. My father was racked with guilt, tormented by it. He went to the German commander's residence, a man named Schwarz, and pleaded with him. They knew each other well, as this man often dined at the restaurant where my father was a waiter. When he finally had Schwarz's agreement that he would release Vassia, my father made arrangements to leave. We took the next boat to Athens, never to return.

Carrie sat in silence as Kris finished reading. Nell had been born with a heart condition, just like Atlas. She remembered thinking that she would do anything, anything at all in her power, to help her child. Did that extend to betraying her own sibling, putting them at risk of imprisonment, even death? She couldn't think, couldn't get her head around being in such an awful situation, having to grapple with such a terrible dilemma. Whatever she herself would, or would not, have done, Andreas had taken the only course of action he had felt possible, and Carrie understood that. 'It's all so sad,' said Nell, breaking the silence. She was clearly overwhelmed by the revelation. 'I mean, don't get me wrong, Andreas shouldn't have done it. But I can see why he did.'

Carrie smiled inwardly at the ease with which Nell had also seen the situation for what it was.

Grimacing, Kris agreed with Nell. 'Yes. He did something terrible, but with a motive we can all relate to. And he paid the price; a lifetime's exile from his homeland and family.'

He began to quickly type. Carrie watched the incomprehensible words take shape. How had she ever thought she could learn this language? It really was all Greek to her.

'What are you saying?' she asked, as Kris continued tapping away.

But Kris just shook his head. 'I'll tell you later,' he said.

It was their last full day on the island, so Carrie, Jack and Nell went to Akrotiri, the archaeological site of the Minoan civilisation upon which much of the Lost Atlantis theory was based. The city had been abandoned before the massive eruption that blew the landmass apart, indicating that the ancient peoples had known what was coming down the line. In that way, it was completely different to the ruins of Pompeii and Herculaneum, where bodies lay among the debris.

Carrie was interested in the site and its history, but she was also preoccupied, happy to let Jack and Nell do the talking. Listening to them burbling away, pointing at various interesting artefacts and poring over the brochure together, her heart turned over with love and contentment.

Nell's start in life had been so uncertain after her heart condition had been diagnosed, and Carrie felt she had always been on tenterhooks. Carrying the burden alone had taken its toll. No wonder she'd spent so many years feeling tired and alone.

That evening, she suggested to Kris that all five of them – including Xanthe, who had returned from Thessaloniki – have dinner together, but he declined, saying he was busy. Carrie wasn't so sure that was really the reason.

The day of their evening flight home dawned as bright and clear as all of the preceding ones. Carrie felt sad at the thought of leaving this mini-paradise, going back to the leisure centre and the chores. She'd been spoiled. It wasn't good for her, all this beauty and luxury; it made her discontent with her lot in life, when she knew how fortunate she really was.

Nell wanted to go into the town and buy souvenirs and little gifts for her friends. *The Undesirables*, thought Carrie, and decided she'd have to give them another name. Now that Nell was safe she felt benign about everything and everyone, calm and sure of herself for the first time in a long while. Jack said he'd go with Nell and Carrie excused herself. She had made a decision.

She found Kris in his office. It wasn't the ideal place, but there might not be another chance. She sat down on one of the chairs at the round table and Kris came to join her.

'I've got some news,' he said, before Carrie could get started. 'I've spoken to Atlas now, as well as emailed, and he's going to come over! With his wife, and their son and two granddaughters. I mean, they're both elderly and they don't want to travel in the heat, so they won't come until the autumn, which will be better all round. I can let them have the best rooms and show them around the island. It'll be quite some homecoming!'

'That's fabulous,' said Carrie, genuinely delighted. 'What a wonderful story of a family reunited. Does your mum know? She'll be overjoyed, won't she?'

Kris nodded. 'She's thrilled. Especially after finding Vassia's scrapbook, she just wants everything sorted, no hard feelings, and so on.'

'I'm so pleased for you all. I wish Sol were still around to join in, and Vassia herself of course. It's so great that we managed to piece the story together. Or most of it, at least.'

Kris eyed her quizzically. 'What's left?' he asked.

Carrie sighed. 'Well, as your mother alluded to, we don't really know why Sol didn't come back for Vassia after the war. He bought that ring, after all, and who could he have meant it for if not Vassia? So why did she never receive it? Why didn't they rekindle their love?'

Kris shook his head. 'I don't know. I suppose things moved on. Life moved on. You know how it does. My grandfather Evangelos, Vassia's husband, was a neighbour of hers, a good village boy. I know how things worked in these small communities in those days. She would have been under pressure to get married and the family would have been keen to find someone suitable. Maybe it just wasn't possible for her to wait for Sol.'

Carrie sighed. 'I'll have to find some other way to end the book, tie up all the loose ends,' she said. 'It's a pity, when we know nearly everything else now.'

'Maybe something will come to light. You never know,' Kris replied. 'In the meantime, I'm going to put all the items on display in the hotel somewhere,' he went on, 'a record of the war and the terrible things that happen during such times.' He looked up at her. 'Perhaps I can include a copy of your book, when you've written it.'

Carrie smiled. 'Of course,' she agreed. 'It would be a privilege.'

A silence followed.

'Carrie...'

'Kris...'

They both spoke at the same time. Carrie laughed nervously.

'Look, Kris,' she said, wanting to say it before she lost her nerve. 'You're an amazing person. You've been so good to us, with everything that's happened, I couldn't have coped without you. I can never, ever thank you enough. But...' She hesitated, clenched her fists, and ploughed on. 'The other evening, on the caldera path, when we nearly... you know. I mean, it was lovely, don't get me wrong. But it's for the best that we didn't spend the night together.' Her voice rose in her desperation to explain things properly. 'I got carried away by all the heightened emotion and everything you did for me when Nell was missing. It distorted reality. Because the thing is, it could never work, could it? You're here and Nell and I are in the UK and she's still got two more years of school and then uni or whatever, so I'm not free to up sticks even if we knew each other nearly well enough to make such a decision... So I just wanted to say I'm sorry. And thank you.'

She stopped abruptly, all out of excuses.

For a moment Kris didn't respond. And then he smiled his gorgeous smile. 'It's all right,' he said. 'I understand. Holiday romances never last, do they.'

A rope tightened round Carrie's heart. He was right. A holiday romance was all it had ever been, just like the first time. Vassia had forgiven and forgotten a wrong done to her that was so much greater than what Jack had done to Carrie. She needed to learn from Vassia's example and make amends, put things right. Vassia had not had that chance, but Carrie did.

Kris was a wonderful man, an incredible friend, but he was not *her* man. In her fear and loneliness she'd let it go too far. The person she loved, had always loved, was Jack.

They would see how it went when they got home. It might work out, it might not. But either way, they had to try. For Nell. And for each other.

# CHAPTER 47

## CARRIE, 2024

As well as working things out with Jack – how to live together, be partners again after so long – Carrie had another important issue to deal with on her return from Santorini. A reconciliation with her sister, Jenny. Vassia's relationship with her brother had been forever destroyed by a terrible betrayal. Carrie could not let history repeat itself with her own sibling, especially over something so minor in comparison.

Making the initial phone call was nerve-wracking enough. Carrie had to pluck up all her courage before doing it, but in the end Jenny had been surprisingly positive and had instantly agreed to drive over from her home in Bristol to meet Carrie in a café in Bath the following Saturday.

Once they were settled with their flat whites and a plate of pastries, Carrie launched straight in.

'I want to apologise,' she began. 'I was an idiot to react the way I did all those years ago, but I've been far more of an idiot since. We could have sorted this out ages ago and it was only my pride and stubbornness that prevented me from doing so. You offered so many olive branches and I refused to take any of them and for that I'm truly sorry.' She picked up her teaspoon and stirred her coffee by way of distraction. Putting the spoon down again, she raised her eyes and determinedly met her sister's gaze. 'I know I don't deserve your forgiveness but I'm asking for it anyway, in case you can see your way to giving it.'

As Carrie watched, she was surprised to see her sister tear up.

'Oh Carrie, you are indeed a complete idiot,' Jenny exclaimed, reaching across the table and grabbing Carrie's hands. 'There's nothing for me to forgive – if anything, I should be asking you for the same clemency. Though I never meant to, I know that I hurt you so badly. What I did – what Jack and I did – was awful. All I can say is that it really was nothing, though I know it didn't seem that way to you.'

Carrie nodded sadly. 'I was so devastated, but I should never have let it get so out of hand or go on for so long. I'm sorry. I wish with all my heart that I could turn the clock back and do it all differently, and better.'

Shaking her head, Jenny pulled a tissue from her pocket and wiped her eyes. 'There's no point having regrets. We just have to move on from here.' She took a sip of her coffee before continuing. 'I've missed you so much, you know. So many times, over the years, I've reached out to pick up the phone because I want to tell you something, or ask you something – and then I remember, as I'm about to dial your number, that I can't. It's been horrid. I'm so glad to have you back.'

Carrie forced back tears as she listened, but try as she might she couldn't prevent her voice from cracking as she responded. 'I've missed you, too. Let's never, ever, let anything come between us again.'

Jenny smiled and ran her hands through her hair. 'Never.' She picked up her phone and fiddled with it for a moment. 'Would you like to see some pictures of the girls? They're going to be so excited to get to know their cousin properly.'

Cautiously, Carrie took the phone from her sister, and

scrolled through the photo album Jenny had opened for her. Zoe and Elsie looked so lovely and it would be wonderful for Nell to have them in her life; Carrie was sure they would get on well and couldn't wait to get them together. To that end, she and Jenny put a date in the diary for a picnic in the Cotswolds, a beautiful spot that they used to go to when they were children.

Carrie and Jenny texted constantly after that. When the day came, Nell was uncharacteristically excited and nervous. She'd only met Zoe and Elsie a few times, at their grandparent's house when holiday stays had overlapped. Carrie had always done her best to limit such times, only letting it happen at all if she were entirely stuck with no childcare when she was working. Looking back on it now, she couldn't believe that she had been so dogmatic about it, so unreasonable. How had she let the past infect so much of the future – her daughter's future, most of all?

As they drove to the rendezvous, Nell was full of questions – where did Zoe and Elsie go to school? What school year were they both in? Where did they even live? What kind of place – a flat or a house, in the city or the country? When were their birthdays? Carrie did her best to answer them all. She was a bit worried about the age gap; Nell at sixteen was the oldest, Zoe was thirteen and Elsie ten. Even a year's age difference seemed a lot in your teens, and Carrie hoped Nell wouldn't find the girls too young to be interesting to her.

Once they'd parked up and got out of their cars, there were a tense few moments during which the three youngsters regarded each other awkwardly, Elsie hiding shyly behind her big sister. Carrie watched anxiously at first, and then, when Nell stepped forward and complimented Zoe on her 'cool' trainers, with pride at how her daughter had broken the ice.

Soon all three were chatting animatedly, discussing their favourite Taylor Swift songs and the best online shops for pre-loved clothing. Nell seemed to be relishing her role as older, more sophisticated cousin, and began restyling Zoe's hair slides, then showing Elsie how to use an elastic band to make a knot in the back of her T-shirt so that it was more 'flattering'.

Carrie raised her eyebrows at that one – did a thirteen-year-old need such an embellishment? – but Jenny just laughed. 'She and I have a fight every morning about the length of her school skirt and the number of rolls she's turned over at the waistband. I make her put it back to normal but I know that the minute she's out of sight, she hoicks it up again! I don't think Nell is going to teach her anything she and her friends aren't already on to.'

Shaking her head, Carrie smiled broadly. 'Been there, bought that T-shirt – literally! Thank goodness it's the end of school uniform for us, with Nell going into sixth form.'

'I can't believe how grown up she is,' said Jenny, with an incredulous sigh. 'She'll be off at university before we know it.'

Carrie grimaced. 'I know and I'm dreading it. But,' she added, more brightly, 'that just means I need to make the most of the last two years I've got with her at home. Fortunately, since the Santorini debacle, she seems to appreciate me a tad more than she did before – I'm still old and embarrassing but she's discovered a kernel of underlying love!'

'Of course she adores you!' exclaimed Jenny. 'And now you and Jack are back together, she must be so delighted.'

'She is,' replied Carrie. 'And surprisingly mature. She told me that I should do whatever I wanted on that front, for me, not for her. *I need to live my own truth*, in her words.' She paused to chuckle at the Gen-Z catchphrase, and Jenny joined in. Then Carrie resumed, more soberly now. 'But despite her saying that, I know how much she wanted me and Jack to heal the rift. We've still got a long way to go though. I hadn't realised how set in my ways I had become – it's been hard to integrate another adult into that, when you're used to doing everything your own way.'

Gales of laughter from the children interrupted Jenny's reply. 'They're having fun,' she commented, before turning back to Carrie. 'But it's all right?' she asked, sounding concerned. 'You're not regretting it?'

Carrie shook her head. 'Not at all. It's great. There's just a bit of adjustment needed. But all good.'

Jenny looked relieved. 'So, shall we break out the picnic? I had a blowout in Marks and Sparks and I am greedy to tuck in to it.'

Carrie picked up her picnic rug and spread it out on the grass, and she and Jenny laid out the goodies. The girls had wafted down to the babbling brook that ran through the tiny village they were in and, shoes discarded, were paddling in the cold, crystal clear water.

Jenny poured them both a glass of sparkling water. 'We'll have to put a night out in the diary before too long that involves a taxi, so we can have a drink.'

Carrie nodded. She hugged her knees to her as she watched Nell, Zoe and Elsie screeching and shouting as their feet sank into the soft riverbed. Though she had written happy endings in her books, she had never truly believed in them.

Now, she was beginning to feel differently. Making amends with her sister was a giant step towards her own happy ending, and she appreciated it so much more knowing as she did that Vassia and Andreas never got that chance.

# CHAPTER 48

## CARRIE, 2024

In her mother and father's musty garage, Carrie stared at the piece of paper she'd pulled out of a cardboard tube. Harriet had recently found some more of Sol's things, including his medals, which she intended to put in a frame and hang on the wall in her hallway, and Carrie had come out to find what else she might find stashed away. Narrowing her eyes in the gloom, she saw that it was another portrait of Vassia, instantly recognisable. But Sol must have drawn it from memory, because it was dated 1947. Slowly, Carrie turned it over. On the back, in Sol's characteristic scrawl, were words that made her heart break with sadness.

*Dear Vassia,*

*I drew this picture for you and took it to Santorini in the hope of giving it to you. I had been meaning to come for ages, but, as is so often the case, circumstances got in the way. At the end of the war in Europe, I volunteered to go to the Far East. I was chosen out of all the SAS and SBS men to be part of a sixty-strong force heading out there, but the atom bombs exploded just before we were due to depart, finally ending the war for good. So I stayed in London.*

*I couldn't admit it to anyone at the time, but it was after this that I fell apart.*

*Once the fighting was over, the stress, strain, exhaustion and trauma of the previous four years all came to the surface. It took a long time for me to put myself back together and, when I'd done so, I knew that the only thing that would help me to heal would be going back to Santorini, the place where, for a few brief weeks, and despite the mortal danger I was in, I was the happiest I have ever been. Seeing you again would make all that I had gone through worth it. In anticipation, I bought a ring to give to you. I took advice from the girl in the shop; something classy, not showy but beautiful in its simplicity, like you. I had it inscribed in Greek, with those words that you embroidered onto the sampler for me, and that we shared at our parting. Faith, hope, love. The greatest of these is love, and I thank you for all eternity for showing me what true love is, what it looks like, feels like, tastes, sounds and smells like.*

*I arrived on Santorini in early spring, not under cover of darkness this time but on a sunny day when clouds scudded across the bluest of skies. On entering Vourvoulos, I saw a crowd gathered outside the tiny blue-domed church where you told me that your cousin Nico and his friends used to play. As I watched, a couple in wedding attire emerged from the dark doorway, and were soon surrounded by well-wishers throwing grains of rice and cheering.*

*For a moment, I felt the happiness in that village square. The war was now consigned to the past and life was continuing as it had done for centuries before. Warmed by the sun, dazzled by Santorini's simple, whitewashed beauty, I was overcome by an enormous sense of peace.*

*And then, the bride lifted her veil and I saw it was you,*

*Vassia, even more lovely than I had remembered you, but taken now, another man's wife.*

*Of course I didn't stay. I had brought the sampler with me for us reminisce over, but I left it on the island, where it blew away in the breeze, just like the love we once shared.*

*For a while, I wondered why I hadn't known that you were to be married, why you hadn't told me. But the truth was that you had no way to contact me. I should have gone back to find you earlier. I understand why you moved on. You had no way of knowing if I was dead or alive.*

*I owe my life to you. Your exceptional bravery and stead-fastness saved me, your kindness and innate goodness illuminate you from within now as they did then.*

*I will always love you.*

*Your very own,*

*Sol Baker*

For long moments, tears pricking behind her eyes, Carrie sat staring at the letter that had never been given to its intended recipient. She recalled that distant, wistful look she had some-times seen in Sol's eyes. She knew now that he had been pining for a girl he once knew, on a sun-soaked Greek island, at a time when all of their lives hung from the most delicate of threads.

Eventually, she wiped away the tears, went outside and walked to the end of her parents' garden, where she leant on the fence and gazed out over the fields beyond. In the distance, she could hear Jack and Nell laughing as they picked windfall apples for a crumble that Harriet was going to make for Sunday lunch. Jenny, her husband and the girls would be here soon; the whole clan together after such a long hiatus.

It had taken a long while for Carrie to stop beating herself up about her mistakes, but now a profound feeling of having learnt some fundamental truths about herself, about the world and human nature descended upon her as she considered everything that had happened since that fateful postcard from Greece had dropped on her doormat all those months ago and had led to her finding the forgotten sketchbook, and everything that had happened after. Above all else, she had discovered the true power of love – for her family but also for herself. Not to mention that she was, indeed, living her own truth.

At the same time, the exploration into the past had given her back her writing mojo, and the first draft of her book was with her publisher. Before too long it would out in the world and others would be able to read the tale of love in the most dangerous of worlds. Whether it sold or whether it didn't, Carrie no longer had to worry about homelessness as, with Jack moved in, their joint income was enough to cover the new mortgage.

And as if all of this wasn't good enough, Spencer had indeed returned to Greece with an engagement ring for Xanthe and the wedding was to take place the next summer; Carrie, Jack and Nell were of course all invited. Carrie could not be happier for her friend.

'Mum!' Nell's voice drifted towards her through the misty, autumnal air, disturbing her reverie. 'Mum! Dad and I need your help!'

A small, pensive smile playing on her lips, Carrie pushed herself away from the fence and turned towards her daughter and... partner? It was still strange to think of Jack that way, but as she did so a sudden feeling of deep gratitude filled her soul.

She was the lucky one. She had been gifted the opportunity of a second chance – the second chance that had eluded Sol and Vassia – and she must make the most of it.

# EPILOGUE

## JACK, 2024

Jack eyed Carrie's mother warily. Why had she summoned him to the kitchen for a 'confab' while everyone else was lying around in the sitting room, holding their stomachs and groaning at the deliciousness of the meal and how much they had eaten? He had always admired Harriet enormously, knowing that he had her to thank for making sure that Carrie had allowed him into Nell's life despite how much he had hurt her. There wasn't an obvious reason that he could think of that he might have fallen foul of Harriet now, and that was why his heart was full of dread. Just when everything had seemed to be going right, surely it couldn't now be going wrong again?

Harriet gestured to him to sit down, which he did, nervously, perching on the edge of the chair. She took a chair opposite him and then, seeming to notice his unease, smiled at him warmly.

'Oh Jack,' she said, 'don't look so worried! I only wanted to take this opportunity to get you on your own for a few minutes.'

Jack tried to act more relaxed, but couldn't really manage it. 'OK,' he muttered, barely able to speak. 'I'm feeling a little bit like a schoolboy summoned to see the head.'

'Don't be so silly,' remonstrated Harriet hastily. 'It's nothing like that. Though I've often thought I might make a good head-teacher. It would be quite fun to be able to quell errant pupils with nothing more than a steely stare.'

'I'm not sure how many heads can do that,' Jack said with a laugh, finally starting to feel less tense. 'According to Nell, Mr Donovan certainly does not have that skill, more's the pity.'

Harriet shook her head. 'Well, she did all right, anyway.' Nell's results had seen a cluster of grade 6s and 7s and even one 8, which had come as a great relief to everyone concerned, not least Nell herself. 'But I didn't want to talk to you about school, or Nell, actually.' She paused and reached over for something on the shelf behind her. 'I wanted to talk to you about this.'

She pushed a small green box across the table towards Jack. Forehead creased in puzzlement, he picked it up and opened it. Inside was a ring, a simple gold band inset with five gleaming diamonds.

'What is it?' he asked, confused.

Harriet rested her elbows on the table. 'It's a ring that Sol bought and never gave away, though we now know that he meant it for Vassia. He entrusted it to me, telling me that either Carrie or Jenny should have it. I've spoken to Jenny about it and she tried it on, but it's too small for her, and anyway, she was clear that she'd rather Carrie had it, that it would make the final amends for what went wrong all those years ago.'

'Oh,' answered Jack, still looking flummoxed. 'That's very kind of Jenny. So why—'

'I'll explain,' interjected Harriet, cutting across him. 'I could just give it straight to Carrie myself. But, when I thought about it, I decided I'd let you do so. It doesn't have to be for anything specific, if you know what I mean.'

'Right.' Jack blinked. Was Harriet talking about a proposal? It had crossed his mind, but both he and Carrie were still at the stage of taking things slowly, one day at a time. Neither of them wanted to rush into anything. There was no need to do so.

'But Sol bought it for someone special, and wanted it to go to someone special, and I just think it would be fitting if Carrie received it from someone special, such as yourself. After all, whatever happens between you two, you'll always be the father of her child. And an excellent dad you've been to Nell, too. She couldn't have asked for more.'

'Well, that's very kind of you to say,' replied Jack, shifting a little awkwardly on his seat. 'And of course I'll give the ring to Carrie. It would be my great privilege.'

'Carrie reliably informs me that the inscription says "faith, hope, love". And I suppose you've had to show all of those, over the years you've been waiting for my daughter.' Harriet smiled wryly, raising her eyebrows at Jack. This gesture dissipated the tension and he laughed, glad the heavy stuff was over.

The kitchen door burst open, making both Harriet and Jack jump.

'What are you doing?' demanded Nell. 'We're going to start a game of Rummikub – are you guys playing?'

'Not me,' answered Harriet, hurriedly. 'I'm terrible at games – I always lose. But I'll watch and cheer you on.'

'OK,' responded Nell cheerily. 'Dad? Shall we be a team?'

'Ye—' started Jack, but did not manage to get the word out before Nell intervened again, snatching up the ring box, asking, 'What's this? Whose is it?'

'It was Sol's,' Harriet said. 'But now it's going to be your mother's. And your father is going to hand it over.'

Nell stopped still and then raised her gaze very, very slowly towards Jack. 'You mean it's a—'

'Not necessarily,' interjected Jack, before Nell could say any more.

'You don't know what I was going to suggest,' she protested.

'I was going to say, it could be a push present for her. You never gave her one at the time.'

'A push present?' repeated Harriet, incredulously. 'What on earth is that?'

Nell had the ring out of the box and was trying it on each of her slender fingers. It fitted the middle one perfectly. She gazed at it, turning her hand this way and that so that the jewels caught the light, admiring the look of it. 'Oh Granny,' she uttered, with an air of overstated patience and forbearance at her grandmother's ignorance. 'It's the present a man gets a woman for pushing a baby out. Everyone on TikTok does it. Some women get like, Range Rovers and stuff.' She glanced back down at the ring, then took it off and put it back in the box, snug in its little padded holder. 'But usually it's jewellery, rings mostly. This is literally perfect.' She handed the box to Jack, turned on her heel and left the room, calling over her shoulder, 'Hurry up, Dad. The game is starting.'

Jack and Harriet caught each other's eye and both began to laugh. Stowing the box in his pocket, Jack said, 'Well, that's sorted then. A push present it is.'

'Wonderful,' Harriet replied. 'I know that, if Sol's looking down on us, he'll be thrilled for his ring to finally have a worthy recipient.'

# A LETTER FROM ROSE

Dear reader,

I want to say a huge thank you for choosing to read *A Santorini Secret*. If you enjoyed it, and want to keep up to date with all my latest releases, just sign up at the following link. Your email address will never be shared and you can unsubscribe at any time.

*www.bookouture.com/rose-alexander*

If you liked *A Santorini Secret*, and I hope you did, I would be so grateful if you could spare the time to write a review. I'd love to hear what you think and it really helps new readers to find my books for the first time.

I love hearing from my readers – you can get in touch through social media or my website.

Thanks,

Rose Alexander

www.rosealexander.co.uk

X x.com/RoseA_writer

# PUBLISHING TEAM

**Turning a manuscript into a book requires the efforts of many people. The publishing team at Bookouture would like to acknowledge everyone who contributed to this publication.**

### Commercial
Lauren Morrissette
Jil Thielen
Imogen Allport

### Contracts
Peta Nightingale

### Cover design
Debbie Clement

### Data and analysis
Mark Alder
Mohamed Bussuri

### Editorial
Kelsie Marsden
Nadia Michael

### Copyeditor
Jacqui Lewis

Printed in Great Britain
by Amazon